Praise for

Nancy Thayer

Summer Breeze

"Nancy Thayer is the queen of beach books. . . . All [these characters] are involved in life-changing choices, with all the heart-wrenching decisions such moments demand."

—*The Star-Ledger*

"Readers will delight in these women's struggles to reconcile their desires and dreams with the cards they've been dealt."

—*Publishers Weekly*

"A novel perfect for beach reading."

—*Sentinel and Enterprise*

"New England's Dragonfly Lake serves as the backdrop for this moving story of self-discovery and friendship, as three women come together to heal their wounds and pursue unrealized dreams. Filled with intrigue and romance, this novel shows how women's unique bonds can survive even the most tempestuous times."

—*Woman's Day*

"This beautifully written novel examines the lives of three women who have recently become neighbors. With unflinching honesty and perspective, the story delves into life-changing decisions that most women can relate to. The characters are wonderful, and the voice and pace of the story pull the reader in right from the start. The Berkshires setting is perfect for a summer read."

—*Romantic Times*

Heat Wave

"Vintage Nancy Thayer . . . Enjoy *Heat Wave* along with a cool drink . . . and plenty of sunblock."

—*Huntington News*

BY NANCY THAYER

Summer Breeze

NANCY THAYER

Summer Breeze

A NOVEL

Ballantine Books Trade Paperbacks
New York

2013 Ballantine Books Trade Paperback Edition

Copyright © 2012 by Nancy Thayer
Random House reading group guide copyright © 2013 by Random House, Inc.
Excerpt from *Island Girls* © 2013 by Nancy Thayer

Published in the United States by Ballantine Books, an imprint of
The Random House Publishing Group, a division of Random House, Inc., New York.

BALLANTINE and colophon are registered trademarks of Random House, Inc.
RANDOM HOUSE READER'S CIRCLE & Design is a registered trademark of
Random House, Inc.

Originally published in hardcover in the United States by Ballantine Books, an imprint of
The Random House Publishing Group, a division of Random House, Inc., in 2012.

This book contains an excerpt from the forthcoming book *Island Girls* by Nancy Thayer.
This excerpt has been set for this edition only and may not reflect the final content
of the forthcoming edition.

LIBRARY OF CONGRESS CATALOGING-IN-PUBLICATION DATA
Thayer, Nancy.
Summer breeze : a novel / Nancy Thayer.
p. cm.
ISBN 978-0-345-52872-8 (acid-free paper)—ISBN 978-0-345-53351-7 (eBook)
1. Female friends—Fiction. 2. Life change events—Fiction.
3. Women—Family relationships—Fiction. 4. Domestic fiction. I. Title.
PS3570.H3475S85 2012
813'.54—dc22 2012010098

Printed in the United States of America

www.randomhousereaderscircle.com

2 4 6 8 9 7 5 3 1

Book design by Mary A. Wirth
Photograph on title page courtesy iStock Photo

FOR JOSH THAYER AND DAVID GILLUM

My knights in shining armor

Acknowledgments

. . . .

On my desk I keep a note I scribbled while talking to my son, Josh. It says: "Quantum theory means that nothing exists by itself."

That's certainly true of a writer working on a novel. Many people inspired and helped me from the first glimmer of an idea to the last punctuation mark of *Summer Breeze*. I'm at a loss for words to express my gratitude to them all.

My brilliant son-in-law David Gillum, associate director of Biosafety and Biosecurity at Arizona State University, is kind enough to talk with me about his significant scientific work as if I could understand what he's saying. Our talks kick-started this book.

His partner, my son, Josh (also brilliant, and that's not just my opinion), continually takes the time to discuss things as grand as quantum physics and as small as whether I've been hitting the right key on my computer keyboard when the damned thing won't work.

Susan McGinniss, Laura Gallagher Byrne, Donald Dallaire, Pamela Pindell, and Deborah Beale keep breaking my heart open with their transcendent artistic talents. Their gifts fuel my writing and my life.

Samantha Wilde (the novelist and, by the way, my daughter) is always on-target when we discuss plots and punctuation while at the same time she and her husband, Neil Forbes, are tending Ellias and Adeline and Emmett, my grandchildren (who are, by the way, her children).

Charlotte Kastner, Jill Hunter Burrill, Martha Foshee, and Laura Simon make even my grayest days sparkle.

Jude Deveraux, you are an angel sent from heaven. Please never go away.

Meg Ruley, thank you for being a magnificent agent as well as my friend. Thanks also to Peggy Gordijn and the crew at the Jane Rotrosen Agency.

Behind the scenes are the magicians at Ballantine who made this book happen: Libby McGuire, Gina Centrello, Kate Collins, Gina Wachtel, Melissa Possick, Kim Hovey, Quinne Rogers, Alison Masciovecchio, and Penelope Haynes. Junessa Viloria is so efficient and witty, she keeps me almost sane. Sue Cohen is a brilliant copy-editor. Dana Isaacson once again added his wise touches to this book. Thank you all.

My editor, Linda Marrow, as always, is pure blazing gold.

And Charley, you *know*.

Summer Breeze

1

· · · · ·

When Aaron's Volvo pulled up to the curb of the Barnaby house, Bella felt just a bit giddy.

She'd met Aaron Waterhouse in December, right after she'd returned home to Dragonfly Lake to help her mother, and the connection had been instantaneous and electric.

Aaron was handsome, sweet, sexy, and smart. He was the first man she'd ever wanted to marry. While Bella was growing up, her own family had been happy—noisy and messy, but happy—and Bella wanted one like that for herself. Lots of children, toys on the floor, flour on the kitchen counter while she taught her son or daughter to make popovers (so much fun for children), a husband who would come home from work with a smile on his face to toss his children into the air—and who could make her melt at the sight of him, the way she was melting now.

She could have all that with Aaron. He had just gotten his master's in architecture. He was putting out feelers for jobs and was sure to get a good one. He was so bright, so reliable. He wanted children. He was in love with her. She was in love with him, and the vision of their life together was enticing.

But there was one enormous problem: Aaron had been invited to interview for a job in San Francisco.

San Francisco excited Aaron. Bella didn't want to leave Massachusetts.

She'd left already, plenty of times. She'd seen foreign places.

She'd traveled to Paris, to Italy, to Amsterdam. She'd lived in Utah and in Texas.

Now she wanted to get started with her own real life. She wanted to live *here*, near Dragonfly Lake, a world she knew and cherished. It wasn't just the landscape and the closeness of her family. It was more than that—it was as if she were falling in love with a new vision of herself, as if at twenty-seven a mist were evaporating from a mirror, allowing her true image to show clear.

It was early June. Bella and Aaron had been together for five months, growing closer every day. She was pretty sure Aaron was about to propose to her. And she didn't know what her answer would be.

"Bell!" Her older brother, Ben, stuck his head into the living room. "I'm driving down to the Hortons' with our beach chairs and the food."

"Okay," Bella answered. "Aaron and I will walk down."

Ben went out the door and headed to his Jeep Cherokee, with its four-wheel drive, good for the snowy months, and its back hatch, good for carrying lots of stuff. Ben was practical, scientific, and methodical. He had a PhD and a tenured position at the University of Massachusetts at Amherst. His life revolved in a precise circle like planets orbiting the sun.

Bella's life felt more like a Slinky flopping down the stairs.

She grinned at her own joke. At least she still had her sense of humor. You couldn't live in a family of four Barnaby children, all with a first name that began with the letter B, without developing a sense of humor. And she *was* happy, and an optimist, glad to be home, full of hope for the future. Her life wasn't *tragic*. Just a puzzle.

Bella had spent the last two and a half years teaching third grade in Austin, Texas, until last Christmas, when her mother, while trying to put the angel on top of the tree, fell off the ladder and broke her leg. Bella's father taught high school English five days a week. Bella's older sister, Beatrice, was busy in her house an hour away with her three little children. Ben, of course, had his own apartment in Amherst, his students, and lab. Seventeen-year-old Brady was still in high school. So Bella abbreviated her contract, left Austin after the first semester, and flew home to take over her mother's shop and help around the house.

She was surprised to discover she didn't miss teaching. She was exhilarated to be back home, which for her was not just the comfortable house she'd grown up in on a lake surrounded by woodland, but the entire region where forests and farmlands stretched like a vast Eden on either side of the wide Connecticut River. This area boasted five of the best colleges in the world, drawing students and faculty from all over the planet.

As a child, she'd hiked with her family up Mount Hadley and Mount Tom, and canoed on the Connecticut River. She'd visited Emily Dickinson's house several times, and heard Billy Collins speak when he was the country's poet laureate. She'd contemplated modern sculpture at the art museums, and she'd witnessed a four-point stag, branched with heavy antlers, step over their lawn and down to the lake to drink in the early-morning light.

She loved this area, her family, their house . . . and that was part of the problem. Perhaps she loved them too much.

Now, as she watched, Aaron stepped out of his Volvo. He waved at Ben as Ben backed the Cherokee out of the drive. Aaron had incredibly muscled arms and thighs, an aftereffect of wrestling in high school and college. She loved the heft of them, the safety she felt in his arms. He had dark, curly hair and wore glasses over his hazel eyes. He was her Superman, looking academic, restraining so much strength and sexuality.

He approached the house, tapped on the front door, and let himself in, as everyone did who knew the Barnabys well.

"Hi, Aaron."

"Hey, Bella."

Just the sight of him made her short of breath. He pulled her to him and kissed her thoroughly.

She gently pushed him away. "We should go."

"Right. I brought some wine. It's in the car."

Together they left the house, picked up the bottles of Pinot, and began walking along the narrow road winding around Dragonfly Lake. The lake was tucked in a hollow snuggled up against a gently rising mountain, or what was called a mountain in New England; in Colorado, it would be downsized to hill. It rose to a ridge running north and south, covered with evergreens, birches, and oaks, home to deer, porcupines, foxes, and numerous other creatures, including the clever raccoons that made human lives miserable if they didn't use the proper tight-locking trash receptacles. Various styles of houses surrounded the lake: A-frames, modernized log cabins, seventies split-levels like the Barnabys' house, and a few fabulous minimansions like the ones on either side of the Barnabys'.

All the homes looked out onto the lake, which curved in a capricious blue oval around the hill, its banks thick with grasses, forest, and wildflowers. Much of the shore was dotted with boathouses and docks, because the lake was big enough to sail on. Here and there, man-made beaches of golden sand sloped to the water. Everywhere there were trees, and over the lawns and road, the sweet green leaves of spring were casting the first delicate shadows. Tulips opened their petals to the light; pansies spilled from window boxes.

Aaron inhaled a deep breath of air. "Nice day for a cookout."

Bella nodded. "Mmm. Funny, it usually is. The Hortons have held the first neighborhood summer cookout for years."

"How many people will be there?"

"Not a real crowd. Lots of these houses are just vacation homes. Like the one to the right of us—"

"That place is just for vacations?" Aaron turned to look back at the house.

"I know. An interior designer from Boston, Eleanor Clark, owns it. She usually comes here in the summer. I heard she loaned it to her niece this year while Eleanor goes around the world with her new boyfriend. She's an artist—Natalie, not Eleanor—about our age."

"Have you met Natalie?"

"Not yet. I think she'll be at the cookout. I hope so. I'd like to meet her."

"I'd like to see the inside of that house," Aaron said.

Bella knocked his shoulder with hers. "Ever the architect."

. . .

Natalie noticed the man when he stepped out of the Jeep [ ] front of the Hortons' house. He was a hunk, with a stern co[ ] nance that gave him an air of intelligence. Judgment. *Responsibili[ ]*

She thought: *Now* there *is a face I would like to paint.*

A wide brow—poets would call it "noble"—over romantically down-slanting pale blue eyes. A straight, slender nose, neat ears, a long face with a firm jaw. Wrinkles at the corners of the eyes and across the forehead, not, she figured, from laughing but from thinking. Here in the five-college area, lots of people thought for a living. The man was perhaps thirty. His hair was golden brown, like toast; she would have bet he'd been a towheaded child.

"That's my son," Louise Barnaby told Natalie. She was sitting next to Natalie, both of them in rockers on the front porch of the Hortons' house. Louise still had to baby her leg, although she could walk on it without a cane, and Natalie had brought her a glass of chilled white wine.

Louise was Natalie's first lake friend. She'd visited when Natalie moved into her aunt Eleanor's house this week, presenting her with a casserole and a vase of fresh flowers. She'd insisted Natalie come to the cookout with Louise and her husband, Dennis, who was out on the front lawn, stabbing croquet wickets into the ground.

"He's awfully cute," Natalie said.

Louise smiled. "I know. The great thing is, he doesn't realize it."

Natalie was grateful for Louise's company. Louise was older, but still chic, her blond hair cut in a sexy shag, her trim body clad in chinos and a blue tee that brought out the azure of her eyes. Louise didn't look like a fifty-five-year-old who'd given birth to four children. For that matter, Dennis was tall, slender, with lots of floppy gray hair. He still looked pretty fine as well.

It was shallow of Natalie to be so judgmental, she knew, but she'd been afraid when she made the decision to move out here from Manhattan she'd find everyone sporting Birkenstocks, feeding chickens, and discussing compost.

she could only claim to be, at most, a
have the pedigree to be a real one.

there were different kinds of snobs. Here,
etts, home of Amherst College, where the
apshire College, where the hip gifted went,
assachusetts at Amherst, where Bill Cosby
e, near Smith College, where poor, brilliant
and Mount Holyoke College, where Emily
Dickinson *ana* w... Wasserstein had gone, the snobbery would
be intellectual.

Natalie felt awkward in her black jeans and black silk shirt. This
was about as cookoutish as her New York wardrobe got. She'd just
moved to Aunt Eleanor's house. She hadn't had time to buy different clothes yet.

Just for a moment, Natalie put her hand to her own head. At
least her hair was growing out. Two years ago, when she had moved
to Manhattan, she'd gone to a hairdresser and had it all chopped off
into a severe, chic, scalp-clinging crop. It had been a part of her
statement. She could still remember leaving the salon, head high
and suddenly weightless, feeling the fresh air on her bare neck,
knowing that now her real life was about to begin. She'd been
twenty-eight. She'd struggled to get there. At times in her life, she'd
despaired of getting there. For years she'd had to drop her studies to
work, often two jobs, to pay for more studies, because her parents
could never help her financially. If it hadn't been for her aunt Eleanor, she would never have made it to Manhattan.

She dropped her hand. As soon as she'd decided to leave Manhattan, she'd begun to grow her hair out. Already dark curls clustered over her ears.

"We're ready!" Morgan called. "Shall I fasten Petey in his stroller?"

Her husband was in his study, tapping frantically at the computer. A sunny Saturday afternoon, and he was working.

"Josh?" She tried not to sound waspish. "The cookout."

"Coming."

Morgan took a deep breath. During the past year, she'd learned to achieve feats of patience she never before dreamed possible. First of all, her adorable boy, just a year old, had taught her a whole new range of deep breathing. Then Josh had taken this job with Bio-Green Industries—and she had wanted him to take it, she had *encouraged* him to take it—and suddenly her husband was too busy to haul out the trash, give her a hug, or notice their child.

Although they did have their house. Their amazing, slightly overwhelming, new house.

The O'Keefes' home was on the shores of Dragonfly Lake. It rose in its concrete-and-glass glory, modern, boxy, space-age. They were able to afford it because the couple who built it had to move to Spain and needed a quick sale. And, of course, because Josh's new job paid so well. They didn't *love* the house, but the location was sublime. A beachfront with sand for Petey to play on. A wilderness to hike in. Morgan and Josh enjoyed kayaking, canoeing, swimming, and dreamed of teaching their children all that and more in the clear, pure waters of this lake. Before the move, they'd been living in a condo on the outskirts of Boston, commuting to jobs on crowded expressways, not getting home until late, too tired to enjoy life, and completely uninspired by the views of malls, highways, and office buildings out their condo windows. This place had seemed like a little corner of heaven to them.

Sometimes, though, to Morgan, it was just a bit like the top circle of hell.

Morgan was a scientist, a hazardous materials expert. Until recently she'd worked in the biosafety department at Weathersfield College outside Boston. She was really good at her work. It challenged her, used all her mental and interpersonal skills; it gave her a sense of accomplishment, of keeping things safe in a turbulent world.

Since Josh had joined Bio-Green, Morgan's life required a whole new set of skills.

First of all, since Ronald Ruoff, CEO of BGI, Bio-Green Industries, was Josh's new boss, paying Josh a salary he'd never even dreamed of before, it was incumbent upon Morgan to make nice to Josh's boss and his wife, Eva.

Morgan had made nice. She and Josh had gone out to dinner last week with Ronald and Eva, and Morgan had been as charming as she could be, which frankly was a big fat private pain for Morgan. She didn't like to do charming, and she *really* didn't like to pretend interest in vapid Eva's frivolous enthusiasms: massages, pedicures, shopping, and whether Kate Middleton was truly suitable for Prince William; Eva's personal and lengthy opinion was that Kate was beneath him, and she didn't even get how her statement was funny. Morgan didn't understand how a woman perhaps only a decade older—Morgan was thirty, Eva somewhere in her forties, already Botoxed and face-lifted—could be so insipid. Especially with a husband like Ronald, who might not be the most debonair dog in the kennel but at least was interested in saving the world. Or, more realistically, in making money while saving the world.

Morgan had hoped—she had *fiercely* hoped—that she would like Eva, that they would have interests in common, that they would make plans to get together, because even though her toddler, Petey, was the beating center of her heart, Morgan was quietly and sweetly going out of mind being a stay-at-home mommy. But if she had to spend more time with Eva Ruoff, she'd hang herself. Okay, that was a bit dramatic, she'd never want to leave Petey, or Josh either, even though these days Josh annoyed her no end. Was she going nuts?

Josh came into the living room, where Petey was babbling to himself as he swept his books off the coffee table and Morgan stood lost in her thoughts.

"Thinking about how to decorate?" he asked.

Morgan almost growled. They had to invite the Ruoffs over sometime, and the Ruoffs believed that their home should *make a statement*.

Josh sighed. "We agreed when I took this job. My part is working at the facility. Your part is networking, socializing, attracting investors."

"I'm not saying I won't do it." Morgan adjusted a *dove* pillow on their *smoke* sofa. "I'm just saying I'm not sure I *can* do it. It's not my field. Not my passion. Not even my interest. Plus, Petey is pretty much a full-time job."

"You could put him in day care."

"Josh, no. We talked about this. We agreed." Morgan snorted with contempt. "How ridiculous would that be, to put a baby in day care so I can spend time making a statement with the house!"

"You don't seem to take my job seriously," Josh muttered.

"What? How did we get to—" They were back on muddy ground, the swampland of their marriage. She didn't want an argument this evening. They were going to a cookout. They were going to meet people. Calming down, she said pacifically, "I know you're working hard, Josh. I appreciate it. I do."

She put her arms around Josh, her husband, her beloved. With his thick, naturally frenzied red hair, sparkling green eyes, and freckled skin, it was difficult for him to appear as brilliant as she knew he was. Thirty-five, yet he looked like a kid. A good-natured, athletic, dreamy boy who fantasized about playing for the Red Sox. "Maybe we'll make some contacts at the cookout," she told him.

Josh kissed the top of her head and swept his son up into his arms. "Come on, champ, we're going to a party."

Outside, they chose the smaller, easier stroller and strapped Petey in. They went down the driveway, past Morgan's SUV and Josh's black Cadillac Escalade, which looked, Morgan thought, like something the CIA would use.

Be good, Morgan warned herself. *Look around!* It was June, perhaps her favorite month, warm and fresh and full of the promise of summer.

Bella and Aaron strolled along the lake road until they came to the Hortons' house. Ben was parked in front, unloading the Jeep. Bella's father was on the lawn, setting up the croquet wickets. Her mother was sitting on the porch in a rocking chair. Beside her sat the new woman from next door, Natalie, very thin and sophisticated, all in black.

Aaron called, "Hang on, Ben, I'll help you." He handed his bottles of wine to Bella and joined Ben at the Jeep. Together the men hefted the folding beach chairs out of the back of the Jeep and carried them around the Hortons' house to the lawn sloping down to the beach.

Bella cuddled the three bottles against her. She noticed the new woman studying Ben. *Good luck to you,* Bella thought.

Ben was good-looking, with the Barnabys' blond hair and blue eyes. Half of her high school friends had had crushes on him, even while he'd been a totally clueless geek, his nose always in a book, staying late to work on projects for the science fair.

In college, he'd had a serious long-term girlfriend, another science nerd. Vickie could have been pretty if she'd cared to, but she was almost aggressively fashion-unconscious. Her nice figure had been hidden beneath baggy jeans and loose tee shirts. Usually, they had arcane quotes on them, like "Resistance is not futile. It's voltage divided by current." In the winter, she wore hoodie sweatshirts instead of sweaters and often forgot to wear a coat. Ben and Vickie broke up after graduation. He went on to Stanford. She went to Harvard. Now she was doing postdoctoral work in London. They remained science buddies who emailed now and then.

When Ben was working on his doctorate in California, he dated other women; Bella knew because she flew out a couple of times to visit him. These women were a new breed—ambitious, intensely intellectual, and not interested in long-term affairs. They were Bella's introduction to the less starry-eyed side of sexuality, and while she placed no value judgment on what Ben had with them, it made her vaguely sad. But then Bella was a hopeless romantic.

When Ben returned three years ago as an assistant professor at U. Mass.–Amherst, he was a grown-up, a serious adult. He rented an apartment in Amherst but came home often for meals or to sail. It was only a fifteen-minute drive. Today he looked familiar, her normal brother, clad in khaki shorts and an old tee shirt.

Bella went up the steps to the front porch. "Hey, Mom."

"Join us, honey." Louise gestured toward the wicker sofa. "Natalie, this is my daughter Bella."

"Hi, Natalie." Bella smiled at the woman sitting next to her mother, even as she cringed just a little inside. Natalie looked so sophisticated with her cropped black curls and no jewelry. She looked like the smart girl in high school, the one who always rolled her eyes at Bella. Bella was smart, but she was petite, only five two, with blue eyes, blond hair, and what older people always praised as a "sweet" face.

Natalie grinned shyly. "Hi, Bella. I think you and I might have met once or twice when we were kids. When Slade and I came to the lake for a week in the summer."

Bella nodded, although what she remembered most about next door was Eleanor Clark. She was glamorous, a wealthy interior designer from Boston's most chichi area. During July and August, her driveway was lined with convertibles and sports cars and even a Jaguar, with license plates from as far away as California. When Bella was younger and Bella's older sister, Beatrice, wasn't married yet, they used to hide in the attic with their parents' field glasses, spying on all the golden people languidly lounging on Eleanor's back deck in their very abbreviated bathing suits. It was better than HBO.

Bella remembered also, vaguely, Natalie and her brother, Slade, from past summers when they visited their aunt Eleanor: two scrawny, pale kids who seemed uncomfortable outdoors. Their mother and father never came to the lake house. The kids would wade from their aunt's beach into the lake, rushing right back out, clutching their arms, complaining that the water was too cold. The girl shrieked when she turned over a log and found bugs. The boy spent a lot of time in the forest, often carrying a book and studying tree trunks, which Bella had thought kind of weird and kind of intriguing.

If she remembered correctly, the brother had been pretty cute. Movie star cute. Black hair, like Natalie's.

"I remember," Bella told Natalie. She settled on the edge of the sofa, cradling the three bottles of wine in her arms. "Seems like a long time ago."

"It was," Natalie agreed. For a moment, she dropped her gaze, looking pensive.

Louise announced brightly, "Natalie's an artist."

Bella said, "Yes, I heard that. What sort of art?"

Natalie cleared her throat. "I paint. I've studied art for several years now, most recently in New York. But I've always had to work full-time as a waitress or sales clerk to pay the rent and buy food, so I've never had a chance to concentrate on my work. When Aunt Eleanor asked me to watch her summer house for her, it was an answer to my prayers." Talking about her work transformed her. She was prettier, more engaging. "What do you do, Bella?"

"I teach," Bella began. "Well, I *taught*. Hey, I've got to get these bottles into a cooler. No one wants warm white wine. Want to walk around to the back with me?"

Natalie glanced at Louise.

"Go on, you two," Louise said. "Grace asked me to sit out front and tell people where to put their stuff." As she spoke, an older couple came up the lawn to speak to her.

Natalie rose, extending a hand. "Here," she said to Bella. "I'll carry one of the bottles."

Bella and Natalie went down the steps and around the side of the house. Almost a dozen people were on the back lawn, setting up tables and chairs, firing up the grill, going in and out of the kitchen. Bella found a cooler full of ice for the wine.

"I don't like to talk about it in front of my mother," Bella confessed to Natalie, "but when you asked what I do—well, it's a complicated question. I've taught third grade for a few years. Last Christmas my mother broke her leg, so I came back to help her and to run her shop for her."

Natalie leaned against the deck railing. "Her shop?"

"Barnaby's Barn." Bella joined her against the railing, and they both gazed out at the water. "She sells children's things, mostly. Handmade clothing. Handmade wooden cradles. She's kind of an artist herself, but not like you. She makes these miniature collections called Lake Worlds." Bella always felt protective of her mother when she spoke about her creations.

"Lake Worlds?" Natalie prompted.

"When we were children, Mom invented stories for us about the creatures who lived around Dragonfly Lake. Darling Deer and her family for Beat—that's my older sister. Her name is really Beatrice.

Timid Toad and his warty family for Ben, and Busy Bunny for me. Barton Bear for Brady."

Natalie's eyes flicked toward the woods. "Are there bears around here?"

"There could be, but don't worry, I've never seen one."

Natalie relaxed. "So go on."

"Well, our friends were crazy for the dolls, so Mom made more animals for birthday and Christmas presents, complete with miniature nests and lairs. I'll show you sometime. She began to get phone calls from parents, offering to pay her if she'd create a set of animals for their children. At the same time, a small barn just on the outskirts of Amherst came up for sale. So she got the idea for her shop. That was sixteen years ago."

"Cool."

"Yeah, the money helped a bit, especially when we all started college, but Mom didn't particularly care about the money. She enjoyed creating Lake Worlds and seeing children's faces when they came into the shop. But while her leg healed over the past few months, I've run the shop for her."

Natalie tilted her head, studying Bella. "Do you enjoy running it?"

Bella looked back at Natalie. She liked her frank question. "Truthfully? I do, but . . . have you ever had a great idea at the back of your mind and it won't come quite clear?"

Natalie threw back her head and laughed. "All the time!"

Aaron approached them, glasses of Pinot Grigio in his hands. "Ladies?" he offered, with a pretentious bow.

"I'd love some." Natalie took a glass.

"Natalie, this is my boyfriend, Aaron," Bella said. She stumbled over the introduction. What should she call him? He was certainly more man than boy. They weren't engaged yet, but they were definitely not merely friends.

Aaron turned toward Natalie, and Bella thought how proud she was to be his girlfriend—or whatever she was. Aaron wasn't provocative like an underwear ad, but he gave off an air of steadiness, rock-solid capability, competence. If he'd been a surgeon, Bella would have let him operate on her. If he'd been a pilot, she'd have boarded any plane he flew.

But he was an architect, and he was aimed toward California.

Natalie was asking Aaron, "What kind of architecture do you prefer? Or perhaps the question should be, who are your favorite architects?"

More guests were arriving at the party, all carrying an offering: a bottle of wine or a casserole or a tray of deviled eggs. Bella saw her mother and father stroll down to the water's edge, leaning toward each other as they talked. Something had happened since Louise broke her leg, Bella thought. Her parents had always been a team, but now they seemed even closer. She'd talk it over sometime with Ben, if she could drag his attention away from his work for a second or two.

As if summoned by her thoughts, Ben came up the steps to the deck and joined their group.

Natalie sensed an eager *click* in her chest when Ben approached. She believed she'd developed a certain sort of judgment from all her years of painting, like an organic and obstinate lock growing right below her diaphragm. She would arrange objects for a still life—a vase, a silver platter, a bunch of grapes—and the lock stayed stubbornly shut. She'd remove the grapes, lay a sheaf of daffodils across the platter, and *click!*—the reluctant lock snapped open. So she knew when a painting was right for her.

That same *click!* startled her when she saw Ben face-to-face. Something inside her opened to him. She thought she gasped; she hoped no one noticed.

Next to her, Bella stirred. "Natalie, this is my brother Ben. Ben, this is Eleanor Clark's niece, Natalie . . . ?"

Natalie supplied her last name. "Reynolds."

Bella nodded. "Right. She's living here this summer."

Ben gave Natalie a preoccupied hello.

Natalie returned a lukewarm "Hi"; she didn't want to appear eager.

"Great day," Aaron said. "Have you been swimming yet?"

Ben answered, "Not yet. The water's still cold. But I got the canoe out last weekend."

Bella slid her arm through Aaron's. "Could you help me set out the salads? I think they're getting ready to eat." She deftly pulled Aaron away.

Ben stood near Natalie, saying nothing.

"So," Natalie asked, "you live on the lake, too, right?"

Without looking at her, Ben answered, "Not really. I mean, I grew up here, but, technically, my parents' house is no longer my home. I'm thirty-two now. I moved out years ago. I live in Amherst."

"I see. What do you do?"

"I teach at U. Mass.–Amherst," he said as he cast a sideways glance at her and blushed deeply.

Well, *ha!* she thought, he was as *attracted* to her as she was to him. She angled her body toward him, lifting her face toward his. "What do you teach?"

"Chemical engineering." He stuck his hands in the pockets of his shorts, as if afraid of what they'd do left out on their own.

She confessed, "I'm not sure I know what chemical engineering is."

"Most people don't."

She persisted. "Give me a try."

He hesitated, then shot her another quick glance. He blushed again. "I heard you say you're an artist."

She smiled wryly. "True. But that doesn't make me an *idiot*."

Ben checked her face, as if to be sure she wasn't ridiculing him, then told her, "Chemical engineering is more or less the combination of chemistry and physics with biosciences to create and construct new materials or techniques. Like nanotechnology or new fuels."

"Oh, well, if you put it that way, then it's perfectly clear," Natalie teased.

Ben had pale blue eyes streaked with white, like shards of icebergs, as if a shield of cold protected the deep and complicated depths. He had long, thick lashes, too, and shaggy blond hair. But he wasn't surfer-boy tempting, he was grown-up tempting. He looked reflective, resolute.

And clueless. He didn't seem to get the fun in her voice. He seemed, in fact, insulted. She hurried to appease him, because she really didn't want to hurt his feelings.

"Maybe I could understand it a bit better if you gave me more details."

"I'm working on hierarchical porous materials."

"Okay . . ."

"We're looking for a way to convert wood-based biomass into oil."

"Fuel."

"Right."

"Got it. Sounds important."

"It could be. I hope it will be." He continued talking, enthusiastic now, explaining his lab, his grad students, the papers he'd had published in scientific journals she'd never heard of. As he talked, it was as if a light had gone on inside him. Natalie understood; she had her own light.

"There you are!" Louise Barnaby came onto the deck, carrying a toddler in her arms, followed by the appealing young couple Natalie had seen two houses down from Aunt Eleanor's. "Natalie, I want you to meet Morgan and Josh O'Keefe. Oh, and I mustn't forget Petey, their son."

Petey clung to Louise with wide eyes.

"Say 'Hi,' Petey," Morgan urged. The boy blinked. "It will take him a while. With the move, all the new people, so much change . . . He's really a pretty gregarious little guy."

Louise asked, "Morgan, didn't you say Felicity Horton has baby-sat for Petey once or twice?"

"She has. Petey adores her." Morgan added, "I do, too. She's fifteen and still more Anne of Green Gables than Beyoncé."

"Well, then, Petey, let's go find Felicity!" Louise carried the baby away.

"Hi. I'm Josh." Robust and red-haired, he sported a Rolex on his wrist.

Morgan held out her hand to Natalie. "I'm Morgan. You must be the artist, right?" She wore her long brown hair loose to her shoulders. She was tall, thin, and lanky, athletic-looking.

The O'Keefes introduced themselves to Ben, and for a while the four chatted amiably about the lake, the party, the long-awaited arrival of summer.

Morgan turned to face the lake. "This is our favorite time of day. I love to sit on the deck with a drink and see the light show."

"It's *your* favorite time of day," Josh corrected mildly. "I'm usually driving home from work, if I'm lucky enough to leave that early."

"Where do you work?" Natalie asked.

"At Bio-Green Industries."

"In that new facility on the outskirts of Amherst?"

"Right. We're working on plant technology, trying to find a way to propagate plants without the use of chemical enhancements."

"I'll drink to that!" Ben lifted his glass. He informed the others, "I'm a chemical engineer at the university. Working on biofuels."

In a wry voice, Morgan said, "Oh, Ben. Just the kind of person who makes my life miserable."

Puzzled, Natalie glanced at the two of them.

Ben asked Morgan mildly, "What do you do?"

"I was a biological and chemical safety officer at Weathersfield College outside Boston. I specialize in hazardous waste management." Noticing Natalie's perplexed expression, Morgan explained, "Chemical engineers and biosafety officers are natural enemies. Chemical engineers are more cavalier with the rules than chemists; they assume that because they're working with small amounts of chemicals, they don't have to be as careful and they can skirt the rules—"

"And biosafety officers take up all our precious time insisting we fill out piles of forms and nitpicking our every move when we're trying to, oh, save the world!" Ben shot back. "*We* do not dump any chemicals down the drain. My lab is spotless."

"Gosh, I'd love to see it someday," Morgan replied wistfully.

Josh chuckled. "That's my wife. Hand her safety goggles and gloves and she's blissed-out."

"I'll take you through anytime," Ben told her. "Did you hear about the terrible accident at UNH?"

"No. What happened?" Morgan leaned forward, fixated.

All around them, families and couples gathered in clusters on the deck and in the yard, sipping beer and wine, yelling orders at their kids, telling jokes, laughing. A teenage girl played on the beach with Petey. A yellow Lab wagged through the crowd, looking hopefully for dropped crumbs. Delicious aromas drifted through the air.

Bella approached. "Hamburgers and hot dogs, hot and juicy, get them on the grill now! Fix your plates, you guys, then join me and Aaron down at the table on the grass. We're saving places for you."

Morgan scanned the backyard. "I'll get Petey. . . ." She went off toward the small beach.

Their group separated, some toward the drinks table, some toward the grill.

Bella took Natalie's arm. "Having fun meeting your neighbors?"

Was it the wine, or the fresh air, or simply how easy it was to talk with Bella? In a whisper Natalie confessed, "I *am* having fun. Your brother's intriguing."

"Oh, please, don't *you* start," Bella moaned. "Ben's got the personality of a turtle."

"Bella." Her father passed her, a glass of wine in each hand. "Be nice."

Bella sighed theatrically. "This is what I get for living at home."

"It's a remarkable place to live," Natalie told her, and she meant it. It was idyllic, not just the scenery but the sense of neighborhood. By the side of the house, several teenagers played volleyball, jumping, yelling, snorting with laughter. At the other tables, families gathered with other families, and Grace and John Horton strolled among the guests, saying hello and asking if they had everything they needed. Grace would never be anyone Natalie would choose as a close friend. She was at least ten years older, and in her ironed white shorts and shirt and gold earrings shaped like anchors, there was something a bit prissy about her. Natalie was certain Grace would find Natalie's artistic dreams too bohemian. But this seemed to be Grace's talent—to hold large, casual gatherings where neighbors got together to enjoy life.

At Natalie's table, the group broke off into separate islands of conversation. It amused Natalie to see how animated Ben was as he argued with Morgan about the Environmental Protection Agency's attempt to bring all universities and colleges into compliance with the current hazardous waste management laws. Odd how Morgan, who'd seemed rather stiff, even aloof, when she first arrived, was vivacious now. Who knew what a few sweet words about waste management could do for a girl?

At her left sat Josh O'Keefe, leaning forward rather aggressively in his chair, pounding the side of one hand into the palm of the other like some revolutionary Russian, clearly trying to convince Aaron of something about Bio-Green. Natalie tuned in; was Josh actually trying to get Aaron to invest in Bio-Green? It sounded like it. Not the most charming way to converse at a cookout.

"Josh?" Bella asked sweetly, rising. "Would you help me clear the table?"

Josh said, "Of course," and stood up to help. Instantly he reverted to the man Natalie had met on the deck: low-key, good-humored, easygoing.

Natalie leaned back in her chair for a moment, letting the talk all around her fade into the background while she lost herself in pleasure at the sight of the water shining as if glazed with gold by the setting sun. She wouldn't allow herself to gawk constantly at Ben, but she was aware of him all during the evening, as if he were a song drifting through the air, or light from the rising moon.

When the party ended, Josh carried Petey home, the child's head lolling on his shoulder, rather than risk waking the boy by placing him in the stroller. Back at their house, he carefully laid his son in his crib.

"I'll take off his clothes and tuck him in," Morgan whispered.

Josh nodded and left the room. As Morgan undid the snaps of his OshKosh overalls and slid them off his chubby body, Petey shifted in his sleep but didn't wake. She checked his diaper—still dry; she'd just changed it at the Hortons' house. He'd be comfortable enough in his tiny white tee shirt, even if a few grains of sand were sifting off his clothes. Her child lay flat on his back, arms and legs spread, as if he were effortlessly falling through his sleep. His lips opened slightly as he puffed his sweet breath into the air. The sight of his innocent face made Morgan feel peaceful in every vein and bone. She etched his face on her brain for the inevitable days to come when he would turn into Hyperactive Tantrum-Throwing Monster Boy.

In their bedroom, she pushed the button (how swank was that!) and the blinds buzzed shut across the wall of windows facing the lake. She undressed, hung up her clothes, pulled on one of Josh's long-sleeved tee shirts she'd appropriated for her own use as a nightshirt.

She was tired. These days it seemed she was always tired, which was weird, because Petey at twelve months slept through most nights. She got comfortable in bed, plumped up her pillows, and waited for Josh to come back upstairs. Now was the sweet time, chatting lazily with him about the evening and the people they'd met. As tired as she was, she wouldn't mind making love tonight. It had been a while.

Josh didn't come up. She went out into the hall and leaned over the railing. "Josh?"

"I'm going to stay down here. I've got some work to catch up on."

Morgan bit back a bitter retort. He was always working, always in his study, even tonight. Since their move here, Josh had spent almost every night on the computer. Sometimes just an hour, often three or four. She didn't nag him about it. She'd known when he accepted the position that he'd have enormous, time-consuming responsibilities. Still.

Sometimes, when she'd had a bad day, missed her job and her

friends, and allowed herself to morph into her Mad Morgan self, she wondered if *work* was all he was doing on his computer. Perhaps he was emailing some gorgeous, sexy secretary from the office—but that was just *ridiculous*! She'd never had anxieties about Josh's fidelity before; she knew he loved her and adored Petey.

She stomped back to bed, shoved her glasses on, grabbed up the *Transfederal Task Force on Optimizing Biosafety and Biocontainment Oversight* report, and settled in. She would read until Josh came up to bed, and then she'd surprise him with an attack of sweet sex like she used to before they were married.

After an hour, she fell asleep, with the bedside lamp still on and her glasses sliding down her nose.

2

.....

Sunday morning, Natalie woke late. Through the open window, a fresh breeze drifted in. She stretched and curled on her side, watching the sunlight flicker against the wall as the wind played with the curtain. An unfamiliar sensation possessed her. After a few moments she identified it, cautiously, as happiness.

When had she had such fun with so many fascinating people? At first, Natalie admitted to herself, her inner snob had been unimpressed by petite Bella with her Alice in Wonderland blond hair and innocent blue eyes, but when they began to talk, Bella turned out to be clever and funny and not unworldly at all. Bella's boyfriend, Aaron, was smart, charming, and incredibly interesting. He was an architect who knew a lot about art and the relationship between the two. Aaron had traveled to Milwaukee to see the Santiago Calatrava pavilion for its famous art museum, and his description made Natalie want to jump on the first plane to Wisconsin. The O'Keefes were cool, too, fascinating and humming with an enigmatic inner tension so palpable Natalie thought she could have painted an abstract inspired by the couple's dynamics.

Bella and Ben's mother, Louise, was a gift, the perfect neighbor, kind and informative, generous and capable, with an interesting face. Natalie would love to paint her portrait someday.

And there was Ben.

Her heart did a drumroll.

She tossed herself out of bed. It was summer, she'd met some brilliant people, and she was living in a spectacular house.

She enjoyed sleeping naked on Aunt Eleanor's million-count sheets, but now, as she roved through a house with so many windows, she needed to wear something, so she pulled on her ancient red dragon kimono and padded downstairs to make coffee. She stepped out onto the deck. Already the lake was alive: Nearby a couple stroked through the water in a canoe, and in the distance a Sunfish sail flashed.

Only a month ago, she'd been sharing a one-room apartment with another waitress in TriBeCa, working at a Starbucks during the day and babysitting at night. For almost ten years, this had been her routine in New York or Boston: a year, or two of working as hard as she could to make enough money to take art classes and paint for as long as her savings held out.

She'd known since junior high that she wanted to paint. She'd worked after high school at a drugstore lunch counter, taking her earnings immediately to the bank down the street to tuck away in her savings account. She'd denied herself cool clothes, bought no makeup or nail polish, and when friends took bus trips down to Boston, she went to the library and spent the weekend poring over art books. When she graduated from high school in Maine, she'd saved enough money for two years of community college near Portland. She'd gone to every art exhibition she could find; she'd taken a drawing class and an art history class before deciding she wanted to find a teacher or an art school and concentrate on oils.

Natalie's mother had scoffed at this. "You'll never make a living as an artist!" she'd predicted with exasperation.

Natalie had shot back, "You should know." Her mother had always struggled financially. When Slade was nine, Natalie and Slade's father had left them and never reentered their lives, never sent child support, not so much as a birthday present. Their mother, Marlene, had worked in the high school cafeteria for years before gradually sliding into the business of breeding and selling purebred bulldogs. She loved those dogs, Natalie had often thought, more than she loved her children. But, then, no doubt the dogs were easier to love.

Aunt Eleanor, Marlene's sister, had been the saving grace in the gloom of Natalie's childhood, not simply because she often arrived like a fairy godmother, giving everyone presents, but because her own life was a model for Natalie. As a young girl, Natalie had seen Eleanor exhausted from cleaning the posh homes of Portland's fat cats. She'd heard Eleanor raving to Natalie's mother about the books on interior design she got from the library and devoured. Marlene had scoffed at that, too. When Natalie was ten, Eleanor had taken her down to Boston to go through the Museum of Fine Arts and later to a concert.

"These are things you have to know," Eleanor had impressed on Natalie. "You don't have to go to college to know them, but you do have to know them."

Natalie had seen Eleanor in sweatpants and tee shirt, on her knees, scrubbing ground-in dirt from the floor of her newly leased shop space on Boston's fashionable Newbury Street. Natalie had been there in her own sweatpants, helping Eleanor. In Eleanor's cramped Charlestown apartment, Natalie had seen Eleanor in a somber suit, hair pulled back in a bun as she prepared to meet a banker to apply for a start-up loan for her interior design shop. Eleanor had gotten it, and quickly repaid it. The last time Natalie had seen Eleanor, she'd been dressed to go out in the evening in a sexy low-cut dress, high heels, and dangling earrings. Recently, Eleanor was interested in finding love—and it looked like she'd found it, since she was spending a year traveling with her boyfriend. Eleanor had asked Natalie to caretake the lake house; she'd even offered her a small salary. Really, Natalie knew, Eleanor was making it possible for Natalie to have one full year to paint.

She was grateful to Aunt Eleanor; how could she not be? She admired her like crazy. And she loved her, truly, but in an unsettling, confusing kind of way. Aunt Eleanor was like lightning. You never knew when she was going to strike or how extreme she would be. She wasn't the kind to remember birthdays or Christmas—but one day when Natalie and her brother were in their teens, they got a phone call from the local car dealer. Eleanor had bought them each a car—inexpensive used rattletraps, but they passed state inspection.

Whatever had happened in the past, Natalie knew she was fortunate to be given this amazing gift of an entire year with a free house and enough money to live on. She shouldn't waste it.

She walked through the house, sipping her coffee. Really, this place was sensational. The living room stretched the width of the house, its cathedral ceiling arching high. A kitchen and half bath were tucked at the front by the entrance hall and downstairs closet. Glossy oak floors lay under hand-woven modern rugs in geometric patterns and vivid colors. Deep sofas faced each other by the high stone fireplace, a hand-carved coffee table between. Upstairs were five bedrooms. Aunt Eleanor had insisted Natalie use hers, and Natalie was delighted—it was the biggest, with the best view.

When she first arrived, she'd been buzzed with determination. She bought groceries and wine, got a card at the local library, and checked out a number of books she'd always intended to read. She'd set up her easel and dragged a table in from a guest bedroom to hold her paints and rags. She'd taken out her portfolio and thought about what she wanted to work on. She studied her own sketches. She arranged her favorite art books on the coffee table.

The first few nights in the enormous house had kept Natalie on edge. After the noise of the city, the sirens and shrieks of tires, the shouts and laughter of passing neighbors, the overall enveloping whir, the quiet of the country spooked her. The brushing of the fir tree against an upstairs window made her jump.

Last night she'd fallen asleep easily, knowing she had nice neighbors.

She hadn't had a chance to get to know Morgan and Bella well, she realized. It was one thing to be in a group, quite another to be with "just the girls." Grinning, she checked her watch to be sure it wasn't too early, then picked up the phone and invited Bella and Morgan over for drinks this Friday night.

. . .

At six, Morgan and Bella arrived. Bella wore a headband to hold back her bouncing blond hair, but she'd changed into skinny capris and a black tee, so she didn't look quite so young and cute. Morgan wore khakis and a loose blue shirt of her husband's. They had all agreed to be comfortable, so Natalie was in jeans and a black cotton hoodie.

"What do you think?" Natalie asked them. "Shall we start out on the deck?"

"Oh, let's," Morgan pleaded. "The weather's so gorgeous."

"In honor of the day, I've made strawberry daiquiris," Natalie announced. "With just a touch of rum, so we can drink all we want without getting hammered." She took the pitcher out of the refrigerator, and the other two women brightened at the sight of the frothy pink liquid, which Natalie carried out to the deck and poured into wide-rimmed glasses.

They settled in Eleanor's comfortable wicker chairs around a table set with a plate of cheese, crackers, and fruit. A strong sun had warmed the deck, and as it slowly moved overhead, it cast slender shadows through the trees.

"It's finally June." Bella sighed, stretching her arms. "I am so ready for it."

"I'm so ready for this." Morgan put her glass on the table. "I don't mean the drink, although I'm certainly ready for it, too. I mean a girls' night out. I had no idea how desperate I was to talk to women my own age."

"I totally understand," Natalie agreed. "Although Louise has been by a few times, to see if I need anything."

"Yes," Morgan said. "She helped me when we first moved in, too. She's a very cool lady."

"She's beautiful," Natalie said. "I'd like to paint her."

"Speaking of work," Bella said, "Natalie, would you show us what you're painting?"

Natalie jumped up. "I thought you'd never ask. Bring your drinks, ladies. The more you drink, the better my work looks."

Natalie led them back into the house and up the stairs to the front bedroom she'd turned into a studio. This week she'd continued to transform the room into *her* place. Now whenever she entered, she stepped into a stimulating, resplendent cocoon. She'd dragged in long tables from the rest of the house and dug out Aunt Eleanor's most vibrant shawls, tablecloths, and pots. She'd stacked the shelves along one wall with her big, heavy, glorious art books: Rembrandt, Monet, Pissarro, Wyeth. She'd hung a few of her own favorite paintings, all still lifes, and against one wall she'd set up a still life of a silver bowl with apples.

Bella studied the beginnings of Natalie's painting on the easel.

"Your work is astonishing," Bella said.

"Thanks. But I don't know, I'm not feeling it." Natalie cast a critical eye at what she'd done. "I think it's the season. I shouldn't be using apples. It makes me think of fall. It's got too heavy a tone. I think I'll start over with, oh, strawberries, cherries. . . ."

"These are all yours?" Morgan knelt on the floor, looking through a pile of painted, unframed canvases.

"They are. In New York I worked on abstracts." She chewed her lips. "But I like other styles, too."

Morgan had pulled a large canvas from the stack on the floor. "This one is amazing, Natalie."

"Thanks." Natalie knew she had to get over the wash of embarrassment that flooded her whenever anyone complimented her. Her art felt so intimate, so personal, and most of all, her inner critic knew that the painting really wasn't amazing. It was, at best, okay. "Hey, my glass is empty. Back to the deck."

It was cooling as the sun drifted across the sky, casting shadows, so they carried their drinks and munchies into the house and settled in the living room.

"All right," Natalie said, "it's your turn for show-and-tell, Bella. What's the deal with you and Aaron?"

Bella groaned. "It's complicated. I met him in December and we've been together every moment since. He's smart, he's good, and I'm in love with him."

"Does he love you?" Morgan asked.

Bella nodded.

"Then what's the difficulty?"

"He wants to move to California. He's been asked to interview at a San Francisco architectural firm he's wild to work for."

"Has he asked you to go with him?" Morgan asked.

"Not yet. But he will. He told me he loves me. I'm sure he's going to ask me to marry him."

Natalie was bending over the cheese board, slicing Brie and dabbing it on crackers. She stopped and gawked at Bella. "You love him, he loves you, he's going to ask you to marry him. And your problem *is?*"

Bella made a face. "I don't want to leave this area. I have a new appreciation of it after being away for a few years. Plus, I don't want to leave my family. I want to watch my sister's children grow up. When I have my children, I want my family around me. I don't want to be way out in California."

Natalie rolled her eyes impatiently. If she ever found a man she loved who loved her back, she'd move anywhere with him.

Morgan was more sympathetic. Softly, she analyzed the situation. "Which is harder? To have a family you don't love or a family you love too much to leave?"

"Um, there are these things called *airplanes,*" Natalie told Bella. "They take you places, like from here to California."

Bella rolled her eyes. "I realize that. But what if my children are sick and I need my family to come over and help me fix dinner and rock the baby?"

"Bella." Natalie spoke in a sensible tone. "You don't have any children yet. Maybe by the time you do, Aaron will have a job back on the East Coast."

Bella shook her head. "Aaron wants to be with a big firm building skyscrapers. Skyscrapers near Dragonfly Lake? I don't think so. What about you, Natalie? You moved here from New York. Do you have a man back in the city waiting for you?"

Natalie tossed back the bit of pink liquid from the bottom of her glass. "Nope. No such luck. Believe me, Bella, I'd love to be in your situation. I haven't had very good luck with men. I don't know if I ever will."

"Well, you *are* kind of scary," Bella told her.

"Well, hey, Bella." Natalie laughed. "Have some more daiquiri!" Morgan snorted.

Bella tried to explain: "All black and sharp points and so serious. You look so *edgy*."

"Sharp points?" Natalie asked.

"You're a size zero!" Bella explained.

"Hardly. Size six. And you should talk. You really are a size zero."

"Ladies." Morgan held out her hands. "It's not about size. Look at me. I'm tall, I'm broad-shouldered, and Josh adores me. It's about meeting the right man, and frankly, Natalie, how can you meet anyone when you're stuck in your studio all day and night?"

Natalie straightened defiantly. "Maybe I don't want to meet a man, okay? Maybe I don't want to get married and have children. Maybe I don't want to believe a man when he says he loves me, and then he leaves me, and leaves my children, and never sees them again, and doesn't care if they live or die, and they grow up feeling worthless."

Bella and Morgan were silent.

After a moment, Morgan tried to lighten the atmosphere. "What did you put in these drinks?"

Natalie waved her hands. "Sorry. I didn't mean to bring you all down. It's jealousy, Bella. Your family is so great. Our father walked out on us when I was one. I haven't seen him since. Haven't heard from him. I *did* see how it warped my mother. All she cares about is her bulldogs. Not to mention how it turned my brother into a psychopath."

"Your brother's a psychopath?" Bella asked, eyes wide.

"No, of course not. He's just kind of turned to stone. It does something to you, you know, when you're a child and your father phones and tells you he's going to come see you and take you with him for a day or two, and then doesn't show up or even call with an excuse. Our father used to call Slade—never me, he only was interested in his son—and tell Slade he'd pick him up some afternoon. Slade would get all dressed in his cleanest clothes. He'd comb his hair, even, because Mom wouldn't do it for him. 'He's not going to come,' Mom would say. 'Don't be a fool, Slade.' Slade was nine years old. He'd stand out at the end of the driveway, watching for Dad's car. We lived out in the country, hardly any cars passed, but when they did, I could see Slade rise up on his toes, his neck craning to see the driver. Then the car would go past, and Slade's shoulders would slump. He'd stand out there until it got completely dark. Our father promised to come for him at least five times, and he never came. Not once."

"Poor little boy," Morgan said softly.

"Poor you," Bella added.

Natalie shook her head impatiently. "We're okay. I shouldn't sound so pathetic. Slade is supersmart. Got a full scholarship to B.U., went there for two years, then dropped out to work full-time with an antiques dealer on Newbury Street. He restores furniture— the more valuable, the better the challenge. He makes a decent living and has a new girlfriend every month."

"How old is he?" Morgan asked.

"Thirty-five."

"Does he want to get married and have a family?"

Natalie chuckled. "Slade? Slade hasn't committed to a girl or a woman in his life. He doesn't have to. He's drop-dead sexy and couldn't care less about anyone but himself." She shuddered. "Enough about him. Bella, tell me about Ben."

"Well . . . I guess he's kind of like Slade."

Natalie rolled her eyes. "Believe me, no one's like Slade."

Bella explained, "I mean, Ben's in his thirties, he doesn't have a partner, he's supersmart, and he's kind of noncommunicative. He's obsessed with his work."

"It's about fuel. Energy. He told me," Natalie said. "Josh said Ben's work is important."

"You're right," Bella agreed. "It's just that he's so different from me. And from my older sister, Beatrice, and my younger brother, Brady. We're all social, like Mom and Dad. We talk all the time, we like people, we're extroverted. Ben's so *interior*."

Natalie thought, *I can understand that; as an artist, I feel that way a lot.* She began, "I can—"

Morgan said it first. "I can understand that. I'm a scientist, too. What I work with is often a life-or-death matter. When I focus on my work, I really dig in."

"Okay," Bella argued, "but you're capable of compartmentalizing your work and also paying attention to other things."

"Perhaps that's only because I'm not working now," Morgan pointed out. "I don't have anything work-related to demand I use my brain. I do read articles online, when I find the time, but basically my brain's filled with a speed-demon toddler and a husband who expects me to act like 'the little woman' for his boss."

"Hey, I envy you," Bella said. "I'd love to have a husband and a toddler."

"You're almost there," Natalie assured her. "You're in love with Aaron."

"Oh, and would that be the Aaron who wants to move to California?" Bella's remark brought them full circle.

Suddenly the roar and sputter of an engine assaulted their ears like a chain saw cutting through the front walls.

"What's that?" Bella asked.

"Oh God," Natalie moaned. "Slade's motorcycle."

A moment later, the front door opened and heavy, masculine footsteps came toward them down the hall.

"Hey, Natalie. Hello, everyone." Slade stood there, every adolescent girl's dream in his tight black jeans and heavy black boots. His glossy black hair, straight as a Cherokee's, fell to his collar. Slade was tall, thin, and terrifyingly handsome, with a two-day beard of black bristles giving him a pirate's exotic allure.

Natalie wanted to pound her head on the table. Several times. This *always* happened! Her friends always went gaga over Slade. Right now both Bella and Morgan were recovering from their first jaw-dropped, goggle-eyed reaction, segueing immediately into the female primate mating pose Slade provoked. Their eyes widened, their eyelashes fluttered, their posture changed so that their chests stuck out, and they smiled like a pair of pointy-breasted models from a 1950s calendar, ready to make his dinner and bring him a drink.

Slade kissed Natalie on top of her head and dropped into a chair across from her, his long legs in the black denim irresistibly attractive. "Aren't you going to introduce me to your friends?"

Natalie waved her hand briefly. "Bella, Morgan, this is my brother, Slade. What are you doing here?"

"I came to see you, of course. You've invited me several times. What are you drinking?"

Bella answered first, her voice breathy. "Strawberry daiquiris. Would you like one?" She half rose from her chair.

"Thanks, Bella." Slade could always remember a woman's name. "I'd prefer a beer if Natalie has any."

"I'll get it." Natalie rose and went into the kitchen.

"Did you come from Boston?" Morgan asked.

"Concord. About an hour out of Boston. Took me just over an hour to get here."

"How long are you staying?" Bella was almost panting.

Slade shrugged. "Depends on how long Nat will put up with me. The weather's so great, I just jumped on my bike without any plan at all. I wouldn't mind staying here for the weekend, doing some hiking, now that it's getting warm." He took the beer Natalie offered him. "Thanks, Sis."

"The weather's supposed to be great all weekend," Morgan announced.

"Yes!" Bella agreed, nodding eagerly. "Even warmer than today!"

"Well, then. Do you have room for me for the weekend, Nat?" Slade asked.

"You know there's always room for you here," Natalie assured her brother, because, after all, he was her brother, even if he did turn her friends into thirteen-year-olds who thought he was Justin Bieber. Deep in her heart, locked in a box sealed inside a casket tied up with ropes knotted a thousand times, hid the hope that someday Slade would actually feel love from another person and return that love in truth and in fidelity.

Of course, she hoped that for herself, too.

Slade sat on a chair at the end of the group, the beer in his hand. He took his sunglasses off, exposing his indigo-blue eyes with their thick black lashes.

"We've just moved in next door," Morgan gushed. "My husband, Josh, works for the new business, Bio-Green, right on the other side of Amherst."

Slade said, "Cool."

Morgan continued, "We've got a little boy, Petey. He's just over a year old."

"He's adorable!" Natalie added. "He's got the fattest thighs!"

"Fat thighs. Nice." Slade's voice wasn't sarcastic; if anything, it was ultrapolite.

Bella's voice had gone husky. "I live next door. On that side. I think we might have seen you sometimes in the summer? When you and Natalie came to visit your aunt Eleanor?"

"Possible." He took a swig of beer.

"I should put Petey to bed." Morgan rose from the sofa.

Slade moved. "Hey. Don't leave because of me," he protested. He put his beer on the table. "I'll take a walk around the lake."

"No, really," Morgan insisted. "I've got to help Josh." She turned to Natalie and hugged her. "This was great! We'll do it at my house next time."

Bella reluctantly rose. "I should go, too." She hugged Natalie, waved to Slade, and went out the door.

3

.....

What was wrong with her? Bella wondered as she drove toward her mother's shop. She was irritable and critical and edgy. She could call it spring fever, but it was June, the air thick with summer humidity and the sky an endless blue.

Of course, she knew exactly what was wrong with her: Natalie. Sophisticated, chic, citified Natalie. Bella liked Natalie, and Natalie was nice to her, so why did Bella feel so uncomfortable around her? Why did Natalie make Bella feel so lame?

Last night had been great fun, drinking those daiquiris with Natalie and Morgan. There hadn't been much alcohol in them, and what there was was soaked up by the cheese, crackers, nuts, and olives Natalie had set out, so this morning when Bella woke, she hadn't had the slightest hint of a hangover. So it wasn't the booze that conjured up the instant sense of camaraderie among the three of them.

Except they weren't old friends, and something about last night had gotten Bella's hair on backward this morning. Was it Natalie's art? Natalie had real talent. Her still lifes were better than her abstracts, or maybe Bella thought that because she didn't *get* abstract art. Natalie had rushed them out of the studio before they could study any of her work, but Bella had had time to be impressed.

Natalie had her art. Morgan had her science. And Bella had . . . *this*?

Barnaby's Barn sat next to the road, with space for cars off to the side so the charming façade wouldn't be obscured. Bella parked. Instead of walking straight to the front door, she crossed the road and allowed herself a moment to stand considering the shop's appearance, trying to see it with a fresh eye.

The barn was white clapboard. The windows were framed by blue shutters with cutout hearts. The Dutch door was blue, and blue window boxes were filled with real flowers in the summer and giant Louise-made striped lollipops and gingerbread people in the winter. Slate steps led in a crooked path from the parking lot to the blue front door. When she was a girl, Bella had believed the place was enchanted.

Her mother had created a magical universe. Louise had delighted in crafting Lake Worlds and seeing children enter the shop—the way their eyes widened with happy surprise.

That was sixteen years ago. These days, Louise didn't seem to have the same enthusiasm for making the miniature worlds or for running the shop. Barnaby's Barn was showing definite evidence of decline.

Was there anything Bella could do to fix the situation? She crossed the road and the raked gravel of the parking lot, unlocked the blue door, and stepped inside. It *was* adorable.

The ceiling was a pale sky blue, the walls a sunny yellow, the floor tiled in light green. Louise had painted enormous tulips and daisies, smiling cows, and leaping lambs on the four walls, and wind chimes and mobiles hung from the ceiling, tinkling and glimmering whenever the door opened. The display cases for the Lake Worlds were the first thing you saw when you entered, and other cases were set around not in rows but at odd angles, making the entire space a kind of maze. Shauna Webb's handmade pottery was sold here, with a special "Cow Jumped over the Moon" set for children. Elizabeth Lodge's handmade, embroidered, and smocked children's clothing shared a case with Lorelei Jenkens's hand-knit cashmere blankets and soft cotton baby clothes. Jim Harrington built cradles for real babies and smaller ones for dolls; he carved hearts and flowers and other designs into them and sold them here along with high chairs and stools. A sweet older woman named Lucy Lattimer made stuffed dolls with stitched faces and Victorian milkmaid dresses. These seldom sold. Louise had no idea why, and she felt so bad about it, she always bought two or three a year to give as gifts, and told Lucy customers had bought them. In one corner was a playhouse complete with table, chairs, sink, stove, and tea set, where customers' children could occupy themselves while their parents shopped.

Bella dropped her purse in the back room, grabbed a spray container of glass cleaner and a roll of paper towels, and began to polish the display cases. Outside, the day was golden with sunshine. She'd be surprised if she had any customers. Everyone would be out enjoying the good weather.

Bella didn't mind working. Her mother had made other plans, and Bella was glad Louise could take a break. Anyway, Bella had always enjoyed running the shop. It allowed her a chance to dream a bit, to remember. She was not drawn to the dolls or blankets or even the Lake Worlds. No, it was the furniture displaying the objects for sale that drew her eye and filled her with an enigmatic pleasure.

Her father's family, the Barnabys, had come over from England around the turn of the twentieth century, bringing with them most of their furniture. As a child, Bella had spent her happiest hours roaming through her grandparents' house, hiding inside the gargoyle cabinet when playing hide-and-seek with her older sister and brother, or reclining on a velvet, claw-footed settee, reading Sherlock Holmes while rain streaked down the windows. A magnificent "bench" stood in her grandparents' front hall, soaring almost to the ceiling, built from dark walnut; intricately carved with scrolls, leaves, and berries; inlaid with ivory cherubs floating upward along the back of the bench and around a beveled glass mirror. Her grandparents had perched there to remove their rain or snow boots, then lifted the bench's lid and stashed the boots inside. That had been a good place for hide-and-seek, too. Armoires, desks, vanities, chairs—all the furniture in the house had a *Secret Garden* kind of feeling about it that Bella loved.

And *that* was what it was—for Bella, each piece of antique furniture was like a novel, rich with layers of history, the patina, chips, and scratches all bearing witness to lives full of adventure, mystery, desire, and drama played out by people she'd never met. Bella day-dreamed about what those drawers had once held: lace handker-chiefs, lawn "waists," cravats and watch fobs, straw boaters, tiaras, jewelry, face powder, and tucked beneath it all, she was certain, love letters. With just one piece of antique furniture in a room, the room was connected to endless histories.

Long ago, when Louise started her shop, she'd asked her in-laws if she could use a few pieces for display purposes, and they had read-ily agreed. "Old elephants gathering dust," Bella's grandmother called them. When her grandparents died, they left everything to Bella's parents, who promptly put most of the antique furniture into a storage unit, sold the old Victorian in Northampton, and used the money from the house to pay for college tuition for their three old-est children.

Her parents thought the furniture was too dark and impractical. They filled their own home with light, bright, easy furnishings that children could bump their plastic fire trucks into without Louise worrying about damage. In Barnaby's Barn, Louise had mixed a few pieces of the most useful old furniture with inexpensive tables she'd found on sale at Target or Walmart. The furniture didn't matter to Louise; it was the displays that counted for her.

But the furniture mattered to Bella. She loved those old ele-phants. When Bella was in college, she'd taken a few courses in in-terior design and art history, although she'd had no real idea what sort of job this might lead to. She was well aware of her father's unspoken hope that one of his children would follow his lead and become a teacher. Her older sister, Beatrice, had married young and now had three children. Ben had gone into science, and her younger brother, Brady, also seemed a scientific type, when he didn't seem like a typical loopy adolescent. Bella was fond of children and she worshipped her father, so in her junior year she declared her major in education and became a third-grade teacher. Teaching had been pleasant enough, but for her it wasn't the passion that it was for oth-ers.

On this quiet morning as she walked around the shop, she admitted to herself that her mother wasn't as absorbed with Barnaby's Barn as she'd been before she broke her leg. Louise had joined a bridge group and a book club; both met once a week. It had invigorated her, Louise confessed, to be with friends her own age, to discuss ideas, to use her mind at cards. She'd started collecting brochures about European cruises.

What did that mean for Barnaby's Barn? Bella wasn't sure. Her mother hadn't yet said she wanted to close it.

Did Bella want to take it over?

If she did, she would certainly change it. Right now it looked tired to her, outdated. The best thing about Barnaby's Barn for Bella was that it was where she had first met Aaron Waterhouse, when he entered the store in December looking for a Christmas present for his niece.

The bell above the door tinkled and a plump white-haired woman entered, wanting advice about a gift for her granddaughter. Bella smiled and gladly went to work.

At noon, the bell tinkled again, and Aaron walked in. He wore khakis and a red rugby shirt and moved with his usual tightly controlled energy. "Lunch!" He held up two white paper bags.

"Aaron, how wonderful." Bella slid out from behind the counter to kiss him lightly. "I didn't think I'd see you until tonight."

"You have to eat, I have to eat, perfect solution. Let's sit outside."

"Oh . . ." Bella thought quickly. "The shop, the phone . . ."

"We'll sit on the bench under the tree. If a customer comes, you can go in. Take the phone with you. If it rings, answer it."

Bella kissed him again. "That's what I like about you. So practical."

He nuzzled her neck. "Is that the main reason?"

She allowed herself a moment's surrender to desire, leaning against him, before pulling away. "You know it's not."

Beneath an old apple tree Louise had placed a wrought iron bench; they settled there. Aaron took out his offerings and set them on the bench between them. "Cheddar with chutney. Turkey with honey mustard. How about we take half of each? Chips. Juice."

"Chocolate?" she asked.

"You'll have to wait and see," he teased.

They ate lunch, chatting companionably. Bella leaned back on the bench, gazing up at the pure blue sky. "I'm glad you got me out here. This is the first perfect day of summer."

"Summer doesn't actually begin until June twentieth," Aaron told her.

"Stop that." She slugged his shoulder in pretend irritation. "Feel the air. Look at the sky. It's summer!"

"Look at the flowers. The lilac bush is still blooming. And over there, peonies. Both late spring plants." He was trying not to grin, but this was a game they played often. Aaron couldn't help it; he had a mind that retained absolutely every fact in detail. When they played Trivial Pursuit or watched *Jeopardy!*, he never missed.

Bella nudged his foot with hers. "You have no soul," she carped, but they both knew she was lying. Aaron had a huge soul; furthermore, Bella admired him for knowing so much. "If tomorrow's this nice, let's get the canoe out on the lake in the afternoon."

"Good idea." Aaron stuffed the used papers into the bags. He brought out a small box and offered it to Bella.

"Godiva!" She gave him a suspicious look. "What does this mean?"

"It's our dessert."

"Aaron." He had plenty of money, but he was frugal, and she liked that about him, and he knew she liked that about him. A Hershey bar would have been just fine.

"I got the call. I'm going out for the interview next Thursday."

Bella's appetite vanished. She stared down at the small gold box without seeing it. "That's great, Aaron."

"But?"

"But California is so far away."

"I don't have the job yet," he reminded her. Reaching over, he held her hand. "Bella, we can work things out."

A silver Range Rover pulled into the parking lot.

The perfect moment for an interruption, Bella thought. "Oh, look. I've got a customer. Can we discuss this tonight?"

"Sure," Aaron replied amiably.

Bella and Aaron stood up. Recognition of the Range Rover suddenly hit her: It was the car Eleanor Reynolds had left for Natalie, and it was Natalie who stepped out of the passenger seat. Her brother, Slade, his eyes hidden by black sunglasses, stepped out from the driver's side.

Bella hadn't expected to see Slade and Natalie again so soon. She'd never expected to see Slade anywhere near Barnaby's Barn. In the glare of the bright June sunshine, next to the silver Range Rover, Slade didn't seem real; he was like a Transformer in a farmyard.

"Hi, Bella! Hi, Aaron." Natalie was in black, too: tight black pants, black tee shirt, black sandals. "Isn't it a great day? Slade and I thought we'd explore the area, and we saw your shop. Aaron, this is my brother, Slade."

The two men shook hands. Bella and Natalie led the way into Barnaby's Barn, Aaron and Slade behind them. The four stood just inside, looking around.

"It's sweet," Natalie said, but her compliment seemed forced.

"It needs a lot of work," Bella admitted. "I hadn't realized how shabby it's gotten."

"It's not *shabby*," Natalie protested. She walked over to the display of Lake Worlds. "These are your mother's? Oh, they're darling. Slade, come look at this beaver family. Perfection. The teeny buck teeth. The flat tail. Incredible attention to detail."

But Slade stalked on his long legs clear to the back of the room and dropped down in a squat. Bella looked at Aaron with an inquisitive arched eyebrow. Aaron's mouth quirked up and his expression clearly read: *I couldn't tell you what the guy's doing.*

Lucy Lattimer's hand-painted stuffed dolls were arranged on the table as if at a tea party, their flounced pinafores and long dresses spread around them. Not, Bella thought, quite what she would have picked for Slade's interest. But really, she noticed, his interest wasn't in the dolls but in the table, painted cream with an edging of ivy and daisies. Slade reached under the drop leaf and pulled out the gate-leg. Without saying a word, he lay on his back and scooted beneath the lifted table leaf.

"Slade!" Natalie threw her hands in the air. "I can't take you anywhere!" She turned to Bella and Aaron. "I told you Slade works in an antiques shop? He's mad about restoring antiques."

"Oh, that table's not valuable," Bella insisted. "I think it was in my grandmother's sewing room, and then Louise painted it to use in the shop to hold things. That leg's cracked, so we have to keep that leaf dropped."

"She shouldn't have painted it." Slade's voice came from under the table.

"Why not? It's her table. She needed it to fit in with the gift shop décor."

Slade scooted out from under the table and rose, all in one sin-ewy graceful motion like an acrobat or an eel. "That's an English tiger oak drop-leaf table with barley twist legs. Restored, easily a thousand."

Slade kept his hand on the table, caressing the wood as he talked. His voice was low and smoky, its timbre resonating deep within Bella's body, gently touching her to open a door so secret even she hadn't known it existed. Her breath caught in her throat; she stared at him, unable to speak.

Natalie misunderstood her reaction. "Surprised to discover you own a valuable piece of furniture? Slade's always doing that. Finding a treasure someone never knew they possessed."

"Good Lord, look at this." Slade crossed the room and inspected the open doors of the cabinet displaying Shauna Webb's pottery. He ran his hands along the wood and knelt down to investigate the carved doors on the bottom. Without turning to look at Bella, he growled, "Do you have any idea what you've got here?"

"Again," Bella explained, "it's a piece from my grandparents' home. It was my favorite, because of the gargoyle carved on top, but now that we use it for a display piece, I have to admit I get frus-trated, dusting all the intricate carvings."

"This is a marvelous piece of work." Now Slade did look at her, and a blue flame of passion gleamed in his eyes. "It's easily—*easily*— worth ten thousand dollars. I'll give you ten thousand for it right now."

"I had no idea." Bella crossed the room and delicately touched her fingertips to the stained glass in the top doors. Slade was running his hands over the long panel of wood on the side. A kind of current of controlled excitement radiated from him like a rushing river she was compelled to enter. "I could never sell it without my mother's permission."

"Slade's not buying it anyway." Natalie stalked across the room, snatched up her brother's hand, and yanked him away from the cabinet. "Slade. Grip. Get one. You are on vacation. We are going to have fun. You cannot buy antiques."

Slade allowed himself to be pulled away. "Sorry," he said to Bella. "Guess I got carried away. It's just that that really is a remarkable piece of furniture."

"We're going into Northampton," Natalie told Bella. "Is the shop open tomorrow?"

"No, thank heavens. Closed Sundays."

"Good. Maybe we can all get together for drinks."

"I'd like that." Bella walked the brother and sister to the door and waved at them as they went out to the Range Rover. "Thanks for coming in!" she called. Closing the blue door, she faced Aaron. "That was intense."

Aaron shrugged. "But profitable perhaps. That guy really seems to know his stuff. Who cares how odd he is if he can help you make some money?"

Bella frowned at Aaron. "I don't know, Aaron. I think my grandparents intended for this furniture to be handed down to their children and grandchildren."

"Well, they have been, and look where they are. Not in your house but in your shop."

"You're right," Bella mused. An idea was taking form in her mind—and in her heart, which was shaking pom-poms of excitement—but she needed to think it through. "But maybe Ben or Brady or I will want them for their homes."

Aaron laughed. "Honey, come on. Look at that cabinet. Gargoyles and stained glass? It's like something from 'The Fall of the House of Usher.'"

Stunned, she snapped, "That's a terrible thing to say."

Aaron held up his hands. "Whoa. *Sorry*."

She wrapped her arms around her chest as if she were holding herself together. Why was she in such a state? She felt as if she'd had too much coffee to drink, as if she'd jumped into a cold river and couldn't catch her breath.

Aaron gave her a few moments to gather herself, then took her in his arms. "Hey."

She spoke into his chest. "Aaron, I'm thinking this through. I guess I'd always assumed that some of my grandparents' furniture would be in my house when I got married. For my children to see."

"Not that cabinet, I hope. It would give children nightmares."

"I totally disagree." Bella pushed away so she could face him. "Aaron, I always treasured that cabinet. I didn't find the gargoyle scary. He was like a magic friend."

"Okay. I get you. It's a great idea to have some of your grandparents' furniture in our house. But, Bella, when the time comes, it's going to be *our* house. Right?"

She searched his honest, open face. She allowed her tense shoulders to loosen. "Of course." She slid past him, out of his arms, and walked to the cabinet. "If we sold this cabinet, it would certainly help Barnaby's Barn financially." A thought tickled her brain like a plant searching to wedge its way up into the light of her mind. "If we changed the shop . . . if we sold some antiques, too . . . We've got old pieces all over the place; we ought to have Slade value them. Ben's got my grandfather's old desk in his apartment. I think it's maple, maybe something that begins with a B." She laughed. "Of course it would; my grandfather Barnaby loved to begin everything with a B."

"Bella." Aaron remained planted in place. "Even if you sell all the furniture your family owns, it's going to run out. Maybe you'll save your shop for a few more months, but then what?"

Uncomfortably, Bella said, "You sound like you want the shop to fail."

"I don't want it to fail, Bella. But I do want you to be open to possibilities elsewhere. I want you to think about something else. I don't want to talk with you about it here, in Barnaby's Barn. I want it to be in *my* space, or at least in a neutral space." He looked concerned. "I'd better go. I can get some work done while you've got the shop open. I'll see you tonight, right?"

"Right." Bella forced herself to walk to the door with him. She kissed him absentmindedly. "Thanks for the lunch."

4

· · · · ·

Petey was taking his morning nap. Morgan was at her computer, so engrossed in a proposed amendment to the solid and human waste management act that when her cell buzzed, she nearly jumped out of her chair.

"Josh!" Her voice was a bit too chipper, her heart pounding as if he'd caught her with a lover. "Hi!"

"Just calling to be sure we're set for tomorrow night."

She was glad he couldn't see her eye roll. "Josh, the Ruoffs are only coming for *drinks*. You went with me to the liquor store." And insisted on buying a full range of unbelievably expensive wines and Scotches. "You saw the cheese and crackers I bought. I can't make the bruschetta until tomorrow night. It has to be heated in the oven for the cheese to melt."

"I'm worried about the bruschetta."

She couldn't believe it. "You're worried about the *bruschetta?*"

"It sounds messy. Something could fall onto Eva's dress."

"Josh. Have you lost your mind?"

"Morgan, we agreed we wouldn't argue." He was in his office, his voice tense.

Morgan took a deep breath. She recalled that when Josh first met the Ruoffs, Josh had nicknamed them "Mr. Wannabe Bill Gates and his wife, Kris Kardashian." Although they had laughed at the Ruoffs' pretentious style, they couldn't help but admire their work ethic and success. The truth was Ronald Ruoff was making significant steps toward a greener world, even if he and his wife were both crass and pushy. And his firm was making money.

Josh was making money now, too—and all for his family.

Morgan could never forget the deciding event that propelled them into changing their lives. Their car failed to pass inspection. Morgan had had to push Petey in his stroller for blocks to the grocery store and back in the pouring rain.

Josh had returned home in time to see his wife and son soaked and shivering.

"That does it," Josh had said, lifting Petey in his arms. "I'm taking the Bio-Green job."

And he had. And here they were.

Softening her voice, Morgan assured her husband, "Okay, sweetie, I'll find another recipe."

"Something that doesn't drip."

"Right." She was an expert in hazardous waste management, and her job was to invent a dripless canapé. "Something that doesn't drip." She choked back an insane little titter.

"Great, thanks, you're a star. Hey, have you joined a health club yet?"

Now she was speechless. The Josh she had married would never have called anyone a *star*. Morgan wanted to warn him: *Don't call me a star. I'm not a client. You're not a Hollywood agent. Stop talking like Ronald Ruoff.* Josh was picking up all kinds of bizarre and unappealing mannerisms over at Bio-Green, and it was making her crazy. But she held her tongue.

"I thought I'd try the gym outside Amherst this afternoon," she told him. "I've read about it online. It has a great children's playroom with a full-time babysitter."

"Great idea, babe. You might meet some prospective clients."

"Hey, *babe*, life's not just about meeting clients." She loved and detested him at the same time.

"I hate it when you use that tone of voice."

"Sorry. I just—"

His own voice roughened with frustration. "Look out the window, for crying out loud. Look where you are. Look at the house we're living in. We've got a beach for our son to play on. We took him out in a canoe last Sunday. What more do you want?"

"I guess I want us to be like we used to be," Morgan said simply.

"Look, I can't get into all this now. Just join a health club."

Josh clicked off without saying good-bye, something else he'd never done before taking the job at Bio-Green. She didn't know if he did it consciously, to reinforce the fact of his incredibly stressful busyness, or if he did it unconsciously, moving so fast from one thing to another, which in a way was worse, because it put her among the other things, no more important.

She sat glumly at her desk, staring at her computer screen. She closed the EPA website and opened one about canapés. Scrolling down, she discovered a recipe for salmon and caviar on crackers. Salmon *and* caviar, that should please Josh. Maybe she'd sprinkle some silver leaf on it all.

But no. She was being petty. After all, she and Josh had talked for hours before he agreed to take this job. He was incredibly lucky to get the offer, and they both knew it. It required just the right mix of odd skills and training that Josh possessed. He'd started off as an English literature major in college, but after two years and an increasing awareness of how few professorial positions there were for English majors, he switched over to chemistry. He had that kind of mind; sometimes she thought he could do anything. By the time she got her master's in environmental health science, Josh had whizzed through the chemistry doctoral program.

They'd met at the university, and before long, they moved in together, sat on the sofa, legs tangled together, poring over chem texts.

They knew they were in a growth industry. For better or worse, the world was speeding down a technological superhighway, tossing its waste out the window and forgetting about it. The potential dangers were stunning. It would not be politicians who saved the world, Morgan and Josh agreed, it would be the nerd with the clipboard and glasses who made sure that the masks protecting lab workers from formaldehyde were up to code.

They were married right after Josh finished his PhD, and both took jobs outside Boston. Morgan worked in the environmental safety office at Weathersfield College, and Josh at one of the high-tech corporations on Route 128. They had tuition loans to repay, and Boston was an expensive place to live, so they decided to put off their dream of having a large family until they could afford a house.

Accidentally, Morgan got pregnant. Don't worry, she told Josh, I'll work after the baby's born.

Then Petey came into the world, pink, perfect, helpless, infinitely precious.

"Don't go back to work, Morgan," Josh had begged her. "You should stay home for a year at least. He needs you. He's so vulnerable. He's so—" Josh had choked back his emotion, unable to find the right words.

Morgan had never loved Josh more than at that moment. "I know," she agreed. "I don't want to leave him. Not yet. But how will we make it financially?"

Josh clenched his fist. "We'll draw up a new budget and learn to economize. I'll work two jobs if I have to."

Morgan had not asked him: *If you work two jobs, when will you see your son? When will you see me?* She knew Josh was doing all he could for them.

Josh met Ronald Ruoff at an ecology conference in Chicago, and they hit it off immediately. Josh, with his big shoulders and blazing red hair, had a charisma about him, not a rock star dazzle that made people shy but a gentle charm and a way of listening that made people feel *they* were the fascinating ones. And it was the truth, after all, Josh did find people fascinating. He was not some phony jerk; he loved learning what made people tick, why they made the choices they made, what their hopes were for the future. Josh had a huge heart; Morgan knew that about him.

Sometimes these days, though, she wondered whether that big heart had gotten buried beneath a pile of money. Sometimes she wondered if he'd drunk a magic elixir that transformed him from the man she loved into this superstressed, fast-talking, GQ-reading, clothes-conscious, Cadillac-driving, overworked, never-home executive who worried about his wife *making contacts*!

Shoving her chair away from her desk, Morgan stalked out of her office—office, hah, she had an office but no job!—and down the hall to the living room. It felt good to walk, and their new house was so damned big she could get exercise just going from room to room.

Be fair, she told herself. *Remember your promise to Josh.* He would be bringing in so much money they could pay off their tuition loans, put money away for Petey's college, and still live well. Or, as Josh put it, live *in style*.

Morgan had tried to keep her part of the bargain. She agreed with Josh to buy this contemporary house even though in her eyes it had all the coziness of a World War II bunker. The best part about it for her was the beach and the lake. Petey would learn to swim, sail, boat. They'd hike in the woods. The Amherst public school district was superb. Anyway, since when had she been so sensitive to the *ambience* of a room? When they lived in their rented condo in Boston, they'd joined their grad-student sofas and tables and used them, ugly, mismatched, but comfortable, and just perfect for life with a spitting-up newborn baby whose bowel movements mysteriously leaked out of his diaper.

Morgan's part of the job at Bio-Green, Josh had told her, was to make their new home *stunning*. They were to have lots of glam parties with new posh friends who would be so wowed by the O'Keefes' sophistication and wealth that they'd feel blessed to be allowed to invest in the company.

How to make their home *stunning*? Morgan had never considered such a project before. Morgan had thought of phoning her mother, because her family's home was so handsomely decorated. Then she remembered how busy her parents were and decided not to bother them. She had shopped the way she lived—online, finding and pricing pieces of furniture before driving to the store to see them. It had been easier to do it on the Internet than lugging her baby in a pack. Immediately she'd decided against black and white;

it had a cool look, but one leak from Petey's diaper and the white wouldn't have the same chic gloss. She'd found a deep smoke-gray sofa with matching chairs. Her genius touch was a chrome coffee table and chrome end tables. The entire living room gleamed softly, and worked perfectly with the floor-to-ceiling fireplace of variegated fieldstones.

Was it too monotone? Morgan chewed on her fingertip, studying the room. One wall was all glass, displaying the lake. Couldn't get better than that! Chrome lamps stood around, casting light, and she'd placed one large red vase (wedding present) in the center of the chrome table, then removed it because it appeared just too *House Beautiful*. This room needed something, though. . . .

Just as a lightbulb went on in her brain, she heard Petey calling out, awake from his nap.

Natalie opened her door, letting sunlight flood into the front hall. "Hi, Morgan! Come in! Hello, Petey!" She wore cargo shorts and a loose white shirt covered with a million dots and dribbles of paint. "I'm so glad you phoned. I've been working all day and getting nowhere but frustrated. Want a Diet Coke? Lemonade?" She took Petey's chubby hand. "Graham cracker?"

"He's fine; he just had his after-nap treat," Morgan told her. "And I came over to see your paintings again. I want to buy one."

Natalie looked staggered. "Man, I should have people over for drinks more often," she joked, but her smile was uneasy. "Morgan. Listen. That's really nice of you, but none of my paintings is ready to be exhibited yet. They're all works in progress."

Morgan shifted her son onto her other arm. "I remember a large abstract of reds and blacks. . . ."

Natalie shook her head. "I don't think my real forte is abstract painting."

"I have to put Petey down someplace," Morgan said. "He weighs about a hundred pounds. Can we go in your kitchen, give him a couple of pans and spoons and spatulas?"

"Sure. Of course." Natalie led them into the kitchen, and Morgan settled the little boy against the wall to stabilize him. "The floor's clean. At least I think it is."

"Don't worry. Petey hasn't quite mastered the art of picking up crumbs yet. He's better with big things. There. Anything rubber is good, because—"

While Morgan was talking, Natalie squatted down and placed a pot and a big slotted spoon in front of him. Petey gave a macaw scream of joy and began enthusiastically banging the spoon on the pot.

"Oh," Natalie said. "I see why rubber is good."

They gave the child a rubber spatula, which didn't interest him. Natalie took out a nest of Tupperware bowls and put them in front of him. Soon he was pounding on the Tupperware, which made much less noise.

"It's almost five," Natalie said. "Glass of wine?"

"In a minute. Natalie, I really want to buy that painting."

"You only saw it once."

"Then let me look at it again." Before Natalie could respond, she said, "Petey, you play with Natalie. Mommy's going upstairs just for a minute!"

Petey had discovered he could hit the spoon on the tea tin, making a new noise. He didn't even notice his mother leave the room.

Morgan zipped through the house and up the stairs. She found her way to the room Natalie was using as a studio and entered. The still life remained set up on the easel. Morgan cast a quick glance at it, noticed how Natalie had softened the colors of the shawl, and felt a momentary twinge of guilt for intruding this way. Weren't artists supposed to be defensive of their unfinished work? She looked away, to the darker corner of the room where the pile of abstracts were stacked on the floor, leaning against the wall.

She rummaged through the paintings, taking care to do so slowly, until she found the one she remembered. It was very large, perhaps four feet by five, an explosion of color. She pulled it out from the others, carried it over to the wall lit by sunlight, then walked away to study it from a distance. It looked like an erupting volcano, or an exotic blossoming flower, or a swirling gypsy skirt, or . . .

She picked it up to carry it downstairs, and saw, on the back, a small white label:

ROMANCE
ABSTRACT IN OIL
NATALIE REYNOLDS
$500

"Aha!" Morgan positioned the painting with the oil facing away from her body and slowly, step by step, went down the stairs, through the hall, and into the kitchen.

By now, Natalie had joined Petey on the floor and added a red colander and a set of measuring cups to their timpani. Petey was intent on his hammering, crawling from one pot to another, and Natalie was hitting various items with a whisk while singing, "I don't want to work, I want to bang on the drum all day!"

Morgan set the painting on the floor, shoved her hand into her pants pocket, and yanked out her cell phone. She took a video of the pair, and just in time, because Natalie looked up and saw her.

Natalie stood up. "My ears are ringing. Don't tell me you got us on video."

"And it's going right to YouTube."

"I don't think so. Look at him. He's still banging away. Doesn't he ever get tired?"

"Not tired, no. He'll get bored in a while and crawl off to wreak havoc somewhere else."

"Let's go down to the beach," Natalie suggested. "Sand is quieter."

"Good idea. Let's take the Tupperware and a spoon for him to play with."

"And I'll bring some iced tea for us."

Morgan scooped up Petey and some bowls. Natalie carried the iced tea and a spoon. They went out the kitchen door onto the deck and down the wooden steps to the flagstones leading through the short stretch of lawn to the beach. When Petey saw the sand, he struggled to get there.

"I could fetch chairs . . ." Natalie offered.

"No, sitting on the ground is just fine." Morgan established Petey in the sand and sat cross-legged next to him, leaning back on her elbows, lifting her face to the sun. "What a great day."

The beach was wide and ran up from the water a good ten feet. A short wooden pier extended between Natalie's house and the Barnabys', with a wooden boathouse a few feet away from the lake, which today reflected a cloudless blue sky. Oaks, birches, and pines grew in all the yards, casting shadows that would be welcome in the heat of deep summer and providing homes for the birds who chirped and rustled among the leaves. From across the water came an occasional note of music or the industrious hammering of the fellow whom they could see repairing the roof of his boathouse.

Natalie handed Morgan a glass of iced tea and took a long sip of her own. "The sun feels so good on my shoulders."

"Is painting hard physically?" Morgan asked.

"Not really. Sometimes I get stiff." She yawned. "This is nice."

"Natalie, I found the painting I want. It's called *Romance*. I saw the label on the back, so obviously you exhibited it at least once."

"And no one bought it," Natalie said.

"Because it was waiting for *me* to buy it," Morgan retorted. Then, because she could tell that Natalie was struggling, she said, "Natalie. Listen. I really like that painting. But I'd be the first person to admit that I know nothing about art. Plus, not to be rude or ignorant, I probably could tell a first-rate still life from a bad one, but with abstract art . . . it all looks incomprehensible to me. But this painting has *spirit*. It has *emotional power*."

Natalie smiled shyly. "Thanks." Her eyes were cast down, her face shadowed.

"I want to buy it." When Natalie didn't respond, Morgan coaxed, "It would only be next door. You could come visit it anytime."

Natalie's posture straightened. She lifted her chin and stared straight at Morgan. "Look. I'm not an abstract artist. That painting is not my best work."

Morgan cocked her head. "And yet, I like it."

Natalie snorted, exasperated.

"Listen, Natalie, what if it were hanging in a gallery? What if I saw it there? I'd buy it, and I'd have no idea what the artist thought about it, right?"

Natalie picked up a handful of sand and let it drift through her fingers as she thought. "I see what you're saying." After a moment, she admitted, "I'm struggling with my still life, too."

Morgan could tell that Natalie was working something through. It had been a long time since Morgan had shared such a moment with a friend. Life was full of decisions, and exposing such personal conflicts was risky.

"What about landscapes?" Morgan asked.

"What do you mean?"

"Have you ever thought of painting landscapes? Of painting"— she held her hand out, indicating the glowing blue lake—"all this?"

Natalie shook her head. "I don't know why, but landscape painting has never appealed to me."

"That's interesting. Why not?"

Natalie shrugged. She relaxed a bit, considering her reply. After a moment, she smiled at Morgan. "Why biosafety?"

"Hmm. Touché." Now it was Morgan's turn to sit in contemplation. She actually knew the answer, but the full truth required personal revelation. "I've always been interested in safety. I love science, but it can be dangerous. When I took chemistry in high school, something lit up inside me at all the safety measures and rules we were taught. One day a girl in my lab was in a hurry and her hair caught on fire from her Bunsen burner." Morgan shuddered. "She was all right—someone dragged her to a sink and stuck her head underwater. Her face wasn't burned, only a bit of her scalp. But I couldn't forget that moment. When I was in college and realized there was such a field as biosafety, I went right for it. And the more I learned about hazardous waste management, the more I wanted to work in that field. Protecting the world as well as people."

"Wow," Natalie said. "That's impressive. You must feel a huge sense of responsibility."

Morgan laughed. "Actually, I do, but my responsibility now is all about taking care of that little guy, which means saving for a college education and all that raising a child requires." She gestured toward Petey, who was carefully adding sand, spoonful by spoonful, into a bowl of water Morgan had carried up from the lake. "I love my work. I miss my work." She sighed. "But I'll get back to it someday." She didn't want to stay focused on herself, and she certainly didn't want to get into her growing dissatisfaction with her husband and his job. "So. Now you tell me. Why not landscapes?"

Natalie tugged at the hem of her cargo shorts. "I think I've been a kind of gypsy artist, wandering from genre to genre. I've been told I can be good. Unfortunately, some of the positive appraisal has come with strings attached, so I don't really know if it's been the truth."

"You're talking about male art instructors wanting to sleep with you?"

"Well, you summed it up very euphemistically, thank you." Natalie's mouth quirked downward.

"You're a babe," Morgan reminded her.

"So are you. So are lots of women. We shouldn't have to have sex with our teachers to get the truth." She ran her hand through her cropped black hair, ruffling it so it stood up like a raven's plume. "That's not all of it, though. I mean, I haven't been able to spend more than nine months at a time working on my art, and that's just not sufficient. I've gotten scholarships at art schools over the past fifteen years, but they didn't cover living expenses so I never could stay long."

Morgan said sympathetically, "That's tough."

"It is. That's why I'm determined to be disciplined in my work now that Aunt Eleanor has provided me with this amazing opportunity. No men in my life, no dating, no flirting. That always leads to trouble. Just *work*."

"You're painting a still life now, right?"

"Right." Natalie exhaled. "And I don't like it."

Morgan laughed. "Okay, then. What would you like to paint?"

Natalie stared toward the lake, and Morgan watched the strain ease from her face, replaced by a dawning hope. "*That*. I'd rather paint that."

"What?"

"Petey. A little boy in blue shorts and a red-and-white striped shirt, pouring water into bowls, his face so intent on his work. Children have done that for centuries, and here he is, one particular child. It would be something eternal and ephemeral at the same time."

"Why not do it?"

"For one thing, how long is he going to keep still?" Natalie asked.

"Here's a solution." Morgan reached into her pocket, took out her cell phone, and snapped a few shots of her son. She handed her phone to Natalie. "The resolution isn't great. . . ."

"And the lighting will change every day," Natalie mused aloud. She stood up, pulled out her own phone, and took a few steps back, clicking shots at different angles. "Clouds, shadow, the earth's angle to the sun, but still . . . Wait. I have a better camera. I'll be right back." She sprinted away.

Morgan held her breath. Her son could grow bored in an instant; she didn't dare move for fear of distracting him. Wouldn't it be wonderful if Natalie did a portrait of Petey!

A minute passed. A bumblebee buzzed over to check out Morgan's hair. She didn't even twitch. The bee flew away. Petey continued to pour sand into the bowl. The sunlight fell on his strawberry blond curls, turning them into a mystical substance, liquid fire. His dimpled hands clutched the spoon fiercely as he cautiously, trying not to spill even one grain of sand, raised the spoon from the beach to the bowl. He would be a good chemist, she realized.

But where was Natalie? Petey wouldn't do this forever! She heard a click and turned her head. Natalie was on the deck with a camera, snapping photos. Morgan relaxed. She sipped her tea.

By the time Natalie returned to the beach, Petey had become bored with this project and was toddling around the lawn, looking for bugs and falling over.

"He's still working on the walking thing," Morgan told Natalie. "Did you get the shots you wanted?"

"I think so. I'll start tomorrow morning to see what I can do, and if the weather's good, maybe you two can come back over."

"Great," Morgan said. "But I do have one stipulation if you're going to use my son as your model."

"Oh?" Natalie was looking down at her camera, clicking through the shots.

"I want to buy the abstract. Today. We're having Josh's boss over for drinks this Friday, and I want to hang the painting in the living room."

"Oh, Morgan, just borrow the damned thing!"

Morgan grinned. "Uh-uh. I'm paying you for it." She picked up her son, whose diaper sagged against his sandy shorts. "I'll carry him. You can carry the painting over. Now."

5

· · · · ·

First, Natalie thought, she'd do a quick sketch of Petey on the beach with a charcoal pencil on a sheet of her less expensive paper. She selected her favorite photo taken of Petey in the sand by the lake, uploaded it onto her computer, and zoomed it as big as her computer screen would take it without distorting it.

Next, she put on her music, some CDs she'd burned, a mix of upbeat and mellow, and set the volume at low. She picked up her pencil and put it down.

Standing in front of her easel, she stared at the digitalized shot of the little boy, letting her eyes blur as she took in the background: the golden sand, blue water, green trees all around him. Her pencil waggled in her hand as she loosened her wrist. She hadn't done portraiture for years. She wasn't sure what she was doing. This would be only a sketch. When she used oils, she could bring out the radiance of the child's hair, the bloom of his fresh skin, the gentle spread of light around him. For now she wanted to capture only line, shape, and shadow. His profile was to her as he squatted in the sand. His hand was halfway between the ground and the bowl, the small spoon heavy, clutched tightly in his hand, his entire body tensed with the effort not to spill the sand.

Her own hand lifted. She didn't think. She hummed to the music. She swayed slightly with the beat. She touched the charcoal pencil to the paper and swooped a line, the plump wrist, the fat fist, the straight handle and curved bowl of the spoon.

She worked swiftly, but still, two hours had passed when she finally stopped, discovering the nape of her neck and the back of her knees moist with sweat. It remained cool in the mornings so she didn't need the air conditioner and she didn't want to use mechanical air if she didn't have to, but by noon the heat had intensified, and even in her shorts and tank top she was uncomfortably warm. She had to take a break. She wasn't hungry for lunch yet. She needed to *move*. As she went through the house, opening all the windows wider, hoping a breeze would sweep through, she caught sight of the lake, glistening in an inviting span of blue.

She didn't possess a bathing suit. It had been years since she'd gone swimming. She wasn't a very strong swimmer, anyway, but right now every molecule in her body wanted to immerse in that cool water. She stepped out of the kitchen onto the deck and looked around. After the still closeness of her studio, the world blossomed around her, an explosion of warmth, fragrance, birdsong, and light. She took a quick peek toward Bella's house. Bella was at the shop today, she knew, but was Louise out on the deck? No. Good. Sometimes—well, probably more than was good for her—Natalie craved solitude. When she'd been painting, she needed time to emerge from her solitary state and rejoin the normal world. Walking to the end of the deck, she peered around at the O'Keefes' house. Both cars, Josh's Cadillac and Morgan's Toyota SUV, were gone.

Lovely. The lake was empty, except for someone in a canoe in the distance. It was, after all, a weekday, when most people were at work.

So no one would see her, and she couldn't wait any longer. She hurried down to her beach, kicked off her sandals, and waded into the lake in her shorts and tank top. The water temperature was heavenly, warm at the top from the touch of the sun, with a teasing coolness the deeper and farther out she walked. She couldn't resist. It was so inviting, especially after two hours of intense mental concentration. She threw herself into the water and began to swim in her own pathetic uncoordinated way.

After a while, she flipped over on her back and floated, letting her arms drift out to the side, kicking her feet a bit, soaking in the

healing power of the warm sun on her face and the cool water supporting her back. Each finger drooped downward as the water ca-
ressed it, and her neck, stiff from working, loosened as her head fell
back, her chin lifting toward the sky. Ripples of water combed the
curls of her hair with delicate swirls. Oh, this was bliss.

She didn't think. She couldn't think. Finally, after all the
months of worrying about the move to the lake, and packing up the
New York apartment and saying good-bye and making the trip, after
wondering if she were just a phony with no talent who would find at
the end of the year all she'd done was nothing worthwhile, after
worrying that she'd meet only people who carried rifles and ate deer,
rabbits, or bears (which was pretty much like the neighborhood
she'd grown up in), after all that, and after deciding to do the still
life and setting up the silver with apples and working on it, *working*
on it and getting twisted in the gut with the instinctive suspicion
that it wasn't *right* and nothing she could do could fix it, after waking up in the middle of the night and stalking into her studio and
inspecting the still life and realizing it really was awful, after seeing
Petey on the beach and getting that massive hit of urgency, that
need to paint him as he was at that moment—after all that, suddenly she was relaxing.

Because she knew her sketch was good. It was going to be extraordinary.

Flipping her feet lightly, she let herself be carried by the water. By
the universe. She was eased to the point of sleep, eyes closed, heart
slowed, tension melting out of her muscles into the lake. She drifted.

She didn't know what made her finally wake from her spell. Flipping
over onto her stomach, she treaded water and gazed around, looking
for her aunt's beach.

She didn't see it.

She dog-paddled a slow circle in the water.

She saw her aunt's house—and it was a million miles away.

A thrill of fear ran down her spine, chilling her, and her feet,
now hanging down into the depths, went cold. How had she drifted

so far? What had she been thinking? Well, of course, she *hadn't* been thinking! *Okay*, she told herself. *Okay*. First of all, she didn't have to swim to her aunt's house. She could swim to the closest shore and walk home.

The closest shore was a million miles away.

Another surge of fear shot through her. *Calm down*, she told herself. The shore is not a million miles away. It's not even a million *feet* away. It only looked like it. And, true, she had never been a strong or efficient swimmer, but she wasn't in a hurry. She didn't have to get back *soon*. She just had to get back. She could do that. She would take her time, head for her aunt's beach, and calmly swim back to shore.

She set out. Left arm, right arm. Kicking her legs. Left arm, right arm. She tried to turn her head and breathe like professional swimmers but she kept getting water up her nose, and then she had to quit swimming and tread water while she blew her nose and caught her breath. Left arm, right arm. She splashed water in her face with each stroke. The water no longer supported her. It sucked at her, pulling her down. She forced herself not to look at the shore because keeping her head up slowed her down, so she turned her head to the side as she swam. But when she did look up, she saw that she'd gotten off course and was almost swimming in a circle.

Well, damn!

She straightened her course and began swimming again. She was tiring. She'd never been much of an athlete, and she could feel her body running out of gas. Still, she continued to plow through the water, sloppily sweeping arm after arm. Her breath tore her lungs. She was wheezing, puffing. She stopped to check: it seemed she was making some headway. The house was closer. She could see the pot of pink geraniums on her deck. She swam.

Left arm, right arm, and then, she didn't know how it happened, she stupidly took a breath and filled her mouth and throat with water. Choking, she paddled frantically in the water, gasping for air. Her body, of its own accord, suddenly just sank. Once again she swallowed a huge gulp of lake. All around her, the water bubbled and frothed as she thrashed.

Fighting now, arms and legs out of sync, she kicked and flailed back to the surface, spitting and gasping and gagging. Gravity dragged relentlessly on her entire body, which had hardened as heavy as stone.

"Help!" she cried, a feeble attempt that made her sink again, water surging into her mouth. Her throat burned. Her lungs were on fire. Her heart was hammering against her chest. All strength evaporated from her limbs as she slapped at the water, struggling to get her nose and mouth up into the air.

Something touched her arm. She screamed, or tried to. Panic flooded her veins, shooting fear on a dazzling course through her body before she understood that it was a hand on her arm, a strong hand hauling her upward. With a monumental effort of will, she forced her body to stop thrashing and blindly turned toward the hand, her eyes flooded with water. Another hand groped at her chin, her shoulder, and finally grasped her under her arm. Her head banged against wood.

She was held like that, her head above water, gasping for air. Someone said something, perhaps "Hang on," and the hand on her wrist moved to her other underarm.

"Just catch your breath," a man said. "I've got you. I won't let you go."

She steadied herself in the water, allowing her legs to sink down, her body to straighten into an I, as her shoulders and head remained in the blissful air. After a moment, the man said, "Okay. I'm going to pull you up."

Her senses focused. It was a rowboat. Her cheek scraped along the wood. She was steadily pulled upward until she could grasp the side of the boat with her hands, but she had no power in her arms to get herself over into the boat. The man moved his own hands to her waist, clutched tight, and hauled her up, her butt and legs unceremoniously plunking down into the bottom of the boat.

She lay there for a moment, breathing hard. She was lying on a couple of fishing rods and a coil of rope, curled in fetal position around a pair of large feet in old deck shoes. The sun beat down on her, but she shivered.

"Can you sit up if I help you?" the man asked.

"I think so." She grabbed the plank of wood serving as a seat and dragged herself up. That took every ounce of energy she had left. She just sat there, head falling forward, chest heaving.

"Take off your top," the man said.

She lifted her head. "You've got to be kidding."

Then she recognized the man. It was Bella's brother Ben, wearing a swimming suit and a cotton polo shirt.

"Your teeth are chattering," Ben told her quietly. "You're covered in gooseflesh. You're probably in shock." In one smooth movement, he peeled off his shirt and handed it to her. "Put this on. It will warm you up." When she just gawked at him, he said, "It's clean. Out of the drawer this morning."

She was encouraged to believe that she was going to live because of the completely frivolous but urgent question that blinked in her mind: What bra had she put on this morning? She had several comfortable and rather saggy old white or nude bras she wore to paint in, and it would be a shame if she were wearing one of those, because she had so many pretty bras, with lace and silk. . . .

"I'll close my eyes," Ben told her, and did as he said.

She wrestled off her sodden tank top, which water had glued to her body. It made sucking noises as she pulled it away, and it felt creepy and suffocating as she pulled it over her head. She dropped it into the bottom of the boat and quickly yanked on his shirt. The dry cotton against her cold skin was like a soft robe after a freezing rain.

"Oh, that feels better. Thank you." Still, she wrapped her arms around herself for warmth.

Ben began to row with quick, rhythmical strokes. "We'll get you in the house. Get some hot tea inside you."

Perhaps it was the rocking of the boat or the thought of tea— Natalie flung herself to the side of the boat in time to vomit into the lake. Most of what came up was water. Afterward, she was so weak that for a moment she just lay against the boat, resting. She became aware of sunlight beating down on her body, drying her legs, her arms, her hair, yet beneath the surface of her skin, she still felt intensely cold. Deep down in her soggy tiny reptilian brain where she was beginning to return to self-consciousness, she also felt humiliated, half drowning like that and then having to be heaved up, helpless, to safety.

She dragged herself back up to a sitting position. Well, a slouching position. With effort, she stared at Ben. "What are you doing here? It's a weekday."

"I don't teach this afternoon. I went in to the lab, checked a few things, decided I wanted to be out here. I like it on the lake when it's quiet like this. People are mostly at work and school. I can hear the birds."

"Well, I'm glad you were here. Thank you, Ben. You saved my life."

"Glad to do it." As he spoke, he looked over his shoulder, steering the rowboat neatly up to the Barnabys' dock. In one graceful leap, he jumped up on the dock and tied the rope around a stanchion. "Think you can make it?" he asked.

Natalie summoned her energy, pushed herself to a standing position, and reached for his hand. He held her steady while she stepped up onto the seat, then onto the edge of the boat, then onto the dock itself. If she hadn't already made a fool of herself, she would have thrown herself down on dry land and kissed it.

"I'm going to pick you up now," Ben said.

"What?" She tried to laugh, but it came out as a croak.

"Look at your legs."

She obeyed. They were shaking. "I can make it to my house," she insisted.

"I'm taking you to our house. You can sit with Louise. She can watch you for any aftereffects."

Before Natalie could argue, Ben simply swept her up, arms under her knees and shoulders, so quickly that she either had to let her head dangle back or wrap her arms around his neck to keep her head upright. She wrapped her arms around his neck. She was painfully—okay, *painfully* was the wrong word—she was *excessively* aware that Ben wore no shirt. *She* was wearing his shirt, after all, so his shoulders were bare, and his torso was bare. Blond hair swirled over his chest. He was slender, not tremendously muscular, but as he walked up the beach and lawn toward the Barnabys' house, he did so with ease, as if she didn't weigh a thing.

"I think I'm fine," she told him, mostly to prevent him from realizing how she was staring at his thick thatch of pale hair, his elegant ear, his thick eyelashes, his strong jaw. Also to prevent him from considering her thighs, hips, waist, breasts. They were in such an intimate proximity.

Very seriously, he informed her, "You almost drowned. You have water in your lungs. That can alter the sodium and potassium levels, which could lead to ventricular fibrillation. You were immersed in water lower than seventy degrees Fahrenheit, so you might be experiencing some hypothermia. And you're in shock. Someone needs to watch you."

"Oh," Natalie said in a very small voice.

"Also, water taken into the lungs can cause problems as long as seventy-two hours after the event. Water irritates the lungs and disrupts the lungs' ability to process air."

Natalie squirmed in his arms. "That's frightening!"

"I'm not trying to frighten you. You should just be aware, and you shouldn't be alone. I'm going to put you down." He lowered her to her feet on the deck of the house and grabbed the handle of the kitchen door. "By the way, what the *hell* were you doing, swimming alone?"

His sudden anger came at her unexpectedly. She'd been dreamily admiring his profile when he so unceremoniously dumped her on the deck. She knew he was right; still, she felt defensive. "I do *lots* of things alone!" She narrowed her eyes. "I'll bet *you* swim alone."

"Sometimes. I was also captain of my swim team in high school. I won state medals. Did you?"

For a long moment their eyes met. All Natalie could think was, *Damn, you are one gorgeous man.* Instead, she admitted, ruefully, "No. Obviously."

He continued to stare at her without speaking. A shiver went through Natalie's body, completely different from anything connected to the lake. *He makes me feel all prickly,* she thought. Then she thought, *Well, that was an interesting choice of words*. She couldn't help it. She smiled at him.

He almost walked into the glass door to the kitchen. Realizing it, he flushed red, glancing away from Natalie. *He's attracted to me*, she realized. *And, good grief, I'm certainly attracted to him!*

Ben pulled the sliding door open. "Mom! Natalie's here. She almost drowned."

Natalie put a hand on the wall to steady herself. A cat lay on the sofa in the sun, stomach up, blissed-out. A bowl of fresh cantaloupes, peaches, and plums sat in the middle of the kitchen table, filling the air with fruity aromas.

Ben asked, "You're okay to walk?" Suddenly he was not coming near her in any way.

"I am." She followed him down the hall and into the living room.

Louise was on the sofa, talking to herself.

"Mom!" Ben bent over his mother and gently removed one of the iPod plugs from her ears. "Turn off your French. Natalie's here. She almost drowned."

In a flash, Louise was up, turned toward Natalie, eyes wide with worry.

"Natalie! Are you all right?"

"I'm fine. Thanks to your son. He saved my life."

Quickly, Louise took in the situation. "Ben, wrap the afghan around her."

"Um," said Ben.

"My shorts are wet." Natalie touched the khaki material. Parts had dried in the sun, but her bum was still soaking.

Louise went into mother mode. "Natalie, go in the bathroom and take everything off. Ben, show her where the downstairs bathroom is."

Natalie followed Ben. In the privacy of the bathroom, she stripped off her shorts and underpants.

"Are you decent?" Ben asked.

"My top half is," she said through the door.

"Just a moment."

She waited. He knocked and opened the door wide enough to toss in a pair of loose black yoga pants, no doubt Bella's. She pulled them on. She looked at herself in the mirror. Somehow she was both pale and sunburned. Her nose had gotten shiny red from the sun, but the rest of her face was white, and her lips were slightly blue. All in all, highly attractive. Another knock came and a patchwork afghan flew into the bathroom. Natalie wrapped it around her, savoring its warmth.

She left the bathroom, returned to the living room, and dropped into a chair facing Ben's mother. She was shocked at how good it felt to sit down.

"Ben said you were swimming alone, quite far out," Louise said gently.

"I know. I'm an idiot. Actually, I didn't swim that far, I was simply floating on my back, drifting. It's so peaceful here. I just sort of melted."

Louise laughed. "I understand completely. It's relaxing on the lake when it's quiet like this. On the weekends, the lake is different, full of people and boats. Are you warming up?"

"I am. This afghan feels so cozy."

"Your color's returning. You must have had quite a scare."

Louise's concern was so unexpected, so poignant, that tears swam in Natalie's eyes. "I *was* frightened," she admitted. "For a moment there I was certain I was going to die." Shockingly, tears flooded down her face. Her shoulders shook. "Sorry," she gulped. "Sorry."

"It's a normal reaction, for heaven's sake," Louise told her. "You deserve to cry."

Grateful for Louise's response, Natalie continued to sob. In truth, she wasn't sure she could stop herself. She'd drawn her knees up to her chest, her feet resting on the chair near her bum, the afghan wrapped completely around her like a nest, and tears spilled down her cheeks.

Ben came into the room, took one look at Natalie in tears, muttered, "Oh God," and hurriedly left.

"Ben!" Louise called. "Was that a mug of tea in your hand?"

No answer.

"Bring it, and be sure there's plenty of sugar in it, and bring the box of tissues, too. It's sitting on the counter near the phone."

Ben returned, mug of tea in one hand, box in the other.

Natalie wiped her face, reached for a tissue, dried her hands, and blew her nose. Ben stood next to her, holding the mug, his eyes aimed at the ceiling. Natalie's fit subsided, leaving her truly exhausted. She took the mug.

"Thanks, Ben." She sipped the tea. It was strong and sweet, and she could feel it sink down through her throat, esophagus, and into her stomach, warming her all the way. She closed her eyes and moaned softly, snuggling into the chair.

"I've got to get back to work," Ben said to his mother.

"Oh, Ben, stay awhile," Louise coaxed.

"Sorry, Mom. Gotta go." Bending down, he kissed the top of his mother's head. "Bye, Natalie," he said when he was pretty much out of the room. Then he left, slamming the front door.

"He saved my life," Natalie told Louise again. "He was so strong. I was so cold, and choking, and the water seemed to be trying to suck me down."

"Honey, don't think about it. You're safe now. Put the mug on the table and rest."

Natalie did as Louise told her. Her body surrendered its final tension of fight-or-flight response, her head nestled into the chair cushion, and she fell asleep.

She woke very slowly. Hearing came first, a whisper of pages. Across from her, Louise was reading. Natalie felt warm, perhaps too warm, but as relaxed as if her bones had dissolved. Secretly, she studied Louise. All the Barnabys had the same cheekbones, high and rounded, blue eyes slightly slanted down. Louise's forehead was etched with wrinkles, and her lower jaw sagged slightly, but she was beautiful, especially now while she was in repose. She had about her the meditative calm of a Vermeer.

Natalie cleared her throat and shifted position.

Louise looked up. "Feeling better, dear?"

"Oh yes." Natalie stretched her arms. "Thanks for letting me sleep in your living room." She sat up straight, feet on the floor, letting the afghan slide away.

"Hungry?"

Natalie stood up. "Not really. I was working on a painting and decided to cool off in the lake. That's what started my idiotic adventure. There's still good light. I think I'll go back to work." She folded the afghan and laid it neatly over the back of the chair. She plumped the chair cushions.

"You're sure you're all right?" Louise asked.

"Perfectly normal. Well, I might take a shower and change clothes." She looked down at what she wore. "I'll wash these things and bring them back." She started to leave, then hesitated. "I wonder, I'd like to get Ben something to thank him for rescuing me. I don't think the etiquette book covers such a situation. Any advice?"

Louise chuckled. "You don't have to give him a present." Her eyes twinkled. "He seemed quite pleased with himself for saving you."

He did? Natalie almost asked Louise how she could spot any emotion Ben might have. But, of course, Ben was Louise's son. She knew him well. Natalie thanked Louise once more and left the Barnaby house, warmed from the tea, the afghan, and the thought of being in Ben Barnaby's arms.

6
.....

Friday morning, Bella left the top half of the blue Dutch door open to let the fragrant summer air sweep into the gift shop. She didn't expect many customers, not on this glorious early summer day, and Aaron was out in California at his damned interview, so she wore sneakers, jeans, and a tank top, planning to move furniture around, experimenting.

Bella could remember when she was a child, tumbling off the school bus and into the house to find her mother at the kitchen table, quietly studying a storybook mole's tilt of nose or whether its whiskers went up, down, or straight out. She sculpted the minute creature in clay, baked it, and sewed soft velvet skin on it before painting its face. Her mother had seemed like a sorceress, capable of anything. Beatrice and Bella would go with their mother to help set up the Lake Worlds in the shop, carrying the boxes of handcrafted animals as if they were made of gold.

That was years ago. DVDs were new. Cell phones were large and clunky. Computers were slow, Facebook didn't exist, and eBay was just beginning. Now children played with games on computers, or Nintendo DS, Wii, Xbox, or their iPhones. Bella's mother still ran her business without the use of a computer, keeping sales, inventory, and tax records in a notebook by hand. Louise sold horse-and-buggy gifts in an Internet world.

The store had to change if it was to continue. Soon—tonight, perhaps—Bella wanted to sit down with her parents and discuss possible alterations to the shop.

The image of Natalie's still life of apples in a silver bowl kept haunting Bella. Well, of course, there was something so symbolic about apples, wasn't there?—the witch offering Snow White an apple, the apple in the Garden of Eden. Her idea was to hang the picture above one of her mother's Lake Worlds: There was one in an orchard with a raccoon family picnicking on fallen apples. Or would that be too weird? Maybe, maybe not. Bella wanted to try it. She wanted to try a lot of things—her mind was teeming with ideas.

She would go through the store today, organize her thoughts, and make a sketch, a kind of presentation to show her parents. They would give her good advice, she knew.

Bella walked around the shop, studying the display cases, the exhibits, the spaces. Lucy Lattimer's stuffed dolls with stitched eyes and smiles were, to Bella's mind, a complete waste of space. She didn't know if they had ever sold even one of the dolls. They were quaint, but in a way they were also a bit creepy, because Lucy's stitching was uneven, giving the dolls cartoon faces, jack-o'-lantern faces. Lucy was the mother of a friend of Louise's; she had been in her eighties, living with her daughter. Bella could remember specifically ganging up with Beatrice against Louise, demanding to know why she wanted to take up space with those bizarro items.

"It gives Lucy something to do," Louise had told them. "It lets her feel capable of making something pretty."

"In other words," said Beatrice—who, as the oldest child, could be caustic with her mother when she felt like it—"you're helping your friend by keeping her mother out of her hair for a while."

"You're a cynical child," Louise had retorted mildly, but her mouth had quirked up and she hadn't denied the accusation.

Lucy Lattimer must be in her nineties now. These dolls were sixteen years old, and their sweet milkmaid costumes were limp. For that matter, Lucy herself hadn't come into the shop for years—Bella didn't know if she was even ambulatory.

If she could get rid of the dolls, cover the corny murals on the walls, focus more on the furniture, and perhaps bring in some art, some of Natalie's work to begin with . . .

She was aware of an approaching motor, and all of its own accord, her heart leapt. Before she could stand up, she heard the bell tinkle and the bottom half of the blue door open and shut.

Bella stood up, turned toward the door, and saw Slade standing there.

"Slade!" Was she blushing or did she just feel hot?

"Hey." He was long and lean in black jeans and a black tee shirt. He took his sunglasses off as he walked toward her. "Wow," he said.

A shiver feathered down Bella's spine. "Wow?"

He walked right up to her, so close they were almost touching. Reaching out his hand, he stroked the gargoyle cabinet. "I thought so," he mumbled, talking to himself. "This is the real deal. It needs to be stripped."

"It's nice to see you again, too," Bella said, lacing her voice with just a thread of sarcasm.

"What?" Slade cast a quick glance Bella's way.

His eyes were the deepest blue.

"*Hello?*" Bella said.

Slade got it. "Sorry. Hi, Bella. I've just been thinking about this piece for days now. I wasn't sure it was original. You don't see many like this, but this is the real thing. Bella, your family must be English."

"Well, duh, *Barnaby*." Something about the man made Bella defensive, like a goofy adolescent talking with a rock star.

"I've been checking. This piece, Bella"—Slade slapped his hand against it gently—"this piece could bring you around fifteen thousand dollars."

She almost fell over. "You're kidding."

"I'm not kidding. This is my field of expertise. This is what I do." He peered at her as if she were a newt emerging from under a rock. "You don't have any idea what you've got here, do you?"

"Well, sort of. I've always loved my grandparents' furniture, and when they died, I insisted on having some of their pieces in my bedroom, even though they're big, dark, and not the slightest bit girly."

He leaned toward her. "You have more pieces like this?" Before she could answer, he grabbed both her shoulders. "Bella, this is something antiques dealers dream about! A find like this!"

Bella was paralyzed by his touch, his nearness, his dark beauty, his passion. She knew her mouth was hanging open and she couldn't locate the intelligence needed to shut it.

"Don't look at me that way." Slade removed his hands from her shoulders. "I'm not trying to cheat you. If I were, why would I tell you what these pieces are worth?"

Bella found her voice. "Then what do you want to do?"

"I want to work with you. I want to sell these pieces on commission for you."

"Slade, these all belong to my parents."

"Then *talk* to them."

"Slade. Do you think you could slow down just a little? How about a cup of coffee? No, wait. The last thing you need is coffee. Come to the back room. I've got lemonade and some cinnamon rolls I made yesterday morning."

He started to object, then nodded and loped along behind her, past the display counter, into the back room. Past the small bathroom (sweetly decorated, because children always needed to go to the bathroom). Past boxes needing to be packed or unpacked. Past worktables and a sink and counter. Past her mother's ancient, scarred rolltop desk, past the ironing board and the cutting table, to the private area with the small refrigerator, microwave, round table, and chairs. Bella's purse hung on a hook, near a mirror. She couldn't resist giving herself a quick glance.

"That rolltop desk is nice," Slade said.

"Sit down." She pointed. "There." Taking a pitcher of lemonade from the refrigerator, she poured him a glass, set it before him, then slid one of her cinnamon rolls onto a plate and placed it in front of him, too. She handed him a knife and fork. She put the other rolls on the table as well, in case he wanted more. She poured herself a glass of lemonade and sat down. By that time, Slade had eaten his roll and was reaching for another.

"Damn," he mumbled, his mouth full, "these are good."

"Thanks." Bella took a roll, though she wasn't hungry. She drew designs in the icing with her fork as she talked, figuring out what she wanted to say as she went along. "Slade. Tell me. How did you learn so much about furniture?"

"I went to New York's Metropolitan Museum School of Antique Furniture."

"Is there such a thing?"

He cast her a withering glance. "No, there's not, and if there were, I couldn't have gone. I barely had the money to go to college for two years. I just like to tell people that when they ask me."

"Well, I'm not 'people,' " Bella told him.

He studied her for a long, drawn-out moment. "No, you most certainly are not."

It took all her willpower not to squirm in her chair. This man was so divine he was undoubtedly used to getting his way, simply by melting a woman's resolve with the flame-tip heat of his dark blue eyes. Add some subtle flirtation, and women probably just fell right over into his arms. "Could you answer the question?" she managed to say.

He sighed, leaning in his chair so that it tilted onto the two back legs. As if he couldn't care less. "When I was a boy, I worked after school and summers for a guy who ran an antiques shop up in Maine. Mostly he carried primitive American antiques, lots of Empire furniture, china, candlesticks. That stuff. Sometimes I'd go off with him on a trip up north to scout out antiques in small towns. Even now you can still find treasures, especially at farm auctions or even yard sales in towns so far away no one ever takes the time to drive there. I learned a lot from him." He dropped forward to munch down another roll.

Bella loved seeing him eat. He was so thin. "More lemonade?"

"Please."

She poured him another glass. "And then?"

"Then I went to college for two years in Boston, and worked for Aunt Eleanor sometimes, helping cart furniture around to other people's homes. I think I learned the most there, seeing the way people with money like to decorate. Some people stick with a period, some like to mix it up. I met a guy named Dave Ralston who was good at restoration, dropped out of college, and went to work for Ralston's Antiques. Learned a ton there."

"You've always been interested in wood," Bella mused.

He quirked an eyebrow. "I have?"

"When you were a kid, you used to go into the forest and stand very still studying tree trunks."

Slade's eyes went dead. "Jesus, what a freak."

"That's not a very nice thing to say," Bella protested. "You could call yourself a child prodigy."

Slade snorted. "A child prodigy of *tree trunks?*"

Bella took a deep breath. "Look. I'm interested in what you know about furniture. I want to update this shop."

"Upscale, you mean."

"No, I meant update, but upscale is not a bad idea either. A lot of the stuff here is inexpensive, and certainly none of it is worth what you say the furniture is worth. But I've been thinking . . . it's not clear yet. . . . I know I don't want to run an antiques store. I want to carry a mix of things. I'm still in the planning process. I had no idea that old cabinet was worth so much, and even though I've taken a couple of courses, I really don't know Early American from British. I wonder, could I hire you to check out all the furniture and give me estimates on its value?"

Slade's eyes had come alive again. He dropped his eyelids halfway in that sleepy kind of "come to bed" look he did so well, and behind the lids was the glint of mischief. "I'd be glad to value the furniture. You don't have to pay me."

"Slade, seriously—"

"Seriously. Or, I'll tell you what, take me out to dinner sometime."

Okay, Bella thought, now he was coming on to her, and her body was making it clear it had no intention of resisting. If Slade were to rise from his chair right now, grab Bella, and press his sensual mouth against hers, she'd knock the lemonade and rolls on the floor and let him ravish her right here on this old table.

From deep in some survival center of her brain, a stern voice that sounded much like her algebra teacher, Mrs. Penner, warned, *Remember what Natalie told you. Slade is a bad boy. He comes on to women all the time. It means nothing.*

Another voice, smaller, slightly ashamed, her own, said, *Bella, for heaven's sake. Remember Aaron.*

She leaned forward, planting her elbows on the table, well aware that this position gave him a pretty fine view of the tops of her breasts pressing against the curve of her tank top. "I'll take you out to dinner. The best restaurant in the area."

Slade considered her. Again, he allowed himself his own sweet time. Bella had no option, unless she wanted to show herself as the coward she secretly felt like, but to hold her pose and stare right back at him.

She was surprised the chemistry between them didn't make the table burst into flames.

Finally Slade spoke. "Bella. Whose shop is this? Yours or your mother's?"

Bella stood up and began clearing the table, using up her nervous energy. She put the glasses in the sink. "That's a very good question." Leaning against the sink, she crossed her arms over her chest, thinking aloud. "I didn't come back here with the idea of taking over the shop. I came back to help my mother. I guess the idea of changing the shop came to me the moment I walked in after so much time away. I realized the shop is dated."

Slade said, "You're a schoolteacher, right?"

"I was. But when I came back to help Mom, I found myself drawn to something about this shop. Not as it is. As it could be. I'm not making much sense, am I?" She nodded to herself, coming to a conclusion. "I need to do some research. I need to run some figures, find out about sales tax, utilities, that sort of thing. I'll talk to my parents about my grandparents' furniture. We've got more of it in the house, and of course Beat's got some in her house, and then there's the storage unit."

"*The storage unit?*" Slade shoved his chair back and stood up. "What storage unit?"

"Slade, do you suppose you could stay with Natalie overnight?

While I talk to my parents? I mean, I have to be here at the shop all day, and Dad's teaching, so I can't talk to them until this evening. Then, tomorrow, perhaps, if things go well with my parents, I could take you to the storage unit."

"Sorry. I've got something going on in Boston tonight." He approached Bella. He stood right in front of her, tall, muscular, lean, giving off warmth. "I'll be back soon."

She had been worrying about talking to her parents, but those worries dissolved in the force field of Slade's magnetism, replaced by a stunning sense of desire. What *was* it with this guy?

The bell on the shop's front door tinkled.

Thank God, Bella thought. "Customer," she croaked, her mouth suddenly dry. When she slid past Slade, her body brushed his for a moment. She shivered with a touch of desire and a stronger surge of guilt.

After work, Bella decided to visit her older sister, Beatrice, who lived in the terribly named Belchertown, not far from the Barnabys' house on the lake. It was a rambling split-level built in the sixties, and for Beat and her husband and their three children, its best quality was its spacious backyard. They owned an acre of land surrounded by woods, most of it a smooth sweep of lawn perfect for a swing set, slide, playhouse, sandbox, water table, and all the other paraphernalia of childhood.

Bella parked her car behind her sister's minivan, walked up the driveway, gathering up fallen towels and lunch buckets as she went. Beat's theory of raising children was different from her parents'. Louise and Dennis had been organized and disciplined. Beat believed in allowing children to raise themselves so their natural, true personalities would have the freedom to emerge. Bella and her siblings would never have gotten away with such messiness, but Beat, in her own ambling, indolent way, managed to keep a semblance of order.

Bella opened the front door and walked in. "Hello!" she called.

"In the kitchen!" Beat called back.

It was about five-thirty. Beat's husband, Jeremy, wasn't home yet from his carpentry job. Her children were in the backyard—Bella could see them through the window. The two little girls were in the playhouse with their dolls, pretending to have tea. Jason was running into the woods with a stick, killing bears.

Beat hugged Bella warmly. On this summer day, she *was* warm—Beat didn't believe in air-conditioning. She was the most easygoing person Bella knew. Perhaps that was because she was so completely luscious, like a Renoir, with wavy blond hair, enormous blue eyes, and a buxom figure. Beat was barefoot, which she almost always was, wearing an old, loose, and stained sky-blue sundress, and she could have posed for Botticelli just like this.

"Wine?" Beat asked.

"Something cold, *please*." Bella leaned against the counter, which was covered with dirty dishes, half-wrapped foil packets, a clean diaper, a vase of dying flowers, and a pile of coins. "How are you? How are the kids?"

Beat laughed as she poured their Chardonnay. "Today Dawn has decided to be a mermaid when she grows up, Jason will be a knight, and Wendy has declared she intends to be a baby."

Bella laughed along with her sister as they went out the kitchen door to the back patio and sank down into the lawn glider with its thick flowered pillows. Bella felt something sharp, rose to remove a small dump truck, and resumed her seat.

Beat curled up on the glider, bringing her knees sideways and sliding her feet onto the cushions. Bella noticed for the millionth time that Beat's feet were dirty, and for the millionth time she slapped herself mentally for noticing. Beat's house was clean enough, even if the kitchen floor was sometimes sticky, and Beat took a shower once a day, so what was Bella's obsession about Beat's dirty feet? It was summer!

"How's the shop?" Beat asked.

"No one comes in there anymore," Bella complained.

"I'm not surprised. Mom's lost interest in it." All at once, she raised her voice. "JASON! COME BACK! WASPS, REMEMBER?"

Bella watched the little boy race back out of the woods onto the open lawn. He began stabbing his stick into the sandbox.

"Wasps in the woods?" Bella asked.

"I don't know, maybe. I just don't like him going so far in I can't see him. And he's terrified of wasps." Beat broke out into one of her long, low, sensual chuckles as she watched her son. "Look at the boy. Could it be more Freudian? Honestly. Stabbing a stick into a hole?" She sipped her wine and stretched luxuriously. "I could watch these little savages all day." She chuckled again. "Actually, I *do* watch them all day."

"They *are* adorable," Bella agreed. And they were, a pack of blond angels flitting around the yard.

"When are you having *your* babies?" Beat asked. "How's Aaron?"

"A pain in the ass," Bella replied succinctly.

"Really?" Beat looked shocked. "I think he's great."

"Yeah, yeah, I know." Bella sighed. "But he wants to take a job in San Francisco."

"And your problem is?" Before Bella could answer, Beat added, "Jeremy wants us to move to the Cape."

"Move?" Bella almost fell off the glider. "Why?"

"More work for Jeremy, and he loves the ocean."

"I hope you don't move, Beat," Bella said, but her sister didn't hear, because just at that moment Jason raced up with his squirt gun, aimed at his aunt and his mother, and blasted them with water, laughing maniacally.

Bella got it in the eyes. "Ouch, Jason, don't aim at faces!"

Beat grabbed her five-year-old son, pulled him onto her lap, and tickled him fiercely. Jason howled with laughter, kicked and thrashed, his foot connecting with Bella's thigh. For a second time, she got off the glider. She strolled across the lawn and peeked in the window of the playhouse to chat with her nieces. They were engrossed in a complicated ritual with their dolls, so Bella went back into the house and leisurely began to clean up the kitchen. She often did this when she visited Beat, and so had her mother before she broke her leg.

It was peculiar, Bella mused as she filled the trash bag, tied it off, and inserted a new one into the plastic container beneath the sink, how different Beat was from what statistics predicted. As the oldest, Beat should be the achiever, striving, energetic, type A, leaving the nest to travel and change the world. Instead, Beat married her high school boyfriend, worked as a secretary until they could afford to buy this house, then began having children. She was perfectly content to stay home with her kids, and even planned to have more. She was still in love with her husband, too. Clothes didn't interest her, nor jewelry, nor trips to Paris or even Boston. She could never claim to have *decorated* her house; it just sort of came together, furniture given to them by her parents or Jeremy's, or found at yard sales and going-out-of-business sales. The only art on the walls was photos of the children at various ages.

Beat had been a happy, successful child, a cheerleader in high school, and prom queen when Jeremy was captain of the football team and prom king. She seemed to have inherited contentment along with her beauty.

Obviously, Bella thought, Beat couldn't comprehend Bella's ambivalence about Aaron and San Francisco, and at the moment Bella herself wasn't certain she could articulate exactly how she wanted to change the shop. Well, there it was: change the shop. It wasn't *her* shop, it was her mother's. But Bella was fixated on it; she couldn't not go forward.

"Dad," Bella said as they were finishing dinner, "could you stay a moment? I want to talk."

Brady had already left the table, rushing outside for one last ride on his dirt bike before dark fell. It was just the three of them—Bella, her mother, her father—at the table.

"Sure," Dennis replied. "What's up?"

Bella took a deep breath. "We had one customer today. Actually, she didn't want anything for a child, she wanted something for an adult."

"She must be new to the area," Louise said.

"There are a lot of people new to the area," Bella pointed out mildly. "The turnover in population is always large because of the five colleges. Students, instructors . . ."

Dennis stretched and yawned. School was out, but he still had committee meetings. "Your point is?"

"I think we need to change the shop. Drastically. If it's going to survive. I think it needs a makeover. I think we should sell to adults. After all, it's adults who buy Lake Worlds and the other stuff for the children. I think we should change our inventory. Keep it unique, but upscale it."

"Upscale it," Louise echoed.

"I've looked at the books. Business has been bad—"

"It always is in the winter," Louise reminded her. "It will pick up this summer."

Bella shrugged. "I don't think so. It didn't pick up last summer."

"What sorts of things are you thinking of carrying?" Dennis asked.

"I'm still working on that. Art, for one. We've got lots of talented artists in the area, starting with Natalie next door. Antiques, for another." She paused, wanting to be sensitive to her mother. "Slade thinks we've got some valuable furniture."

Louise surprised her. "All that Barnaby stuff. More than we need." She looked over at her husband.

"If you can sell it, do it," Dennis told his daughter.

Louise continued, "I can see where you're coming from. I'm not opposed to your ideas. But, Bella, as I see it, the main question is: How long are you prepared to run the shop?"

What an enormous question. "To be honest, I don't know."

Bella's father weighed in. "Bella. We don't want you to feel obligated to run the Barn."

"But what will happen to it if I don't run it?" Bella asked.

"Louise and I have talked about this," Dennis told her. "I think we'll close it. Maybe put the building up for sale."

Bella gawked. Why did she feel like her father had just run a stake through her heart? "I didn't know you and Mom were thinking of *closing* Barnaby's Barn."

"Honey, we've been thinking about it for months." Louise

smiled affectionately at her husband. "We think it would be nice to have some fun. We've worked hard for a long time. You children have all turned out so nicely. We have a feeling that Brady's going to want to follow in Ben's tracks. He's going to science camp this summer, you know."

"The point is," Dennis said, because he loved summing things up and making everything perfectly clear, "don't give the shop a second thought, Bella."

Louise nodded, agreeing. "Of course, if you want to change the Barn, go for it. Although if you're going to move somewhere with Aaron, it seems like a waste of time, doing anything to the shop. Sweetheart, why are you looking so worried? Dad and I are telling you that you're *free*."

Bella frowned, struggling to marshal her thoughts. "I don't want to be *free*, Mom. I can't articulate it well, but I love the shop. At least my idea of how that shop could be." Reaching into her book-bag, she brought out a notebook. "I've been running some numbers. You guys own the barn, so you don't have to pay a monthly mort-gage. If you let me run the shop for a few months without paying rent, I think I could make the utility bills, pop for some ads, plus squeeze out a few pennies for myself as a salary. I have enough in savings to pay for paint. I'd like to spruce the place up, and—"

"Bella." Leaning forward, Louise put her hand on her daughter's. "Honey, what about Aaron?"

An odd cramp squeezed Bella's heart. "He's in San Francisco now, for the interview. But that doesn't mean he'll get the job. It doesn't mean he'll take the job. I don't want to put my life on hold."

"Just for the summer," her father suggested, "couldn't you simply enjoy the lake?"

Bella shook her head. "I really want to try to realize my idea of a shop. This seems like the perfect opportunity for me. Come on, a rent-free building near a large, cultured community? Where would I ever find that? I know I don't have a complete business plan yet. But it excites me. It seems *important* to me."

"I know exactly how that feels," Louise said. "You're right. This is the time and the place. Go for it!"

7

After much research, Morgan chose Judy's Gym for Women. Morgan liked the idea of exercising in a male-free area; plus, Judy's had an excellent children's room with lots of toys and several certified child caregivers. The showers were sparkling clean, the locker room also, the equipment new and first-class, the towels thick and sweet-smelling. It was a forty-five-minute drive from Morgan's house, which was a drawback, but it was by far the most expensive gym in the area, which earned Josh's seal of approval.

She worried a bit when she took Petey into the child-care room, but one look at a pedal tractor just his size and her son waddled away from her without looking back. A few other toddlers were playing there, too, and the attendant was a cozy older woman on her knees with building blocks. She waved at Morgan and mouthed, "He'll be fine."

She went down the corridor and into the workout area. Morgan had an athletic body, trim and muscular, and she'd usually gone to a gym, especially in the winter. She preferred the weights, the bikes, the treadmill. Lifting Petey or pushing him in his stroller had kept her in pretty good shape, but Elise, her personal trainer, immediately spotted all sorts of problem areas, especially around Morgan's abdomen, where pregnancy had loosened the pelvic and abdominal muscles. Also, her blood pressure was on the high side—and it never had been before. Elise scheduled Morgan for thirty minutes a day on the treadmill, and in addition a series of exercises to tighten her torso.

Morgan climbed on the treadmill, plugged the iPod buds in her ears, and kept the volume on Coldplay low. She needed this free time, this quiet, to think.

About her marriage. About Josh.

It would have been so helpful if Natalie or Bella were married! Morgan knew marriages went through phases. She knew that people changed. She knew that she and Josh were still in the new-house-new-job level of stress. Still.

A kind of space had opened up between them. It was as if they couldn't reach around it to touch or even see each other clearly. Her sweet, darling Josh had become Armani Man, slickly dressed and always in a hurry. When he wasn't rushing off to work, when he was actually at home, he was down in his study on his computer. Last Friday morning in a fit of pique, Morgan had stormed into his study and sat down at his desk. She'd opened his email and his files to see what the hell he was always doing, and to her relief, it was work, all work.

Except for one file that wouldn't open without a password.

What?

Why would Josh have a protected file? She had her own laptop; she never used his, and no one else ever came near his study. She knew Bio-Green was working on some potentially profitable innovations, but that was done, *had* to be done, at the facility. Although it was possible that Josh was working out a formula or a logarithm too complex to be created in a day or even a month. Perhaps his mind kept going even when he was home. Certainly he acted like it, always staying up late at night, here at the computer. Once, she'd come down in the morning to see him asleep in his desk chair, slumped like a dead man, snoring like a bull elephant.

He was working too hard. She needed to talk to him about that. She worried about him. Their marriage was suffering.

Before they moved here, back in their dinky undecorated apartment, they'd been so close. Both read whenever they could grab even ten minutes. Morgan loved nonfiction, especially involving science. Josh loved science fiction. On weekends, they pushed Petey in his stroller around the nature preserve near the Charles River, talking about books, science, and TV series they loved—they hadn't had the money to go to movies. Saturday nights they stayed up late, watching *Saturday Night Live* or DVDs, doing silly voice-overs and eating popcorn. On Sundays they hiked, or if there was snow, went snowshoeing, with Petey snuggled cozily in a BabyBjörn on Josh's back.

The best had been Sunday mornings—ah, Sunday mornings. With Petey cheerfully playing on the floor, Josh would give Morgan long, luxurious body rubs, starting at her head and working his way down to each and every toe.

Now on weekends, Josh slept till noon, something he never used to do. She had to nag him to get out on the lake with her and Petey.

She knew Josh was under pressure. He was new at this job. He was being paid a hell of a lot and was determined to earn it.

Morgan was trying to do her part. Their evening with the Ruoffs had been successful. Morgan had created canapés that didn't drip on Eva's silk dress. Even better, both Eva and Ronald had been impressed by Natalie's abstract, hanging on the living room wall opposite the window facing the lake. Eva had trailed around the house with Morgan, concluding in her plummiest tones that Morgan had style. The rest of the evening Morgan and Josh listened to the Ruoffs describe their beach house on the Cape and their ski house in Stowe. Eva had asked if they played bridge—they did not—so the Ruoffs suggested they take lessons. She asked Morgan if she'd be willing to do some volunteer work for the Amherst library—it might lead to a position on the board. There were some heavy hitters on several of the boards in the area; Eva was already on the hospital board and the symphony board. Excellent way to meet people. With Josh standing next to her, Morgan smiled her best smile and agreed that absolutely she'd volunteer for the library.

Josh had been happy after that evening. In fact, they'd made love when they went to bed that night, and it had been a long time since that had happened. It had been so heavenly, not just the sex but the cuddling afterward, the nuzzling, the silly endearments they used for each other when they were in especially romantic moods. He really was her darling, with his red hair sticking up like a porcupine's, and his long legs and torso and arms lightly covered with freckles, and his powerful ribs like the staves of a boat sheltering his warm, beloved beating heart.

That night she determined to work with him, to ease some of his tension by doing her share and more.

So here she was, at Judy's Gym, on a treadmill. She'd seen a couple of posh yummy mummies around. After she'd come here a few times, perhaps she could introduce herself, meet them for coffee, network.

Right now, next to her, a much older woman labored away on her treadmill. Morgan had noticed the woman when she came in. She was probably around sixty, with an impressive bosom and what clothing manufacturers were now calling a "bold" bottom. She was actually pretty cute in her turquoise tights and her fuchsia tunic, with a matching headband holding back her white hair. Morgan nodded hello to the woman, giving her a big and genuine smile of encouragement. *Good for her*, Morgan had thought, twenty minutes ago.

But now she noticed the older woman struggling. Her hands were clamped onto the support bars so tightly her knuckles were white. Her legs were shaking. In fact, her entire body was trembling, and her eyes darted frantically around the room.

Morgan scanned the room, too. Where was Elise? Where were any of the perky personal trainers? She looked back at the older woman, who was staring at her, mouth open, no words coming out.

Morgan clicked off her treadmill and jumped onto the floor, hitting hard, her own body lurching from the sudden change.

"Do you want to stop? Or slow down?" she asked the older woman.

The older woman nodded. Her face was red, almost purple. Her hairline was soaked with sweat.

Morgan reached over and moved the speed lever so that the conveyor belt gradually slowed, then stopped. The other woman almost fell onto one of the bars. Morgan stepped on the conveyor belt and grabbed her waist and steadied her.

"Breath," the woman gasped, her chest heaving.

"Okay. Take your time. I've got you. You won't fall. Your breath will come back naturally. We'll sit down, right here, on the belt."

"Faint," the woman said.

"Okay, we'll sit down right now." This was Morgan's territory. She'd actually never been with a person who fainted before, but she had the training to deal with it. Besides, anyone knew it would be a much better situation for the woman to fall while sitting than standing. The whole hitting-the-head consequence was lessened. Morgan didn't have the strength to completely support the woman, but she put her arm around her shoulders and carefully helped her turn away from the control panel until she was facing sideways.

"Can you put your feet on the floor?" Morgan asked.

The woman nodded.

"Try one foot at a time. I've got you. Good. Next foot."

Once the woman's feet were firmly on the floor, Morgan stepped down, too. "Now we're going to sit down. I'll keep my arm around you."

Cautiously, they sat. The older woman nearly folded in half, sagging forward, her torso heaving as she inhaled.

"I believe my trainer was a bit optimistic about my abilities," she panted.

"They can be that way," Morgan agreed. "How do you feel now?"

"I'm dizzy. I don't think it was entirely my trainer's fault. I told her I wanted to push myself." After a few moments, she straightened, although her legs still trembled. "It looks like I did." She laughed creakily.

"You should drink some water." Morgan rose, grabbed the bottle of water from the holder on the machine, and handed it to her.

Suddenly another trainer, a stocky gymnastic type named Shari, rushed up, her ponytail bobbing. "Mrs. Smith! Are you all right? What happened?"

"I'm fine," Mrs. Smith replied. "I think perhaps the pace was a bit fast for my first time. This young woman helped me since you weren't around."

"Oh, I'm so sorry. I was with another client." Shari squatted down to face Mrs. Smith. "How do you feel now?"

Mrs. Smith blurted, "I need to go to the bathroom."

"Let me help you." Shari held out her arms. "Put your hands on my arms and we'll stand up."

Mrs. Smith drew back. "I'm not an invalid."

"Of course not. But you *are* trembling and your color isn't what it should be."

"My color is never what it should be," Mrs. Smith joked, but she put her hands on Shari's arms and allowed herself to be heaved to standing. Tilting slightly toward Morgan, she said, "Thank you so much, my dear. I think you saved my life."

"You're welcome," Morgan replied.

Slowly Shari and the older woman progressed away from the machines, out of the equipment room, toward the ladies' restrooms.

Morgan left Judy's Gym with a glow on, partly from exercise, partly from performing a good deed. The day was overcast and muggy, and in the lush heat the trees around the lake waved their leaves like a multitude of green banners. After Petey's nap, Morgan buckled him into his stroller and went out for a brisk walk.

"Look, Petey." Morgan bent down to show him. "Daylilies!" On the side of the road, a cluster of wild lilies was opening from candles to a lavish display of orange.

"Hi, Mrs. O'Keefe!" Their babysitter, Felicity Horton, brought her bike to a halt. "Hi, Petey!"

Morgan watched as Felicity kicked the bike stand down so she could bend over to talk with Petey.

"He's such a doll," Felicity cooed.

Petey shrieked with joy and waved his arms.

Before the thought had cleared her brain, the words spilled out of Morgan's mouth. "Felicity, how would you like to babysit him for a couple of hours? I just want to run into Amherst to do some errands."

"Oooh, I'd love to! Can I take him to my house? Mom is home and she'd love to see him."

"Absolutely," Morgan agreed.

. . .

She changed her shirt, combed her hair, put on mascara and lipstick. Kicked her walking shoes into the corner and slipped her feet into some pretty beaded sandals. Jumped into her SUV and drove away, singing.

She'd seen the outside of Bio-Green Industries, but she'd never been inside, in spite of the fact that labs and technical facilities were her favorite places in the world. Okay, she was weird, but test tubes and lab coats turned her on. She saw a garden center by the side of the road and pulled over, jumped out, found a great bright azalea plant, and bought it. She'd give it to Josh for his office.

Bio-Green had the same brick-and-glass exterior of many tech businesses along Route 128 near Boston. The access road was landscaped, the grass green, slender newly planted trees blooming profusely. The road curved around to the side, where a parking lot for employees faced more construction at the rear of the large building. Morgan found a slot with the sign Visitor Parking and slipped in. She grabbed up the azalea and headed for the front entrance.

Glass doors slid open at her approach. The lobby was cool and, not surprisingly, painted and furnished in a pale spring green. Behind a high curved desk a gorgeous young woman in a tight gray suit showed Morgan her snowy teeth.

"Welcome to Bio-Green. May I help you?"

"Hi. I'm Morgan O'Keefe. I just want to give this to my husband, Josh. Could you direct me to his office?"

"Of course, Mrs. O'Keefe. This way." The receptionist slid out from behind the counter and headed down a corridor to a set of elevators. She pressed a button. "Fifth floor. The top floor, actually! Turn right. Dr. O'Keefe's office is at the end of the hall."

Oh Lord, Morgan thought. She knew that Josh, even though he had a PhD, didn't like being referred to as "doctor" because he considered it a medical appellation. She'd bet that Ronald Ruoff had instructed the staff to use the word.

"Thank you." She stepped onto the elevator and was whisked up.

The hallway was carpeted in pale beige. The walls were light green here, too. She passed ornately framed pictures of forests, waterfalls, flowers, and polar bears as she headed to the end of the hall and Josh's office.

The office wall and its door were glass. Morgan had spoken with Josh's secretary on the phone before. Her name was Imogene, so Morgan envisioned her as an older woman, precise, efficient, and perhaps a wee bit plump, in a plaid suit.

But the secretary who saw Morgan and jumped up to open the door was centerfold pretty.

"You must be Mrs. O'Keefe!" the girl gushed. "I'm Imogene, Dr. O'Keefe's secretary. I've seen your picture on his desk with your cute little boy, Petey. What a gorgeous plant! You are so lucky, Dr. O'Keefe is actually in his office right now. Often he's down at the labs, you know. Shall I buzz him to let him know you're here?"

Overwhelmed by the cascade of words, Morgan took a moment to breathe. "Hi, Imogene. Please call me Morgan. And, yes, I'd be grateful if you'd buzz Dr. O'Keefe to let him know I'm here."

Imogene zipped back to her desk. Morgan saw that the rest of the room was paneled in wood. The door to Josh's office was wooden, thus blocking the interior from sight. As if secrets were hidden inside. Perhaps that was the purpose, to make his office look significantly restricted.

"Dr. O'Keefe? Your wife is here to see you."

Morgan strained to listen; she couldn't hear his response. So the door and walls were thick. Interesting.

Josh's door flew open and he stepped out, a wide smile on his face. "Morgan! What a surprise!"

"I've brought a plant for your office." Seeing him like this, in his fabulously cut suit, a Ralph Lauren today, in front of his luscious secretary, in this imposing building, Morgan felt suddenly shy, as if she were meeting a stranger, or someone for a first date.

Josh laughed. "How nice." He ushered her into the office and shut the door tightly. "Now," he said. "Where shall we put it?"

The room was enormous, lavishly equipped with sleek furniture. Behind his desk, behind the sofa, behind the table near the window, were potted plants: a ficus tree, a lemon tree, and a palm tree.

Why hadn't she foreseen this? Of course, *Bio-Green* Industries would have plants in all its offices.

"Oh dear." Morgan put her azalea, which was getting heavy, on the end of a table. "I didn't realize."

"I'll find a place," Josh assured her. "It's thoughtful, Morgan." Coming close, he pulled her to him and kissed her mouth.

She smiled up at him. "This place is amazing."

"I know, right?"

"This whole building is great. I'd love to see the labs."

Josh frowned. "Oh, honey, I've got a pile of paperwork to get through and a load of calls to return."

"But just a peek—"

Josh put his finger beneath her chin and tilted her face up so her eyes met his. "Morgan. Think. You? In a lab? Just a *peek*?"

She conceded the point. "True. But you'll show them to me someday, right?"

"Of course." He kissed the tip of her nose. "How's Petey?"

"He's fine. I left him with Felicity for a while—"

He interrupted her. "So everything's good?"

He was impatient. His entire body was straining to get back to work. He wanted her to *leave*. It was irrational, she knew, but her feelings were hurt.

"Everything's fine. I just wanted to see you."

She stalked across his office, yanked the door open, and exited. She twinkled her fingers at the luscious secretary as she passed her desk.

"Bye, Imogene."

"Bye, Mrs. O'Keefe." Imogene twinkled her fingers back.

Morgan made it to the SUV and out of the parking lot before bursting into tears.

She sat for a while, indulging in a good cry, then got bored with herself, blew her nose, wiped her tears, reapplied her mascara and lipstick, and started up the car.

The University of Massachusetts at Amherst was nearby; she'd passed it several times when driving along East Pleasant Street, but she'd never spent any time there and was curious about its layout. The university had a vast campus, spread across fourteen hundred and fifty acres of rolling green land. It had over twenty-seven thousand students and over a thousand faculty members. It was a city of student centers, lecture halls, dormitories, libraries, dining halls, and laboratories. The environmental safety office, where she'd work if she ever worked again, was on Campus Center Way; she'd Googled it once, just out of curiosity. She didn't dare go to the environmental safety office. She knew a position was open there; she knew if she walked in the door, she'd be hooked.

She knew where the department of chemical engineering was, because after she'd met Ben Barnaby, she'd Googled it, too. The two buildings weren't far from each other, except for the spaghetti of streets between them. She drove to Draper Hall, which housed the chemical engineering faculty. It was an elegant Victorian brick building, softened by age, with an arched doorway. She drove past it, found the parking lot, searched for an open space, and finally slid into a space marked Staff Only.

When she'd worked at Weathersfield College, just north of Boston, she'd memorized the campus map, not a difficult feat, because that campus had been so much smaller than the massive U. Mass.–Amherst campus. It had existed in her mind like a hologram so that if there were ever an emergency, she could make her way to it instantly. She'd overseen the installation of OSHA-approved eyewash and deluge showers in several departments and especially the mercury-reduction initiative. Spilled mercury was highly toxic to the central nervous system, hazardous to the ecosystem, and could not be disposed of in the trash. She'd personally supervised the deacquisition of mercury-based instruments—hydrometers, manometers, pyrometers, sphygmomanometers, and so on—and replaced them with nonmercury alternatives. With each step she'd felt a sense of real achievement. People talked about saving the earth; she took action. She couldn't save the entire world, but she could do her bit.

"Morgan?"

The male voice broke into her thoughts so suddenly she almost screamed. She'd rolled her window down for fresh air, and there in the window stood Ben Barnaby. What was he doing here?

Of course, the question was, What was *she* doing here?

"Ben, oh, hello." She shook her head, emerging from her reverie.

"Are you okay?"

He had such clear blue eyes. He seemed so sympathetic.

"To be honest, no, and you might be one of the few people to understand why. I miss working, Ben! I miss the labs, the computers, the offices, the emergencies. I must sound totally crazy."

"No, you don't. I understand. Look, want me to show you Goessmann Lab?"

"Oh, Ben, that would be incredible!"

He laughed. "I hope you're not disappointed."

He stepped back. She opened her door, left the car, beeped it locked, and set off walking with him.

"Petey's with a babysitter. Felicity. I was just touring the campus. I guess for me it's like going to the world's most fabulous mall."

Ben chuckled. "Perhaps an eccentric point of view." He walked along beside her, going left out of the parking lot onto a sideway. "You're lucky your husband's a scientist."

Not today I'm not, Morgan thought, but said simply, "True. Although we study different things."

They crossed the street and wound past buildings, bike stands, lampposts, trees, and barrels labeled Trash and Recycle.

"Are you teaching during the summer session?" she asked Ben.

"One morning class three days a week. Plus, I've got some papers to write and some grants to apply for."

"You're working on bio-oil upgrading?"

"Correct. A bit like what Josh is doing over at Bio-Green, but different. Everyone's rushing to find an alternative to oil, or a way to improve its efficiency." He opened the door into a modern building constructed of what looked like giant real-life LEGOs.

She followed him down a corridor, past doors with windows in them and numbers on them and people moving back and forth inside them, and then he opened a door and said, "Here we are."

His lab was probably thirty by twenty, with high windows at the other end, track lighting in the ceiling, the walls lined with countertops, refrigerators, cupboards, sinks, and fume hoods for proper exhaust and ventilation. In the middle of the room ran a long workbench, covered with computers and microscopes. Two men and one woman sat on stools staring down into the microscopes or tapping at the computers.

"Hey, everyone," Ben said. "How's it going?"

The three grad students glanced up, smiling. "Hey, Ben."

"This is my friend Morgan O'Keefe. She's a biosafety specialist."

The three grad students froze.

Morgan waved. "I don't work here," she assured them. "I'm a stay-at-home mom these days. I just miss seeing labs."

"So she's welcome to come in and visit here anytime, okay?" Ben told them.

They nodded, but Morgan could tell by their body language they weren't comfortable with her presence. All scientists were a bit paranoid, not surprisingly. Everyone was racing to find the Big Answers to so many questions.

"Want to stay?" Ben asked. "Look around?"

She shook her head. It wasn't just the sight of a lab that Morgan craved. "No thanks. This was great." As they walked away from the building, Morgan said, "It's terrible, Ben, how much I miss all this."

"Why is that so terrible?"

"Because I have a child to take care of. Because the formative years are so important. Because I need to protect him and nurture him and teach him."

"He'll be ready for preschool soon, won't he? Beatrice has two of her kids in preschool."

"True. I shouldn't be so impatient." She looked up at the tall blond man walking next to her. "But if you were in my shoes, wouldn't you be?"

"Honestly?" Ben answered. He took her arm to pull her back as a car came down the road and kept his hand on her arm as they crossed the street. "I think I've let my life get too narrow. It seems all I do is work, work, and worry about whether I'll get the grants done in time, and meanwhile, entire seasons pass."

"Do you have a girlfriend?" Morgan asked, surprised at her own audacity.

"Not now." Ben frowned. "Don't have time for a girlfriend." Then, as if she'd gone a step too far, he literally backed off. "I've got a meeting." He pointed. "The parking lot's over there. See ya."

"Ben, thanks for the tour!" Morgan hurried to say.

But he was loping away from her, toward Draper Hall, hands in his pockets, head bent forward, and she could tell his mind was already on his work.

Natalie was in her aunt's immaculate blue-and-white laundry room putting clothes in the dryer when her phone rang.

"Hey, Nat, I've got an idea. Let's have a cookout Sunday night and invite the Barnabys and the O'Keefes."

She nearly dropped the phone. Then, her voice sarcastically sweet, she said, "Excuse me? Who's calling, please?"

Her brother said, "Very funny."

A charming white wrought iron chair with a blue-and-white-checked gingham cushion waited next to the ironing board, also covered in blue-and-white-checked gingham. Natalie dropped into it. "*You* want to have a cookout."

"Yeah. Listen, you don't have to worry about a thing. I'll swing by Angelato's and get it all—potato salad, macaroni salad, gelato— and I'll pick up some hamburger and hot dogs and buns when I get the mixers. I'll bring the booze, too."

"Slade. What the hell are you up to?"

"What do you mean? It's summer. It's hot here in Boston. I want to spend the weekend on the lake. I want to swim, see you and your friends."

A light flashed in Natalie's brain. "You want to check out the Barnabys' furniture."

"Oh, get over yourself, Nat."

"You're shameless."

"Hey. No reason to get mean about this. I just want to have a cookout."

"You never just want to do anything."

"Fine. Forget I ever said anything." Strangely, he sounded hurt.

Natalie sagged. "Oh, Slade."

"Don't worry about it. I've got other friends." He hung up.

Now Natalie felt awful. Quickly she punched in the number and called him back. When he answered, she said, "Look. I'm sorry. I simply can't forget the way you treated all my girlfriends in high school. Plus, you are a wheeler-dealer with the antiques, you know you are."

"That's true. I am. It's my *business*, Natalie. I have learned a lot of stuff over the years, and you know what? I'm proud of it. I've talked with Bella about the furniture her family has, you're right about that, but I don't intend to rip the Barnabys off. Bella's thinking of changing her shop, and I offered to help her bring in some antiques. And that's the truth."

"Slade, so help me, if you break Bella's heart—"

"Hold on. Bella's practically engaged to Aaron. She's not interested in me. I'm not interested in her. I thought you wanted me to come out this summer and enjoy the lake house. If I have to go through this kind of interrogation every weekend, forget it."

"No, you're right, I do want you to come out."

"Well, thanks. And, PS, did I say I wanted to go on a date with Bella? No. I said I wanted to bring out a lot of stuff and have a cookout. I like your friends. Is that so weird?"

"No," Natalie agreed. "All right, let's do it. Do you want me to invite them, or you?"

"You. You see them all the time. I'll try to get there Sunday morning. That way I can enjoy some sunshine. I'll do all the cooking in the evening. It's going to be fun."

"It's a good idea, Slade. It really is."

Still, when Natalie hung up the phone, her stomach felt funny.

. . .

Sunday was a perfect summer day: hot and cloudless with the slightest of breezes sweeping away any visiting mosquitoes and filling the sails of the small boats drifting on the lake.

Natalie worked in the morning. She had gotten into a good work routine and almost begrudged the weekends, when people expected her to do something as worthless as having fun. Her charcoal of Petey had surprised her with its unexpected resonance. It was so good she couldn't give it to the O'Keefes; she wanted to keep it for a show, when she ever had one. Until then, she needed to refer to it, to keep looking at it—it was leading her somewhere. So she was doing an oil of the same pose of Petey for the O'Keefes. They would prefer the oil, she knew. In it, Petey looked like himself, the real boy in living color; the charcoal had something more art museum, even antique, about it. She wouldn't give the oil to the O'Keefes this weekend, not when everyone was around. She'd wait for a special time.

She worked in a new black bikini and an ancient paint-covered work shirt until she heard a van pull up in her drive. Not even her talented brother could arrive with all the picnic goodies on a motorcycle. She hurried downstairs to help him unload one of Dave Ralston's vans. They lugged in beer and wine, soft drinks and sparkling water, and bags of groceries. They stocked the refrigerator, emptied bags of ice into a Styrofoam cooler, and shoved cans and bottles down into the sparkling ice. They set up beach chairs on the sand, and put out a table and a cooler of ice.

"That's about it," Slade said. "It's hot. Let's get out on the water."

He disappeared into the downstairs bath, returning in surfer-boy boxer-short bathing trunks that slid down his skinny hips just a tantalizing inch. His long, lean body was muscular, but white.

"You're pale," Natalie teased as they left the house and tapped down the wooden steps from the deck.

"(A) I am not, and (B) not everyone lounges around on a lake all day."

"I don't lounge," Natalie shot back.

Together, they dragged the old canoe out of the boathouse down to the edge of the water.

"Get the paddles," he told Natalie. "They're on the wall."

In the shed, the summer fragrance of sun-warmed wood and packed earth surrounded her. She breathed in, closing her eyes just for a moment, then found the paddles and the flotation cushions and carried them down to the shore.

"You get in," Slade directed. "I'll shove off."

Slade pushed the boat into the water and stepped in, rocking the canoe until it settled down as the lake embraced it.

They dipped their paddles into the water and stroked. The boat obligingly moved forward. They slid away from shore as gracefully as a swan. A beguiling silence enveloped them, broken only by the musical splash of their oars. The sun splintered the surface with streaks of dazzle. Along the shore, trees dappled the lake with shade. They passed the piers and docks and beaches of other houses, and people they didn't know waved at them from their decks and porches. A pair of mallards bobbed near a fallen maple branch. A green fall of willow leaves bowed from the ground into the water; they slipped beneath the arch it created. Droplets of water fell from Natalie's oar, each one a shimmering gem.

Natalie turned to look at her brother. "Hey, we're like canoe pros! I don't remember Aunt Eleanor teaching us."

"She didn't. We learned by trial and error." Slade chuckled. "More error than anything else, if I remember right. And my swimming style sucks."

"I'm terrible at it, too. I almost drowned last week. Bella's brother Ben had to rescue me."

Slade laughed. "You're kidding me."

"Nope."

"Awesome."

They continued along the lake in silence.

When do childhood emotions loosen their hold, allowing you to see the world, be in the world, as the adult you've worked so hard to become? Natalie wondered.

Today was like the Sundays of her childhood memories. The air smelled sweet and felt fresh on her bare skin, the sky arched higher than ever before—she could scarcely see the blue behind the shimmer of sunlight—and grasses, ferns, and green bushes drooped down the banks of the lake in a thick, verdant tapestry. Children's laughter and the splashing of oars rang all around.

The Barnabys were already out. Louise was on the deck, reclining on a chaise with an umbrella angled over her to protect her from too much sun. Ben and his father were at their boathouse, carrying out deck chairs, oars, sails. Bella sat at the table on the deck, bent over a book. Brady and a friend were already on the lake, side by side in kayaks.

At the O'Keefes', Morgan was fastening Petey into his life jacket while Josh stepped the mast on the Sunfish. All three were in bathing suits. Morgan and Josh waved at Natalie and Slade, then returned to the business of getting Petey into the sailboat. The little boy was so excited he was jumping up and down.

Happy families on either side. Happy families all around the lake. Natalie remembered this so well from visiting as a child, remembered the sense of difference she carried like a hump on her back—something visible to everyone else, something that set her and Slade apart. Their mother would drive them down in her rattling old station wagon and drop them off for a few days, scarcely bothering to come in for even a short chat with Eleanor. Which was fine with Natalie, because it hurt her to see her mother and aunt together.

Natalie's mother was three years older than Eleanor, but she was so worn-out, overweight, and defeated in appearance she seemed more like Eleanor's mother. Aunt Eleanor would be wearing something glamorous over her toned, lean body. Natalie's mother would be in old jeans and a shapeless tee shirt, usually stained. Natalie knew that her mother was just as pretty as Aunt Eleanor, or would be if she could pull herself together, but over the years it became clear that Marlene would never change. And why should she? The loves of her life, her bulldogs, didn't care what she looked like.

So there they would be, Slade and Natalie, stick children, all elbows, knees, and ribs, wearing the wrong clothes, feet pinched in old shoes, hair drooping shaggily and probably greasily over their eyes.

"Dear God," Aunt Eleanor would always say. "You look like you stepped straight out of Dickens."

When she was very young, before she knew who Charles Dickens was, Natalie had interpreted her aunt's remark to mean she'd just left the Devil, which mystified and worried Natalie terribly, because even though her mother was poor and often cranky, she certainly wasn't *evil*. She would huddle next to Slade, who would be rigid with anger at the entire situation. Of course, Aunt Eleanor always had other people staying at her house, gorgeous, wealthy, carefree playboys without a worry in the world—that was how it seemed. They'd glance at Slade or Natalie, widen their eyes, arch their glossy shaped eyebrows, and murmur "My, my" to one another before sauntering off to the deck.

Aunt Eleanor would hug Natalie and Slade. "Darlings, you know where your room is. Take your luggage there and change into your bathing suits," she'd say before rushing to join her friends.

They were all younger then. Natalie and Slade were painfully aware of the Barnabys, who lived next door, with their badminton net set up in the side yard, their croquet set in the front yard, their deck and beach and boats and swarm of friends. Slade was about Ben's age; Natalie about Bella's. But they never met. Ben and Bella were too busy with their own friends, screaming with laughter as they splashed in the water, swimming with the natural ease of dolphins. Aunt Eleanor didn't try to introduce them. She had no experience with children; she was trying to be kind and generous to her nephew and niece, whom she did love in her own grown-up way.

Still, no one taught Slade and Natalie how to swim. "Go swim," Aunt Eleanor would order them, knowing at least that on a summer day children shouldn't be lurking in the house. It was humiliating to walk down to the beach in their last-year's faded swimming suits, pale as slugs from under a log. Sometimes, if the Barnaby kids weren't around, they'd really try to swim, occasionally succeeding, more often sinking and choking horribly. Slade was mean to Natalie in the water if other kids were around. He'd shove her under, or knock her off balance, or splash water in her face. She was younger and more sensitive to the opinion of others. Instead of getting into a fight with Slade in front of Aunt Eleanor or the neighbors, she'd stagger out of the lake, water dripping from her nose, her arms clutching her skinny body.

They didn't belong there. Slade and Natalie knew it. They told their mother they didn't want to go there, but she always answered with searing honesty that it was the only chance she had to provide them with any kind of summer vacation.

"I'm hot." Slade's voice broke into her thoughts. "My shoulders are getting sunburned. I'm thirsty."

Natalie burst into laughter. "You *are* a tender flower!"

"Yeah, well, you should see your shoulders," Slade challenged.

She looked. Bright red. "Ah," she said. "We should have worn sunblock."

They concentrated on turning the canoe back toward home, which suddenly had grown far away.

"How long have we been out here?" she asked.

"Over an hour," Slade told her.

"We're idiots," she said mildly.

"I know," he agreed.

A woman and her daughter sailed past in their kayak and waved at them. Far away, the O'Keefes glided through the water in their Sunfish. Birds flitted among the trees or swooped high in the sky, and a belly laugh boomed over the lake.

"Slade," Natalie said, "do you think you'll ever get married?"

He was quiet for so long she didn't think he would answer. She heard only the silken dip and slide of the oars.

"Oh," he said at last, "I don't know."

"You're thirty-five."

"You're thirty."

"I can't seem to meet a decent guy. I'd like to get married, though. I'd like to have a family."

He didn't reply. They paddled along companionably.

"Bella's nice," Slade said.

Natalie almost fell out of the canoe. Turning around, she looked at him. "Bella? Bella is *sweet*. Bella is almost engaged to Aaron. Bella wants lots of babies!"

"I just said she was nice," Slade replied defensively.

"Do you want children?" Natalie asked.

She could almost hear him shrug. "With the right woman."

They drew near their beach.

"Slade," Natalie said. "Listen, really. Don't play around with Bella, okay?"

"Give me some credit," Slade replied tersely.

Then they were back onshore, busy with the effort of getting the canoe up onto the grass, and turning it over, and hurrying into the house to shower and dress.

9
.....

By nine-thirty that Sunday evening, the sky was still luminous with a pale lavender glow. The lake was empty of boats, but the porches and decks rang with laughter and conversation. The tempting aroma of grilled food drifted through the air. All around the lake, trees, shrubs, and sheds lost their edges, blurring into shadows, while lights at the houses gleamed like points of gold.

Morgan sat on the Barnabys' wicker glider, comfortable on the deep pink-and-green floral cushions, with Petey sleeping in her arms. From here she could look over at Natalie's deck, where most of the party was gathered. Her muscles were pleasantly tired from the day's activities: Not only had she and Josh taken Petey out sailing, but later, after Petey's nap and before the cookout, they'd played volleyball, badminton, and croquet with Ben, Aaron, Slade, Bella, and a hesitant and uncoordinated Natalie. Louise and Dennis had kept Petey occupied, pulling out dump trucks and backhoes that Beatrice's children played with; the older people had insisted they loved being with the toddler. So Morgan was able to run and jump for the ball, feeling the slam of it against her palm, right down to her shoulder; she was able to swing her racquet forward to whack the birdie over Aaron's head—she'd felt, for a while, young again, back in a body that could leap and spin and smash, an athletic body meant for movement. She didn't have to prepare dinner either. It had been a perfect summer day.

Louise and Dennis had gone into the house to watch *Masterpiece*

Theatre on PBS. Natalie had sat with Morgan for a long time, talking desultorily, lulled by the fresh air and all the delicious food they'd eaten. Natalie was back on her own deck now, slipping around inconspicuously tidying up: tossing used cans and bottles into a recycle barrel, covering the cupcakes and carrying them inside. Bella leaned against the deck railing, snuggled up against Aaron, who had his arm around her and from time to time bent to kiss her forehead. Morgan remembered those early-love days, the sweetness, the tug of connection. The others, Slade, Ben, and Josh, were arguing about the Red Sox.

One of the men pulled away from the others, went down the steps, crossed the lawn, and came up to the Barnabys' deck.

Slade sat down next to Morgan, gently, so he wouldn't rock the slider. "Hey. Where'd the Barnabys go?"

"TV. It's after nine."

Slade stretched. "Yeah. I've got to go soon. It's been a long day. Everyone has to work tomorrow."

Morgan spoke before thinking. "I don't. I mean, of course, I've got Petey. . . ." She gazed lovingly down at her sleeping son.

"Does he sleep through the night?"

Morgan stared at Slade.

"I have friends with children," Slade said defensively. "I know a couple whose daughter still won't go to sleep unless she sleeps in their bed, and she's two."

Morgan shifted the heavy lump of her precious boy over to her other arm. "Petey's been sleeping through the night for about six months now. Thank heavens. And he sleeps in his crib." Slade wore cargo shorts and a black tee. Now in the dusk, the red streak of burn across his nose, forehead, and cheeks was less noticeable. She couldn't really see his face, and yet amazingly, she was still intensely aware of his extraordinary good looks. Of his sexuality. It was like having a sleek panther curled on the glider with her, something feral, sensual, patient, aware of her, biding its time.

"I should put Petey to bed." She struggled to rise.

"Let me carry him." Slade stood up in one uncoiled move and held out his arms.

She thought for a moment. "Okay."

Slade bent down; together they maneuvered the child into his arms. For the briefest moment, Morgan inhaled Slade's scent, a mix of fresh air, clean cotton, and an unfamiliar aftershave. She arched her back and stretched, free of the child's weight. "Let's go in through the front door," she suggested, "so all the talk won't wake him."

Slade followed her quietly down the steps, around the side of the house, across the lawn, and up the steps into Morgan's house.

"Wow," he whispered when they entered. "Posh."

She wasn't sure how to respond, so she only answered, "His bedroom's upstairs."

In Petey's room, she quickly turned on the night light, then smoothed out the bedsheet and lowered the bars on the crib. With great gentleness, Slade bent to lay the sleeping child in his bed. Petey stirred, murmured, his pink lips twitching. Curling on his side, he continued sleeping. Morgan reached past Slade for Petey's light cotton blanket and covered him, then stood for a moment, watching the boy sleep, as she always did. Only this time she was aware that it wasn't Josh next to her—not that Josh was around much these days to help put Petey to bed. She was aware of Slade's tight muscular concentration. He lived with a shield around him. Right now the shield drew her like a magnet.

"Okay," she whispered, and went out into the hall. Slade followed. She pulled Petey's door halfway shut.

"What about his diaper?" Slade asked.

"He's not wearing one," Morgan confessed with a grin. "We allowed him to water the bushes by the side of the house. He was thrilled. I think he's pretty much drained himself dry. Anyway, I'll have to change his sheets tomorrow. He's got sand on the bottom of his feet and heaven knows what in the pocket of his shorts, but I decided I'd deal with that tomorrow rather than wake him up for a bath tonight."

"Gosh." Slade stopped by an open door. "Is that your bedroom? Do you mind?" Before she could answer, he stepped inside. He strode across to the window overlooking the lake, then came back to the door, flicked on the overhead light, and surveyed their room before focusing on the bed. "Waverly, right?"

"Hey, you're good." Their queen-size mattress, bound in crisp white sheets, sat on a long, low heavy black frame with two black bedside tables, creating a kind of Asian look. It was lower to the ground than most beds, which for Morgan had created difficulties when she was nursing Petey and had to get them both into the bed in the middle of the night. But the look was spectacular.

"It's my business." Slade looked at their chest of drawers. "Although I can't place this."

"It's Thrift Shop, circa 2009," Morgan joked. "I haven't found time to buy chests that will look good with such a—what the saleswoman called—a *statement* of a bed." Morgan flashed on the days when they first bought the bed, how she and Josh had made love in it over and over again, turned on by its expensive unusual lines, feeling as if they were in another country, on another planet.

Slade squinted, thinking. "In our shop in Boston, we have a black lacquered table cabinet with five drawers, antique Chinese, probably 1880, similar severe lines."

"Sounds like it costs a fortune."

"About two thousand. But I could get a deal for you." He didn't look at Morgan when he said this, but his voice was an invitation, an overture.

"I'd have to talk with Josh about it before I decided."

"Sure. Tell you what. I'll take a photo of it and email it to you and Josh."

"Okay." Morgan was uncomfortably hot, even though she knew the air-conditioning was on low, keeping the temperature just right for Petey. She turned away and hurried down the stairs, and then, as if prompted by something she didn't know resided within her, she went into the living room. She flicked on the overhead light.

"What do you think about this room?" she asked Slade.

"It's cool. Minimal. Low tones. I like it. I really like the picture on the wall over there, too. Who did it?"

Morgan laughed. "Your sister."

"No way." He crossed the room to stand in front of the painting, arms folded, studying it. "Wow. I had no idea." In a flash, he changed subjects. "Your dining room—you need a buffet or something."

"I know. But, remember, we've only owned the house for a few months, and Josh thinks it's important for me to get it right."

Slade ran his hand over the dining room table surface, feeling the wood. "*Josh* thinks it's important? Don't *you?*"

"I'm kind of decoratingly challenged," Morgan joked. "I can't get too excited about 'creating a statement.' To be honest, I loved the furniture in the house I grew up in. All big, fat comfortable sofas and chairs in chintz, with miles of thick carpet. It was deliciously homey, which was great, because my parents are both physicians and seldom were around."

Coming back into the living room, Slade plopped down on one of the long gray sofas. "It's comfortable enough." He glanced around. "But perhaps the room is a bit cold." He stood up, squinting, thinking. "Here's what I'd do. Over there by the window facing the street? A Victorian settee. It would be eye-catching. A contrast to this modern stuff."

"No one ever sits over there," Morgan told him.

"That's because there's nothing to sit on," he shot back sensibly. "I'm just saying. If you mixed it up a bit, I think you'd feel more at home here."

"I suppose you have the perfect piece," Morgan said cynically.

"Ah, you've insulted me." Slade pretended to be hurt. He crossed the room and went out into the hall, just slightly brushing Morgan's arm with his own. "Now, even if I had the perfect piece, I wouldn't tell you," he teased.

She started to follow him out the front door, then stopped. She had sat out on the deck in the late evenings, waiting for Josh to come home, with Petey asleep in his crib, but if she went back to Natalie's, she wasn't sure she'd hear him if he woke crying.

"Slade," she called, "I'm going to stay here."

He turned and looked at her with a quizzical, even worried expression.

"Because of Petey," she explained. "In case he wakes."

"You want me to tell Josh before I take off?" Slade asked.

For just a moment, Morgan wanted to say no. No, let Josh wonder where she'd gone. Let him wonder if she'd ridden away with Slade. But of course Josh wouldn't think that, and he wouldn't wonder where Morgan was. He'd know she'd be somewhere near Petey.

"Sure," Morgan said. "Tell Josh I'm on our deck. And, Slade, thanks for the advice."

"I'll email you some photos," he said, and disappeared into the dark.

She went out the kitchen door and leaned on the railing of their deck. By now night had fallen but lights from the houses nearby allowed her to see what was going on two doors down. People were dispersing. Ben waved at Morgan as he walked around Natalie's house to his car. Bella had gone. The lights were off on the Barnaby deck. Josh was helping Natalie and Slade carry the last of the party glasses, bottles, plates, and napkins inside. The soft, dark air carried sounds to her like drifts of blossoms: laughter, the murmur of conversation, music from across the lake, a whip-poor-will's call. She breathed in deeply, savoring the fragrance of some flower she couldn't name. For a few moments she could believe she was in paradise. So much happiness around her, her little boy safely asleep, her muscles aching with the pleasure of use, her body filled with delicious food and wine, and her life surrounded by such interesting friends.

She wanted to share this contentment with her husband.

After a while she heard an engine start up; Slade, she assumed, on his way back home. Leaning on the railing, Morgan watched Josh say good night to Natalie.

"Great party," he told her. He sounded happy. Relaxed.

"Thanks for coming," Natalie told him, waving as he went down their steps and across the lawn to his own home.

Morgan turned to lean in what she hoped was a seductive pose, arms and back on the railing, hips canted forward. Josh came up the steps.

"Hey," he said. "Petey in bed?"

"Out like a light."

Instead of approaching her, Josh went into the house. "Aren't you coming?" he called over his shoulder. "It's late."

She went into the kitchen, slid the glass door shut, and latched it. "I spent some time in the house with Slade," she remarked, hoping to catch some kind of attention from her husband.

"Oh yeah?" Josh was at the sink filling a glass with water. He wore his bathing trunks and a rugby shirt, and his red hair stuck up in every direction. His skin was pink from the sun. She could see the muscles of his shoulder blades moving under the fabric of his shirt.

"He had some interesting suggestions about furniture."

"I'll bet." Josh's tone was sour.

Hope perked up in Morgan's heart. Could he possibly be a bit jealous?

"Yes," she said calmly. "He helped me put Petey to bed. He looked in our bedroom, really liked our bed, suggested an antique Asian chest for our clothes."

"Not a bad idea. But I bet the price tag is high. I think he's a wheeler-dealer."

So he wasn't jealous. Snippily, Morgan replied, "I thought you wanted me to purchase upscale items."

"Right." Josh drank his water thirstily. "I had too much sun and beer today."

"We all did. We needed it." Crossing the room, she leaned up against him.

Josh jerked his shoulder as if twitching off a fly. "Sunburn."

"Everywhere?" Morgan asked, using all the sexiness she could find to flavor her voice. In the early days of their marriage, that was all it would take for Josh to turn and take her right there up against the refrigerator.

"I've got work to do, Morg," he said grumpily.

She hated it when he called her Morg. And he knew it. Who would want to be called Morg, with its echoes of *morgue?*

Still, standing this close to her husband, feeling his body heat, her own mood so mellow, all combined to make her persevere. Gently, she leaned her hips against his. "I promise not to take too long," she teased. Affection for her husband swelled inside her, a sense of love and longing she hadn't felt for months. "Sweetie," she whispered, lightly touching his back, "this was such a lovely day. And all because of you, because you work so hard, because you took the job that made it possible for us to live here in this great place."

She sensed his tension ease. Josh turned around, put his hands on her shoulders, and touched his forehead to hers. How long had it been since they had been with each other like this, like lovers, man and woman, husband and wife, instead of adversaries or merely employees in the business of running a family?

"Morgan." He pulled her against him, hugging her close.

She could feel a struggle inside him, could feel how something was fighting to break through. "What is it?" she asked, leaning back to search his face.

He swallowed. "I just . . . I'm glad you had a good day. It matters a lot that you thanked me, that you know my work means something for us as a family. That's why I took the job. I know I work long hours. I'm not home as much as you'd like. It seems like I'm always on the computer, but it will get better. This is just my first year. It's hard for me, too."

"Oh, Josh," Morgan murmured, nuzzling into his neck.

He took her hand. "Let's go to bed." He added, with a rueful smile, "But do me a favor."

"Anything," she promised.

"Try not to press my shoulders. I was an idiot not to wear a shirt all day."

She laughed and let him lead her upstairs.

10

·····

By the time Bella and Aaron left Natalie's and returned to the Barnaby house, Louise and Dennis had turned off the television and gone upstairs to bed. Bella pulled the sliding glass door shut from the deck, locked it, and did a quick survey of the kitchen. All was tidy. She flicked off the kitchen light and began to walk into the front hall, but Aaron put his hands on her waist and stopped her.

He whispered into her ear, "Come back to my place." He smelled warmly of Coppertone and sun, and his hands were strong and sure.

Bella hesitated. She knew she existed in an uncomfortable arrangement in this house, where she'd lived all her life. She'd had sex. She was on the birth control pill. Her parents were aware of that. Yet, she couldn't manage to invite Aaron to spend the night with her in her bedroom.

The image was amusing, because Bella's bedroom remained girlish, with two twin beds covered in floral patchwork quilts. Muscular Aaron would look peculiar in such a setting. But more than that, Bella wouldn't want to make love with Aaron, not in this house where her parents were sleeping, or, worse, not sleeping.

Aaron's hands smoothly roamed around to her midriff, lightly touching her breasts. "Come on. You know you want to."

Bella pulled away, turning to face Aaron. "I do want to," she agreed. "But, Aaron, first—we need to talk."

Aaron stepped close to her, only inches away. "No we don't. We don't need to talk tonight. We can *talk* tomorrow."

"Aaron, please. Listen. I feel so—uncomfortable about everything."

"You mean about my job in California."

She echoed his words sadly. "Your job in California."

"All right," Aaron said. "I put it the wrong way. I don't know that I'll get the job. I'm one of the top three candidates. That's what they told me, and that's all I'll know for the next few weeks." The light from the hall illuminated the dark kitchen enough for Bella to see Aaron's face. He was such an honest man, and his gaze was clear. "Let's not think about California. Today was a perfect day. Let's have a perfect night."

She kissed him. Upstairs a toilet flushed and water ran. For a moment Bella froze, like a high school kid caught in a misdemeanor.

"You'll have to bring me home tomorrow so I can get dressed for the shop," she reminded him.

"I can do that."

"Okay. I'll grab my purse and leave a note for my parents."

They went out into the night, easing the front door closed behind them. In the Volvo, on the way into Amherst, they passed Barnaby's Barn, barely visible in the darkness except for a soft glow from the security lights inside.

"So," Aaron asked, "what's going on with the shop?"

Bella hesitated. "Slade came back. He thinks some of our family furniture is really valuable."

"Hey, that's great. Your parents might be able to sell enough furniture to give them some security for retirement. Or even for some luxuries."

The lights of Amherst flashed against the car windows. They passed Subway, 7-Eleven, a gas station, and Aaron turned down a side street toward the apartment complex.

"I had a good talk with Slade today," Aaron continued. "He knows his stuff. We're at opposite ends of the spectrum—I'm modern, he's antique—but I respect his opinion."

"Let's not talk about the shop right now," Bella suggested as Aaron parked in front of his apartment building.

Bella had seen Aaron and Slade talking this evening at the cookout. Slade had been flipping burgers on the grill and drinking a beer; Aaron had been holding out a platter of buns and drinking a beer, too. Men multitasking. They'd both been barefoot, in bathing trunks and polo shirts, with sun-dried hair ruffled by the wind. Aaron was shorter, but much more muscular. Sturdy. Slade was tall and lean. The back of Aaron's neck looked powerful and sunburned. The back of Slade's neck was obscured by his shaggy black hair.

Bella tried to erase the image of the two men as she and Aaron went up the walk and inside the converted Victorian house. Aaron's apartment was on the second floor, which meant they got noise from the apartments below and above, but in the summer the air-conditioning unit drowned out most sounds.

Aaron didn't turn on the overhead light but pulled Bella to him and whispered, "Did I tell you how good you look in a bikini?"

The terrible thing was that Bella was so glad Aaron didn't want to continue with a serious talk that she wrapped herself around him, kissing him passionately, not quite sure exactly who the passion was for.

Later, in the shadows of Aaron's bedroom, they lay together like spoons, with Aaron's arm around Bella's waist. The air conditioner hummed reliably, making the room cool enough that they needed a sheet over them.

"This is an important time for me, Bella," Aaron murmured.

"Mmm," she agreed sleepily.

"In a way, it's *the* time."

The tension in his voice stirred her into wakefulness. "What do you mean?"

"All my life I've dreamed of creating buildings. Since I was a child playing with blocks, actually. The completed vision interests me, but more than that, I like the challenge of creating something that looks impossible and yet is structurally sound."

"I know." She nestled closer. "Safe. Reliable. Like you."

Encouraged, Aaron continued, "The thing about San Francisco, Bella, is that they love history as much as you do. They're not interested in a spaceship landscape. If you saw the art museum, you'd be surprised; you'd fall in love with it, I know."

She stroked his hand. "I've heard that San Francisco is awesome."

"It is. And the company that wants me—I hope—well, Bella, I know you'd like them. Most of the architects are young, in their thirties or forties, married, with children. I interviewed with several different people, including the president of the firm, who is older, in his fifties, but very cool, not arrogant. You'd like him, too, Bella. The atmosphere out there is so—I don't know how to describe it—*open*. Fresh. Exciting. Expansive. I think they liked me, Bella."

"Of course they liked you."

"No, I mean, they liked my ideas. My designs. My sketches." He stirred his legs against hers, restless in his thoughts. "And the city has everything. We could sail, we could hike, just like we do here. The restaurants are amazing, the schools are excellent—"

Bella turned over to face him. "Aaron. Honey. You've got to wait until you hear from them to get so excited."

"I'm sure I'll get the job, Bella. I *feel* it. They said things, they implied things, like they said '*when* you join us' instead of '*if* you join us' a couple of times. Jorge Meridian—he's in charge of a new parking garage, which doesn't sound like anything, but he's tasked with making it modern, useful, and eye-catching. Jorge took me out to lunch and we were absolutely on the same wavelength."

His excitement was electric, radiating from him. He was being so open, so honest, that Bella didn't want to hide her own aspirations from him any longer.

"Aaron." She pulled away from his arm, sat up, and tugged the sheet up to cover her breasts. "I need to tell you something."

He sat up next to her, both of them leaning against the headboard. "That sounds ominous."

"It's not," she assured him. "It's good. Just . . . complicated. Aaron, some people, like you, are lucky. You've always known what you've wanted to be. Natalie's known, too, even if she's had to struggle to be an artist. Morgan's mad for her weird biohazard safety stuff. Ben's always been a scientist, and my sister, Beat, has always wanted to be a mommy with a big family. I suppose, in a way, I've been searching for what I want."

"You're a third-grade teacher."

"True. And I'm pretty good at it. I enjoy the children, and I know how to keep them on task. But it's not my passion. I thought, since Dad is so crazy about teaching, I would be, too. I do *like* it. But it's not *the thing* for me, like architecture is for you."

Aaron studied Bella as she talked. "Okay. Go on."

"Well . . . just because I haven't gotten *there* yet doesn't mean I'm not on my way." She touched his shoulder. "Listen to me. I feel like I'm *waking up* somehow since I've been home. Not because of my family, although I love being around them, and when the time comes for me to have children, I really want to be near them. But it's more than that. For one thing, it's this area. I feel good here, like a cat with her fur stroked the right way."

"San Francisco is pretty nice," Aaron reminded her in a mild tone.

"I know," she agreed. "But also, Aaron, it's the shop. Not Barnaby's Barn, but *my shop*. The shop *I* could create." The words spilled out of her in a rush. "I'd sell antique furniture, and art, and . . . I'm still working on what else. I suppose I'm not being clear, but one thing I'm sure of is that I feel excited by the possibilities. But I need some more time."

"Okay." Aaron stroked her arms. "Okay," he repeated thoughtfully. "I know what it's like to pursue a dream. I guess I'm chasing my own dream with the San Francisco job offer." He pulled her next to him. "You know, Bella, I want us both to have our dreams come true."

"So you can give me time?"

"Am I rushing you?" He nodded to himself. "Perhaps. We haven't been together very long. What, six months? But I love you,

Bella. I'm planning my future—my *real life*. You're the woman I want in my life. I haven't proposed to you because I realize it would freak you out, but you've got to know I'm going to."

He was so steady. So sure of himself. She curled against him, nuzzling his neck. "I love you, too, Aaron."

"I know. We'll work it all out."

They turned off the lights and snuggled down into bed together. Aaron began the deep rhythmic snore of sleep almost immediately. Bella lay staring into the dark.

The next morning they didn't continue the discussion. Aaron's mind was on his work. He had a couple of classes to teach for summer school, and research he was doing for a paper he was writing for an architectural journal. He'd received his master's degree, but any publication increased his credibility and status as an architect, and while he waited to hear from California, he was glad to have this to keep his mind occupied. He drove Bella back to her house, gave her a quick smooch on the lips, and told her he'd see her that night.

Her parents were already up when she went in, even though it was early. She said a quick hello, then raced up the stairs to shower and dress for work. It was another lush summer day, hot verging on muggy, so she wore a sundress and sandals. She had time to grab a bagel and a to-go cup of iced coffee as she went out the door.

She opened Barnaby's Barn, turned on the air-conditioning, and leaned on the counter, thinking. *Plotting* was the more appropriate word, she decided. She was waiting for someone special to arrive.

In her cyclone of ideas about the shop, she recalled how her mother had started it, as a venue for her own creations, and then as a showroom for the handiwork of others as well. That was sixteen years ago. Bella's friends had grown up, and while some of them had moved away and some of them were teaching, working on degrees, whatever, some of them were artisans. She realized this when she ran into Penny Aristides, who'd been in her grade all through school, in an Amherst coffee shop. Penny had been Penny Watson;

she'd married Stellios Aristides, a physician practicing in Amherst, and she was pregnant with their first child. Bella and Penny chatted about old times and caught up on the past few years, and then Bella asked Penny where she'd found her fabulous earrings.

Penny made them. It was only a hobby, she confessed.

"Do you ever sell them?" Bella asked.

"Oh, Bella, I'll make you a pair if you'd like."

"No, what I mean is, do you ever consider selling them?" When Penny continued to look confused, Bella explained, "I'm going to change Barnaby's Barn. I want to make it completely different, aimed at adults, with a range of unusual, cool merchandise, and your earrings are something I'd love to carry."

Penny had chewed her lip, thinking. "I do have several pieces. . . . Let me bring a few things in Monday," she said. "We'll talk."

It was after ten on Monday when Bella heard the crunch of tires on gravel. After a few moments, Penny lumbered in, one hand carrying a velvet box, the other supporting her swollen belly.

"Hi, Penny!" Bella came around the counter to greet her friend.

Penny stopped just inside the door. "Oh, wow. I haven't been in here for years."

Bella waited for Penny to say more, to say, *Oh, I love the murals with the daisies*, or *I should get a Lake World for my baby*. Instead, she stood there, silent, looking uncomfortable. "I'm not sure . . . ," she began, and grimaced.

Embarrassment flashed down Bella's spine. "You're not sure this is the right place for your jewelry," she finished for Penny. "I agree completely." Guilt zinged her as she spoke; she was betraying her mother's taste and commercial judgment. The guilt seemed to rip at her heart. Still, Bella kept talking, the words spilling out of her from some unknown source. "I'm getting rid of most of this stuff. I'm going to sell antique furniture—upscale, valuable furniture. And art. I'm not sure what else; I'm only beginning to put details into a general picture. Let me see your jewelry."

Reassured, Penny set her case on the counter and opened it.

Carefully she lifted out a large velvet cloth and laid several pieces on it for Bella to scrutinize.

The jewelry was heavy, ornate, even baroque, but also somehow modern. Two pale peach cameos were held in a twisted silver web, hanging from more twisted silver with topaz stones caught in them—spectacular, unusual earrings. A necklace thick with brilliant stones, silver birds, and old-fashioned charms had a medieval appeal. Another necklace hung from a stainless steel chain, its showpiece a dazzling starburst of stones shaped like petals, with smaller stones set deep in the core.

"I've always made my own jewelry," Penny told Bella. "But I don't know about doing it professionally."

"These pieces are *exquisite*," Bella said. "How did you do it?"

Penny laughed. "For one thing, I take apart my grandmothers' costume jewelry. They used to wear so many huge brooches with matching earrings. I used to buy drugstore magnifying glasses and use tweezers and my dad's pliers. After I married Stellios, I started stealing things out of his medical kit. Medical tools are fabulous for jewelry making—long-handled tweezers and so on. For my birthday a few years ago, Stellios surprised me with a complete set of real tools, and some sheets of silver, and a professional-quality magnifying glass."

As Penny talked, Bella held the jewelry up to the light, watching it dangle and sparkle. Here was someone else with a natural passion for work, and a true talent.

"I never thought of selling it," Penny was saying, "until you mentioned it. The truth is, I've made more than I can ever wear. It's like I can't stop myself. I wake up in the morning with an image in my mind of a new necklace, or a cuff, and my fingers *itch* to make it."

"After you have your baby," Bella pointed out, "you won't have much time for jewelry making."

"True. But I know I'll get back to it eventually. This may sound odd, but it keeps me sane."

"I can understand that."

"And, Bella"—Penny smiled smugly—"when I say I have a lot of it, I mean *a lot*."

"I want to sell your jewelry," Bella said decisively. "I've got an image in my mind of the way I'm changing the shop." Not until she spoke did she realize this was absolutely true. "I want to spotlight your jewelry. It's spectacular, and frankly, it should sell for a substantial price."

"It will all be one of a kind. That's valuable in itself. But, Bella, how will people know it's here? I mean, Barnaby's Barn looks so *sweet* from the outside, and my creations are far from sweet."

"I know. As I said, I'm making changes. I'm going to repaint the outside, get rid of the flower boxes. I'm going for a kind of Italianate look. I'm going to put topiary in huge pots outside the door, and lavender, and vines up the front of the building, and of course the inside will be completely redone."

"That will take you a long time, won't it?"

"No," Bella told her. "I can move fast when I need to."

11
.....

Yesterday at the cookout, Natalie had asked Louise if she could draw her.

Louise had laughed. "As long as you're not expecting me to pose nude."

Natalie tilted her head, squinting, imaging the setup. "No. You can keep your clothes on. I have to warn you, though, Louise, if this turns out like I think it will, I'll want to show it. Sell it."

"Sweetheart, you need a younger woman if you want to make money."

"I don't think so. This will be classic. I'll do an oil copy for your family," Natalie offered as an enticement.

"But aren't oils better than drawings?"

"Not necessarily. Charcoal drawings have depth, timelessness, resonance."

"What kind of pose did you have in mind?" Louise asked.

"I want you reading," Natalie told her. "I want to do *Woman, Reading*."

"I do plenty of that," Louise said. "Fine. When should we start?"

"Tomorrow morning."

At nine, Natalie showed up at the Barnabys' house with her easel, paper, and charcoal. Louise was in jeans and a tee shirt, barefoot, no makeup, no jewelry.

"Perfect," Natalie told her. "I want this to be contemporary, realistic, but also with a kind of mystery about it. I want you curled up in a chair. Do you have a book that will hold your interest?"

"Absolutely. A new Jonathan Kellerman mystery." Louise obediently arranged herself in an armchair.

Natalie said, "Get comfortable. I want to draw you looking down."

"Hmm." Louise adjusted herself. "Just don't make me look like a melted candle."

"Damn," Natalie joked. "That was my exact plan."

Her heart bubbled with hope, excitement, and a bit of apprehension as she set up her small movable easel and gathered her paper, charcoal, erasers.

"Okay," Natalie said. "Go ahead and read." Grabbing up her charcoal, she started sketching.

Time vanished as Natalie worked. She stepped back to eye her subject, stepped forward to draw a line.

"Natalie, I need to scratch my nose."

"Of course," Natalie said. "Sorry! Go ahead and stretch, too. I don't want you getting stiff."

Louise stood up, shook her shoulders out, then resumed her position.

"We can talk," Natalie told her. "But try not to move your head."

"Oh, good." Looking down at the book, Louise said, "You know, Natalie, I've spent some time over the years with your aunt Eleanor. She's quite a remarkable woman."

"She is," Natalie answered, her mind allotting about five percent to conversation.

"But I don't believe I've ever met your mother," Louise continued. "Your mother is Eleanor's sister, right?"

"Right."

"I know her name—it's Marlene, right?"

"Right."

"I know she used to drive you and Slade down here in the summers to drop you off for a vacation, but she never stayed." Louise looked at Natalie, a question in her eyes.

"Face the book," Natalie told her. Still drawing, she said, "Mom raises purebred bulldogs. That's how she makes her living. Dad left us when we were young."

"Oh dear, I'm sorry."

"It's okay. But that's why she couldn't ever stay. She had to get back to her bulldogs."

"She sounds very enterprising," Louise commented, eyes on her book.

Natalie was working with the eraser now. In charcoal drawings, erasing was as much a part of the art as the charcoal. "Mother is *insane* about bulldogs," she told Louise. "I don't think she was as enterprising as she was infatuated."

"Well, she was clever to make a living with what she loves," Louise remarked. "Isn't that what we all hope for?"

Natalie paused. She'd never thought of her mother as *clever*. Continuing to draw, she muttered, "My mother didn't plan to make her living that way. It just happened."

"That's the way it was for me," Louise said with a chuckle. "My plan when I was young was—no making fun of me, now!—to become an airline stewardess!" She lifted her head as if gazing right through the ceiling up to the sky.

"Eyes on the book," Natalie ordered gently.

Louise obeyed. "Back then it seemed the most glamorous occupation a girl could have! I would get to wear one of those darling chic uniforms, maybe with a scarf around my neck and a perky cap. I'd fly all over the world to exotic places. I'd meet fascinating pilots and marry one and all our life together we'd fly everywhere, until we'd seen every corner of the globe!".

Natalie grinned at the vision. "Why didn't you become a stewardess?"

Louise chuckled. "I met Dennis. I was a sophomore at U. Mass. He had just graduated. We fell in love, and the minute I saw him, I knew all of the world I ever wanted to see was right inside that man."

"Oh, that's so romantic."

"It was."

"Louise, I'm sorry, but could you stop smiling? I need you to look meditative."

"Meditative. Hmm. All right."

For a few minutes, Louise gazed at her book and Natalie worked. Natalie had to ask. "Did you ever regret it? Not becoming a stewardess?"

"Honestly? I had my days. When the babies kept me up all night crying and teething and we lived in a dreary little apartment, I allowed myself to remember my old daydream. But even then, regret my decision? No. My goodness, I'm so in love with Dennis. And my babies! My children! That's adventure enough for me. I'm extremely fortunate and I know it." Louise allowed some silence to pass, then remarked, "I believe most mothers wouldn't trade anything for their children. They might long for better *circumstances*, because it can be such hard work."

"I suppose," Natalie replied noncommittally.

"Tell me about your mother," Louise invited. "She must be a knockout if she looks anything like you and Slade."

"That's from Dad," Natalie said. "Mom's hair is just brown. She's pretty, I guess, but she doesn't keep herself up. She says the dogs don't notice."

Louise laughed. "I can understand that. Children can be so critical! Dogs never say you need to have your hair styled or to get out of those old jeans."

"Don't laugh." Natalie concentrated fiercely on her drawing. It had never occurred to her that she and Slade had been critical, but of course they had been—there was so much about their mother to criticize!

"I was lucky in my in-laws, too," Louise mused, looking down at the book. "Dennis's parents were reserved, their parents had come over from England. Dennis's father taught literature at Smith. They were stuffy, but basically kindhearted. They helped us out quite a bit financially. We couldn't have bought this house without their assistance. We didn't have to ask. They offered. Lorraine, Dennis's mother, helped with the children when they were small. They had only the one child, and she was especially enchanted by the little girls." Louise went quiet, remembering.

Good, Natalie thought. *Stay in your memories.* This was the expression she wanted.

Around noon, Natalie needed to shake her hand out. She could tell that Louise was fatigued from remaining in one pose. Probably she should stop for today, although she hated to. When Natalie got going on something she loved, she became a very still, utterly focused maniac.

Louise went to the kitchen to fix them iced tea when a knock came at the front door.

"I'll see who it is," Natalie offered.

Before she could get there, Morgan had opened the door and come in, with Petey in her arms. "Oh! Hi, Natalie. I didn't expect to see you here. I came to say hello to Louise."

"Hi, Morgan. Hey, Petey!" Natalie tickled the boy's tummy. He giggled and squirmed.

"Oh. My. God!" Morgan exclaimed. "Natalie! How stunning!"

Louise said, "I haven't seen it yet. Let me see."

Natalie protested, "It's far from finished! I've got another few days' work to go on it. . . ."

Morgan set Petey on the floor. He made a beeline for the toys.

"My goodness," Louise said. "Do I look like that?"

"I haven't finished," Natalie repeated.

"You don't look exactly like that," Morgan told Louise. "When we see you, you're always smiling, talking—"

"Eating," Louise joked.

"I've never seen you so . . . *still.* Thoughtful. Gosh, this is contemporary and somehow, what's the word I want—archetypal. Natalie, we've got to call Bella and make her come home right now."

"Why?" Natalie asked.

"Because Bella wants to make some changes in Barnaby's Barn." Her eyes whipped toward Louise. "You know that, right?"

Louise waved her hand as if brushing away a fly. "I know that, and Dennis knows it, and we're fine with it."

"When I was talking with her yesterday at your cookout, Natalie, Bella said she wants it to become more of an art gallery. She has a friend, Penny Aristides—"

"I know Penny," Louise chimed in.

"She makes fabulous jewelry," Morgan continued. "Bella is considering displaying that, and some antique furniture, and, Natalie, she should hang your work, both your abstracts and your charcoals. I mean, you did say you wanted to sell your charcoal of Petey. And this of Louise, too. My gosh, it looks like an old master!"

"An old *mater*, you mean," Louise joked.

"I'm calling Bella right now." Morgan took her cell out of her shorts pocket.

While they waited for Bella, they organized a platter of cold cuts, cheeses, red grapes, and crackers. They set it on the dining room table with a pitcher of iced tea just as Bella came in the door.

"Hi, Morgan; hi, Natalie— OH!" Bella slammed to a halt, hand on her heart, looking at Natalie's drawing. "Oh, wow."

"Thanks. It's not finished, though. I've got several more days of work to do on it. The shading is really important, the contrast between dark charcoal and light—" Spotting a section that irritated her, Natalie stepped to the canvas, picked up her charcoal, and lightly added a blurring of gray.

"So what I'm thinking," Morgan suggested enthusiastically, "is that you carry Natalie's charcoals and some of her abstracts. You've seen her charcoal of Petey, right?"

"I don't think I have," Bella admitted. "I've seen the oil of Petey. It's in your living room. Where's the Petey charcoal, Natalie?"

Now Natalie was working with the eraser, dabbing lightly. "In my studio."

From the corner, Louise spoke up. "Will you want to keep anything I've been selling? Just asking."

Bella answered, "Mom, of course I want to keep your Lake Worlds.

For the rest, I'm not so sure. I've been looking at the records. Not much has been selling. The Lucy Lattimer dolls have to go."

"Poor Lucy." After a moment Louise added, "But, you know, I haven't spoken with her for a while, and I'm not sure she's in good health. We'll just box them up and store them in the back."

They gathered around the table. Morgan held Petey on her lap and handed him a cracker to gnaw. "Did I tell you the Ruoffs were over about a week ago? They saw the abstract I bought from Natalie and went wild for it."

"What are the Ruoffs like?" Bella asked. "I've never met them."

Natalie listened to them with part of her mind while she continued drawing and erasing on Louise's portrait. She preferred working in relative privacy, and her stomach was growling, but she couldn't stop. This really was going to be an amazing piece. Perhaps her best.

"*Whoa.*"

The voice, low and masculine, hit Natalie like an electric shock, passing through her ears straight down her torso. She turned.

"I didn't know you could do *that*," Ben said. He wore khakis, a blue-and-white striped button-down shirt with the sleeves rolled up, and a dark blue tie.

Natalie was flooded with so many emotions she couldn't sort them out. Her eyes found delight in the sight of him, her senses yearned to be nearer to him, while at the same time fierce self-protection rose up in her. She didn't like people to see her work before it was finished, especially not people who *mattered*.

And it was the emotional news flash that Ben *mattered* that rocked her. Defensively, she asked, "What are *you* doing here?"

Ben was too entranced by her drawing to be surprised by her question. "I finished teaching. I have only morning classes in the summer. I want to go out on the lake." He was walking toward Natalie.

Actually, Natalie realized, as she forced herself to breathe, he was walking toward the portrait. She stepped back from the easel. "It's not finished," she protested. "I just started it today. I've got a lot of work to do on it."

"How do you do that?" Ben asked, like a child who's just seen a magic trick. "That's amazing. Can I watch you?"

Natalie felt a rush of blood warm her cheeks. Ben was looking right at her now, and standing close enough to reach out and touch her. It was embarrassing to be so attracted to this man while in the same room with his mother and sister! She struggled to be light-hearted. "Some of us can swim long distances, some of us can draw."

"That's more than drawing," Ben said. "That's really something, Natalie."

Her name in his mouth was like a caress. She smiled helplessly. "Thank you."

Morgan interrupted the moment of intimacy that so sweetly en-closed them. "Hungry, Ben? We've got tons of munchies here. And we've got the best idea about your sister's shop."

Ben tore his eyes away from Natalie's. "Food, yum. Hi, every-one." He sat down at the table.

"What did you teach today?" Morgan asked.

Ben piled cheese onto a cracker. "I had a lab. We worked with transmission electron microscopes."

"On your bio-oil catalyzing?" Morgan asked.

"Right."

Natalie touched her charcoal to the paper, but suddenly all in-spiration had vanished, replaced by an irritation that Morgan had stolen Ben's interest. Was Morgan *flirting* with Ben? Certainly she was fascinated by whatever it was he was talking about, leaning toward him, gesturing, nodding, totally *into* the conversation.

Natalie couldn't work now. Her interest was fogged. She dropped the charcoal onto the tray and stretched her arms. "Done for the day."

Ben didn't quite look at Natalie but angled his head toward her. "Want to go for a sail?"

Surprised, she didn't answer for a moment. "I'd love to."

Petey dropped his cracker, wriggled off his mother's lap, and toddled to Ben as fast as his fat legs could carry him. "Sail!"

Morgan reached for her son. "No, sweetie, not today."

Petey's lower lip trembled. "*Sail.*"

"Honey, Mommy can't sail our Sunfish with you unless Daddy is with us. It's just not safe."

Petey's sweet, innocent face crumpled with disappointment.

"I tell you what," Ben told the child. "Why don't I take you and your mommy for a sail first. Then I'll take Natalie out."

Natalie thought: *Hey!* At the same time, she mentally kicked herself for feeling usurped by a toddler.

Morgan lit up. "Oh, Ben, that would be so kind. Afterward, I can put Petey down for his nap. I just don't feel confident sailing alone with Petey, even when he's wearing his life jacket."

"You're right," Louise agreed. "Accidents can happen in an instant."

"And I'm not the best sailor in the world," Morgan confessed.

"I'll just get out of these clothes." Ben left the room for the downstairs bathroom, where a multitude of bathing suits hung.

"Louise?" Morgan asked. "Could you watch Petey while I run across and get our bathing suits and some children's sunblock?"

"Of course."

Morgan ran out the door.

Bella said, "Natalie, know what? I'd love to go over to your house now and look at your abstracts again. More carefully this time. I mean, I'd love to show some, but I want to think about space, and what else I'll put on the walls, if anything."

Natalie hesitated. The humming invisible bond that she had felt drawing her close to Ben was stretched to breaking now. Yet this could be a real start for Natalie as an artist in the area, having her work shown at Bella's shop. *If* Bella were really going to change the shop.

"All right," she told Bella. She grabbed some cheese and crackers. "Louise, I'd like to leave the easel here. Is there a place where I can put it that's out of the way?"

Louise pointed. "In the corner. It won't get knocked over there."

"So you're really changing the shop?" Natalie asked as they made their way across the lawns to Natalie's house.

"I really am," Bella stated defiantly, softening her words with a funny face. "I guess."

"What do your parents think?"

"They're delighted. I guess Mom's ready to let it go. It kept her buzzing along for years, but now she's at the point where she wants to slow down and enjoy life. Plus, the shop isn't doing well."

"How are you going to change it? What else are you going to carry?" Natalie opened the door and led Bella into the house and up the stairs.

"I don't have it all worked out yet. Slade's coming tomorrow, I think, to help me value some of the furniture in our storage locker. We have some pretty pricey antiques we never really knew about, and I have a friend who makes amazing jewelry. Sort of antique and modern at the same time."

"What about Aaron?" Natalie went around the room flicking on all the lights and raising the blinds on the north windows.

"Good question," Bella moaned. "We don't know exactly when he'll learn about the job in California." She waved her hand. "Let's not go there. Let me concentrate on your paintings."

Bella chose four of the abstracts and went into a fit of compliments over the charcoal of Petey, begging Natalie to let her hang it in the shop. They placed the pieces at one corner of the studio, then hurried downstairs again.

"I've got to get back to the shop. Even if we never have any customers, I hate to not be there when I'm supposed to be," Bella explained. "I mean, we do still have *some* customers. I'm glad Morgan called me, though, Natalie. I really want to hang the charcoals of Petey and Louise, and do you suppose you could do another one or two charcoals? I'll bet you could by the time I get the shop repainted and reorganized."

Natalie laughed at Bella's enthusiasm. Bella wasn't an art dealer, she didn't run an art gallery, she was only a friend with a half-baked idea for a shop, and yet her conviction that Natalie's work would sell and her eagerness to show it was manna to Natalie's soul. It was as if she were in a colorful hot-air balloon, shooting high into the wide blue sky, carried by Bella's bright spirits.

They stepped outside, and the balloon popped.

Ben was at the Barnabys' beach, lifting Petey out of the Sunfish. Morgan was stepping out on the other side, and Morgan was wearing a bikini. Not the modest, sporty Speedo she'd worn the day of Natalie and Slade's picnic, but a teeny bikini. *Red*. Her legs were longer than Kate Middleton's. Her stomach was flat; how could that be possible when she'd had a baby? She'd twisted her long brown hair up into a knot at the back of her head. Fetchingly, strands of it had come loose, curling around her face. She was a sexy woman, and Natalie's self-image shriveled.

Morgan bent over to pick up her son, presenting a flawless backside.

"Natalie!" Ben waved to her from the beach. "Ready for a sail?"

"Sure! Just give me a minute." She dashed into the house. She could wear her painting clothes, who cared if they got wet? But the afternoon had grown hot, relentless with sunshine, and besides, how pathetic was she? She might not be ten feet tall and sleek like Morgan, but her own body was not to be ignored. It never had been; she'd sat nude for several life painting sessions and seen the admiration in the other artists' eyes—and more than admiration in some. She knew as an artist that her body was shaped like an hourglass. Just because for some freakish, incomprehensible reason Ben Barnaby's opinion mattered to her did not make her some kind of abject coward.

She put on her black bikini. It emphasized her black hair and pale skin. She grabbed a tube of sunblock and whipped out the door before she could change her mind.

Morgan and Petey were gone by the time Natalie reached the beach. She waved to Ben. "Ready. Thanks for waiting."

"We've got a good wind today," Ben told her. He wore a funny floppy canvas hat to protect his face from the sun. "Want a life vest?"

Natalie cocked her hip and gave him a saucy look. "Nah. If I fall over, I'll tread water until you rescue me."

He laughed, and perhaps blushed—he moved too quickly for her to see. "Help me shove the boat out."

They pushed the boat off the sand into the water, then climbed aboard. The sail filled with wind, smoothly carrying them away from the shore and out into the lake. Froth flew up all around, cold and bright as snowflakes as they sped along. Ben handled the tiller with the earnest solemnity of someone racing for his life while Natalie perched on the side, creaming her skin with sunblock and then letting her head fall back, face raised to the sun, the wind ruffling her hair. The breeze sent them skipping along past docks, beaches, houses, and open fields scattered with daisies and wild berry bushes.

After her morning of work, the heat of the sun relaxed Natalie down to her bones, and her mind drifted away from its usual concerns. She felt sweat break out on her skin, until the breeze fluttered over her, cooling her in little shivers. They whipped along so far down the lake she couldn't see her own house, then Ben tacked and they headed back. She closed her eyes and soaked in the sun.

"Duck," Ben said.

She felt the boat turn and opened her eyes. Ben had lowered the sail and was slipping them beneath the trailing gray-green branches of a leaning willow tree reaching in an arch from one bank to another. They entered a small cove, all three sides a wilderness of evergreens, thickets, and innumerable grasses and wildflowers tangling together, falling down the bank into the water. The trees shadowed the area. The air was cooler here, the water still. It was intimate, its own sheltered world.

Ben let the boat gently bump alongside a bank.

"Gosh," Natalie said. "It's like a sanctuary."

"I know." Ben stretched, looking around with satisfaction. "We've got a lot of lakes in this area, but few of them have any uninhabited coves like this."

"Who owns the cove?"

Ben tied a line around a nearby tree trunk. "Some guy from New York who comes up here to play Boy Scout. I'm serious. He brings a tent, walks around his property, hikes the mountain, folds his tent, and goes home. Does it once a season."

"In a weird way, I can completely understand that," Natalie mused. She scooted to the edge of the deck, letting her feet dangle in the water.

Ben crossed the short space to sit next to her. "Me, too. When I was a boy, I thought of this place as my own. I don't think most people on the lake even know it exists because that willow tree was blown sideways by a storm, so it sort of blocks the entrance."

"Maybe it *is* your own," Natalie told him.

They sat for a while, listening to the birds sing and rustle in the trees. The water was flat calm, and in the shade it was more black than blue.

"When I was a girl, I had a special tree that I'd climb," Natalie reminisced in a quiet voice. "Whenever I needed privacy, I'd be up in it. It was an oak, very tall. I could sit at the top, hidden by branches, and survey my world. Of course, because it was in rural Maine, I mostly saw other treetops. But I felt protected. Completely on my own. Nobody's child, nobody's sister, nobody's student, just myself. I could stay up there for hours. Sometimes I wore my backpack and took up crackers and a thermos of juice."

"Me, too. I mean, I did the same thing." Ben grinned at the memory. "Well, not juice, Coke. Not crackers, cookies. But even without food, I could stay hidden away here for hours. Just thinking, or not even that. I liked lying here with my eyes closed, letting the sun play over my eyelids, my eyelashes—"

"Yes!" Natalie broke into a smile. "I know just what you mean. Sometimes I'd close my eyes and rub them and see circles and lines and dots that aren't really there, so it's as if you're seeing a different world."

"They're called phosphenes." Ben shook his head. "Sorry. Don't mean to get all analytical."

Natalie replied, "I think I can handle it. After all, David Bohm said, 'Physics is a form of insight and as such it's a form of art.' "

"That's stretching the point," Ben began, then stopped. "You know who David Bohm is?"

"If you study art, you study color, which means you study light, which means you learn about physics. Not to mention perspective, space, movement, time."

Ben stared at her. "You're really an interesting person."

His scrutiny unnerved her. She responded immediately, unthinking, with her usual protective irony: "I know. I'm not just the fluffy little sex object I seem."

Ben stared at her for a long, silent moment. "I wouldn't call you fluffy." He angled his body toward hers. "Could you take off your sunglasses?" he asked. "Because I'd like to kiss you."

Natalie took off her sunglasses and lifted her face toward Ben's. He kissed her, his lips warm and tasting slightly of sunblock. She scooted closer to him, her legs squeaking unromantically against the fiberglass hull. Ben put his hand on her face. The kiss deepened. Natalie wanted to press against him. She put her hand on his chest. His naked skin was hot. Beneath them, the boat rocked and tipped.

Ben pulled away. "Okay, now is the time when I need to jump in the lake."

She blinked, confused.

He grinned. "Like a cold shower?" He went into the lake, feetfirst.

Natalie didn't want to lose the sensation of the kiss. It had been like one of those expensive chocolates, delicious on the outside, hiding in its depths a hint of champagne or Grand Marnier. She wanted to keep kissing.

"Come in the water," Ben coaxed.

She squirmed. "There are green things in there."

"Weeds. They won't get you. They're just near the edge." Ben swam to the stern. "Jump over here."

She jumped, embarrassed by her awkward belly flop. The water was exquisitely cool after the heat of the sun.

"Aaah," she breathed. Having Ben near her filled her again with a playfulness, a childishness she had not experienced for a very long time. She dove under the surface with her eyes open. She saw weeds swaying near the bank and the tree trunk that seemed, beneath the water, to waver. Surfacing, she swam toward one of the willow branches, reached up with both hands and grabbed it, hanging from it slightly, water dripping off her.

Ben swam toward her, faced her, put his hands on the branch on either side of hers, and let his body lightly touch hers all up and down. Their legs touched and twined beneath the water, but he held his chest and head back, looking at her, watching the effect his touch was having. She could feel his erection through their bathing suits.

"Ben," she whispered.

He kissed her again.

This time the kiss lasted so long Natalie's arms dropped of their own accord to wrap around Ben. She ran her hands over the long muscles of his back, through his wet hair, over his jawline. Ben let go of the tree branch and clasped her against him. They both sank under the water, still kissing. Ben kicked his legs. One of them was between Natalie's legs. She thought she was going to faint from desire. Their heads broke the surface of the water, and they both gasped for air and, of necessity, let go of each other to tread water with their arms.

"I think I'd better go for a swim," Ben said, and struck out, away from Natalie. He dove beneath the willow branch and disappeared out into the wide lake.

Natalie grabbed the branch again and hung there, eyes closed, dazzled.

After a while, Ben reappeared. "It's getting late. We'd better go back."

"I have no idea what time it is," she confessed with a smile.

"Well, physics girl, if you look at the way the sun has moved, and notice how the shadows have changed . . ." Seeing her face, he laughed and held one arm up, displaying his waterproof stainless steel Seiko. "A watch is good, too."

She kicked out, splashing his face. He caught her ankle and yanked her away from the branch and next to him. They both sank. Natalie got a nose full of water and started coughing. Immediately, Ben had her by the waist, lifting her above the surface. He swam her to the boat and helped her get aboard, then pulled himself up.

She sat on the hull, gasping.

"You okay?"

"I'm fine."

"Yes," Ben said. "You are fine."

He undid the line, shoved the boat hard away from the bank. They both ducked as he steered them through the narrow opening between the willow branches and the bank. He raised the sail and headed toward the end of the lake where their houses were. Natalie put on her sunglasses and lounged in the boat, feeling just like Cleopatra triumphantly returning home on her barge.

12

.....

Bad Bella.

She'd been emailing Slade. About Penny's ornate jewelry. About her ideas for redecorating the shop. About furniture.

Slade emailed her back, mostly links to websites of fabulous shops, homes, churches, restaurants, all over the country, all over the world. Her mind swarmed with ideas.

You need to change the name of the shop, Slade emailed her. *"Barnaby's Barn" is not right.*

I agree, she emailed back. *Ideas?*

Something short. Maybe just one word.

"Barnaby's?"

No. Something too Mother Goose about that.

Oh, thanks so much.

Also, it's got the word "barn" in it. How about "Bella's"?

Bella sat staring at his last email with her heart thumping away like a brass band. *Bella's!* She didn't know how to respond.

Slade sent another email: *Bella's: Art, Antiques, Jewelry.*

After a moment, Bella got her breath back and emailed Slade. *Yes. I like that.*

Another email:

I have to go to the Berkshires and southern Vermont to check out some antiques for our store. I think you should come, too. I've thought about it, and you can't keep a shop running on the stuff your parents have in their storage unit. You'll need to be able to find other pieces. I'll show you how it's done. I'll pick you up early Thursday morning, have you back Thursday night.

Bella hesitated. This wasn't a *date*. It shouldn't make Aaron jealous. She remembered with guilty relief that Aaron was driving down to the Cape on Thursday to see his family for a long weekend. He wanted Bella to come with him, but she'd declined, claiming she needed to stay in the shop. And while this wouldn't be staying in the shop, it would be *work*.

I'll be ready, she emailed Slade.

Thursday morning, in the privacy of her bedroom, Bella tried on just about everything she owned to find the right outfit for the antiques jaunt with Slade. Should she try to look impoverished so the owners would take pity on her and she could get the bid down on a piece of furniture? But she wanted, as much as she refused to let herself dwell on it, to look really good in front of Slade. Also, to look professional. Also, to look sexy. Stop. How did *that* thought get in there? She didn't want to look trashy, or easy, and she had to remember this was work, so she *shouldn't* look sexy. She needed to look casually intelligent. In a summery way.

She wore a severely cut, sleeveless brown linen sheath and high brown heels that made her look taller, therefore more grown-up, and also, just as a side effect, sexier. She told her parents what she was doing and that she'd be back late. She wasn't keeping this a secret from Aaron—she'd tell him about it tonight, when he called from the Cape. He was driving there now.

Slade arrived in a big white Chevy Suburban that said "David Ralston Antiques" in gold print on the side. Bella waved at her mother, grabbed her enormous purse, and clicked down the steps to the driveway. Slade hadn't gotten out to knock on the door; he'd only tapped the horn. Businesslike.

"How many cars do you own?" Bella asked as she climbed with as much grace as possible into the passenger seat.

"This van belongs to my boss," Slade explained. He wore a white

button-down cotton shirt, khakis, and loafers without socks. Aware
of her curiosity, he said, "Work clothes. Disguise."

"So the real Slade Reynolds wears all black?" Bella inquired.

"Maybe. Maybe I'm a man of many façades."

"But are you *all* façade?" she asked flippantly. Her hand flew to
her mouth. Slade's presence made her act so strange! She hoped she
hadn't insulted him.

Slade threw back his head and laughed. "Stick around and find
out." He put the key in the ignition and started the massive engine.
Off they went.

She'd been nervous about being alone in the car with this man
for the roughly two hours it would take to drive through the moun-
tainous countryside. Of course they could discuss antiques. She'd
been researching them online while she sat undisturbed by customers in Barnaby's Barn.

Slade hit the button on the CD player. "Radiohead?"

"Love them," she answered, relieved when the music filled the
air.

Slade drove north from Northampton, zooming up I-91, taking
an exit to a smaller road, turning off that to an even narrower road
winding through farmland. Trees flickered past; green leaves fluttered and parted to expose a stream flashing with water racing over
rocks. Hills rose and fell as they sped by rocks embossed with moss,
ivy, and wildflowers like badges in a garden show.

After almost an hour, Slade turned down a dirt lane fenced in
wire. He stopped in front of an old house smaller and less freshly
painted than the barn next to it.

Slade slipped out of the driver's seat, stretched, tucked his shirt
in. Bella stepped out, too, glad to move. She followed him up to the
front door, which was open. An old dog hurried to the screen door,
barking and wagging his tail.

"Spot, old fella, how are you?" Slade asked.

The dog wiggled all over at the sound of Slade's voice.

"Is that who I think it is?" An old man appeared in the gloom of
the hall. "Slade, as I live and breathe. You son of a gun, where have

you been?" Dressed in overalls and a torn light flannel shirt, the old man was bald, wrinkled, and stooped, but his brown eyes were bright. "And who is this you've got with you, you lucky guy?"

"Mr. Wheeler, this is Bella Barnaby. She's learning the antiques business."

"She is, is she? Well, she's got a good teacher. Come in, come in." With a liver-spotted, veined old hand, Mr. Wheeler reached up to unlatch the screen door.

Bella followed Slade into the dusty hallway.

"Business first, then cider?" Mr. Wheeler asked.

"If you don't mind. You know I hate being kept in suspense."

Mr. Wheeler opened a door to the front room. He went in. Slade went in. Bella froze in the doorway, stunned.

The room was chockablock with furniture in no particular order. Desks, armoires, chaises, headboards, chairs, tables, secretaries, in all styles and woods. In some cases, towels were laid over tables or chest tops so that smaller pieces, trunks, and benches, and cabinets, could be stacked on top.

"Mr. Wheeler is not a dealer," Slade told Bella.

The old man laughed, "Hee-hee-hee. That rhymes. Plus, it's not the God's pure and honest truth. I can deal all right when I want to."

"I mean he doesn't own an antiques shop," Slade continued.

"Couldn't if I wanted to! I'm still running the farm my parents and my grandparents ran before me." The old man waved at Bella. "Come on in, darlin'. Look around."

Bella stepped inside. She squeezed herself down a crooked aisle between a dry sink and a glass-front bookcase.

"Mr. Wheeler is my unofficial assistant." Slade's voice came from the other side of the room. "He knows everyone in the area. If someone moves out—"

"He means if someone kicks the bucket," Mr. Wheeler corrected, and did his wheezing "hee-hee-hee" laugh again.

"—Mr. Wheeler knows what kind of furniture they have, who the relatives are, and drops by to offer a fair price to help clean out the house."

"These young people, you know," Mr. Wheeler said, shaking his head. "They move clear across the country. Seattle. Phoenix, for Christ's sake. No interest in their own home, in the farm, in the furniture. Just want the money."

"I come out about four times a year to check on Mr. Wheeler's discoveries," Slade said. "I pay him what he's paid the original owner, plus a finder's fee."

"Adds to my Social Security. The farm don't make a dime. I need the money; plus, I will admit I *am* a nosy old bugger."

"I like this." Bella paused in front of a slant-top mahogany desk. "I really like this." She ran her hand over the wood. *Silk.*

Slade slid sideways down the narrow aisle. Standing next to Bella, he surveyed the desk, his arm brushing hers as he bent. "Yeah. That's nice."

"Slade," Bella whispered, fighting to keep her voice steady, "I've been doing some research. I'm sure this piece is English. Georgian, I'd say."

Slade squatted down, pulled out a drawer, looked at the pulls. "You *have* done your homework. Mr. Wheeler, how much for this desk over here?"

Another "Hee-hee-hee" came from across the room, behind rows of furniture. Then, "Five hundred."

Slade snorted. "You *are* a wheeler-dealer."

"I ain't worked with you for three years without learning something."

"I'll take it," Bella called.

Slade gazed at Bella with a light of admiration dawning in his eyes.

"And what about you?" the old man yelled from the other side of the room. "You find anything you like?"

Slade was pressed almost against her. "Yes. I have."

Bella wanted to kiss Slade. She wanted to lick his neck. Among all this antique furniture, she felt caught in a dream: She was the maid, he was the master; she was the peasant selling flowers, he was the soldier. He was the pirate. She was his plunder.

But, Bella thought triumphantly, her hand on the desk, she was the one who had found the treasure.

She pulled away. Her heart was beating so fast she was afraid it showed beneath the light linen of her dress. She stepped away from Slade, squeezing between an Early American pie cupboard and a high-backed bench, aware of Slade's eyes on her body as she twisted and slid. Her skin felt so hot she was surprised she didn't ignite the furniture. Her senses screamed at her to go back to Slade, but Natalie had told her that Slade was a flirt, a scoundrel, a user, a hound dog. Bella needed to wear Natalie's warning words like a shield of armor.

The rest of their time in Mr. Wheeler's amazing room, Bella spent in rows as far away from Slade as she could get. When she'd chosen three pieces, and Slade had chosen four, they were invited back to Mr. Wheeler's kitchen for cider and cookies while they concluded their business.

Mr. Wheeler's kitchen was tidy and immaculate. His cider was homemade and sweet, taken from the freezer that morning in honor of Slade's arrival. They sat at the table—a scarred but steady walnut drop-leaf—and talked. Slade opened his briefcase. He lifted out a pastry box of fresh cookies, sweet rolls, and doughnuts from Boston.

"You are a fine fellow." Mr. Wheeler laughed, clapping Slade on the shoulder. He explained to Bella, "My wife died two years ago. I can't bake and I can't tolerate the sight of the poor old widows who used to drive all this way to bring me a casserole or cake, so I wasn't as appreciative as I should have been. But this guy knows what I like, and he doesn't want to marry me and iron my tea towels. Hee-hee-hee."

"Do you have other dealers who come to check out your finds?" Bella asked.

"I do. A few. No one as nice as Slade. Usually in the autumn, when they can combine it with some leaf peeping. Mostly people who want antiques don't want to spend so much time driving this far out into the boondocks. If it ain't down in Sheffield, they can't be bothered."

After they enjoyed some pastries, they wrote out checks and proof of ownership documents, and then Slade and Mr. Wheeler carried the furniture out to the van. At first Bella worried that the furniture was too heavy for such an old man to be lifting, but Slade shot her a glance when she started to object, and as she watched, she understood that Mr. Wheeler might be old, but he was wiry and plenty strong.

When they said good-bye, Mr. Wheeler shook Slade's hand and patted his shoulder with real affection. To Bella he said, "Now you treat this young man right."

Her jaw dropped. Are you *nuts?* she almost cried. Aware of Slade's mocking grin, she replied sweetly, "It was a real pleasure meeting you, Mr. Wheeler. I hope I see you again."

Driving away, Slade said, "I should have told you about him. He is one foxy old devil. For one thing, he's not as old as he looks. I phoned to tell him we were coming, so he went into his local-yokel act. He's not stupid. He *is* lonely. And sometimes the furniture he finds is amazing. He's got a real eye, and the farmers for miles around welcome him into their homes when they wouldn't let us in."

"I can't believe what we got," Bella said. The furniture was wrapped in quilted pads and secured by bungee cords in the back of the van. She wanted to crawl back, peel off a quilt, and gaze at her purchases.

"You did well, Bella. You found some prizes. This was probably the best part of the day. Mr. Wheeler is one of a kind, I'm afraid. This is prime antiquing country. Sheffield, down in Massachusetts, is basically an antiques town. First-rate stuff in pricey shops. Near Williamstown, Bennington, both college towns, you've got some great shops, too. Between here and Albany, you've got, basically, mountains. Snow in the winter, mud in the spring. Still, most old farmhouses like Mr. Wheeler's have been tapped. Antiques dealers have checked out attics and barns. Or they attend auctions."

"How do you find something for your shop, then?" Bella asked.

"Just this way. Searching. Driving far out on no-name roads. Buying, like we're going to buy from a few dealers. We won't make as much profit as we will from Mr. Wheeler's pieces. But still. The thing is, Bella, lots of people want what they want *now*. They don't want to drive all the way from Boston or New York or the Vineyard to find their Chippendale side table. Basically, they'll pay a whole lot more for something if they can just walk into our store in Boston and point."

"What about my store?" Bella bit her lip, thinking. "You've got a much bigger population in Boston than we do out in the middle of the state."

"True. Also, more of your population is earthy-crunchy, hippy-dippy, less-is-more, and mobile. Students won't buy. Lots of professors won't buy, because they aren't making any money and they're planning to move to another college sooner or later. But you've got some established, distinguished scholars with historic homes and lots of rich parents coming up from Connecticut to visit their brilliant offspring. You're close enough to New York and Boston that you'll get some of that traffic."

"Gosh," Bella said. "You really do know a lot."

Slade smiled. "You'd be surprised."

Bella dropped her eyes.

Near Troy, New York, they stopped in a shop carved out of a garage attached to a white colonial house. The owner was an elegant woman with a snooty nose, savvy eyes, and a piercing voice. Bella saw at once that Slade's charm bounced off Mrs. Eachern like bullets from Wonder Woman's bracelets. Still, Bella found a table on which Slade promised her she could double her price, and Slade bought a cabinet. They drove west, stopping twice on different roads with the word *Hollow* in the name. At one shop, set up in the front rooms of a Victorian farmhouse, they found nothing, but at the other, located in a barn, they each made a purchase. They grabbed a late lunch to go from a drive-through fast-food place and headed on Route 2 back over the mountain into Massachusetts.

Near Williamstown, they stopped at a shop straight out of Marie Antoinette, or some ancient French monarch with a taste for chandeliers and nude marble statuary. At first Bella thought the owner, clad in a dapper white summer suit, was Rob Lowe. *Couldn't be*, she told herself, and as he came closer, she saw that of course it wasn't.

Gary Errick's eyebrows arched with delight when he saw Slade.

They fell when Slade introduced Bella. Slade talked with Gary about business while Bella strolled around the shop, nearly tripping on antique Far Eastern carpets piled on top of one another. She picked up a marble statue of some old Greek god overwhelming some poor female, saw the price tag, and set it back down with extreme caution. Nothing here was anywhere near her price range, and she was glad when Slade said they had to leave.

She thought he'd put on music again for the hour they had left to drive back to Dragonfly Lake. Instead, Slade was in an expansive mood.

"So you've seen a variety of antiques shops. What do you think?" he asked.

She took a moment to deliberate on his question. "Each shop is unique," she decided. "What is your shop like, Slade?"

"I suppose Ralston's is most like Errick's. Very posh. Quite pricey. But excellent value, never any doubt about provenance or authenticity. We know our clients and what they're looking for, so they don't have to search far for what they want."

"I can't do that," Bella mused. "I don't want to do that. I want a range of prices, and lots of different people coming in. I want a young couple to fall in love with one of Natalie's abstracts and be able to afford it. But I want to price her charcoals high. They look like museum pieces. I don't want Early American furniture. Half the shops in New England carry Early American. I love the more ornate, but I want the shop to have an airy feeling, so people can walk around and not be afraid they'll knock something off a pedestal like at Errick's."

Slade laughed. "He does crowd pieces in." He glanced over at Bella. "You've done a lot of thinking."

"I guess I have. This trip has been enormously helpful, Slade. I can't thank you enough."

"What's your next step?"

She counted off on her fingers. "I've got to close Barnaby's Barn. Which means advertising a huge sale, so I can get rid of as much as possible. I've got to completely redo the look of the place, inside and out. I can envision the exterior. . . . I want to paint it sort of umber, instead of white, with huge topiary plants on either side of the door."

"You need to replace the door."

"You think? Aren't Dutch doors kind of . . . European?"

"What about hanging big wooden shutters on each side of the door, and leaving the door open? You could have a glass inner door for cold or hot weather, but an open door is inviting."

"Oh, what a good idea!" They were on a small, curvy road now, winding through forests, but Bella saw the shop, not the trees. "What color do you think I should paint the interior?"

"What color do *you* think you should paint the interior?"

"The floors are dark-stained pine. They've been polyurethaned against use and they've held up pretty well. I'm thinking something between beige and pale coral. *Not* pink. But pale brown with a touch of pink. Do I mean a pale umber? I need to look at paint chips."

"We can have a painting party," Slade suggested.

Bella cocked her head. "A what?"

"Some weekend, after you've had your sale and are ready to redo the place, we can all get together and paint the interior and exterior. Natalie and I, you and Ben, Morgan and Josh. Maybe your parents. Maybe Brady."

"What a good idea. That sounds like fun. Although I'm not sure Brady will want to help."

"Pay him. I'll bet he'll be useful to you as time goes by. He's a big kid; he can help move furniture around and hang pictures. You're going to need a strong man around to help you, you know."

"Aaron." Bella suddenly and guilty remembered. "He'll help paint. Help move furniture."

"Will he?" Slade's voice was dismissive as he turned onto the narrow lane around Dragonfly Lake.

"Of course!" How insulting Slade was, implying that Aaron wouldn't help her!

Slade turned the van into the Barnabys' driveway. "It's late. We've had a long day. I'm going to spend the night with Nat. Maybe tomorrow you can round up another male to help me unload your furniture."

"This is going so fast!" Bella panicked. "I don't know where to put the furniture. I mean, I'll have to move some of Mom's displays to make room."

"You've spent some money buying these antiques, Bella." Slade clicked off the engine and turned to look at her. "You know the saying 'Put your money where your mouth is'? You've done that. Now you need to put your body where your heart is."

She frowned, working to untangle his meaning.

Slade undid his seat belt. Without warning, he leaned over and kissed Bella on her mouth. His lips pressed gently, teasingly. Just when she thought he'd draw away, he put his hands on her shoulders and pulled her to him so that her head fell back and her lips parted. Their breath mingled.

Then he drew away. Her heart raced. She wanted more. She stared at his wonderfully bewitching pirate's face, such black hair, his eyes so dark blue they were almost ebony, and the look in those eyes so compelling, full of desire. Full of lust.

She didn't want to sit there like a deer frozen by the presence of a panther. Natalie's warning rang in her mind: *Slade's a rogue, a playboy, not to be trusted.*

She said weakly, "I have to go in."

"Do you?" He kept his gaze fixed on her.

She was not clueless. She certainly wasn't *easy*. She didn't want him to know how much he had aroused her, not when she was fully aware that for him she was only a plaything. He probably kissed every woman he could. He probably bedded every woman he could, and a man who looked like Slade could bed lots of women. She wanted to keep her dignity.

"Slade, you bad boy," she teased. She undid her seat belt and pretended to be insouciant. "Thank you for helping me. This has been an amazing day. Can I phone you tomorrow morning? Maybe take you out for a big breakfast to thank you for today?" She was proud of herself; she sounded so sophisticated!

His eyes grew even darker. In the irises gleamed a momentary light that reminded Bella, suddenly, of the tough boys she'd taught in third grade, the boys too proud to show hurt. But, of course, Bella had no power to hurt Slade!

Embarrassed by her thoughts, overwhelmed by her emotions, she slid out of the van onto her unstable high heels. "Thanks so much, Slade. *Really.*" She hurried toward the safety of her house.

13
.....

Now at the beginning of July, the foliage around Dragonfly Lake was so green it almost hummed. The temperature in the Amherst area would reach into the nineties today, and so would the humidity, but near the lake it seemed cooler, especially when a light breeze rippled the water. It was a weekday, so most lakeside residents were at work, but here and there teenagers free from the confines of school raced down the dock, whooping as they jumped into the water or paddled around in inner tubes or on rubber rafts.

Morgan sat in the grass, still damp with morning dew, near their small private beach, watching Petey fill a bucket of water and carry it up to fill the hole he'd dug in the sand. She had one eye on her son and one on her laptop. She'd just gotten an email from Slade.

Hey, Morgan, here's a photo of that Victorian settee I mentioned. It's only a thousand dollars. A deal, I promise. Plus, what do you think about this big chunk of marble? The veins make it look like a piece of modern art. Petey could climb on it, but it's not so high he'd get hurt if he fell, and there are no sharp edges. It would "make a statement," don't you think?

Keep cool,

Slade

She clicked on the link to the photo of the settee. She could see what Slade meant. It would work well in their living room in that

holstery was cream with cream embroidery.
photo of the rock. It was amusing to imagine
of rock in the living room—clever of Slade
him lots of points for considering Petey's
was still toddling, not that steady on his
n the rock, though, he could sustain some
e, that was true of many places in the house.
She had taped cushioning Bubble Wrap around their coffee table
and the edges of the hearth. She'd put safety latches on all the
kitchen and bathroom cupboards and stacked any cleaning materials up high above the sinks, out of reach. Safety gates barricaded the
top and bottom of the stairs to the second floor and the stairs to the
lawn from the back deck. Josh had gone over their yard with a
fine-tooth comb, checking for sharp rocks protruding from the
ground.

You could drive yourself mad protecting your child, Morgan
thought. How did people manage not to melt down? How did they
allow their precious children to toddle off into the world, knowing
they might stub their toes and fall?

Slade, we'll take the settee. Let me think about the rock. Morgan

I'll bring it out next weekend when I come.

Great.

Slade spent more time helping her with the house than Josh did,
Morgan mused. But, of course, Josh was working hard to pay for all
this stuff. Slade was making money from selling it. She had to remember that. Still . . .

She was losing her mind. She was sitting on the shore of an idyllic lake and quietly going nuts.

"Okay, sweet Pete!" Morgan slammed her laptop shut, grabbed
it up with one hand, and grabbed her sandy boy with the other.
"We're going to the playroom!"

One of the great qualities about kids was that they usually accepted sharp swerves in the activities of the day—because, really, what choice did they have? She stood him on the deck and brushed his clothes free of sand. She carried him and her laptop into the house and shut and locked the sliding door. She dropped her laptop on the kitchen table, rinsed her hands and Petey's hands, and slid his sandals over his chubby feet. She grabbed her bag, his diaper bag, the car keys, and strode out the front door as if on a mission.

Well, she *was* on a mission. She was going to help her husband. She was not going to sit in the sand daydreaming about Slade while Josh was working so hard to give them this perfect life. She buckled Petey into his car seat—he arched and wailed, as always—handed him some rubber toys, jumped into her own seat, keyed the sliding doors closed, and drove away from the house toward the gym.

"We're going to Judy's Gym!" she reminded her son encouragingly. "Petey *loves* the playroom. It's got so many toys, and lots of kids will be there, maybe Luke or Camden. Miss Amber will be there or Miss Caroline. You love Miss Caroline."

It took forty-five minutes to get to the gym, which was in a rural setting on the other side of Amherst, but once Petey heard Miss Caroline's name, he stopped gibbering and settled down. To his great delight, and Morgan's, it was Miss Caroline who watched over the playroom today. Short, round, and rather trollish, Miss Caroline greeted Petey with genuine pleasure, hugging him and carrying him off to show him the new backhoe they'd just gotten.

Morgan gave herself a moment to enjoy the sight of her son bravely toddling around this place without his father or mother. Then she raced for the locker room. She shed her summer clothes and tugged on her exercise gear. She yanked her hair back in a high ponytail. She headed out to the equipment room, found a treadmill, jumped on, and began to walk.

She'd forgotten to bring her iPod, but that was all right. Wide-screen TVs hung high on the walls of the gym. She focused on the news channel, but while it occupied her eyes, it was her own thoughts raging through her mind that accompanied her as she worked out.

What was *wrong* with her?

She *knew* what was wrong with her!

She was not a natural mother. She adored her child, she even could foresee the day when she'd want to give him a brother or sister, but right now, day after day after day after day, with the conversation of a thirteen-month-old as her only society, she was going mad. Of course, she saw Bella as often as possible, but Bella worked at the shop six days a week, and spent most of her evenings with Aaron. She saw Natalie only when Natalie was through painting or drawing for the day and collapsed, happily exhausted, on her deck for a drink.

She saw Josh, of course. He was her husband. Her companion. Her lover.

Just not recently. Recently, he was all about his work. He left early for Bio-Green, came home too late for dinner, took a moment to peek in at his sleeping son, changed out of his suit into shorts and a tee, and disappeared into his study, tapping away on his computer. If Morgan happened to wander in, she saw how he closed whatever screen he was on in a flash, and he always looked perturbed by her presence. Some companion. Some lover.

Still, she refrained from showing her disappointment. She knew he was pressured, anxious about his job and his ability to do it. She didn't doubt that he loved her . . . *most of the time*. Sometimes when she called his office at BGI, and loquacious Imogene answered the phone only to chirp that Josh wasn't there at the moment, a chill of dread snaked down Morgan's spine. He was a desirable man, used to lots of adulation from high school and college athletics. Married life was not a daily challenge ending with victory, cheers, and praise. Was Josh looking somewhere else for the stroking he believed he deserved? Certainly he wouldn't be the first man to do so.

Dripping with sweat, huffing and puffing, Morgan clicked off the treadmill, stepped down on wobbly legs, and staggered over to the weight bench. This took more concentration, for which she was grateful; it made it impossible for her mind to continue on its own hamster-cage treadmill. She was strong and in good shape. She always had been. She'd enjoyed working out even before she'd been married to a workaholic. She used the rowing machine and the re-cumbent exercise bike until she was almost shaking with exhaustion. The gym had a gorgeous locker room with excellent showers and all the hot water you could ever need. When she came out of the gym with Petey in her arms, she was glowing with health and clean hair and skin. And she was starving.

In the parking lot, next to her SUV, an old lady stood by the open door of her ancient Toyota. She wore a track suit, sneakers, and an expression of despairing confusion.

It was the woman who had almost passed out on the treadmill in the gym. "Mrs. Smith?" Morgan approached her. "Are you okay? Can I help you?"

The woman sagged with relief and took a few steps toward Morgan. "It's my car. I'm afraid it's broken."

"Oh." Morgan keyed open her own vehicle, dumped her purse and Petey's bag inside, shifted Petey to her left hip, and walked around to stand next to the woman, peering into the car. "What's the problem?"

"It started, but then it just . . . stopped."

"You're Mrs. Smith, aren't you?" Morgan asked. "I'm Morgan O'Keefe. I met you a few days ago in the gym."

"Oh yes. Of course." Mrs. Smith shrank into herself a bit. "You must think I'm a walking disaster."

"Not at all. Look, I know something about cars. Would you mind if I tried starting your car?"

"Please."

Morgan bent down to slide Petey into the passenger seat, then settled in the driver's seat. She shut the door. The car was immaculate inside and smelled like peppermints. The key was in the ignition. She turned it and scanned the dashboard.

"Mrs. Smith, the problem seems to be that you're out of gas."

"Really?" The older woman's eyes widened, as if Morgan had imparted news of earth-shattering importance. "Oh dear." She scanned the area, as if expecting a gas pump to rise up out of the ground. "Perhaps you could drive me to a service station?"

Morgan smiled. In the back of her SUV, beneath the carpeted

floor, was her automotive safety kit, complete with jack and lug wrench, spare fuses, tire sealant for minor punctures, jumper cables, kitty litter for ice, flashlight, first-aid kit, and a six-foot length of clear plastic tubing.

"I can do better than that," Morgan assured Mrs. Smith. "I'll siphon some gas from my tank into yours. Enough so that you can drive to a gas station."

Mrs. Smith gawked, speechless.

Morgan keyed open the back of her SUV. "If you'll just sit in your car with Petey, I'll have this done in a matter of minutes."

She could see Petey in Mrs. Smith's passenger seat, holding on to the door, bouncing up and down, exploring the unfamiliar door handles and buttons. The older woman settled in the driver's seat and showed Petey how to lift the console lid in the middle.

"Petey." Morgan knelt to face her child. "Mama's going to move the car closer to Mrs. Smith's."

But Petey wasn't concerned. Mrs. Smith had handed him her keys.

Morgan started up her SUV, and with the warning signal beeping because she hadn't fastened her seat belt, she maneuvered her car so that its gas tank was just about two feet from the old Toyota's. Her SUV was a good foot higher than the Toyota; this would work. She got out, opened the Toyota's gas tank door, opened her own gas tank door, and threaded in one end of the clear hose. She held the other end in her hand and began to suck. The gas quickly rose. The second she saw it, she stuck her end in the Toyota's gas tank. She watched the dark liquid flow downward. It didn't take long. It didn't have to. Mrs. Smith didn't even need a gallon of gas to get to a station. After a minute or so, Morgan pinched the hose tight, yanked it from her car, and held it high, letting the excess flow down into Mrs. Smith's tank. Then she pulled the empty hose from the tank, wiped it down with paper towels she carried in the car, and coiled it. She screwed on the gas caps and shut the doors. She cleaned her hands with antiseptic baby wipes.

"Now," she called to Mrs. Smith, "try starting the engine."

Mrs. Smith turned the key. The engine rumbled to life. Quickly she turned it off and scrambled out of the car. "You are a genius!"

"I have my moments." Morgan opened the passenger door and lifted out Petey. "You'll have enough gas to take you to a station now."

"How can I ever thank you?" Mrs. Smith held out her hands helplessly. "If you hadn't come along, I'd be out here broiling in the sun!"

Actually, Morgan thought, Mrs. Smith would have been in the air-conditioned gym office, waiting while someone arrived from a garage with a five-gallon container of gas. "It was nothing," she assured Mrs. Smith. "I'm glad to help."

"You know," Mrs. Smith said, "you are."

Morgan blinked.

"I am what?"

"You *are* glad to help. Just like the other day in the gym when I was having trouble on the treadmill. You are a person who likes to help other people. A very admirable quality. I am most impressed."

Morgan flushed, surprised and shy at this sudden estimation of her qualities. "Well, thank you. I'm glad—" She stopped herself. Mrs. Smith's words had touched something sensitive, tender, and yearning deep inside Morgan's soul. For a moment Morgan was afraid she was going to burst into tears. "Okay, then, we've got to get along. I'll see you again here at the gym." She lifted Petey's arm. "Say bye-bye, Petey!" That was another thing babies were good for, providing distractions from conversation.

"Bye-bye." Petey flapped his arm in a wave.

"Oh, but I feel so grateful," Mrs. Smith called. "I'd love to repay you somehow for your kindness."

"Don't give it a second thought," Morgan told her. "It was fun."

The truth was, it *was* fun, Morgan thought. Was that pitiful? That she got a kick out of doing what she'd learned to do as a teenager when she crawled out her window one night to go joyriding with friends? Even now she could remember how thrilled she was that dark night, to learn how to siphon gas.

It was after noon, and she was starving, and Petey was crabbing away in his car seat. She drove into the center of Amherst, stopped near the Black Cow, hefted her son onto her hip, and ordered sandwiches and an iced latte to go. She handed Petey an oatmeal cookie to gnaw on while she drove through the labyrinth of roads into the heart of the U. Mass.–Amherst campus until she found a parking spot near the pond. Once more she unstrapped her big boy, clasped him on her hip, grabbed the paper bag of lunch goodies and the picnic blanket she carried stuffed under the seat. She locked the car and headed for a long strip of shade underneath the trees overlooking the pond.

Petey loved to eat. Once they got settled, he focused intensely on his peanut butter and jelly sandwich, which he took apart and licked, allowing Morgan to take a deep breath, sip her latte, enjoy her own sandwich, and gaze around at the college campus. It was like a city. A world. She had loved every campus she'd set foot on. The professors, the students, the residences, the ivy-covered towers of classrooms, the libraries, the labs, and especially the maintenance buildings that kept this world running. Funny thing about maintenance: It was essential, yet no one paid any attention to it; no one praised it, yet the most brilliant scholar couldn't function without it. It was like motherhood, Morgan thought, grinning to herself.

After lunch, she held Petey's hand and they slowly ambled down to gaze into the pond, but Petey was tired and ready for his afternoon nap, so they turned around and toddled back up toward the sidewalk. He clamored for Morgan to carry him; she wanted him to walk as much as he could, and this particular debate took all her attention as they made their way toward North Pleasant Street, where she'd parked her car.

"Cawwy!" Petey lifted his arms pathetically.

"You're a big, strong boy. You're full of jelly sugar," Morgan reminded him. She needed him to use up all his energy so he'd have a good, long nap.

"Cawwy, Mommy, pwease." In his blue shorts, white shirt, and sneakers, he resembled a tiny track star who could go no farther. Petey knew how to push her buttons, knew how to make his voice full of pathos.

She was kneeling to pick him up when a very polite, accented voice asked, "Is the child okay?"

Morgan looked up, but not very far, for the voice came from a short, exceptionally neat Japanese man in a crisp linen suit. To her surprise, Ben Barnaby stood next to him.

"Ben!" Morgan rose awkwardly, Petey in her arms.

"Morgan! What are you doing here?" Ben was impressive in his suit and tie.

"We just had a picnic by the pond. I had to come into town, and I thought I'd give Petey the opportunity to see the campus."

Petey waved an exuberant hello at Ben.

"Hi, guy." Ben high-fived Petey. "Morgan, this is Dr. Takamachi from Tokyo. He's an expert in nuclear engineering. He was the keynote speaker at our conference here this week."

Morgan extended her hand and shook the scientist's tiny white paw. "I'm honored to meet you, Dr. Takamachi."

Dr. Takamachi bowed slightly. "And I, you. You have a most pleasing son."

The charming man was so doll-like in his perfection, Morgan almost bowed back to him. "Thank you."

"I am availing myself of fresh air, which is excellent for the brain, while at the same time I am having a most thought-provoking conversation with this young scholar," Dr. Takamachi told her.

Petey was squirming in her arms now, turning into octopus boy. "Well, I have to get my excellent child home for a nap before he has a meltdown," Morgan announced.

"Meltdown." Dr. Takamachi first looked concerned, then barked out a laugh. "I see! I see!"

"It was nice meeting you, Dr. Takamachi. Bye, Ben!" Morgan strode away, hurrying toward the car.

Petey fell asleep in his car seat on the way to Dragonfly Lake. Fortunately, the heat of the day and the excitements of the morning had used up his energy, so when Morgan unlatched him from his seat, he scarcely woke.

14

.....

"I'll call you," he'd said.

But he hadn't called.

It had been over a week since that startling, magical, unexpectedly lovely sail on Dragonfly Lake. When Natalie and Ben had returned to shore, she'd helped him drag the boat up onto dry land, unstep the mast, and fold the sail, both of them working quickly, without speaking. *What happens next?* she'd wondered. She had been opening her mouth to invite him over for a drink when Brady came whooping out of the Barnaby house, followed by several of his teenage buddies.

Brady had rattled out his words so fast he was almost incomprehensible: "Mom says we can cook hot dogs tonight but we're out of hot dogs can you go get some?"

Ben shot Natalie a glance filled with dismay, but his brother didn't notice. Brady and his friends surrounded Ben like enormous hyperactive jumping frogs, hooting and bumping into one another.

Brady continued, bouncing on his toes, jiggling all over, "And I have my driver's permit, so if you ride with me, can I drive, huh?"

"Yeah!" Zack yelled, and the two other boys chimed in.

Ben was helpless, encircled by such exuberance. "Sure," he said.

The boys exploded with cheers and raced for the driveway, knocking and shoving one another as they went.

Ben had smiled ruefully. "I'm sorry."

The heat still trembled between them. It wouldn't vanish easily,

Natalie thought. "I'm sorry, too." She summoned her courage. "Want to come over for a drink after you get back?"

"Yes, I want to. But I can't. I've got something else on. I'll call you."

Those were the last words he'd spoken to her. *I'll call you.*

Right. How many times had any woman heard that from any man?

Still, she had totally believed he would call her. She hadn't even tortured herself wondering what if that "something else" he had on tonight was a date with another woman. She'd sauntered into her house, humming an old Beatles song. It was late in the afternoon, but she'd been full of energy.

When she was happy like this, she wanted to work. She almost couldn't keep herself from working.

There was an oil on canvas by Margaret Foster Richardson titled *A Motion Picture* painted around 1912 that Natalie had always adored above all other paintings. It was a portrait of the painter moving toward her easel, a young woman with her hair pulled back, wearing glasses and a gray painting smock, holding brushes in each hand, staring intently at the viewer, her smock rippling with movement. The painting was compelling, dramatic, dynamic: a woman artist, alive, at work!

This was what Natalie had always wanted to do, and right now she was in the mood to do it. She had the courage; she had the *passion*. She went into her studio, and as if on autopilot, put a fresh canvas on the easel. She found mirrors in two of the guest rooms, wrestled them off the walls, lugged them into her studio. She set them up, shoving furniture around to support them, angling them so that when she stood at her easel, she saw her own reflection.

She began to work.

That was last week.

Today Natalie could not get the painting of herself to live. She turned the mirrors to the wall. She lifted off the canvas and put it in the corner. She paced her studio, chewing on her nails. She wanted to work, she still wanted to work, but she needed a new subject. She didn't want to do oils, she wanted to go back to charcoal. Her charcoal portraits of Petey and Louise were by far the best things she'd done, and she wanted to keep at it. She wanted to do another charcoal, of a man. She needed a man.

She'd be dammed if she was going to phone Ben and ask him to sit for her! If he had called her as he'd said he would, it would be the easiest thing in the world for her to ask him, and she knew his schedule was flexible in the summer. And his body was so beautiful, his long limbs an artist's dream. His shoulders, so wide and strong, his collarbone, his throat . . .

Maybe she *could* call him. Wasn't it a new world, couldn't women call men, weren't all the silly old rules of courtship thrown out the window? And besides, this wasn't about courtship, it was about her work!

In a daze, she showered, dressed in shorts and a clean tank top, and wandered down to the kitchen for a bagel spread with peanut butter, which she washed down with a glass of juice. She tied on her sneakers and forced herself out into the heat of the day to walk the circuit of the lake.

It was always early afternoon when she took her walk. During the week, most houses were quiet, only the hum of air conditioners breaking the silence. Natalie stayed on the shady side of the street, where it was a few degrees cooler under the trees. Occasionally a brilliant spot of summer flowers would catch her artist's eye, but usually on this walk her attention was inward, on her artwork.

Today, her mind was on Ben. Pathetic.

Her pace quickened as she finished her circuit of the lake and came toward her home. Aunt Eleanor's home, of course, but by now Natalie thought of it as her home.

A white SUV passed her and turned into the O'Keefes' driveway. Morgan stepped out, hurrying around to unbuckle Petey.

"Hi, Morgan!" Natalie jogged up the drive toward her friend.

"Hi, Nat." Morgan's son was dozing in her arms. "We're just on our way to *nappy* time." Her singsong voice and the look on her face warned Natalie that now was not a good time for a visit. "We just had lunch at the university, and Ben was there, and Dr. *Takamachi*, who knows everything about nuclear *engineering*!" She touched the

SUV door handle and it slid closed. She lugged her purse and diaper bag and her drowsy little boy up to her house. "See you later, gator." Her voice was now almost a whisper.

Natalie waved, not wanting to break the silence. She walked back to her own house, let herself in, and then stood in the hall, frowning.

Morgan had had lunch with Ben at the university? Morgan had had lunch with some nuclear engineer? Well, of course, Morgan was a scientist. So that made sense, kind of.

But Morgan wasn't a nuclear engineer. She wasn't a chemical engineer. She wasn't even employed. Why would Ben ask her to meet him for lunch?

Morgan was married. So Ben wasn't interested in her that way, was he? He certainly wasn't like Slade, who tried to get every woman he met into bed. It had to be a purely intellectual friendship. . . . Still, for one blood-red moment, Natalie *hated* Morgan. She hated Ben, too. She was so full of anger she didn't know what to do with herself.

In the next moment she knew she didn't hate Morgan or Ben, she hated herself. When was she going to grow up? Why was she such a basket case? So what if Ben had asked Morgan for lunch! Natalie hadn't come out here to fall in love; she'd come here to paint. What she needed right now wasn't a man. She needed some stimulation, some life, people, city stuff.

She took another quick shower and pulled on one of her few dresses. It was black, like everything else she'd worn in New York. Suddenly she had a fierce yearning for a pretty sundress. Aunt Eleanor was paying her to "look after the house," so for the first time ever, Natalie had some money to spend on herself. Maybe she'd get some new sandals, too. Stop by the used-book store in Northampton. Perhaps she could find some nice art books. Aunt Eleanor had a few books scattered around the house, but they were mostly thrillers, paperbacks with water-stained pages.

As soon as she was in the silver Range Rover, she felt better. She punched in the classic rock station on Sirius and sang along as she drove. Northampton was a funky little town, its streets trailing away from the dignified campus of Smith College. Mixed among massive, fortresslike stone buildings were coffee boutiques, Afghani restaurants, and hole-in-the-wall shops selling tie-dyed bedspreads from India. She found a parking spot on the main street and ambled along the sidewalks, the tension flowing out of her shoulders as her eyes filled with the sight of so many young people, men and women, many of them dressed in colorful hippie garb. It was like photos she'd seen of the seventies.

At the Mercantile, she found several sundresses in filmy cool prints, priced for a college student's wallet, swirling with color and easy to wear, draped material falling from a sort of rope tied around her neck. She bought three and wore the purple one out of the shop. Much better now, much cooler. As she walked, the material belled out and gathered in around her knees, creating her own summer breeze.

The used-book store was around the corner and down a hill. Inside, it was cool and slightly dampish, and packed wall to wall with books. She settled in the art section and surrendered to delight. She discovered a book with several Lilian Westcott Hale portraits in charcoal on white board or paper and a more modern drawing by Margarett Sargent, a fourth cousin of John Singer Sargent whom Natalie had never known existed. She found a biography written by Margarett Sargent's granddaughter, entitled *The White Blackbird*, and grabbed that as well. And a book called *A Studio of Her Own: Women Artists in Boston, 1870-1940*. She went to the cash register, dazzled with riches, stunned at how inexpensive the books were.

"Natalie?"

She turned. "Aaron!"

Bella's boyfriend was holding as many books as she was, and it didn't take more than a second to spot that they were all various histories of San Francisco. "Oh," Natalie said. "San Francisco! Did you get the job?"

"I'm one of the final three contenders," Aaron said. Rather sheepishly, he gazed down at his books. "Whether I get the job or not, the city fascinates me. Not just the architecture now, but the way it changed and evolved throughout the city's history."

The cashier cleared her throat.

"Oh." Natalie dumped her books on the counter. "Here you are."

The cashier herself was a mobile work of art, so covered with tattoos and piercings she shifted like a hologram of herself as she rang up the purchases and took Natalie's money.

"Want to get some coffee?" Aaron asked as he laid his pile on the counter.

"Sure." This was just what she loved about the city, just what she needed—clothes, books, friends with interests that complemented hers.

"The Golden Gate Bridge," Aaron was saying as they left the shop and headed uphill toward the main street, "is both practical and romantic. It's been called one of the wonders of the modern world."

Natalie stopped walking and talking. She stared at Aaron. Her blood thundered. "You're a man!"

Aaron stopped, too. He frowned at Natalie. "What?"

"You're a man, Aaron!" Natalie took a few steps to the left, estimating the depth of his rib cage beneath his shirt. "And I really need a man."

In a monotone, Aaron replied, "You really need a man."

She shot a question at him with her eyes, then burst out laughing. "I mean for my drawing, Aaron! I want to *draw* a man. I need a male model. I don't want to sleep with you, for heaven's sake!"

Aaron hesitated. "How long will it take?"

"Just a few hours a day for four or five days. It will help *Bella*, Aaron, think of it that way. She's going to hang my drawings in her shop. Look, we can go home and set up the sketch now. I'll make you iced coffee, or give you a drink, whatever you want, just follow me home, okay?"

Aaron shrugged. "Okay."

The studio was cool and quiet. Natalie made an iced coffee for Aaron and one for herself, but she was too psyched to drink hers as she calmly but quickly set up her easel with fresh paper near the table holding her charcoal.

"Could you take off your shirt?" she asked Aaron.

He hesitated.

"Oh, Aaron, come on. I saw you in your bathing trunks, what, two weeks ago, when we had the picnic and we all swam and played volleyball? Take off your shirt."

Aaron took off his shirt.

Natalie studied him. Aaron was compact, more fleshy and muscular than Slade or damned Ben. His chest was also extremely hairy—she'd forgotten that, and it made the drawing of his pecs difficult. But he had an extremely strong-looking neck, with a powerful sternomastoid running down to his trapezius, and his deltoid muscles bulged. He'd worked out. A lot.

"Did you wrestle in high school?" she asked.

"Yeah." Aaron was staring at the ceiling, uncomfortable with her inspection.

"Okay, I got it! Here. Sit on this chair. Now raise your arms and push them back as far as you can, and turn your head to the side and bend it back, too." She showed him the pose she wanted. Aaron wasn't really *trying*; he was reluctant, as most people were in unusual poses. "You've got fabulous musculature, Aaron. I want to take advantage of your trapezius and deltoids."

Those were words he understood. Immediately his pose improved.

"Great! That's great! I know it's a strain on your muscles, but you can take a break every so often. Hold it just like that for me as long as you can. It's like, oh, let's say you're being held down by a lion, you're twisting away so he won't get to your face, but your muscles, your body is tensed, ready for one last struggle, you're at that moment just before you lunge—"

She drew rapidly, inspired. Her charcoal scratched against the paper. This was going to be *awesome*. Quickly she sketched in the broad outline, his profile, his ear, his jaw, his shoulders, stressed and straining, his sturdy chest and abdomen. It was a hard pose to maintain, especially with his arms held out and back, and after a while she could tell he was tiring.

"Let's take a break. Shake it out. Get up and walk around."

Aaron headed for his iced coffee. "I've never sat for an artist before."

"You're fabulous," she told him. "Want to see? I think this is the best thing I've ever done, Aaron. It's going to be . . ." She searched for the right word. "It's going to be *epic*. And *masculine*. I'm not just painting roses in a bowl here."

Now Aaron was studying Natalie. He said, "You're ambitious."

"Gosh, yes." She sipped some of her coffee. "Not for money. Not even for fame, although I'd like my pictures to be bought and hung and shown. I'm ambitious for myself, Aaron, for"—she waved her arm, indicating her entire studio—"for this. I want to keep pushing myself, I want to see what I can do. I never knew until today that I could do anything like that portrait of you, although you do understand that's not *you* on the page, it's something else; it's Struggle, or Endeavor, or—"

"Survival," he offered.

"Yes! Survival, that's it, that's what it's becoming. That's what I'll call it." Impulsively, she wrapped Aaron in a big hug. "Oh, Aaron, thank you! I'd never have gotten to this without you!"

Aaron flushed bright red from his chest, up his neck, to his entire face. "You're welcome," he muttered.

"Oh God." Memories suffused Natalie: all the times artists she'd posed for had hit on her, assuming that her nakedness, her willing arch and arrangement of limbs and torso, constituted some kind of invitation. Assuming that posing was some kind of tacit agreement. "Aaron, I'm sorry. I wasn't hitting on you, I promise. I'm just excited. Intellectually excited, artistically excited. I would *never* hit on you!"

Aaron was grinning. "You're assuming my reaction was embarrassment."

"What else could it— *Oh!*" Now it was Natalie's turn to blush. "Well, Aaron." She began to dither. "I'm not saying you're not, or rather that I couldn't be, but, come on, you're practically engaged to Bella!"

"Am I?" Aaron was no longer smiling.

"Aren't you?"

They stared at each other. Natalie did not feel the urgent chemistry she'd felt with Ben. On the other hand, it was quite possible Ben hadn't felt the urgent chemistry himself. Certainly he hadn't called her. He'd had lunch with Morgan! But Bella was a friend. A new friend, but a good friend.

"I don't know," Aaron answered. "I was planning to ask Bella to marry me, but frankly, I think she'll refuse because she doesn't want to leave this area."

This was between Bella and Aaron. No place for Natalie to intrude. "Sit down again," she ordered. "I want to work a bit more."

Aaron took his position, turning his head away, straining backward. It was impossible for him to talk now, and Natalie was glad. She needed to concentrate on her drawing. Aaron was a classy, good-looking guy. He was strong, confident, kind, easygoing. Bella would be a fool not to marry him.

She worked for another forty-five minutes, allowing Aaron to stretch at intervals.

At last she folded. "That's it for the day. I might shade in some background tomorrow. Can you give me some time tomorrow?"

"I've got lots of time until I hear from San Francisco," Aaron told her, his voice slightly muffled as he pulled his shirt on over his head.

"Tomorrow after noon?" she asked.

"I'll be here at one."

They thumped down the stairs together.

"Would you like a drink?" she asked.

"Not today, thanks." Aaron leaned over and kissed her cheek. "I'm really proud to be part of this, Natalie. I think you've got quite a talent."

"Thanks, Aaron." Natalie stood in the doorway, waving at him as he drove away, and she couldn't stop smiling.

15

.....

Online, Bella ordered a "Going Out of Business" banner. She placed an ad in all the local papers: the *Daily Amherst Gazette*, the *Valley Advocate*, the *Belchertown Sentinel*, the *PennySaver*. She put an ad on craigslist. She made up flyers on her computer and drove around all the local towns, thumbtacking them up on every bulletin board she could find.

Her father called a friend who was a reporter with the *Gazette*, and suggested he write a hometown story about the closing of Barnaby's Barn, but Harry Warton was reluctant. The paper was already full of closings; it was depressing. So Dennis suggested he write about a new business taking over the spot where Barnaby's Barn had been, and Harry thought that was a great idea. He agreed to cover the opening of Bella's.

Bella dusted each individual item of stock, polished the display cases until they shone, swept and mopped the floor. She was glad to be so busy—first, because this was an enormous change taking place and she was eager to make it happen, to see it *done*; second, because she was driving herself crazy trying not to think about Aaron and Slade. When she did, her mind went around in circles. No, not even circles, more like one of those weird Escher drawings of stairs that went nowhere and led back to themselves.

Plus, she didn't know what to think about Aaron posing for Natalie.

Natalie had phoned her the first evening he posed. "Come over after dinner, would you? I've got something to show you. Well, you've seen it before, of course, but not this way."

Well, *there* was an intriguing invitation! Aaron was having dinner with some colleagues, old friends from college who were in the area, and Bella was eating dinner at home with her family. She bolted her food and raced across to Natalie's.

Natalie was over the moon about this new drawing. "Look!" she demanded, gesturing toward the paper on the easel, as if Bella could do anything *but* look. "My God, Bella, the musculature that man has, the vigorous lines of his torso, the power just *shouting* from his biceps! It's almost mythic. What a beautiful human being."

Bella had swallowed. She'd never thought of Aaron as *beautiful*. Certainly he was handsome, but he was short, stocky, hairy-chested, and kind of . . . "Primitive," she whispered.

"*Primitive*," Natalie echoed. "You're right." Stepping forward, she picked up a piece of charcoal and lightly shaded an area. "I don't know why I suggested this pose. It was spontaneous. I knew at once what I wanted as soon as he took his shirt off. Do you see the line here, his sternomastoid? It's thick. Pure."

Bella hugged herself with her arms as she listened to Natalie praise the anatomical parts of her lover's body. It was one of the odder experiences of her life. Natalie spoke so freely, so openly. *I knew at once what I wanted as soon as he took his shirt off*. What?

"Why don't you draw Slade?" Bella asked. She was really curious.

"Oh, for heaven's sake, Slade is nothing but bones," Natalie responded contemptuously. She jerked to a stop and pivoted suddenly to face Bella. "Bella! You're absolutely right! Why didn't I think of it myself?" Almost lunging forward, she grabbed Bella in a hug. "You're a genius!"

Surprised and confused, Bella could only ask, "Really?"

"I should draw Slade! In the same pose! Think of it!" Natalie was almost levitating.

Bella thought of it. Slade, with his shirt off, his neck twisted away, his arms raised, his chest bare . . .

"The difference will be stunning!" Natalie burbled on. "Slade is long and lean, and if he has any muscles, they'll be like threads compared to Aaron's."

"That's not a nice thing to say," Bella told Natalie.

Natalie laughed. "For heaven's sake, Slade's my *brother*. That's hardly the worst thing I've said about him." She paced around her paper, jabbing forward now and then with her eraser, touching the tip to a line, a shadow. "I'll have to phone Slade, ask him to come stay for a few days."

That night, Bella slept at her parents'. Aaron phoned her as he was driving home from dinner with his old friends. He told her about them—both were married and already had children—and asked about her day.

"I saw Natalie's drawing of you," Bella told him. It was late. She was alone in her old childhood bedroom, in her twin bed with the pink sheets.

"What did you think? She's good, isn't she?" Aaron answered.

"She's really good," Bella agreed. She kind of wanted to pick a fight, to accuse him of something, but really, what could she accuse him of? It wasn't like he'd been totally naked in front of Natalie.

And if he had been, should she have cared?

"She thinks you're beautiful." Bella opted to be pleasant, complimentary, and why not, that was what Natalie had said.

Aaron laughed, a deep grumbling in his throat. "Honey, men aren't beautiful. She's just an artist, and they perceive stuff differently. If she was painting, oh, I don't know, a mushroom, she'd think it was beautiful."

"Oh, Aaron." Bella smiled. Her heart was touched by Aaron's instinctive protection of her feelings. As if he didn't want there to be any chance at all that she'd be jealous, that she'd think Natalie was hitting on him, that she'd wonder whether something happened between Natalie and Aaron up in that studio, something not overtly physical, not so much as a kiss . . . and she found herself thinking of the way Slade kissed her before she got out of the van. And there she was, talking to Aaron and melting all over about Slade.

. . .

So it was a good thing, a saving grace, that she had so much to do to close her mother's shop and start Bella's.

On the second Saturday in July, Bella pulled on a sundress, grabbed a cup of coffee, and drove to Barnaby's Barn. Ben met her there as he'd promised. They'd already hung the Going Out of Business banner at the beginning of the week, and it had drawn some people in and moved some inventory out, as well it should have, at seventy-five percent off.

This morning Ben helped her carry Jim Harrington's furniture out to the drive in front of the store. Low-to-the-ground, handmade wooden cradles for real babies, as if mothers still rocked them with their feet while they worked their spinning wheels. Cradles for dolls. High chairs, stools, and cupboards carved with hearts and flowers. Some items Louise had taken on commission, and those Jim had already collected. Some Louise had paid for years ago. At seventy-five percent off, she would be taking a huge loss, but Bella knew that if someone didn't buy them, they'd be given away for free to preschools in the area at the end of the day.

Around ten, Bella's parents arrived. Dennis took out his digital camera and snapped shots of Louise in front of Barnaby's Barn, and inside Barnaby's Barn, near several of the displays.

"Gosh," Louise exclaimed. "I'd forgotten this was here! Oh, honey, have I been living in the dusty old past!" She tilted her face up to Dennis's. He took her hand. Their faces shone with pleasure. "Definitely time for a change!"

Very few people came by. At noon, Aaron arrived with bags of sandwiches and drinks for everyone. They sat at the table under the shade of the tree and chatted, ready to jump up if anyone came, but no one did. In the early afternoon, it clouded up, driving a few families away from other activities, and for about an hour Barnaby's Barn had a minirush of business. The hand-smocked children's clothing went to a woman with a victorious glint in her eye. She probably owned a specialty clothing store in someplace like Nantucket where she could sell handmade garments at enormous markups—but fine, Bella thought, more power to her.

Shauna Webb stopped by around four with some boxes and

newspaper and packed up the Cow Jumped over the Moon pottery that hadn't sold.

"I'm into bellies now anyway," she told Louise and Bella.

"Excuse me?" Louise asked.

"Porcelain bellies. Or thighs. Breasts. Whatever you want. For your coffee table."

Bella cleared her throat. "People buy porcelain body parts for their coffee tables?"

"You'd be surprised at how well I'm doing. It's the rage."

Bella supposed Natalie would understand what Shauna meant, but she couldn't imagine have a belly or thigh just lying there in her living room. But this was an artisty area, with a lot of interchange with New York and Boston, and body parts were certainly edgier than children's tea sets.

At five, it was obvious that no one else was coming. They packed the remaining inventory into the back of Dennis's Volvo and Louise's SUV, ready to take to the various preschools Monday morning. Louise surprised them all by nodding at Dennis, who brought out a bottle of champagne and their crystal stemware.

"Good-bye to Barnaby's Barn!" Dennis toasted. "Hello to Bella's!"

Bella was emotionally choked up. When she took a big sip of champagne, the bubbles went right up her nose and she physically choked up, too. A piece of her history, her childhood, was ending. But her mother laughed, holding her husband's hand and acting like a woman who'd just had a mountain removed from her shoulders.

The Barnabys drove home. Aaron followed in his car. Ben ordered pizza and they all ate while watching baseball on television for a while, catching up on the Red Sox. Bella put together a platter of grapes, strawberries, and melon slices and set it on the coffee table next to a platter of cookies.

"Now," her father said. He clicked the remote and the TV went blank. "Your mother and I want to chat just a bit."

Bella sucked in a breath. Why did this "chat" send her anxiety level soaring? She wondered if it had anything to do with Brady, who was over at Zack's for the weekend.

"Your mother and I have been talking," Dennis announced.

"Okay," Bella said.

Louise said, "I don't feel old. Your father doesn't feel old. We are in good health. But Dennis is going to be sixty, and he wants to retire. We've decided that while we're both in good health, we want to buy an RV and explore the United States."

"So we need to think about this house. Our house," Dennis added. "We might want to rent it."

"This isn't about money. It's about our lives." Louise raised her hands, as if holding an explanation they could see lying right there, like a scarf or a picture. "We love this house, but perhaps we'll want to sell it eventually. It's big for two older people."

Stunned, Bella asked, "What about Brady?"

"Brady has another year of high school. It's going to take us at least a year to get this house in order for a renter. We've got to go through all the stuff in the basement, attics, bedrooms, the shed. . . ."

"Simplify," Louise said quietly, nodding to herself. "Simplify."

Dennis continued, "We're not saying this is happening *tomorrow*, Bella. We just want you to know our plans."

Louise went on, "Nothing is going to happen *fast*. You'll have plenty of time to make your own plans. And, Bella, while we're all sitting down, there's something else you need to know."

"I can't imagine what more there is." Bella tried not to sound like a petulant child.

"Beatrice and Jeremy are moving to the Cape."

Bella sagged. "I was afraid of that."

"Why are they moving?" Ben asked, his voice mild.

"They love it down there," Louise told him. "There's more work for Jeremy, too."

"The Cape's great," Aaron said. "What town?"

"Chatham."

Aaron nodded. "That's out on the elbow of the Cape."

Bella complained, "So it's another thirty minutes to get there from Hyannis."

"You've hardly seen Beat at all this summer," her father reminded her. "You've been working so hard. She's been so busy with her kids."

"True," Bella admitted.

"Brady wants to apply to Stanford for college," Dennis added.

Bella echoed, "Brady wants to go to California? What next? Ben, are *you* moving to Mars?"

Ben rolled his eyes. "Bella, I'm staying right in my apartment in Amherst."

"So," Dennis concluded, "that's our news."

"These changes are enormous," Bella told her father, her voice soft. Sitting so near him, she noticed how the laugh lines around his eyes had deepened, how thin and gray his hair had grown . . . and were those age spots on his hand? The world was shifting beneath her feet. She could almost feel it.

Her father patted her arm. "I'll teach this coming year. I've talked to the principal. I'm giving a year's notice. They're eager to get rid of me anyway, get some new young blood at lower salaries."

"So nothing," Louise repeated, "is really going to happen for a year."

Dennis looked at his older son. "How do you feel about all this, Ben?"

Ben shrugged. "Me? I'm fine with it."

"Me, too." Bella forced herself to be happy for her parents. Well, she *was* happy for them. "I'm glad you guys are going to see the country. You'll have a blast."

Dennis kissed Bella's forehead. "Thanks, Bell." He stood up. "Back to the Red Sox. If they don't win this game, they'll be down to fourth place."

Aaron stood up, too. "Bella. Want to go for a ride?"

She didn't know what she wanted to do right now. "Sure," she agreed, numb.

Aaron said a polite good night to everyone. Bella went out the door and climbed into the passenger seat of his car. Aaron got in the driver's seat. For a moment they sat in silence, allowing the steamy night air to fill their lungs. In the distance, a bird called.

"A lot of developments in one day," Aaron said quietly.

"Aaron, I'm changing, too. I mean . . . well, I don't know how to express it, but I want—I *need*—to give Bella's a chance." She drew her hands through her hair. "Could I be more inarticulate?"

Aaron was silent for a few moments. "I was hoping you'd fly out to San Francisco with me. So I could show you around."

"Aaron, I love it *here*." She spoke to him, but they were both facing forward, as if talking to the windshield.

"And you love me."

She lifted her chin. "And you love me."

Aaron turned and took Bella in his arms. His eyes glittered in the ambient light falling from the houses around them. "I do love you, Bella. That's why I want you to come to San Francisco with me. If I get the offer."

"But if you love me, why can't *I* say the same thing? That's why I want you to stay here with me," she countered, her voice reasonable.

Aaron chuckled. "Honey. You can't equate Barnaby's Barn with one of the most distinguished architectural firms in one of the most glamorous cities in the world."

"It won't be Barnaby's Barn," Bella reminded him.

"Whatever it's called, it's hardly going to make enough money to support us, is it? Not to mention the children we want to have."

He was right. Glumly, she nodded agreement.

"Winston Churchill said, 'We shape our buildings, and afterwards, our buildings shape us.' " Aaron said.

"What?" Bella's fighting spirit was up again. "What does that even *mean*?"

"Come on, Bella, think of cathedrals. Courthouses. The buildings in Washington, DC. Think of corporate headquarters touching the sky."

"And compare them to the Barn, is that what you're saying? That your work is so much more *significant* than mine would be if I ran Bella's."

"Bella, I love you. I want to marry you. I want to have children with you. I want you to be my wife. I know you've got a talent for putting together antiques and art. You'd go wild about the shops in

San Francisco. You could set up your own shop." Aaron sighed. "I just don't get what your problem is."

Cruelly, Bella reminded him, "You may not get the job. There are two other candidates."

Aaron rubbed his eyes. "Right. Believe me, I think about that constantly."

"My painting party's tomorrow," Bella told him.

"What?"

"The painting party. Everyone's going to help me freshen up the Barn. Slade and Natalie, Morgan and Josh, 'cause it's a Sunday and he's free, Ben and Dad, and Brady, too. And you, remember?"

Clearly Aaron hadn't remembered. "I didn't realize it was scheduled for tomorrow. So soon. Bella, why don't you wait? I mean, why go to all that work when . . ." He let his sentence trail off.

"I'm going ahead with it," Bella said. "I've made a lot of plans." Suddenly she wanted to hurt Aaron. "Slade's staying for a few days. He promised to help Ben and my dad move some furniture into the shop next week after the paint dries."

"You didn't tell me this."

"We just agreed on it by email today," Bella explained. "Aaron, you can't be angry with me for discussing the shop with Ben and Slade instead of with you."

"No. No, I know you're right about that." He ran his hands over his face. "You know what? We are in what my grandmother would call a pickle."

Bella smiled at him, grateful for his attempt to lighten the atmosphere.

"I think we should both just go to bed, get some rest, and see where next week takes us. Perhaps I won't get the job, and then I'll have to figure out some new plans for my life. Or perhaps I will get the job, and we can talk about it then. What do you think?"

"I think you're wonderful, Aaron," Bella told him.

They kissed for a while, tender, affectionate kisses without a trace of urgency or lust.

Aaron pulled away. "Good night, Bella."

"Night, Aaron." She stepped out of his car and went up the walk to her house. To her parents' house. She slipped inside and made her way up the stairs, calling good night to everyone in the living room before hurrying into the safety of her own room. She was too tired for any more conversation. She threw herself on her bed. She heard Aaron's car start up and drive away.

16
· · · · ·

Morgan absolutely could not believe it! It was Sunday, and Josh had gone in to work! Furthermore, he'd gotten up before she had and sneaked out of the house like a ferret, leaving her a note on the kitchen table: *Have to work. Sorry.*

"*Have to work. Sorry?*"

She was so angry she burst into tears. They really had to talk, because this was no way to live. It was summer, it was Sunday, they'd made plans to help Bella paint, taking turns playing with Petey, and then their new gang would get together for beers and burgers afterward—and all of a sudden, without forewarning Morgan, without even having the decency to wake her this morning and talk to her about it or sit down last night and explain it to her, Josh just took off.

She dialed his office phone. He didn't answer. She dialed his cell. No answer, straight to voice mail. She said, *Josh, you'd better call me!*

When her cell trilled, she snatched it up.

"Hey, Morgan, it's Bella. Ready to paint?"

"I am, but Josh has gone into Bio-Green and I don't know when he's coming back." She knew her voice had taken on a note of self-pity and she tried to sound less pathetic, but she added, "So I don't know if I can help, because I've got Petey, and Petey and paint are a sure recipe for disaster."

"Can Felicity babysit?"

"I'll call her," Morgan said.

"Good. Let me know when you're ready. You can ride down with me."

Felicity was thrilled to babysit, but Morgan still felt cranky as she threw on shorts and an old tank top and slammed out of her gorgeous husbandless house.

As they settled in Louise's SUV, Morgan said, "Don't even ask me why Josh had to work."

"Well, too bad for him," Bella sympathized.

Morgan glared at Bella. "Too bad for *him*? Too bad for me and Petey. We never see him. He's always working. And why couldn't he at least have woken me up to tell me he was going in?"

"Perhaps because he knew you'd be angry?" Bella suggested.

Morgan snorted. She felt like Bella was taking Josh's side.

"Men and their work," Bella continued, and now her own voice grew thick with discontent. "Aaron really wants to take the job in San Francisco."

"San Francisco is amazing," Morgan said quietly.

"So everyone says." Bella was practically shooting sparks, she was suddenly so fired up. "Why is a big city better than a small town? Why is his dream more important than mine?"

"I didn't realize Bella's has been a dream of yours," Morgan said.

Bella inhaled deeply. "I didn't realize it either." She grinned a bit sheepishly. "I've been such a good girl, doing what was expected of me all my life, teaching because Dad taught and I admire him, coming home to help Mom when she fell. This shop idea is new to me, too, but, Morgan, it's so strong, getting stronger every day. It makes me happy thinking about it, and excited."

Morgan laughed. "You sound like you're in love." As they pulled into the parking lot, Morgan suggested, "Why not give yourself a chance to see how it works out? It's not like there won't be planes to San Francisco in four months or a year. It's not like you can't visit Aaron, and he'll come back and visit you. Who knows, you might get bored with the shop. But you don't have to make a huge black-and-white decision now."

Bella brightened. "You're right, I know." Grinning, she added, "Since you put it so well, want to tell Aaron for me?"

"No," Morgan said, getting out of the car. "I want to *paint*."

Ben, Louise, Dennis, and Brady arrived with buckets of paint, brushes, rollers, plastic sheets, masking tape, and ladders. They divided up the work: The men would take the outside; the women, the inside.

Natalie showed up with her brother. She slipped inside without talking to the men, and Slade ambled in after her.

"Hey, ladies." He wore ratty old jeans and an Arcade Fire tee shirt. "Morgan," he said, coming close to her. "I've got something for you in my van."

"Is it the settee?"

"Would you like it to be the settee?" he teased. His grin was roguish. Slade flirted as he breathed; could he do one without doing the other? He jerked his head toward the door. "Come out and I'll show you."

Morgan was aware of how Bella was staring at her, a glint of—could it really be *suspicion* in her sweet blue eyes? "It's a piece of furniture for our living room!" she called to Bella. "Slade's emailed me photos, and I've been eager to see it. I'll be right back." She hoped Bella got the tacit message: *And I'm not going to have sex with Slade because I'm mad at my husband!* Although that was not the most repulsive thought she'd ever had. . . . *Stop it!* Morgan told herself. *Concentrate*.

She followed Slade out to the van. He keyed the doors open so she could peer inside. The white Victorian settee was protected by sheets of Bubble Wrap and held in place with wide straps.

"It looks perfect," Morgan said.

"Want to go over now and put it in your house?" Slade asked. "It wouldn't take long, and then this afternoon when you walk in, it will be in place, you'll be able to tell how you react to it."

"I don't know. We should be painting, helping Bella." Morgan tilted her head questioningly at Slade. "Shouldn't we?"

Slade rolled his eyes at her twinge of conscience. "We'll paint. But let's move this while we've got the energy." He ran his eyes over Morgan. "I think you and I can do it. We won't need Josh."

"Good thing," Morgan muttered. "Josh isn't around."

"Oh?"

"He's at work."

"On a Sunday?"

"Don't ask." Morgan went around to the passenger side of the van and climbed in.

They drove out of the parking lot just as Aaron was pulling in. "That will make Bella happy," Morgan said, waving at Aaron.

"What—that Aaron showed up?" Slade didn't seem particularly interested.

Morgan filled him in on the whole dilemma: Aaron wanting to move to San Francisco, Bella wanting to stay here, how would they decide? Aaron would know this week if he got the job in San Francisco.

"Yeah, marriage," Slade said. "Cramps your style."

"It certainly does," Morgan agreed.

Slade looked over at her. "Cramps *your* style?"

"Slade, I'm trained in biosafety. I know how to handle bacterial and parasitic agents. I've written a pamphlet on sewage spills—"

"Whoa!" Slade yelled. "That's *extreme*. You are completely grossing me out."

Morgan gave a wicked laugh. "The things I could tell you."

"Please. Don't."

"Who would dream you were so squeamish?"

"Who would dream a babe like you enjoyed sewage spills?"

"Ah," Morgan bantered. "Now you're getting sexist. Anyway, I didn't say I *enjoyed* sewage spills."

"Come on. You implied as much. Anyway, what do you mean? What *do* you enjoy?"

"The safety aspect of it," Morgan replied instantly. "I love knowing how to protect people from things they don't even realize are dangerous. For example, Slade, let's say there's a blockage in a dorm toilet. Normal, right? Happens every day. A custodian dealing with the problem could be exposed, which could lead to something entering his digestive system and causing bacterial disease like salmonellosis and hepatitis A. To start with. He might have symptoms like vomiting, fever, abdominal pain, diarrhea—"

"Okay, *stop!*" Slade shuddered. "You are the weirdest chick I've ever met."

"Well, Slade, you have to understand, I've got a master's degree in biosafety. I don't go around campus with rubber gloves cleaning up shit. I supervise. I run programs. I train and I test, people as well as equipment. I do most of my work at the computer and at the phone. I work with an enormous team. . . ." Morgan went quiet. After a moment, she said, "Rather, I *worked* with an enormous team. At Weathersfield College. I gave it up to come here. With Josh, because he got such a plum job at Bio-Green."

They'd arrived at her house. Slade pulled into the drive. "I'll unlock the door and just check the house phone," she told Slade hurriedly. Josh hadn't called her on her cell yet.

He hadn't called on the house phone either. She fixed the screen door to remain fully open and went back down the steps to the van. Slade was inside, undoing the packing straps. Morgan climbed up to join him. It was warm, shady, even gloomy inside the van.

"Let's edge it to the end, then I'll jump down and take it until you have to get down," Slade instructed. "We can rest it on the floor while you jump down."

Morgan checked to be sure her hands were clean. The settee was so white. But it was protected by lots of Bubble Wrap. She hefted the far end of the settee and slowly moved forward as Slade inched backward.

"You're at the edge!" she called. "Don't fall!"

"Thanks, Mom." Slade jumped down.

Raising his arms, he took the far end of the settee and carried it out of the van into the light of day, pausing for Morgan to jump down. Together, they lugged it across the lawn, up the steps, and through the open door into the house. They turned into the living room and gently positioned it in the spot in front of the window facing the street.

"Got scissors?" Slade asked.

He wasn't even sweating, despite the hot day, but Morgan was puffing after carrying the solid old piece of furniture.

"I'll get scissors and some ice water," she told him, and went off to the kitchen.

She returned to find Slade lifting one end of the settee to slide protective rubber squares beneath the ornate mahogany claw feet. She handed him the scissors, not sure where to start the process of unveiling, and stood back to watch. He sliced at the top, cutting quickly and surely, and before long they were both tearing at the wrap, pulling it away to expose the exquisitely carved, curled, and embossed back and arms of the settee and the Arctic white silk of the seat and back.

"What was I thinking?" Morgan chuckled. "Petey will turn this into a Mondrian in two minutes."

"Really?" Slade asked, looking at Morgan.

"Actually," she replied, "maybe not. Mostly he plays in the kitchen or the den or his playroom or his bedroom. In fact, Josh and I are hardly ever in the living room unless we have company."

"Lots of rooms in this house." Slade had an odd expression on his face. He said, "Let's sit on it."

"What?"

"Sit on it. The new settee. It *is* a piece of furniture meant for sitting on. Don't you want to try it out?" He wasn't sweating, yet he gave off heat. Or, no, not *heat,* more like an exotic incense, as if he were some sort of plant she wanted to lean into and inhale.

Why did Morgan suddenly feel so flustered? "Of course!" She pretended more enthusiasm than she felt. "It's just . . ." Bending, she tried to scan the back of her shorts.

"They're clean," Slade told her. "So are mine."

Morgan sat down on the new settee. Not at the far end, because that might seem rude, but not in the middle either. "Ooooh." She hadn't expected it to be quite so cushy.

"When we refurbished it, we added foam stuffing to make it softer. When they were first built, the seats contained horsehair and were about as hard as wood." Slade sat down next to Morgan.

Their arms almost touched.

It had been a long time since Morgan had been alone in a room with a full-grown male other than Josh.

"It's luxurious," she said, running her hand over the silk. She was aware of her bare legs extending from the hem of her shorts. His legs, next to hers, were longer, leaner. She was aware of her bare arms, her bare neck.

"It suits you," Slade said, and he ran his eyes up and down her body.

She knew she should pull away, stand up, grab her glass of ice water and hold it to her burning cheek, but she only croaked, "Hah. First time anyone's equated me with luxury."

"I think you're very luxurious," Slade assured her. Angling his body toward hers, he lightly touched her hair, which she'd pulled up in a high ponytail to keep it out of the way when painting. "Such thick, glossy hair. Skin like satin." He drew the tip of one finger down the side of her face, down her neck, stopping at her collarbone.

"Slade."

"Did you know this old settee is long enough for most people to lie down on? To sleep on? Or . . . whatever?"

She could feel his warm breath on her cheek. He looked like some dark prince materialized from one of the gothic romances she'd read as a teenager.

And he had said what no one else in the world had ever said about her. That her skin was like satin.

Turning, she rammed her face at his before she could change her mind, and smashed a kiss on his mouth. Taken by surprise and by the force of her lunge, Slade fell backward, but he was quick enough to wrap his arms around her and pull her with him. On top of him. They tangled together on the white satin, adjusting arms, torsos, mouths. Slade was too tall to get all of his long body onto the couch, so he had to keep his legs turned sideways, and Morgan slipped onto her side, only the embrace of Slade's arms keeping her from falling to the floor. His mouth was salty, hot, and much more knowing than any other mouth she'd ever kissed. As she pressed forward, Slade gently brushed his lips along her cheek, her jaw, the pulse in her

neck, the tender tip of her ear. She arched upward, eyes closed, sur-
rendering to a kind of lust she couldn't even remember.

"This isn't working." Slade struggled to sit up, forcing her to sit
up, too.

"It's not?" Morgan's hair had come out of the band and hung
down on one side of her face and against the back of her neck. "It's
working fine for me," she panted.

"I mean, the settee. It's long enough for a short man, but not
long enough for me and not wide enough for two people." Slade's
eyes were half closed, his lips wet with her saliva, his cheeks flushed
with heat. His chest was heaving. He was as vivid as a poppy, as
breathtaking as a thunderstorm.

Morgan understood what he meant. He didn't have to say that
if they were going to continue what she had started, they'd have to
move to a bedroom.

She couldn't do that. She was married. To that irritating jerk
Josh.

"Slade," she apologized, pulling away. "I'm sorry. I shouldn't
have kissed you. I don't know what came over me."

Slade's grin was crooked, astute. "Beauty queen, we're just getting started."

Beauty queen. Morgan had never been that. His words, and the
desire in his eyes, tugged at her, pulling her into the force field of his
sexuality. Morgan had never been sexually wild. She'd never surrendered, she'd never been *taken*. She had always been interested in
safety.

She still was, if only for Petey's sake.

Morgan stood up on trembling legs, walked to the coffee table,
picked up a glass, and held it out to Slade. "Ice water?"

His laugh exploded. "Yes, please." He stood up, arranging his
clothing.

Morgan slugged back her own ice water as if it were an anesthe-
tizing Scotch. "We should get back. Help paint."

"Right." Slade walked away, carrying his empty glass out of the
living room, down the hall, and into the kitchen. He returned. His
face was blank, his posture stiff. "I'll wait for you in the van."

Morgan carried her own glass to the kitchen. Petey's toys were on the floor. No sign of Josh, not even a coffee cup in the sink. He'd left so quickly he hadn't even taken time for the coffee he loved. What the hell was Josh doing?

She locked the house and climbed into the passenger seat of the van. Slade wasn't there. For a moment, her heart stopped—she had no idea why. Then she saw him coming out of his aunt's house with a portable CD player in one hand and a pile of CDs in the other. He tossed them in back, then slid into the driver's seat.

"Natalie called," Slade told Morgan. "She wants some music." He didn't look at Morgan.

"Slade." Morgan's throat was raspy. She cleared it. "I'm not sure what to say—"

"No need to say anything," Slade told her. He seemed to have recovered, and the smile he sent her was gentle, even kind. "It's like it never happened, okay?"

"Okay, Slade. Thanks." Morgan smiled, but she was all at once on the verge of tears. *As if it never happened?* Was she sure that was what she wanted? Could the sheer power, the *deliciousness*, of those few moments be erased from her memory?

Slade blasted the radio as they drove back to Bella's. He didn't speak again; his mind seemed to have retreated into a privacy she could sense he did not want invaded.

The van turned into the parking lot. Dennis, Brady, and Ben were up on ladders, painting one wall, and Aaron was squatting by a gallon of paint, prying the lid open with a screwdriver.

Saying "I'll help the men," Slade was out the door before she could speak.

Morgan jumped down from the van. "Right. I'll go inside."

Bella, Louise, and Natalie waved at Morgan with their paintbrushes.

"Look at what we've accomplished!" Bella called triumphantly.

"Well, I've got a great new piece of furniture," Morgan told them. As she headed toward a ladder, she experienced a bubble of relief in her chest: She hadn't done anything stupid. She was glad to be back among her friends.

17

·····

Inside the shop, Natalie and Bella started painting the walls. Bella had chosen an umber shade to give the place an antique aura. They would have to do at least two coats to cover Louise's murals.

She noticed Morgan going off in the van with Slade, and she noticed Bella noticing. Honestly, her brother. But she was glad for a few moments alone with Bella.

Trying to sound nonchalant, Natalie said, "Morgan told me she had lunch with Ben the other day. On campus."

Bella was squatting next to a gallon of paint, stirring it with a wooden stick. Preoccupied, her only reply was "Hmm."

"With Dr. Takamachi," said Natalie. She opened the sturdy metal ladder, pulled down the shelf, and slowly mounted the steps, lugging her own paint and brush.

"Doubt it," Bella said. "Ben would never mix work with pleasure."

Pleasure? Natalie wanted to shriek. Ben would consider being with Morgan *pleasure?*

"I don't know much about what Ben does," continued Bella, "but I do know there was a conference Ben had to attend. Takamachi's visit to campus is a very big deal. Morgan is a scientist, true, but she's in a different field. She wouldn't speak their language."

"Well." Natalie couldn't think what else to say. She was all too familiar with the experience of girls being her friend so they could attract her brother's attention, and she didn't want to go anywhere near that sort of thing. She liked Bella for herself. It would be too childish, anyway, too high school, to whine, *Bella, Ben kissed me and said he'd call me and he hasn't called, what can I do? Plus, Morgan had lunch with him*. No. Natalie was a grown-up now. If Ben hadn't called her, it was her own problem to deal with.

Although she *was* glad to hear about the conference and that Dr. Takamachi's visit was a big deal.

She began to paint, swiftly, with great concentration.

"Morgan and Slade are certainly taking their time," Bella remarked from the other side of the room.

"Don't worry," Natalie mumbled. "I don't think even my brother would mess around with a married woman."

"Oh, well, that's not what I mean," Bella hastily replied. "Damn. Got a big glob on my shirt."

"We should have brought some music," Natalie said. "I've got a portable CD player and some good discs. I'll phone Slade and tell him to pick them up and bring them over."

"Great idea!" Bella agreed.

Natalie carefully backed down the steps; crossed the floor, which was covered with protective plastic sheets; and went into the back room, where she'd dumped her purse. She dug her cell out and hit Slade's number. As she waited for the phone to ring, she leaned against the door jamb and let her eyes rest on the windows and open door. She could see Dennis, Aaron, Brady, and Ben crossing back and forth, carrying ladders, paint cans, rags, hammers. She'd been inside when Ben's car pulled into the parking lot this morning, and she hadn't wanted to rush out, all dewy-eyed and eager, to say hello, and he hadn't come inside. Ben and the other men were talking and laughing, their voices low, rumbling, and lighthearted. She couldn't hear their words, but Natalie knew they weren't discussing personal relationships.

Slade picked up his cell. She told him what she wanted; he said he'd bring it and grab some CDs of his own from his van. She didn't ask him why they were taking so long, and he offered no explanation. She tossed her cell phone into her bag and went back to her ladder.

"Did you get Slade?" Bella asked.

"I did. He's going to pick up my CD player, and they'll be here soon."

Natalie had carefully edged in one wall before she heard the crunch of tires on gravel: Finally Slade and Morgan were returning. She heard the van doors slam. Morgan and Slade called to the men working outside; Natalie strained her ears to hear whether Morgan was chatting with Ben, but could detect no exact words. Finally, Morgan swept in, lanky and flushed.

"Damn, it's hot! Bella, don't you have air-conditioning?" Morgan demanded.

"I do," Bella replied from the top of her ladder. "But it doesn't seem fair to use it when the guys are sweltering away outside."

"Oh, for heaven's sake," Morgan said. "They can deal."

Slade sauntered in, carrying the small portable CD player. "Here you are, Sis." He put it in the middle of the floor and hit a few buttons. Heavy metal guitars screamed.

"HEY!" Natalie yelled.

Slade hit the volume control. "Sorry." He took out the CD. "That was one of mine."

"Surprise," Natalie said.

"What do you ladies want?" Slade asked.

Morgan was looking through the discs. "Let's hear some ABBA. That should get us moving."

Natalie wanted to say, snippily, *Bella and I have been painting for an hour.* But she kept quiet.

Slade left. Bella climbed down her ladder, closed the door and windows, and turned on the air conditioner. Morgan opened her gallon of paint and set to work on her own wall. ABBA sang "Take a Chance on Me." Occasionally Natalie caught a glimpse of Ben passing a window. He'd taken off his shirt and put on a baseball cap to shade his face.

They broke for lunch around one o'clock. The women had finished the walls and were beginning the doors and baseboards. With the air-conditioning pumping into the big room, the first coat would dry soon enough for them to add a second coat after lunch.

Bella had made sandwiches, macaroni salad, potato salad, and coleslaw. Her father and brother lugged out a cooler filled with ice and soft drinks and another one filled with ice water. Natalie had brought chips, brownies, and cookies, and Morgan had added cold spicy fried chicken. The picnic table wasn't big enough for all of them, so they tossed a couple of old blankets from the trunks of their cars on the grass. Everyone was craving salt, and conversation was at a minimum as they ate and drank.

Natalie had taken her loaded paper plate to the blanket under a tree and arranged herself there as alluringly as possible, hoping Ben would join her. So far, he hadn't even looked at her. He'd gone straight for the food, sat at the table, and eaten like a starving man. She wondered if he cooked for himself. She wondered a lot of things about Ben—most of all, why he wasn't talking to her. He could at least say hello.

"This chicken is amazing, Morgan," Natalie said, watching Ben out of the corner of her eye to see if he sent any kind of glance at Morgan.

"Thanks," Morgan said. "I got the recipe off the Internet."

"I do that all the time," Bella chimed in. "It's easier and quicker than using a cookbook. But when I'm relaxing, I love to look at cookbooks."

"Me, too," Natalie agreed, and then no one else spoke.

The group seemed rather out of sorts today, Natalie thought as she ate and looked around. Morgan was not flirting with Ben or Slade; she seemed sunk in her own thoughts, and didn't look happy. Bella and Aaron weren't sitting together; they weren't even talking to each other. All the men looked tired after painting outside in this heat. It had to be in the nineties, and the humidity was killing.

Still, it was just so strange how Ben wasn't paying any attention to Natalie at all. It was as if he had amnesia. As if he hadn't kissed her. She'd never had an experience like this, so she had no idea what to do. She wasn't going to sidle up to Ben and wiggle her shoulder and give him a sexy hello. The more she thought about it, the angrier she got, and it was a relief when the group decided lunch was over. Time to get back to work.

Of them all, Bella, not surprisingly, was the most determined. "Natalie, since you've got such a steady hand, how about you start on the trim while Morgan and I give the walls a second coat?"

"Fine with me," Natalie agreed.

The smaller brush was lighter, and the trim required concentration and an unfluctuating line. She couldn't allow even one bristle to touch its drop of cream paint against the umber of the wall. Bella put on the Beatles' *Sgt. Pepper's* album; soon all three women were singing along, and Natalie's spirits rose.

At three o'clock, Bella's father came into the shop.

"That's it for today," he announced. "I've made a unilateral decision."

"The windows—" Bella began to protest.

"—can wait," Dennis decreed. "No arguing. It's just too damned hot and muggy. Anyway, we've all been working so hard, if we keep it up, we'll get sloppy, and you don't want that. I'll come over tomorrow and help you with the final bits, Bella."

"I'll come, too," Morgan added.

Natalie felt obligated to pitch in. "I'll come—"

But Bella preempted her. "No, Natalie, not you. You've got to work on the charcoal of Aaron so I can hang it in the shop."

"Well, anyway, ladies," Dennis interrupted, "let's quit for the day, okay? Go home, take a swim. Or a nap."

"Or a shower," Natalie said, grinning.

"It's looking good, don't you think?" Bella asked. "Kind of elegant?"

"It will once the plastic drop cloths are gone," her father told her as he went out the door.

The men carried in their ladders and laid them on the floor. They brought in their cans of paint and various tools and set them inside. The women tapped the lids on their cans, wiped their hands on rags, and took turns rinsing the latex paint off their brushes under the tap in the bathroom sink.

By the time Natalie came out of the building, she saw that Ben's car was gone. She drove home, saw Slade's van parked in the driveway, did not see Ben's car parked in the Barnabys' drive.

"I hate him," she said aloud to no one.

Slade was already in the guest room shower. Natalie showered in the master bedroom, put on clean shorts and tee, and immediately felt better. Looking out her window, she saw Morgan playing with Petey on their beach. Aaron and Bella were swimming out to the raft they'd moored in the lake. Dennis was lying on the chaise in the shade of a beach umbrella, the Sunday newspaper over his face. Natalie felt drowsy, too lazy to work, too grumpy to try to swim. She shut her bedroom door, sank onto her bed, and fell asleep.

"Hey."

She opened her eyes to see her brother standing there. "Hey, what?" she yawned.

"You've been snoozing forever. It's dinnertime. We're all going in to Mama's for some crazy cocktails and dinner."

Natalie scooched up in bed and stretched. "All who?"

"What am I, your social secretary? Bella, Aaron, Morgan, and Petey, I guess."

"What about Josh? And Ben?" She rubbed her face, as if trying to wake up, not wanting to let her brother catch a glimpse of anything. He could read her so well.

"Josh is still MIA. Bella phoned Ben; I don't know if he's joining us or not."

"Listen, I'll stay and take care of Petey," Natalie decided.

"Suddenly you're Mother Teresa?" Slade asked, puzzled.

"No, I'm an artist, and eccentric and sometimes reclusive. I've been with people all day and I want some time to chill." Natalie swung her feet off the bed and stood up. Outside, the sun was low in the sky, gilding the green leaves and bronzing windowpanes all over the lake. "Besides, Morgan should have a chance to enjoy herself, and Petey would be miserable at Mama's."

"You've got your period," Slade said.

"How did I deserve such a sensitive genius for a brother," Natalie shot back, knocking his shoulder as she left the room.

They clopped down the steps to the living room and then into the kitchen.

"Aren't you hungry?" Slade asked.

Natalie shrugged. "I don't know. Not really. I had a huge lunch."

Yawning, Slade said, "Well, I bet Morgan would probably love to have you take care of Petey. I know Bella suggested that she leave Petey with Felicity, but Morgan said no, Felicity had Petey all day."

Natalie slammed the refrigerator door shut. "Let's go over to Morgan's."

Morgan's front door was open. They let themselves in and wandered through the house.

Slade pointed. "There's the settee I sold her. Sharp, isn't it?"

Natalie cocked her head. "Slade, it looks *amazing* there. You really have an eye."

"Aw, shucks, ma'am," Slade said, but Natalie could tell he was pleased by her compliment.

Morgan came down the stairs. "Sorry, guys," she whispered. "I'm not going. Petey wiped himself out at the Hortons'. I just fed him and got him down to bed. He couldn't wait to fall asleep. Josh hasn't answered his phone, so I've got to stay here."

"Natalie's going to stay," Slade said.

Morgan blinked.

"I'm tired, too, Morgan," Natalie said. "I'd like nothing more than to sit here in the absolute silence with a book. And, of course, to keep an ear out in case Petey cries."

"I can't let you do that," Morgan said. "You must be hungry."

"Nope. Just tired."

"She's an *artist*," Slade said, sounding only slightly sarcastic. "She vants to be alone."

"I get that way, too," Morgan said. "Oh, Natalie, if you really want to—"

Slade's cell rang. He looked at it, clicked it on, listened, clicked it off. He said, "That was Bella. She got hold of Ben. He's coming, too."

Natalie forced a blithe smile. "I really want to stay here. Just let me run home and get a book." She hurried out the door, nearly falling down the porch steps. So now she'd arranged it that Morgan could be with Ben, and she, *Natalie*, couldn't. Oh, well, what did it matter? Ben didn't seem to notice if she was there or not.

She grabbed up the novel she was reading and one of the library's heavy art books and headed back to Morgan's. Morgan was all aflutter with excitement about going out.

"Natalie, you are the *best*!" She grabbed Natalie, hugged her, kissed her cheek. "I need tonight, I really do."

"Yeah," Slade said. "We can discuss sewage."

Morgan chuckled and gave Slade a light punch on the shoulder.

Slade and Morgan went off, both tall, lanky, and tanned, chatting away, leaning toward each other, and Slade said something as he opened the van door for Morgan, and Morgan laughed, throwing back her head so her long hair tumbled past her shoulders. *Morgan is just sexy*, Natalie thought. *She can't help herself.* Maybe Natalie ought to grow her own hair long like that. Like a damned shampoo ad.

Natalie tiptoed up the stairs and peeked into Petey's bedroom. The toddler slept in a crib. He was on his stomach, knees up, bum high in the air, wearing light summer pajamas covered with baseballs and catcher's mitts. He was sleeping soundly, his dimpled hand twitching now and then, his eyelashes curving against his cheek.

He was the most beautiful thing in the world.

She wanted to draw him, just like that.

Her paper, easel, and charcoal were of course at her house. For a moment she debated phoning Dennis to ask him to come over for just a moment while she ran home, but decided against it. Bella's father had seemed pretty whipped this afternoon. She couldn't take a picture of Petey; the flash might wake him.

She tiptoed back downstairs and into the kitchen. She spotted plenty of pens and pencils in a cup by the phone book and notepad. The notepad was too small even for a sketch. She searched around until she found where Morgan had neatly stashed the folded brown grocery bags. She fished a pair of scissors out of the utility drawer and cut the bag apart until she had a good-sized piece of paper. She grabbed a black pen and tiptoed back up the stairs.

Downstairs, a door slammed. Startled out of her own private world, Natalie jumped. Fortunately, her pen was not on the paper, so she didn't mar the drawing.

"Hello?" a man called.

In his crib, Petey shifted, turning over so that he faced the wall. Quietly, Natalie rose and crept away from his door and down the stairs.

Josh was in the kitchen, drinking water from the faucet. He was wearing khakis and a polo shirt. Not really business attire, but perhaps on a Sunday he didn't need to wear a suit into Bio-Green. When he saw Natalie, he frowned. "Natalie?"

"Hi, Josh. I'm babysitting for Morgan. She went out to eat with the rest of the painting gang."

"Painting gang?" For a moment, Josh looked puzzled. Then he remembered, and his face fell. He sagged against the sink. "Oh shit. I am in deep trouble now."

"Why is that?" Natalie was thirsty, too. She wished he'd move away from the faucet.

"I forgot about the painting party. Morgan will be pissed." He rubbed his face with his hands.

"We didn't finish," Natalie informed him helpfully. "There's still a lot of window trim to do."

Josh went to the refrigerator and took out a cold beer, then slumped in a chair at the kitchen table. "I've got to work tomorrow."

Natalie grabbed a glass and ran herself a long drink of water. "After working all day today?"

"It's a demanding job," Josh told her. "Morgan knows that. Knew it when we agreed to move here." Natalie had put the drawing on the kitchen table, and suddenly Josh noticed it. "Wow. Did you just do that?"

"I did." Natalie slid into a chair, welcoming the support of the curved back. "I peeked in on him and he was so irresistible. . . . I didn't wake him," she hastened to add.

"He's hard to wake." Josh pulled the sketch over closer to him. "This is amazing, Natalie."

"Thanks." She loved the way Josh's face softened as he studied the image of his sleeping son. Something else shadowed Josh's expression—Natalie couldn't read it. She shifted in her chair to check the clock behind his back. "I have no idea how late it is. When I'm drawing, I lose track of time."

"I know how that is," Josh murmured.

She raised an eyebrow. "Are you writing a publication presentation for Bio-Green?"

"No." Josh looked up at Natalie, and once again something flashed over his face. His green eyes sparked with a decision. "No, Natalie, I'm not. What I'm writing is a novel."

Her jaw dropped. "You're writing a *novel?*"

He slapped his forehead. "Damn. I shouldn't have told you. Please don't tell Morgan. She'll go out of her mind. I don't want to tell her until it's a done deal."

"And that could be years, right?"

Josh almost squirmed with electric energy. "Wrong. I'm deep into it. I've got an agent. He's seen the first three chapters, and he's pushing me to hurry up and finish it. He's got two different publishers interested."

"My God, Josh! That's *huge!*"

Josh lit up at her words, but attempted a modest shrug. "I wouldn't say *huge* exactly. For me, it's huge. For me, it's a dream come true. But whenever I finish, whatever advance I get for the book, it's certainly not going to compare with the kind of money Bio-Green's paying me. And that's the kind of money that makes it possible to live in a place like this. That's the kind of money that's going to pay for Petey's college education. Do you have any idea how much it costs to send a kid to college? Over fifty thousand dollars! A year!"

"Oh God, money." Natalie shook her head. "The evil necessity.

I couldn't spend a year painting here if my aunt hadn't given me her house and a stipend to keep me 'caretaking.' I don't know what I'll do when she returns from her trip around the world."

"Where did you live before?" Josh leaned back in his chair, arms crossed behind his head.

"Manhattan. For a couple of years. Boston before that. I took lessons, and I drew when I could, but I spent most of my time working as a waitress, and I lived in a shoebox with cockroaches and slutty roommates."

Josh laughed. "I've been there." His face went solemn. "It's fine, if it's just you and your work. The work is all that matters. If you have a good day, you can sleep on an old mattress in a closet and not care. But once you love someone, and especially once you have a child, the whole game changes. I couldn't let Morgan and Petey live that way."

"I see what you're saying, but, Josh, isn't there a kind of halfway spot? I mean, this place"—she spread her arms out, indicating the gleaming state-of-the-art kitchen and the modern house around them—"is a palace. Do you guys have to live in quite so much luxury?"

"It's a long story," Josh told her, then corrected himself. "Actually, it's not a long story. It's very simple. This house is part of the Bio-Green package."

"You mean they're paying for it?"

"Hell, no. I mean the CEO of Bio-Green wants me to be a living advertisement for the success of his company. Part of the deal was that I buy a house that would 'represent' Bio-Green's eminence in the scientific race."

"Ah," Natalie said. "I see." She considered this. "Tell me about your novel."

Josh tilted his head so his eyes scanned the ceiling. After a moment, he said, "I don't know. I feel kind of bad even telling you I'm working on a book." He clunked his chair back down on all four legs. "I haven't told anyone else. It's just that seeing this drawing of Petey . . . It's hard not to tell Morgan. I want to tell her, but I know it's going to freak her out."

"Why?"

Josh shrugged. "We're not in a very good place right now. She already thinks I spend too much time working. If she knew I was working for Bio-Green *and* writing a novel . . ."

The front door opened and closed. Natalie and Josh both jerked in surprise. They stared at each other guiltily. Natalie rolled up her drawing of Petey; she'd show it to Morgan another time.

"You won't mention this, right?" Josh whispered.

"Right," Natalie promised.

"Hi, Natalie." Morgan ambled into the kitchen, giving Natalie a great big smile. She stretched her arms high, swaying her head so that her long hair wafted sensually from side to side. She was a wee bit lit.

Natalie stood up. "Petey didn't wake up at all. Slept like an angel."

"He *is* an angel," Morgan cooed. Leaning forward, she kissed Natalie on the cheek. "Thanks so much for staying with him, Nat. I needed tonight. I don't know when I've had so much fun with people I *like*."

Morgan still hadn't spoken to Josh, and Natalie was aware of some hidden message in her words about people she *liked*. Time for Natalie to leave the O'Keefes alone.

"Okay, then, see you tomorrow." Natalie reached over, picked up her drawing of Petey, and headed for the door.

"I'm off to bed," Morgan purred. "I'm just exhausted. All that painting, and the heat . . . and the margaritas." She laughed and left the room, heading for the stairs.

Natalie shot Josh a funny face. "Bye."

Josh said, "Bye." He plunked his elbows on the table and buried his face in his hands. Actually, Natalie couldn't help thinking, it was an arresting image. That thick red hair going in all directions, the droop of the big, wide shoulders, so expressive of despair or at least discouragement. It was a posture every human being had taken at some time in life . . .

She forced herself to walk down the hall. By the time she was out the door, Morgan had disappeared at the top of the stairs.

18

......

Bella, Slade, Dennis, and Brady carried furniture from the Barnabys' garage and the back of the building into the front of the shop and arranged it where Bella, with Slade's help, decided. They carefully leaned ladders against the glowing walls, held Natalie's abstracts and charcoals up, waited patiently for Bella's decision, hammered in nails and picture holders, and hung the artwork.

Aaron wasn't there. He was posing for Natalie. That was what Bella wanted him to do, because she wanted to hang that charcoal drawing in Bella's, too.

In the late afternoon, Brady jumped on his bike and cycled away, legs pumping, to join his friends. Dennis kissed Bella and drove home to take a nap. Slade and Bella stood in the shop, looking around with admiration and excitement. Upon entering the opened front door, the eye fell immediately upon the long carved antique desk Bella had bought from Mr. Wheeler. Above it hung one of Natalie's abstracts. The combination of new and old was arresting. To the right, against the wall, was one of Louise's display cases, now arranged with Penny Aristides's jewelry, glittering beneath the lights. Pieces of furniture stood against two other walls, some paired with an abstract, and by themselves on a wall were two of Natalie's large charcoal drawings. Louise. And Petey. Matted in white, framed in gold, they were breathtaking.

"It looks good, doesn't it?" Bella asked Slade.

Slade grinned. "I've got a surprise for you. Stay here. No. Go in the back. Sit down at the table and stay there until I call you."

"Oh, Slade . . ."

"Trust me?"

She had to laugh. "Okay." She went into the back.

Actually, it was a relief to sit at the table. Her back ached from hefting furniture and paintings. She yawned. She heard shuffling noises in the front room, and odd thumps she couldn't figure out.

"You can come in now," Slade called.

When she entered the large room, she saw at once what Slade had done. The pine floor was now covered with several thick Persian carpets, their deep hues and exotic patterns truly magical.

"I brought them from Boston," Slade explained. "A friend of mine's a dealer. Art Hannoush. I said I wanted to try them on commission. I mean, I think *you* should try them on commission."

"They're magnificent," Bella breathed, kneeling to run her hand over the silky pelt.

"I think they add something to the shop," Slade said. "They complete it."

"You're right. Brilliant, Slade. But you'll have to help me with the pricing and the commission."

"You got it." Slade bent down to comb out the fringe of a rug with his fingers. "So are these where you'd like them? The positioning okay?"

Bella went outside and walked through the door, trying to see the room with a fresh eye. "Perfect," she decided.

"When's the grand opening?" Slade asked.

"This Saturday. I've got an ad in the paper, and Dad's friend is coming out to take some photos and do a write-up."

"Cool." Slade studied the room. "You know, don't you, that it takes about three years for a new business to show a profit?"

"Now you tell me," Bella joked. "Of course I know. And I know expensive inventory like this doesn't move fast. Still, oh, Slade, I'm so excited! Saturday evening, I'm having a champagne celebration here, and Penny Aristides will bring her husband and her gang, and Morgan's promised to bring Josh's boss and his wife, and they have money out the ying yang, and maybe they'll bring friends. Of course, Dad and Mom have invited a lot of their friends—and you'll come, won't you, Slade? I know it's a drag, driving back and forth from Boston, but it would mean so much to me if you'll come."

"Would it?" Slade asked. He was standing just three or four feet away from her, but his look was so intense, it was as if he were touching her.

"Would it what?" Bella's mouth went dry.

"Would it 'mean so much' if I came?"

"Well, of course." She answered immediately, and she could hear the cheerful, good-hearted *friendliness* in her voice, the spontaneous tone she'd use with anyone. She saw the light change in Slade's dark blue eyes; she saw his mouth turn down scornfully.

She stepped toward him, reached out, put one hand on his arm. "Slade. That was thoughtless of me. You know I never could have gotten to this place without your help. I can never thank you—"

He jerked his arm away. "I don't need and I certainly don't want your indebtedness."

"That's not what I meant!" she protested.

Slade strode around her to the door.

"Stop it, Slade!" Bella ordered. "Just *stop it*. Wait! Give me a chance to get my thoughts together, will you?"

Slade stopped. Turned. Looked straight at Bella. His eyes met hers. He said, "Okay. How long do you want me to wait?"

Bella's voice trembled. "Slade, you're a playboy. Natalie told us about you. You don't want to settle down. It's not your style." He didn't respond, but continued to keep his gaze focused on her. She swallowed. "Whatever I feel for you . . ." Oh God, this was hard! Never before had she been the first to declare her feelings. Not with Aaron, not with her early boyfriends. As she spoke, she realized she was admitting, aloud, in words that could not be erased, the truth. "Slade, I do feel something for you. It isn't simply lust, although of course lust is there in the mix." She knew she was blushing fiercely. "But, Slade, I don't know you. I can't trust you. You're like—like a falling star. So brilliant, but moving away while I watch."

Slade's voice was low. "Bella. You know me." He seemed completely open, honest, and vulnerable. "For you, I could stop. I could stay."

His words paralyzed her. She whispered, "Slade—"

"Oh, good! You're here!" Shauna Webb strode through the open door, her arms full of Bubble-Wrapped porcelain. She didn't seem to notice Slade leaning against the door, or the tears in Bella's eyes. "God, these are heavy, but I wanted to show you as many as possible, and I didn't want to package them up in boxes—that takes forever. Where can I put them? Oh, I'll just set them on this table." She leaned over the barley twist leg table and gently laid down her burdens.

Slade crossed the few steps to Bella. He touched her cheek with the palm of his hand.

"It's okay," he whispered. "We've got time, Bella."

Bella thought she'd faint from wanting to wrap herself around him. At the same time, a neon sign flashed *Danger* through her mind—and she didn't know if that made her want to run toward Slade or away.

"So I thought when I saw the abstracts," Shauna was babbling on, "this would be the perfect place for my new sculptures. Because they really are selling in Northampton, but I need more than one venue, and this will be perfect." Carefully, she peeled away the Bubble Wrap, exposing a rounded white *something*. She lifted it up and set it on top of the antique desk. "What do you think?"

Bella and Slade approached it, bent down, and peered at it. It was shaped rather like a very large . . .

"Shauna," Bella asked. "Is that a *butt?*"

"Yes, isn't it clever?" Shauna was unwrapping another piece. Lifting it away from the Bubble Wrap, she carried it to the display counter and delicately placed it there.

It was a giant, anatomically correct foot, the toes lying just inside a large mouth.

It was the ugliest thing Bella had ever seen. But Slade burst out laughing.

"That's pretty funny, Shauna."

"I know, right?" Shauna was a chubby woman, cool in a loose

muumuu with a fish pattern. Her dark hair stuck up in ringlets all over her head. "Gosh!" she said, her attention caught by what lay inside the display case. "Look at these earrings! They're fantastic! Bella, how much are they?"

"Penny Aristides made them." Bella came to stand next to her at the counter. "We're not going to sell them until the grand opening this Saturday."

"Oh, damn, so you won't show them to me now?"

Slade slid behind the counter. "Of course we'll show them to you, but you'll have to come to the grand opening to buy them." He opened the case and took out the velvet tray of earrings. "Are these the ones you like? They're twelve hundred dollars."

Shauna gulped. "Don't I get a discount as someone with work on commission with you?"

Bella stepped in. "We'll think about it, Shauna. I'm not even sure your pieces are right for this shop."

"Look at the bum from here," Slade told Bella.

She turned. The white object gleamed as if lit from within. It curved and swooped and hinted at crevices and clefts.

"I don't call it *Bum*," Shauna corrected Slade sniffily. "Its title is *Home*."

"You're showing in Northampton?" Bella asked thoughtfully.

"Yes. At Warner's. He's sold a pair of hands of mine for a thousand dollars. The collection is called 'I Sing the Body Electric.' " She walked back to the table to unwrap the final piece. "This piece is called *Clever*."

Bella and Slade took turns examining the object, which was a knee in all its articulate complexity. The femur, tibia, and patella were clear, and the knee could be bent slightly and restraightened.

"That was a bastard to create," Shauna said. "It's a genius design."

Slade said, "Bella, I think you should try these three pieces at the opening. See how people react to them."

"Hey, they'll love them!" Shauna declared.

"Maybe," Bella mused. "They *are* unusual, Shauna."

Shauna narrowed her eyes.

"But I agree with Slade," Bella continued smoothly. "I'd like to exhibit them this Saturday. Let me get some paperwork on them."

Bella went to her desk in the back room and found her folder with the legal contracts for commissions. She brought it to the showroom, took out the relevant papers, and had Shauna read them. For Shauna and Natalie, Bella would take a forty percent commission on each piece. The furniture she was free to price as she wished, and as Slade advised. Shauna was older, and had never been a close friend; she had an established reputation in the area and had had her work praised in the *Boston Globe*. Bella realized with a jolt that during this transaction all her emotions and lust had smoothed themselves down, like feathers effortlessly, naturally, gathering themselves into tranquillity. Odd.

Shauna energetically signed, gathered up her papers and her Bubble Wrap, and left. "See you Saturday night!" she called from the door. "Don't sell those earrings before I get here or you're in big trouble!"

"She's a bit of a character," Slade said softly as they listened to Shauna's car pull away.

"Yes, and her artwork is bizarre," Bella replied.

"But kind of fascinating."

Bella was standing on one side of the glass display case with the folder of papers in her hand. Slade was on the other side, holding the porcelain knee. Bella looked up at him.

"I'll, uh, just put these papers back in the desk," she told Slade.

"I'll put the knee over on the cabinet," Slade said. His voice had thickened.

Bella's pulse picked up as she returned to the back room and settled the folder in its spot again. *What was she about to do?* Whatever it was, wherever it took her, she knew she had never wanted anything so much in her life.

She smoothed her hair. Licked her lips. A slight trembling was overtaking her.

She returned to the front of the store. Slade was across the room, just standing there, waiting for her.

Tires crunched on gravel. Bella froze. A door slammed.

Aaron walked into the shop. He wore khakis and a white button-down shirt and a red tie and an enormous smile. "Bella! I got it! I got the job!"

"Oh, Aaron!" Her response was genuine. "Congratulations!"

Aaron had never looked happier, healthier, stronger, or more impressive. In two steps he crossed the room, grabbed Bella up, and swung her around in his arms. Head thrown back, he laughed, and Bella laughed with him. Whatever came next in her life, she knew that, first of all, she wanted Aaron to have this moment fully, this jubilation.

"They chose me! Over twenty-three candidates, they chose me! Seven of them were from San Francisco! And they chose *me*!" He gave Bella a long, hard kiss.

"Aaron," Bella gasped. "I can't breathe!"

Laughing, he released his embrace and set her on her feet. At the same moment, he noticed Slade over at the back of the shop, lounging against the wall, all black, thin, and somber. For just a fraction of a moment, Bella felt a chill when she saw the deadness in Slade's eyes. The blankness. As if a light had gone off. Then Slade came to life, smiled, walked across the room with his hand extended.

"Congratulations, Aaron."

"Thanks, Slade." The two men shook hands. "I've got to say I'm excited. Well, obviously." Aaron looked around the room. "Hey, Bella, it looks great in here. I can't believe it's the same place that used to be your mother's store."

"I know," Bella agreed. "Slade helped so much. He knows everything about furniture, and if he hadn't recognized some of the family pieces as valuable antiques, the store probably wouldn't exist. Certainly not as it is now. But this furniture changes everything." She sensed she was babbling. She felt as if she were treading water between two powerful currents, both forces rushing at her, sweeping off in opposite directions while she struggled to remain in place. "Slade brought in these carpets, Aaron. Aren't they gorgeous?"

Aaron looked. He walked from one to another, to another, and bent down to brush his hand across the silky nap. "They are. Such intricate patterns. And amazingly soft." Standing up, he announced,

"I'm feeling like buying a bottle of really expensive champagne! Shall I get it and some glasses and bring it back here?"

The pause, the moment of held breath among the three of them, was probably less than a second, but it seemed to ring like a clarion in the room before Slade broke the silence.

"Thanks for the offer, Aaron, but I've got to go. Congratulations again." He strode across the room and out the door. A moment later, the van roared away.

Aaron turned to Bella. "Want to share some champagne with me?"

"Absolutely. Just let me lock up the shop."

"Hey, Bella," Aaron called. "I have an idea. Let's bring the champagne to your parents' house. Then I'll take everyone out to dinner. Your parents have been so good to me these past few months, and, oh, I don't know, I feel like a party."

Bella burst into tears.

"Hey," Aaron said. Gently, he put his hands on her shoulders, studying her face. "Why the tears?"

"You're just so *thoughtful*, Aaron." Bella wept.

"And that's a bad thing?"

"No, it's a good thing. I guess I'm just so happy for you. I'm so proud of you. I know this is absolutely a huge achievement, Aaron." She wiped her eyes. "It makes me want to, oh, I don't know, set off fireworks in your honor."

He grinned. "We'll set off fireworks. Later."

19

.....

For the fifth time in as many seconds, Morgan checked the clock on their bedside table.

"If Josh isn't here in five minutes, I'm divorcing him," she said through clenched teeth to the empty bedroom.

Downstairs, Felicity was feeding Petey his dinner. She would take care of him tonight while the O'Keefes attended the opening of Bella's.

At least Morgan would attend the opening.

She ran her eyes over her reflection in the mirror. Good. She looked good. She'd gone shopping with Natalie and Bella yesterday, all of them trolling for the perfect dress, and the other two women had convinced Morgan to purchase something more daring and edgy than she'd ever consider by herself. The dress was pale beige, tight fitting, with a straight-across bateau neckline in front and a plunging back crisscrossed with straps. Morgan's skin was tanned to almost the exact shade of the silk, so in certain lights she appeared nude. She wore the sensational diamond studs Josh had given her when he signed with Bio-Green, and no other jewelry. She wore her lowest high-heeled sandals because tonight she didn't want to tower over Bella, who was going to wear new four-inch heels and still would be shorter than Morgan, and tonight, really, was Bella's night.

Still, Morgan looked fabulous. All she needed was a husband who would occasionally cast a glance her way. They'd been fighting so much about his not being home that they'd driven themselves into a rut; every time Morgan opened her mouth to say anything, Josh looked wary, guilty, defensive. And he always looked so tired.

He was going to look *dead* if he didn't make it home in time for Bella's opening!

The front door slammed. Footsteps thundered up the stairs. Josh burst into the room, undoing his tie as he ran.

"I'm here. I just need to shower and I'm ready." He began ripping off his clothing, dropping his pants, jacket, shirt, and boxers on the floor. "Is Bella's air-conditioned?" he yelled from the bathroom.

"It is," she told him.

The shower drowned out anything else he said. He was quick, soon striding back into the room, a towel wrapped around his waist, when Petey came toddling eagerly in, Felicity behind him.

"Daddy! Daddy! Daddy!" The little boy threw himself at Josh, who grabbed him up and kissed tickles into his tummy.

"Um, I'll just wait in Petey's room." Felicity scurried away, closing the door behind her.

Morgan glanced at the clock again. Okay, they'd be late, but she couldn't begrudge her son these precious moments with his father, who seldom got home before Petey went to sleep for the night. Josh fell on the bed, lifting his son up high, lowering him to kiss his belly, and Petey giggled, squirmed, and chortled in an ecstasy of happiness. Josh's towel fell away from him, exposing his long, strong body in all its glory. Damn. Would she ever stop being attracted to the man? Why would she want to? She just wanted him to be equally attracted to her. Didn't he ever think, *The hell with this project, I'm going to go home and seduce my wife?*

Josh saw her looking. His smile turned mischievous. "I'll tickle your tummy later."

Oh, Josh! It all flooded back. Morgan grinned. "I hope so." She swept Petey up in her arms. "Enough excitement, big guy. You need to settle down for your bedtime story with Felicity. And Daddy needs to get dressed. We've got a gala evening ahead."

She carried Petey into his own bedroom, where Felicity awaited on the floor, building a tower with blocks. She was both familiar and enough of a novelty for Petey to want to be with her, and he immediately switched his attention to his babysitter. Morgan kissed his cheek, but he wasn't interested in his mother right now.

Back in their bedroom, she watched Josh slipping on a black silk tee shirt and his Armani suit. "The Ruoffs are coming. Definitely," he told Morgan. He ran a brush through his wet red hair. "Should I take time to shave again?"

She ran her palm along the bristles on his jawline. "You look sexy as hell like this. And I promised Bella we wouldn't be late."

"Great, then, let's go." Josh bounded out of the room and down the stairs.

"Thank you," Morgan said to the empty room. "I'm glad you like the dress."

She hadn't slept at all last night. She hadn't slept well for a week. At three or four in the morning, roaming Aunt Eleanor's darkened house, Natalie would sink to her knees, overcome with a terror she could never expose to any person who knew her.

In New York, when she worked on abstract painting with Archibald Mackintosh, a huge sandy-haired Scot with a captivating accent and a tendency to roar, Natalie had thought she might have talent simply because Mackintosh was so very picky about which students he'd admit. He'd admitted her; therefore, she showed promise.

Natalie had liked the freedom of abstract painting—the swoop of the brush, the impulsive splat and dot, the fun of it, the play, the color, the movement. It opened her up to new insights into her own art, whatever that would turn out to be. It was childish for her, like finger painting, playing in the sand on the beach, like dancing with her shadow.

Yet for her it was superficial. It was not work; it did not call up from her depths the kind of determined involvement, the soul-baring struggle, the exertion, the reach, and the gloating *Yes!* of her still lifes. Because she'd paid good money for the course, she did not let herself drop out.

Quickly, Natalie became friends with some of the other painters. They got together after every class in a local coffee shop or bar, depending on their moods. Everyone criticized Archie—he was manic-depressive, irrational, inconsistent in his instruction and his criticism. He exaggerated terribly, he raged and tore up their work, he wept and begged their pardon, he fell on his knees in front of a painting that pleased him. He was nuts. He was brilliant. He was amazing. He was someone important to know.

At the end of the first year, Archie actually admired one of her canvases. He praised her. She felt the other students watching enviously. She signed up for his next class.

Larry Somerkind was in the abstract class, too, and after a while, in an, well, *abstracted* sort of way, Natalie and Larry started dating. Like Natalie, Larry had a day job to support his art habit. Both were so busy with work and classes, snatching any spare moments for painting, that a relationship didn't really interest either of them, although they did become friends and, briefly, lovers.

That had more to do with Natalie's imagination than with Larry or lust. When Natalie first attended art school in Boston in her early twenties, she and a group of other students had become enchanted by the Pre-Raphaelite brotherhood of painters in England: Dante Gabriel Rossetti, Holman Hunt, Millais, and their women models— especially Lizzie Siddal. Siddal painted also, becoming briefly famous before her tragic death. Natalie had idolized Rossetti and Siddal. Romanticizing love with an artist, in New York for the first time, Natalie had met a man who she thought had real artistic and romantic potential.

She spent Christmas with Larry, and New Year's Eve. They critiqued each other's work, they gossiped about the other artists, they were good friends. Natalie had never imagined a man caring much about her; her father certainly hadn't. So she was satisfied with Larry's lukewarm affection, and he seemed to be with hers.

Then came the exhibition organized by Archibald Mackintosh. It was held in a gallery on Second Avenue, and the work of only five of Mackintosh's students had been chosen to be shown along with the works of students from other teachers. The exhibition dazzled with champagne, canapés, chic art lovers, and critics from other art schools and Manhattan newspapers. Natalie wore her highest heels; Larry, who wore glasses and a plaid muffler around his neck no matter the weather, accompanied her, because his painting had been chosen for the exhibit as well as Natalie's.

Natalie's painting sold. Larry's did not.

Of course, they had discussed this possibility before, both of them claiming with humble insistence that their own particular piece wouldn't sell, that his, or hers, certainly would, and no matter what, they understood that someone else's reaction to a piece of art was a purely personal emotion that would not make a bit of difference to their relationship.

Yet, when it happened, when the lights went out and the gallery door was locked and Natalie and Larry went with other artists to a pub to celebrate, Larry was so obviously miserable that he couldn't wholeheartedly congratulate Natalie. And she was so sensitive to his hurt feelings that she couldn't celebrate as flamboyantly as she wished.

Then Aunt Eleanor's offer came. Buoyed with the knowledge of the sale, Natalie was willing to risk leaving the New York art scene and move to the country. By then it was obvious that she and Larry were not going to become a true couple. He raised no objection when she mentioned moving to the country. He didn't suggest coming with her. She guessed that in his deepest heart, he was glad she was going.

Now here she was, the afternoon before the opening of Bella's, and Natalie was hit with a panic attack like she'd never experienced before, not even in New York.

She was accustomed to these fits of fear before a show. She had always had a mini–nervous breakdown before any formalized exhibition of her work, but this time it was different. This time, for some reason, it seemed *real*.

Because this time, she had put her heart and soul into her work. Because with the three charcoal drawings, of Petey, Louise, and Aaron, she had truly surrendered, in a way she'd never dreamed of, to whatever mysterious flame burned within her, flaring through her to reach out to the world. Of course her friends thought the pieces were good. They were her *friends*. But was her work genuinely good?

She wasn't certain she could allow herself to trust her instincts. She'd been so absolutely sure that Ben Barnaby had been attracted to her that summer day in the boat when he took her to his private cove tucked behind the willow tree. It was the same kind of natural belief arising from the depths of her cynical heart that made her draw those lines of charcoal on a piece of paper. It was the knowledge, immediate, definite, undeniable: *This was hers*.

And yet, "I'll call," Ben had said. He hadn't called.

She hated herself for equating her emotions, her physical response to a man, with her judgment of her own creative work. This was wrong; she knew it. She just couldn't help it. Everything seemed to be off. The universe had tilted. Ben had never called, so Natalie couldn't trust that when she walked into Bella's this evening, she wouldn't find people laughing at her work.

Still, she reminded herself, tonight was not just about Natalie. It was about Bella. It was the opening of her shop, Bella's own creation. Natalie had to go there to support her, and she was going to look as fabulous as she could, and certainly Ben would be there, and perhaps another, strange man would be there, and Natalie could flirt with him in front of Ben. . . .

Natalie stood wrapped in a towel in her bathroom. It was almost time to go.

"You are an idiot," she said to her reflection.

The phone rang.

It was Ben. "Natalie, I thought you might like me to drive you to the opening."

Natalie actually looked at the phone in her hand. She looked at her shocked face in the mirror. Were her thoughts transmitting themselves without her control? She collapsed on her bed. "Are you kidding me?"

"Why would I kid you?"

"Um, because you said you'd phone and you didn't." Pressure pushed against Natalie's rib cage, against her throat, beneath her eyes. "So how would I know you'd actually show up to drive me to the opening?"

"Damn, Natalie, I'm sorry. I was going to call you—"

"Oh, please. I have *so* heard this all before!"

"No, wait, you haven't! Listen, there was a conference at the university."

"I know. Dr. Macharacha. Morgan told me."

"Dr. Takamachi. I had to present a paper. I had to get it ready. When I'm working, I go mentally underground. I don't remember to eat or see other people—ask my parents, ask Bella! It's like something's wrong with me. Like some of my systems shut down. But, Natalie— Jesus, why am I talking to you on the phone? I'm next door. I'm coming over."

"No, Ben, don't." There she was in the mirror, excited by the sound of this man's voice and angry at him and hopeful but also determined not to let tonight of all nights be about whether or not some guy wanted to get in her pants. "Ben, I want to drive myself in."

After a long silence, Ben said, "So you're really mad at me?"

"No, Ben, this has nothing to do with you. It's just about me, about how I feel right this minute."

"Are you nervous?" Ben asked. "I'll bet you are. Before I give one of my papers, I almost throw up. It's not just stage fright. Lots of people have fear of public speaking, but it's not that for me. It's shyness, sure, but it's also excitement because I'm revealing what could become an important scientific breakthrough."

Natalie laughed. "It must be what striptease artists feel before they go onstage."

"Yeah," Ben agreed. "That's it exactly. Months of lab work, charts, and statistics to prove a point. Exposure of my intellectual abilities." He paused again, then confessed, "I'm good with science, but not so great with people."

"You had lunch with Morgan," she interrupted.

"What? No, I didn't. I have no idea— Oh. I did see her and Petey on the campus one day during the conference when Dr. Takamachi and I were taking a walk. Why would I have lunch with

Morgan? She's all about hazmat stuff. I'm all about chemical engineering. Dr. Takamachi and I were discussing biofuels. I'm not good at small talk." Another pause. "If I spend time with anyone, I want to spend it with you."

She caught the ring of honesty in his voice. She smiled at the realization that he was just next door, probably in the kitchen, perhaps the living room, bent over his cell phone because any moment Brady might come stampeding in.

"Natalie?" he asked.

"I'd like that," she told him. "I'd like to get to know you."

"So, then, can I drive you to Bella's opening?" His voice was eager.

"I think this is something I have to do on my own this time," Natalie told him gently. "But I'll see you there. Soon."

20

Saturday night, Bella wore a tight black dress and black four-inch high heels. She'd let her hair grow so it was long enough for the hairdresser to sleek into a little knot at the back of her head. She wore dark eyeliner and red lipstick, and she'd practiced holding her head high and standing quietly. Her parents said she looked like Grace Kelly. Well, Bella thought, maybe a *short* Grace Kelly.

She gave herself a lecture during her shower, reminding herself not to be eager and sweet. Especially not sweet. She was smart, she had an eye, and she was savvy. The art critic of the *Hartford Courant* was coming to her opening, and a reporter from the *Daily Hampshire Gazette*. Morgan said Josh's boss and his wife, Ronald and Eva Ruoff, were coming, and they were trendsetters. Of course, her parents and their friends were all coming, which alone ought to fill the room.

Earlier in the day, her father and Ben and Aaron had set up a table inside Bella's, then covered it with one of her mother's best white tablecloths and all the washed and shined wineglasses from the Barnaby, O'Keefe, and Reynolds' houses. Bella had planned to rent glassware—she didn't want to use plastic, even though it would make cleaning up easier—but Natalie had nixed that idea, pointing out that her aunt Eleanor had enough goblets and flutes and glasses for a party of hundreds. Bella's father and Brady had bought two new plastic tubs from the hardware store, rinsed them out, and filled them with ice. The refrigerator at the back was stocked with white wine and champagne, and the red wine was already on the table.

Louise had been occupied in her kitchen all day, making canapés—dripless, she laughingly agreed with Morgan—to put out on silver platters. She and Dennis drove over early to set up the food table before the crowd arrived.

Bella prayed there would be a crowd.

At a quarter till six, Aaron knocked on the front door.

"Wow," he said when he saw Bella.

"Wow back," she told him.

Aaron wore a navy blazer, white shirt, yellow tie. His dark curly hair had been combed into submission, and he was freshly shaved. He was a hunk, and tonight he also looked distinguished. The night they'd gone out to celebrate his job offer, he'd been boyish, expansive, and slaphappy, but tonight Bella knew she was seeing the man who had walked into a prestigious architectural firm on the other side of the continent and comported himself with such distinction he was chosen from all other applicants.

"Ready?" Aaron asked.

"Ready," Bella said. Tonight she was a woman who had created a shop full of magnificent treasures.

Aaron parked at the far end of the parking lot so there would be room for all the guests' cars. He took Bella's arm as she navigated across the pebble drive in her high heels.

Bella stopped in the doorway and looked around the room. Without display cases in the middle, the space looked larger than it had as Barnaby's Barn. On one hand, she thought with a pinch of worry, perhaps she didn't have enough inventory. On the other hand, in order to see the artwork, people had to be able to stand back and have an unobstructed view. Earlier in the day, her parents, Aaron, the O'Keefes, and Natalie had had flowers delivered. They were set around the room on the various pieces of antique furniture.

"It's wonderful, Bella," Aaron said.

"Thanks." She chewed her lip and looked back out at the parking lot. No cars were turning in.

Aaron read her mind. "It's one minute till six. Let's have some wine."

Bella nodded, and they walked over to the table where Louise and Dennis waited as the evening's bartenders.

"Madam, what will you have?" her father asked formally, a twinkle in his eye.

At five after six, the O'Keefes arrived, and a few minutes later, Natalie stalked in all by herself. They gathered together at the table, animated and laughing too much at nothing—nervous, hopeful.

At ten after six, Bella's older sister, Beatrice, arrived alone. Taller than Bella, she was curvaceous and still moved with the confidence of head cheerleader. She hugged and kissed Bella, then rubbed the lipstick off her cheek where she'd kissed her. "Jeremy couldn't come. The babysitter canceled at the last minute, but that's okay—you know he'd be bored stiff in this place. You look fabulous, Bella. I can't believe you're my baby sister."

"Maybe not so much a baby anymore?" Bella responded.

"Honey, you'll always be my baby sister." Beatrice sauntered off, sure of herself, over to greet her parents and get a drink.

Bella took a moment to interpret her sister's remark. She knew Beat loved her, but she also wondered whether Beat was a bit jealous of what Bella had achieved: this exquisite room. Bella had usually been the jealous one. She *was* the younger sister. She did want a home, loving husband, and children. But obviously Bella wanted something more—something different. For here she was. Even if it was only for one night, she had created *Bella's*.

At a quarter after six, Ben entered. He kissed Bella's cheek. "Break a leg."

"Thanks," Bella said. "But Mom's already done that for me."

At six-twenty, Penny Aristides and her husband arrived, and a few minutes later Shauna Webb and her partner came in.

It looked more festive now, Bella thought, as people carried their wine around the room, studying the pieces.

At six-thirty, *finally*, came a rush of people. They were all friends of Bella's parents, or her friends from high school, but they exclaimed loudly over the shop, the art, the rugs, and transformed the evening into a party.

Then! Two women entered whom Bella had never seen before. Both were coiffed so simply the cuts had to be expensive. They wore Lilly Pulitzer dresses. Were these Bella's first real customers?

Morgan poked her in the back. "Go."

Bella gulped. She approached the women. "Hello. I'm Bella Barnaby. I'm so glad you came. Would you like some wine?"

"We'll just wander," the woman said, and her eyes were all over the walls, taking everything in.

Another couple came in, a man and woman Bella didn't know, and then another.

And another.

Bella stayed near the door, greeting people. Soon she had to raise her voice slightly to be heard over the chatter and laughter of the crowd. Time blurred. At one point, Josh quickly crossed the room to join her.

"Bella, I'd like you to meet Ronald and Eva Ruoff."

Eva Ruoff was almost frighteningly perfect, with a lifted, Botoxed face and a tight dress displaying a sculpted body. Her smile was taut and looked painful. She extended a limp hand to shake Bella's. The rings on Eva's hands bit into Bella's palm.

"Pleasure," Eva said succinctly, then turned, scanning the room. "Hmm. You've got abstracts like the one the O'Keefes have in their house."

"Yes," Josh said. "Let me introduce you to the artist." Smoothly, he led the Ruoffs over to talk to Natalie.

Bella turned to greet more people. The Gilberts, Hoffenbys, and Watsons, all friends of her parents, showed up in a cluster, made a fuss over Bella, then strolled around the room. Madeline Gilbert chirped, "Oh, there's Eva Ruoff. She's new to the area, she's volunteered for the museum. She's got such exquisite taste." She hurried over to chat with Eva.

Around seven, the flow ceased. Bella was grateful, because it gave her a chance to wander around and talk with her guests, but beneath the relief was a thin layer of terror: *What if nothing sold?*

Keeping a bright smile on her face, she ambled around the room until she came to the first two women who'd appeared. They were standing in front of Natalie's charcoal of Aaron. They were giggling.

"Twenty thousand is a bit much," one woman said.

The other said, "I'm divorced, I'm fifty-five, I'm a professor of art history, I have nudes all over my house. Really, Dorie, you shouldn't imply that I'd buy it simply because the man is gorgeous."

Bella held her breath.

"It *is* rather brilliant," the first woman said. "This line here . . . this sweep. The curve, the sense of power . . ."

Should she introduce them to Aaron? Should she say something or keep quiet? Bella hadn't thought this through. With her mother's inventory, it hadn't mattered so very much; Louise's offerings had been inexpensive, easy to discuss.

Decisively, the woman announced, "I'm going to get it. Where's the owner?"

Bella thought she would giggle deliriously. Instead, she heard herself say silkily, "I'm right here, actually. I'm so glad you like it. The artist studied in New York. She's here tonight. Would you like to meet her?"

She led the two women over to meet Natalie. As they conversed, the art history professor effortlessly slipped her credit card to Bella. Natalie charmed the two women while Bella took care of the business side, and it was with a thrill that ran from her scalp to the soles of her feet that she placed a red dot for *Sold* on the label next to the drawing of Aaron.

Almost at once, Eva Ruoff was at her side. "I want that one." She pointed to one of Natalie's abstracts.

"Oh, lovely," Bella said. "Have you met Natalie Reynolds? She's the artist. She studied at the Art Students League in New York."

"Yes, Morgan told us about her. Up-and-coming, isn't she?"

At that moment, the reporter and photographer from the *Hartford Courant* appeared. Eva Ruoff went nearly neon with delight at having her photo taken next to the painting she'd just bought.

As Bella answered the reporter's questions, she noticed, almost accidentally, that while she was working, Slade had arrived. He wore, as usual, all black, and he looked sleek, glamorous, and surly. It was an excellent look for him. He was behind the display counter, taking out a velvet tray to show a customer Penny Aristides's jewelry.

"Oh, Slade, thank you," Bella whispered to herself. The crowd parted, and she saw Aaron—he and Morgan were chatting as they walked around the room together, subtly removing empty glasses and wadded napkins from the surface of various antiques. Her father was out in the crowd now, talking with friends, and Ben had gone behind the counter to take over the bartending. "Oh, my friends!" Bella murmured. How did anyone do this alone?

The reporter and photographer cruised the room, took more pictures, and left. Bella concluded the sale of the abstract to Eva Ruoff. She found a moment to say hello to Slade, who was still behind the counter, showing someone else jewelry, and then Morgan tapped her shoulder.

"Bella? I'd like you to meet a friend of mine."

Bella turned. The woman before her was as short as Bella would be if she weren't wearing her high heels, and she was nearly as wide as she was tall. She seemed to be wearing a shirtwaist dress from the 1950s, complete with pearls and a rhinestone brooch shaped in a starburst. Her hair was white, her eyes brown, her expression grandmotherly. A nice little old lady.

"This is Bella, Mrs. Smith," Morgan told the woman.

Mrs. Smith held out her hand. "Charmed, darling. You've got quite a nice gallery here. Very interesting taste."

"Thank you," Bella replied.

"Some of the furniture brings me back to my childhood," Mrs. Smith continued. "Well, staying with my grandparents, the appointments in their homes. As a very young girl, I used to hide beneath a table rather like that drop-leaf, pretending I was in a cave."

"Oh, I know. I used to do that sort of thing, too," Bella confided.

"But it's the gargoyle cabinet that really takes me back. I haven't seen one of those in years. And all the stained glass in the top doors looks original. Is it?"

"Oh yes," Bella informed her. "I know that personally."

"Well, in that case, how can I not take it? Fifteen thousand doesn't seem out of line at all. I looked all over at the Winter Antiques Show in New York this spring and didn't find anything nearly close."

Bella just stared.

"Bella?" Morgan prompted.

"Oh my goodness," Bella sputtered. It was only now that she realized she had never expected this particular piece of furniture to sell. It was huge, ungainly, odd, hard to dust, and it was topped with a hideous gargoyle. Her old friend. The mythic monster she'd thought her own children would wonder at and gradually learn to love. But she had been the one to type out the label, name the price, describe the piece and the provenance, and affix the label to the wall.

A crowd had gathered around them, watching as Mrs. Smith opened the middle drawer. It slid out smoothly. She bent down to open the bottom doors and peer inside at the glossy, recently polished wooden shelves.

"Yes, I know exactly where I want to put this," Mrs. Smith murmured to herself.

Slade appeared at Bella's side, deftly slipping her the sales clipboard.

Eva and Ronald Ruoff joined the crowd.

"Morgan," Eva prodded sotto voce, "why don't you introduce us to your friend?"

Morgan nodded agreement, but waited until Mrs. Smith had finished her inspection of the cabinet.

"Will you take a check?" Mrs. Smith asked Bella.

Bella's mouth went dry. "A check for fifteen thousand dollars?" Mrs. Smith's starburst brooch was not, Bella swiftly realized, costume jewelry.

"You can let it clear the bank before you deliver it," Mrs. Smith informed her.

"Yes, of course," Bella said.

The moment Mrs. Smith handed Bella the check, Eva moved in. "I'm Eva Ruoff. I'm a dear friend of Morgan's."

"Yes," Morgan agreed, and with what she hoped was an elegant gesture, indicated her husband's boss, "and this is Ronald Ruoff, Eva's husband."

"You're new to the area," Mrs. Smith observed. "You're that new business outside Amherst."

"Bio-Green," Ronald said with a courtly dip of his head.

"Chemicals," Mrs. Smith qualified.

"Chemicals," Ronald agreed, preparing to launch into his saving-the-world speech.

"I like chemicals," Mrs. Smith told them. "I like to invest in new companies. I need to sit down. Find me a place to sit and then tell me all about Bio-Green."

Smoothly, Slade announced, "I'll bring two chairs from the back and put them in the corner."

Bella remained for a moment standing in front of the gargoyle cabinet, just slightly paralyzed.

Morgan whispered in her ear, "Buck up, chum. Lots more going on tonight."

Bella nodded. "Thanks, Morgan." She fastened the blessed check into the clipboard, filled out a sales receipt, and handed it to the buyer. Josh escorted Mrs. Smith to the chairs. Beatrice wandered past, her long multicolored peasant skirt and white tank top showing off her abundant hourglass figure. She wore flip-flops, no jewelry. Anyone else would look out of place, but Beat's long, wavy curls and her carriage, at once erect and careless, gave her a movie star aura. If Gypsies could be blond, Beatrice would be a Gypsy queen.

"Your sister looks like one of the models for the Pre-Raphaelites," Natalie whispered to Bella.

She watched her sister head for the drinks table to kiss her father and mother and chat with them. She watched as Slade's eyes zeroed in on Beatrice, slowly taking in the charms of this flip-flop princess, her lazy, ripe curves and sensual movements. She didn't blame Slade. Beat was a marvel to watch.

Beat strolled around the gallery; she spent the most time staring at the charcoals of Louise and the one of Petey.

Sliding up to Bella, she whispered, "Aren't you the clever one."

Bella frowned. "Am I?"

Beat gestured vaguely around the shop. "You've pulled together a world, Bella. Would you call it an *ambience*? I don't really know. I just never realized you had all this"—Beat held out her hands—"in you."

"I never knew either, until now," Bella confessed, warmed by her sister's praise. She wanted to hear more, but Beat gasped.

"Who in sweet heaven is *that*?"

Bella hardly had to glance his way to know whom Beat was gawking at. "Slade Reynolds. Natalie's brother. He's an expert in antique furniture. He was a great help to me in setting up the store."

"I'll just bet he was." Beat sashayed away, toward the jewelry counter.

Aaron and her father were following Slade's example and bringing folding chairs out from the back, setting them in conversational groupings around the gallery. People dropped into them with relief, leaning toward one another, talking. More people strolled the gallery. Penny Aristides was at the jewelry case, displaying her creations to a clutch of glamorous young women Bella hadn't even noticed entering the shop.

A reporter from the *Daily Hampshire Gazette* was interviewing the Ruoffs and Mrs. Smith while a photographer snapped shots.

Bella put her mouth next to Morgan's ear. "Who the *hell* is Mrs. Smith?"

Morgan answered, "I don't know. I met her at the gym. And I siphoned gas into her car."

"You siphoned gas into her car?"

"She was on empty. Her car is an old wreck. I had no idea she could pay fifteen thousand dollars for anything."

"She has to have some money to belong to that gym," Bella mused. "I certainly can't afford to go there."

Morgan grinned. "Maybe you can after tonight."

Pearl Dennehy, one of Bella's high school friends, came to her side. "I can't believe you did all this, Bella! It's awesome. Of course,

I'll never be able to afford even a pair of earrings here, not with the twins and a new one on the way." Smugly, she patted her belly.

Bella listened to Pearl recount the many wise and witty things her twins did. As she listened, Bella surreptitiously checked her watch and scanned the room. It was almost nine o'clock! Bella's had been officially open for three hours. People were beginning to leave, coming up to tell Bella good-bye or simply drifting out the door into the dark summer night. As soon as the first group left, more people followed. Beat came up, hugged Bella, and said, "Congratulations, you funny little thing," then left.

By nine-thirty, Bella was alone with her family and friends.

"We're exhausted," her father said. "We're going home to put our feet up."

Bella hurried over to kiss her parents. "Mom, Dad, thank you."

Morgan was beaming. "Josh and I put the wine and seltzer in the back room. All the canapés are long gone. I've checked the furniture: no sign of stains."

Bella laughed. "Morgan! You don't have to do all this."

"I'm delighted to do it, honey." She enfolded Bella in a warm hug. "What a success tonight was! Congratulations!"

Ben and Aaron were hefting the barrels of ice out the front door, tipping them so the melted ice splashed onto the gravel drive. Slade and Josh were folding the legs of the wine table and carrying it through the door into the back room. Bella cruised the gallery. Everything was already in place.

Natalie had been standing with her arms around her waist, staring at her charcoal of Aaron. Now she threw herself at Bella, grabbing her in a fierce hug, nearly knocking her over. "Oh, Bella, you *genius*." She burst into tears.

"Hey," Bella said, holding her friend. "I'm not the genius. You're the one who sold two pieces tonight. You're the artist."

"I am," Natalie blubbered into Bella's neck. "I am the artist."

"All right, everyone!" Josh bellowed. "Time for a celebration dinner. My treat."

"Oh, Josh, that's not necessary," Bella hastily insisted.

"I know that," Josh said. "But, Bella, I'm feeling very expansive tonight."

They drove in various cars to Judie's in Amherst, a noisy, crowded restaurant, a place to be seen, and as Bella and her group followed the waitress to their table, she noticed how heads turned to stare at her and her friends. She felt high on the success of the evening, sleek in her black dress, tall in her high heels. She felt dazzling, charismatic, mysterious.

They were all *starving*. They ordered everything—fried shrimp tempura, sweet potato sun spot fries, nachos, drunken scallops and bacon, steak and mushroom risotto, seafood gumbo, lobster ravioli, lots of Caesar salads. They shared it all, exchanging plates, eating from one another's forks, crying "You've got to try this!" The men drank beer, and the women drank sparkling water, all of them confessing they'd already had enough champagne at the opening.

The table was long and rectangular, and after she'd eaten enough to quiet her hunger, Bella noticed how the group had spontaneously arranged itself into pairs. Aaron and Bella sat on one side, Josh at the end, on Bella's right. Morgan sat at the other end of the table, chatting with Ben. Ben and Natalie sat across from Aaron and Bella, and so it would have been symmetrical, except that Slade made seven, and he was squeezed in next to his sister.

"Oh, Slade," Bella leaned forward, raising her voice to be heard in the crowd. "Thank you for your help tonight."

Slade's face gave away nothing. "Welcome. Glad to help."

"You sold several pieces of Penny's jewelry, right?" Bella asked.

Slade nodded. "The only one who didn't sell anything tonight is Shauna."

"Her pieces are unusual," Morgan commented.

"Her pieces are *weird*," Josh added.

Slade had seemed aloof, even cold, but the business talk drew him out. "Oh, and the rugs," Slade added. "No one bought a rug."

"No one could *see* the rugs," Bella pointed out.

Natalie laughed triumphantly. "Too many people standing on them!"

More seriously, Slade agreed. "True. I have a suggestion. We do this at Ralston's. We hang one of the smaller rugs on the wall, like the work of art it is. That draws attention to it and leads into a discussion of the ones on the floor."

Bella nodded. "Good idea." She filed the idea in one of the buzzing corners of her overwhelmed brain. Suddenly her feet, trapped in the four-inch heels, hurt like crazy. She yawned. "I'm whipped."

Aaron patted her knee. "You deserve to be. It was intense."

"It was *fabulous*," Natalie crowed. "It was *magnificent*!"

Just like that, the evening was over. Their plates were empty. Their glasses had been drained. Conversation faltered. Bella's yawn was contagious.

Only Josh remained effervescent as he called for the bill and whipped out his credit card with a proud flourish. "Anyone up for a swim?" he dared.

Bella groaned, hand on her stomach. "I'm so full, I'd sink straight to the bottom."

Natalie stretched and confessed lazily, "And I'd just drown."

Next to her, Ben said quietly, "No, you wouldn't."

Bella saw how Natalie and Ben looked at each other. *Well, well,* she thought.

The group rose from the table and filed out of the restaurant, nodding at the waitress and hostess, and then they were out in the night.

Aaron had his arm draped lightly over Bella's shoulder. "My apartment?" he whispered.

"Yes," she agreed, "but only because it's closer and I'll be able to fall asleep faster."

Aaron laughed. Taking her hand, he led Bella toward his car. They waved at all the others splitting off in different directions to their cars, and it was only through a haze of exhaustion that Bella heard the roar of Slade's motorcycle as it peeled off into the dark.

21

......

During the meal, Natalie paid special attention to the way Ben interacted with the others at the table. He followed the topics of conversation, and while he seldom spoke, what he'd said was appropriate to the subject. He listened, he participated, he was *there*. So it wasn't that he couldn't do it. Never once did he talk about his chemical experiments, and even though he was next to Morgan, who sat at the end of the table, he didn't go into a huddle with her about science.

As the party ended and they filed out of the restaurant, Natalie woozily attempted to recall the conversation with Morgan when Morgan said she'd had lunch with Ben—*had* that been exactly what she said?

More kisses from Morgan and Bella, lots of calls of "Good-bye!" and Natalie headed for her aunt's silver car.

A tall figure loomed up beside her. "Could I catch a ride?"

Natalie looked at Ben. Light and laughter spilled out of the restaurant onto the sidewalk. Bella and Aaron had waved good-bye, and Slade had roared away on his motorcycle. Morgan and Josh were just down the street, on the way to their car.

"Don't you have your car?" Natalie asked.

"I rode in with Morgan and Josh. But I don't want to go home with them."

His words carried an ambiguity that cut straight through the fog of her adrenaline- and alcohol-fired evening. And she couldn't forget how, just minutes before in the restaurant, when she said she'd drown if she tried to swim, Ben had looked at her and said, "No, you wouldn't." Something had passed between them again, intimate and connecting.

"Sure, you can ride back with me." Natalie wanted to touch the man, lean against him, hear his heart beat, hold his hand. *So do it,* something told her, and she reached out and took Ben's hand. "Come on. The car's this way."

He loped quietly along beside her. His hand was much bigger than hers, and cooler. How could it be cooler? Her own body was steaming, and it wasn't just the heat and humidity of the summer evening.

"I'm so hot." She sighed. She hoped her palm wasn't damp with sweat.

"Thermogenesis," Ben said.

"Oh, of course," she snorted.

"Heat production by the body. Digestion is one source, and we've just had a huge meal."

"I don't know how much I ate. I'm afraid I had more alcohol tonight than food."

"Hormones also increase the body's temperature," Ben told her.

They'd arrived at the Range Rover. Natalie paused next to Ben. He was so tall.

"I had only one drink at the restaurant," Ben told her. "I hate feeling drunk."

"Oh, all right, then. Would you like to drive?" she asked. Swaying slightly, she said teasingly, "Or are your *hormones* increasing *your* body temperature?"

Ben said, very seriously, looking her in the eye, "Actually, they are."

She almost swooned.

"But the air-conditioning in the car should help," he added.

She rolled her eyes. He was hopeless. "Could you *be* more romantic?" She handed him the keys and started to open the passenger door.

"Yes, I think I could." Ben's voice was low and husky.

He took her in his arms, bent down, and kissed her. Natalie reached her arms up to wrap around him, pulling him closer. His mouth tasted salty but fresh, like ocean water. She dreaded to think what her own mouth tasted like—champagne and, oh, what was that drink they all had tried?

Ben drew back. Keeping hold of her with both arms, he said lightly, "Do you realize you're sagging?"

"I'm *sagging?*" Immediately, she thought of breasts. Hers were fine!

"I think you're tired," he told her. "Let's get you home."

Ben opened the passenger door and helped her slide in. He walked around to the driver's side and got in.

Ben steered the car away from the curb and out through the streets. Natalie focused on her interior, body and mind. So much was happening there. She wasn't really *drunk*, not sick-to-her-stomach throwing-up drunk like she got when she was younger. She'd had plenty of water throughout the evening, a sensible trick she'd learned long ago. She was stuffed with food, and she was tingling all over from Ben's kiss, but something else was fighting to reach the surface of her consciousness—

"Ben!" She turned toward him. "Ben, I sold two pieces tonight! The charcoal of Aaron and an abstract. Good grief, I made a ton of money! Well, *Bella's* gets forty percent, of course, but still I made more money tonight than I've ever dreamed I'd make from my art. And they liked the works, Ben, they *liked* them."

Ben glanced at her with affectionate tolerance. "Of course they *liked* them. They bought them."

"Yes, but . . . they weren't *friends*. Bella's doesn't have any reputation yet, so they weren't showing off, they can't say casually to their other rich friends, *Oh yes, I got it at Sotheby's*. Wait, I'm not trying to insult your sister. Obviously she's going to have a super reputation; look at the success of her opening!"

"You're babbling," Ben said, and he sounded happy.

"I know. Do you mind?"

"Not at all." They left the lights of the town streets and wound along the dark country road toward the lake.

"Well, since you hardly talk, this way we can have a conversation and both of us can be comfortable."

Ben laughed out loud. Reaching across, he took her hand. "I think, in your own bizarre way, you've hit on something."

At home, Ben parked in the driveway, then came around and helped Natalie out of the car.

"I'm not drunk," she insisted.

"I'm not saying you are." He held her elbow as he ushered her up the walk to the front door. He still had the keys, so he opened the door.

He stepped inside with her.

"I think I'll sleep here tonight," he told her, looking down at her.

Heaven forgive her, she almost batted her eyelashes at him. "Are you going to take advantage of me?"

"Actually, no. I'm not a college kid, Natalie."

"But . . ."

"I just think it would be nice to sleep with you."

She bit her lip. How could anyone ever be this happy? "Because you don't want to drive all the way back to your apartment in Amherst?"

"Natalie, I could simply walk next door and sleep in my old room," he reminded her. "No, I meant what I said. I only want to sleep with you."

"I don't know if I'm complimented or not," she worried.

"You'll find out in the morning."

Once again, he took her hand. They climbed the stairs and entered her bedroom. It was almost two a.m. The air-conditioning had kept the house pleasantly dry and cool, and the queen bed stretched before her like the very definition of softness.

"Oh," she said. "I'm so tired, but I might be too excited to sleep."

Ben had slipped off his khakis and was unbuttoning his shirt. "You'll sleep." He unzipped her black dress.

She let it fall to the floor. "You've seen me in my bikini," she rationalized blurrily. "That's like seeing me in my underwear."

"Yes, Natalie, that's true. And vice versa." He removed his shirt and tie.

She sank onto the bed and eased her feet out of her high heels. The pleasure was exquisite. "Ben," she said, "people actually liked my work!"

He said, "I know. You're an amazing artist." He went around the bed, climbed onto it, took hold of her shoulders, and pulled her back down so her head rested on the pillow. They stretched out together on top of the light cotton quilt, two people in their underwear, too tired to make love, but two people together, like an old married couple.

"Ben," Natalie murmured.

"Natalie," he answered.

They fell asleep.

Sun splashed across the room, spotlighting itself right on Natalie's eyes. She raised her lids slightly, expecting the stab of hangover pain, only to discover she didn't feel bad at all. She thought: *Last night I sold two pieces! I made over seventeen thousand dollars!*

A man snored. Turning her head, she saw Ben sleeping soundly beside her. Carefully, she raised herself up on one elbow and surveyed his body. He was perfection. She wanted to draw him. She'd ask him to sit for her; he would be her next charcoal, but would she be able to sell it? Which angle should she draw him from? From the side, the high barrel of his ribs rose, concealing his private heart, then his skin slid tautly down to his flat belly. A trail of hair led beneath the band of his briefs.

His legs were very long. His torso was long also. His feet were bony and enormous. What if she drew him straight-on? The whole person—head, shoulders, torso, pelvis, legs . . .

Sitting up, she cocked her head and considered. The sun illuminated every aspect of his body. She scooted to the bottom of the bed and tilted over his feet, studying him from this angle.

He opened his eyes. "Um, hello?"

Natalie jumped. "Oh!"

"I don't even want to imagine what you're doing." He stretched, his long bones elegant.

"I want to draw you."

"*That's* what you want to do with me?"

She lay down on her side next to him. He turned onto his side, facing her.

"How do you feel?" she asked him.

"Fine. You?"

"Fine, too. It's so odd. I thought I'd have a crashing hangover. I'm glad I kept drinking water last night." She put one fingertip on his hand. "Thank you for driving."

"You're welcome." He turned his hand over and captured her hand. "I have an idea."

"Oh, gosh."

"Actually, it's really a dare."

"That sounds scary."

His eyes were as blue as summer.

"I dare you to spend the day with me without mentioning your art."

She drew back. "Huh?"

He repeated his dare. "And I'll go all day without mentioning my work."

She narrowed her eyes at him. "I think you're trying to make a point."

"Which would be?"

Crankily, she twitched her shoulders. "That our work is part of us. Maybe even the most interesting part of us, or the *defining* part of us." Suddenly she brightened. "Did you say we'll spend all day together?"

"If you'd like." He let go of her hand and slid his palm along her wrist, up her arm to her shoulder.

Everything changed in the intensity of that moment of physical connection. Her chest and neck went rosy with a flush that flashed up her cheeks. "I know a way we could get to know each other without using any words at all," she murmured, inching her body toward his.

"Oh, I'll make you use words," Ben said.

Afterward, they slept again, wrapped in each other's arms. Natalie woke to a snuffling sound—her nose pressed against Ben's chest. She rolled away from him and smiled up at the ceiling.

He had made her use words.

Mostly, his name. *Ben. Ben.*

As if she'd spoken aloud, calling him, he opened his eyes. "Good morning."

She snuggled against him. "I'll say."

He gently pushed her shoulder back. "I don't want to be rude or, God forbid, unromantic, but I'm starving."

She realized she was, too. They pulled on their underwear and padded barefoot down the stairs and into the kitchen.

"I'll make eggs," Ben announced. Opening the refrigerator, he peered inside. "With cheese and stuff."

"You can cook?"

"I live alone. I usually do cook for myself. Besides, I like to cook."

"Oh, right, I suppose it's sort of like chemistry for you." She filled the glass coffeepot with water and poured it into the reservoir. "Do you like your coffee strong?"

"I do. With a spot of milk, no sugar."

He cracked eggs into a bowl, grated cheese, chopped vegetables. Natalie set utensils and napkins on the table, poured orange juice, prepared his coffee, and set it next to him.

They ate quickly, not talking.

Natalie cocked her head at him. She was going to try to stick to the dare. "How do you usually eat your breakfast?"

He looked puzzled. "With a fork and knife. I raise my hand from the plate to my m—"

"That's not what I meant!" she protested, laughing. "I mean, do you eat cereal standing over the sink before rushing to work?"

He thought for a moment. "No. I like a big breakfast. With protein. I usually make eggs and bacon, or cream cheese and salmon on a bagel. I like to fuel up in the morning because later I sometimes forget to eat. I usually watch CNN while I eat. Catch up on the news of the world. See if anyone's solved the energy problem while I slept." He neatly laid his knife and fork on his empty plate. "What about you?"

"Coffee for me, first. The biggest cup in the house. Orange juice while I wait for it to brew. I take my coffee up to my studio and get to work." She skipped ahead. "I don't usually eat until around lunchtime."

"Do you like to cook?"

"I don't know, really. I've waitressed so much, I've always had my biggest meal wherever I worked, and of course in New York I usually grabbed takeout. Your mother's such a wonderful cook, so you probably learned from her without even thinking about it."

"What about your mother?"

"Oh." Natalie flipped her hand, waving her mother away. "She was more interested in making dog food."

"Tell me about her." Ben leaned forward, elbows on the table.

Natalie rose, got herself another cup of coffee, and looked out the window. "It's a perfect day. We could go swimming."

"Or you could tell me about your mother."

Natalie sank back down in her chair. As concisely as possible, she described her early life: her father leaving, her mother and the bulldogs, the ramshackle house on a dirt road outside a depressed town in rural Maine.

"Your mother must have been pretty strong," Ben said. "And brave. Raising two kids alone without financial support, or any kind of support, from their father."

Natalie murmured, "I never thought of Mom as strong. Louise said the same thing, though, so maybe I wasn't fair to her."

"I'd like to meet her."

Natalie made a scoffing noise. "Meet my mother? Ben. She's not a thing like your mother. She's a tough old bird."

"She would have to be, wouldn't she?"

"Are you trying to be contrary?"

"I'm trying to get to know you."

"My mother never once encouraged me in my desire to be an artist. In fact, she discouraged me. That's what you need to know."

"Your mother probably knew that artists seldom support themselves financially. I'll bet she worried about that." Ben's voice softened. "Is she pretty, like you?"

Natalie quirked her mouth sideways. "I guess. Slade and I look like our father. He's handsome, like Slade. Or he was, when he was younger. I don't know what he looks like now."

Ben carried his plate to the sink, rinsed it, and put it in the dishwasher. "Let's go for a sail."

She stood next to him, looking out the window. "If we leave this house to go down to the beach together, your entire family will know where you spent the night."

Ben drew her against him with an easy hug. "I don't think they'll be too surprised."

22
.....

Morgan phoned Natalie and Bella first thing Monday morning.

"Drinks here at five," she told them. "Josh won't be home until dark probably, and I'm going to have Felicity take Petey to her house to play so she won't be able to hear anything we say."

The O'Keefes' deck reflected, like the rest of their house, what they thought it *should* reflect: expense, striking lines, originality. The chairs were Lafuma, from Europe, tightly tailored, bright turquoise or cranberry mesh, with padded headrests and "integrated suspension." A wrought iron table with matching chairs filled one corner of the deck, an umbrella opened over it for protection from the sun, and next to the various lounge chairs were heavy glass tables on wrought iron stands to hold drinks and munchies. Privately, Morgan thought she'd barf if she saw another potted geranium on a deck, which the Barnabys and even Natalie had set out. She had gone to a garden shop and bought a lemon tree, an orange tree, and various striped grasses planted in terra-cotta containers.

"It's like a little jungle here," Bella remarked as she gently arranged her body in one of the contemporary lounge chairs.

Morgan looked at the grasses. To say they had flourished would be modest. "I suppose I should cut them back, trim them, or whatever."

"They're fabulous," Natalie decreed. "And they provide a great screen. No one can see what's going on up here."

"Oh, have you tried?" Morgan teased.

"Why should I try?" Natalie shot back. "You're an old married woman."

"You'd be surprised." Morgan arched an eyebrow.

"*What?*" Bella tried to sit up but only managed to slip around.

Morgan looked pleased with herself. "Later. Right now I want to get the drinks. I'll be right back."

Morgan stalked into her kitchen. She was barefoot, in shorts and a halter top, her long hair yanked high on her head, held with one long pin.

It was still hot on the deck at five, but a summer breeze played over the water, swirling cooler air up around them. Flocks of clouds like white woolly lambs clustered and slowly rambled across the blue sky, and all around the lake, the trees and shrubbery were heavy, flush with summer green. It was a sated, verdant, satisfied time of year, everything juiced up on photosynthesis and plenty of rain, all the flowers so thick and rich they splayed their bright petals as if drunk on the sun.

On the deck, waiting for her drink, Natalie removed her painting shirt and hung it over the back of her chair. She was in her black bikini—she'd run out in the middle of the day for a quick, refreshing dip in the lake. Not a real swim, though, just a playful paddle near the shore. Bella had changed out of work clothes into a tiny pink sundress with spaghetti straps. She kicked off her sandals and wiggled her toes.

"I hope you worked today," Bella told Natalie.

"I certainly did," Natalie answered smugly.

Morgan returned, beaming. On a silver tray, she carried three very tall flutes filled with mouthwatering liquid.

"Peach Bellinis," she announced. "Made with Prosecco, which is light on the alcohol, so we won't get hung over. Plus, think of all the vitamins in peach nectar." She set a flute on each side table, adding a plate covered with salted almonds, stuffed olives, and wasabi peas.

"Very nice," Bella said, reaching for her drink.

Morgan sank into her own recliner. For a moment the three

women lay side by side looking out at the shimmering azure lake. Overhead, birds were beginning to wake from their hot afternoon siestas and sing their plans for the evening. Across the lake, a lawn mower hummed. The sun slanted down on their brown limbs.

"Sunblock, anyone?" Morgan asked.

"No thanks," Natalie said. "I slathered myself before coming over."

"Me, too," Bella said.

"Okay, then." Morgan lifted her glass. "Let's toast. What shall we toast to? Bella's?"

"We did that Saturday night," Bella said. "Let's toast to friendship."

"To friendship!" They lifted their glasses but were too far apart to clink. They sipped. And sipped again.

"So, Bella," Natalie asked. "How was your first real day at the shop?"

"Nothing like the opening, that's for sure," Bella told her. "No one came in until around eleven, and then, happily, it was some women who'd seen Penny's jewelry. They each bought a piece."

"That's great," Morgan said, stretching her long legs on the lounge chair.

"Yes," Bella continued, "but then Shauna Webb came in with some more body parts."

"Sorry, Bella," Natalie said. "I think Shauna's stuff is kind of creepy."

"I know. I agree. Shauna was upset that no one bought anything of hers at the opening; plus, she brought in a box of other pieces she wanted me to add to what I'd put out. . . ." Bella took another sip of her drink. "I told her I didn't want them."

"Uh-oh," Natalie commiserated. She could guess what was coming.

"Shauna flipped. She tried pointing out how unique her pieces are, and she tried getting mad at me, and she tried crying. . . . It was kind of awful, actually."

"How did you handle it?" Morgan asked.

"I'm proud to report I was perfectly professional. I said I was sorry, but it was apparent to me that Bella's wasn't the right venue for her work." Bella tilted her head. "I was quite rational. I didn't insult her. I didn't get upset when she insulted me."

"She insulted you?"

Bella smiled. "She called me a reactionary, soulless, lowbrow opportunist and a leech who lives off the lifeblood of artists."

"Whoa!" Natalie cried.

"Nice," Morgan added.

"I can understand. She needed to vent. She needed to save face. The good news is that she got so angry she insisted on taking everything out of the shop. She refused ever to set foot inside Bella's again."

"Were you really as calm with her as you seem?" Natalie asked.

"You know," Bella announced, "I was. All my work with third graders came in handy."

"Good for you," Morgan said.

"Thanks. And this afternoon, Natalie, a woman came in with her husband. She'd been at the opening and loved your charcoals, and she wanted her husband to see them. They didn't introduce themselves or buy anything, but they did stay for quite a while, studying the charcoals and talking about them. Are you drawing anything else?"

Natalie smiled. "I'm drawing Ben."

"Really?" Bella was amazed. "Is that where he spent all day yesterday? I was at Aaron's, but I talked to Mom and she said Ben didn't come over."

"Natalie!" Morgan sat up in surprise, peered over Bella's body to stare at Natalie. "You minx! Is something going on there?"

At the same time, her voice chiming along with Morgan's, Bella asked, "When will the drawing be ready for the gallery?"

Natalie laughed. "Not for a few more days. He posed for me on Sunday, but he's at the lab today, and you know your brother, he'll be at the lab constantly, so I probably should start something else."

"How about a young woman?" Bella suggested.

"Good idea," Natalie agreed. She sipped her drink and stretched expansively. She'd been working today, actually; she'd taken some

digital shots of Ben in the pose she'd chosen, and she'd played with
the shading of the background. She was drawing him as a swimmer,
arms extended, legs kicking, head turned sideways, face partly obscured by water. It was the biggest, longest work she'd attempted
yet. Ben had been an excellent model, putting tension and strain in
his muscles, as if actually racing. The final piece would have a sense
of movement. "Bella," Natalie asked, "would you like to pose?"

Bella shook her head violently. "Absolutely not! How weird
would that be, hanging a drawing of myself in my own shop?"

"I see your point. But I could obscure your face." Natalie grabbed
up a handful of nuts and munched, thinking of the possibilities.

"Besides," Bella added sensibly, "when would I have time? I've
got to be there six days a week."

"True," Natalie agreed. The Bellini was relaxing her. The memory of her Saturday night sales still flowed through her like a heavenly drug, and the memory of Ben—oh, wow, that made her tingle
and blush.

"You didn't answer *my* question," Morgan reminded Natalie.
"About you and Ben."

"I'm drawing him," Natalie answered evasively.

"Yeah, and what else?" Morgan demanded.

Natalie took a fortifying gulp of her Bellini. She felt the cold
liquid sliding down right between her breasts. "I suppose you could
say we're seeing each other."

Bella sat up straight. "Oh. My. God. Are you and my brother
lovers?"

"That's such a sappy word," Natalie protested, but her face gave
her away.

"But what if Ben does something stupid?" Bella asked. "Ben can
be so frustrating. He forgets to keep appointments. He forgets to eat.
He—"

Morgan interrupted. "Whatever Ben is like with you, he's different with Natalie."

Natalie smiled smugly. "That's correct." She turned to Bella.
"What about you and Aaron? I heard he got the job in San Francisco."

Bella's face dropped. Settling back in her chair, she allowed herself a moment to think before admitting, "I really don't know. We celebrated when he found out, and then he celebrated with me for the opening of Bella's, and he really focused on what I had achieved. He knew I needed him to do that, so he did it. Now what? I really don't know. Today he drove down to the Cape to talk with his parents and his brother. Then tomorrow night . . ." Bella paused. "And there's something else—"

"Wait. This calls for more drinks." Morgan rose, went into the house for fresh, chilled Bellinis, returned, and poured. Sinking back down in her chair, she said, a tang of mischief in her voice, "I notice no one's asked me about *my* love life."

"*Your* love life?" Natalie snorted. "You're married."

"Wait." Bella turned on her lounge chair toward Morgan. "We were talking about *my* love life."

"Sorry." Morgan tossed some nuts into her mouth. "Proceed."

"It's just that— I don't know quite how to say this, or even what it is I want to say. . . ." In one quick word, Bella got it over with: "*Slade*."

Natalie groaned. "I knew this would happen."

"Slade what?" Morgan prompted.

"Slade . . . You know he's been so helpful with the shop. We've had such fun going antiquing together. We get along so well. He's really been a kind of mentor, guiding me toward what sorts of things I should sell, but more than that, helping me discover what it is *I* like."

Natalie muttered, "I'll bet."

"Bella." Morgan set her glass on the table and sat up straight in the lounge chair. "Look, honey. I think Aaron is the best husband material I've ever seen in a man. He's real. He's reliable. He's thoughtful. Slade is more—let's call it *glamorous*." She hesitated. "Remember, Slade was 'really helpful' to me, too." She made quote marks with her fingers. "He suggested the Victorian settee for our living room, he sent me photos of it online, he brought it to the house."

"That's his *work*," Bella reminded Morgan. "Slade and I have something personal."

"Bella," Natalie asked, "tell me. Have you slept with him yet?"

At the same time, Morgan said, "Bella, Slade came on to me."

Bella blinked. "What?"

Natalie sighed. "Oh God."

Morgan explained, "It was when he delivered the Victorian settee. The day we painted your shop. We left for a while in his van, remember? He'd brought it out from Ralston's in Boston. He'd suggested it to sort of jazz up the ambience. So we carried it into the house. We sat down on it. To kind of test it, you know. It's extremely soft and comfortable, the fabric is very expensive quilted silk—"

"Forget the stupid settee!" Bella cried.

Morgan hurriedly continued. "Hang on, this is *relevant*. We sat next to each other on the settee. I'm trying to remember this exactly as it happened. I think I said the silk was soft or something. Slade said, *Just like your hair*. He said my hair is silky. No. He said *luxurious*. He said the settee was luxurious, like me."

"What a tool," Natalie muttered.

"Go on," Bella insisted.

Morgan shifted her gaze away from Bella. "He touched my hair. He said my skin is like satin. He . . . he *looked* at me. He told me the settee was long enough for people to lie down on." She paused, remembering. "We kissed. I'll admit the kiss was my fault. I instigated it. Actually, I sort of jumped him . . . but you've got to understand, Josh and I have been like strangers lately. I don't even know if we'll stay married. He doesn't seem to care for me anymore."

"Oh, honey," Natalie cried, full of concern. "Of course he loves you! He's writing a novel, and it's almost ready for the agent, and then—"

Morgan swung around so abruptly she knocked over her glass. Peach-tinted fluid spilled across the glass tabletop and dripped down onto the wooden deck.

"Josh is writing a novel?"

"Yes!" Natalie held out her hands. "Morgan, Josh loves you so much! He wants to complete the novel, and—"

Morgan stood up, hands clenched at her sides. "Josh told *you* he's writing a goddamned *novel* and he didn't tell *me?*"

"Wait a minute!" Bella sprang out of the lounge chair and stood towering between them in all her five foot two quivering rage. "Morgan. Finish about you and Slade!"

Morgan forced her attention back on Bella. "What? Me and Slade? There's nothing else to say! We kissed, that's all. We didn't commit any kind of infidelity as serious as telling someone else a really, really HUGE secret!" Tears flooded her eyes.

Bella wouldn't let go of it. "Please. Morgan. This is important to me. Is that all you did? *Kiss?*"

Morgan looked at her petite, optimistic friend, and with great effort, she wrenched her mind back to that moment with Slade, and not only to that moment, but to the significance of it, the reason she wanted to *warn* Bella. But she was also still fueled by her hurt, her *anger* at Josh and Natalie. "Oh, this is important to you? So I should forget Josh conspiring with Natalie?"

Natalie sighed. "We hardly conspired. Morgan, I apologize. Let me explain."

But Morgan was speeding down some mental slide as if shoved, and emotional gravity was not about to let her stop. "Okay, Bella, here's what happened. I kissed Slade. He did not push me away. He did not say, 'Stop, Morgan, I love Bella.' "

"Morgan," Natalie interjected. "No need to be harsh."

"He pulled me down on top of him on the settee. Our bodies were all tangled up together. We kept kissing. He had a hard-on, I could feel it through his jeans. He said—not me, *he* was the one who said—the settee was not wide enough to have sex, and he wanted to go up to my bedroom. I was the one who put the brakes on."

Bella was pale.

Seeing Bella's shocked expression, Morgan hit the bottom of the slide, and it felt like slamming down into the water, feeling the impact of collision and her actions flying out to slap other people. Abruptly ashamed of herself, she cried, "Bella, listen, I'm not trying to hurt your feelings. I'm not trying to compete with you. I'm your friend. I care for you. I think Aaron is a great guy, a wonderful guy, who loves you truly, I can see it on his face every time he's around you. What happened between me and Slade was *nothing*. Nothing to me, and nothing to Slade. But I can tell it means something to you, and you really should think about it before you make any life-changing decisions."

Bella's face was miserable, but her voice was calm. "Okay. I know you're right, Morgan. I'm glad you told me about Slade. It helps me. . . ." Her voice trailed off as her thoughts went interior.

Morgan walked around Bella and towered over Natalie. Natalie was still seated, although she'd drawn up from the lounge position and turned sideways to set her feet on the deck, her arms crossed over her chest defensively.

"Okay." Morgan spoke with clenched teeth. "Tell me again. Josh told you he's writing a novel?"

"Sit down, please, Morgan." Natalie waved at the end of her chair.

"Why? Am I going to faint?" Morgan shot back sarcastically.

"Fine. Stand. It just hurts my neck to look up at you." Natalie reached her hand out and touched Morgan's arm.

Morgan flinched. Stepped back.

"Morgan," Natalie said, "I apologize. I made an enormous mistake, letting it out like that. I can't tell you how terrible I feel."

"I can tell you exactly how terrible *I* feel!" Morgan retorted.

"Let me explain. It was the night of the painting party."

Morgan remembered. She wanted to know all of it. She sank down onto the lounge chair, careful not to touch Natalie. "When you babysat Petey."

"Right." Natalie let it all out in a rush. "Josh came home, only a few minutes before you got back, and he saw the drawing I was doing of Petey, and I suppose that made him want to talk about his own creative work and how worried he was because even though he has an agent who thinks the novel will sell, he won't ever make as much writing as he will working for Bio-Green."

"He told you *all that?*" Morgan was dumbfounded.

Earnestly, Natalie said, "He loves you and Petey so much, he feels a tremendous sense of responsibility to protect you both financially, to make enough money to send Petey to college. . . ."

"Thanks," Morgan said curtly. "Thanks so very much for telling me all this private stuff my husband shared, not with me, but with *you*. You're really reassuring me about the state of my marriage, you know; you're really a loyal friend, listening to my husband and keeping what he said secret."

Natalie protested, "He asked me—"

"—to stand right in the middle of our marriage? To go around every single minute of every single day knowing something about my life, my marriage, that I didn't know? How could you do it, Natalie?"

Bella interrupted. "Maybe we're all getting kind of carried away—"

"Oh, you *think*?" Morgan was shaking.

"You didn't tell me about kissing Slade," Bella pointed out.

"Slade is not your *husband*!" Suddenly Morgan's anger transformed into a terrible self-knowledge. "What kind of a wife am I?" she asked herself aloud. "What have I done to Josh that he couldn't confide in *me*? Why would he tell you, Natalie, and not me? Am I a *monster*?"

"No," Natalie said soothingly. "It's not like that, Morgan."

Morgan buried her face in her hands. She'd plunged down the slide, hit the surface, and now she was hitting bottom, the cold, dark truth of the state of her marriage. Sitting on this expensive furniture on the deck of this magnificent house, she was caught in the murky reality of her marriage, how this house was anything but a home. So this was why Josh never came home at night. So this was why he worked so late in his study. So this was his secret file. She knew how much he loved reading; why hadn't she ever talked to him about the possibility of his writing? How could she love the man and not be aware of his deepest needs? She was angry with Josh. And she hated herself.

"I've got to be alone." Morgan stood up. She walked away from the spilled Bellini and the glasses of gleaming yellow liquid, from the two women who sat watching her with tears in their own eyes. She walked into her fabulous house, slid the door shut, and locked it.

23
. . . . .

After Morgan stormed into her house, Bella and Natalie stood helplessly while the peach Bellini drizzled down the table onto the deck.

Bella grabbed her napkin and tried to soak it up.

"Morgan can hose it off," Natalie told Bella. "Still, what a mess."

Bella added softly, "All kinds of messes."

Natalie sank back down on the side of her chair. "I don't know how I let Josh's secret out. It was just the heat of the moment."

"Maybe it's best that she knows." Letting her napkin fall, Bella sat down facing Natalie. "I wouldn't want my husband keeping a secret like that from me."

Natalie flinched. "You think I should have told Morgan right away?"

"I'm not saying that. I don't know what I think, actually." Bella looked miserable, too.

"I'm sorry about Slade," Natalie told Bella.

"It's hardly your fault. Besides"—Bella opened her hands, as if offering an explanation—"Slade has a sweetness about him, Natalie. Truly."

"If he wants to," Natalie agreed with reservation. "Bella, Slade can act the wounded baby bird if it will get him laid."

Bella cringed. "Charming." Narrowing her eyes at Natalie, she asked, "Did you ever consider that perhaps you're possessive of your brother? That you go around warning women off him so he won't choose a woman who will be more important in his life than you?"

Natalie gawked. "You've got to be kidding."

Bella stood her ground. "I know your father left you. Slade is the man in your family now. Slade—"

"Oh, stop this." Natalie rolled her eyes. "You think *I* made Slade come on to Morgan? You think I was behind that seductive Victorian settee whispering, 'Go, boy, go'?"

"That's disgusting."

"No more disgusting than what you're saying!" Natalie reached over to take Bella's hand. "Bella, I would be *thrilled* if Slade fell in love and married and had someone who was truly his. I'd be over the moon if he had a family. You've gotten way off track here. Slade is hardly the man in my life. I scarcely saw him in New York. It was only after I moved into Aunt Eleanor's that he started staying with me."

"So maybe he *is* interested in me," Bella said.

"Maybe he is," Natalie agreed. She paused, seeming to think her words over. Slowly, she pieced together her thoughts. "Bella, you warned me about *Ben*. How he's got a one-track mind, he's the absentminded professor, he's consumed by his work."

"True." Bella squeezed Natalie's hand. "Perhaps Ben will be different with you. I hope so."

"I hope so, too. So maybe I'm wrong about Slade, Bella. Maybe he'll be different with *you*."

"Has he said anything about me?" Bella asked hopefully.

Natalie thought. "He did, several weeks ago. We were out in the boat. He told me he liked you."

"Liked me."

"That's a huge thing for Slade to admit. I'd forgotten that. And it's true, he's been around here, helping you all the time."

The two women looked at each other. A flash of white caught their eye as a neighbor sailed his boat out onto the lake. Overhead, birds chirped, endlessly cheerful.

Natalie looked toward the glass door leading into Morgan's house. "I wish Morgan would come back out."

"Bella!" Next door, Bella's father appeared on the Barnaby deck, waving a newspaper at her. "The paper's here! The review!"

"Coming, Dad," Bella called back. "Want to come, too?" she asked Natalie.

"You couldn't keep me away."

They went down the deck steps, across Morgan's lawn, and up the Barnabys' steps to their deck.

"Let's sit inside," Dennis suggested.

They all gathered around the kitchen table: Louise, Dennis, Bella, and Natalie listened while Dennis read the review from the *Hartford Courant*.

Bella's, a new art and antiques shop located on Route 202, held its grand opening last Saturday night to a crowded and appreciative coterie of connoisseurs of crafts and creations of all kinds.

Most impressive were the works of Natalie Reynolds, recently from New York, whose abstracts are dazzling and whose charcoal drawings are worthy of comparison to the old masters. The furniture, mostly nineteenth-century antiques, pulled the eye with its polish and panache as it sat on luminous Persian carpets, also for sale. The prices, I must warn, are high, but deservedly so.

Stunning jewelry handmade by Penny Aristides, wife of local surgeon Stellios Aristides, added a contemporary gleam. Perhaps the only puzzling pieces were the ultramodern sculptures by Shauna Webb. Neither attractive nor comprehensible, these were at least small enough to overlook.

As the Amherst area becomes more raffiné, Bella's should fill the bill for the discriminating buyer. My only caveat is the location. Route 202, a few miles from Amherst, seems too rural for such a boutique and may be its downfall.

"Oh." Bella slumped in her chair. "Rural."

"He does end the review on a negative note, Bella," her father told her, "but the rest of it is pure praise!"

"Poor Shauna Webb," Louise mused.

"Raffiné?" Natalie snorted. "Who even knows what that means?"

"All the raffiné people know," Bella groaned. "Whoever they are."

"We still have the *Daily Hampshire Gazette* article." Louise patted Bella's hand. "That will come out in the Style section next Sunday."

"It's always more fun to be critical than approving," Natalie reminded Bella.

Bella just nodded, considering the consequences of the review.

"Bella." Louise squeezed her daughter's hand. "Let's have some dinner before we think about this anymore. It's easy to get discouraged on an empty stomach."

"I'm not discouraged, Mother," Bella said. "I'm not hungry either. I'm just . . . thinking."

Natalie understood exactly where Bella's mind was. She'd been there many times herself. "I'm going to head home." She stood, kissed the top of Bella's head, and said, "Congratulations, Bella. It really is a splendid review."

"He certainly liked *your* work," Dennis said heartily.

"Yes, he did. And I'm so grateful to Bella for showing it." Natalie waved at the three of them gathered around the table and let herself out the sliding glass door.

"What shall we have for dinner?" Dennis asked. Now that Bella worked at her shop all day, he and Louise were sharing cooking tasks.

"I made a potato salad earlier," Louise told him. "Is there enough cold roast chicken left over?"

Bella spent a moment gazing fondly at her parents, then excused herself. "I think I'll go for a walk."

"Oh, darling, it's so hot out."

"No, it's fine. It's cooled down from earlier today."

Before they could object, Bella hurried down the hall and out the front door.

She clipped along down the slate sidewalk bordered with her mother's flowers, then turned left, toward the main road. Toward *rural* Route 202. She didn't want to walk the route around the lake. Too many people knew her and might come out to chat with her about the newspaper review, and right now Bella wanted to be alone with her churning thoughts.

The verges of the two-lane road were narrow and thick with grass twined with Queen Anne's lace. A forest, cool and dim, stretched endlessly on either side. In the silence, her mind calmed, and the disturbing revelations of the day settled down, shrinking in significance.

Slade and Morgan. How could she be surprised?

The review of Bella's. Natalie must be thrilled.

Aaron. San Francisco.

Her shop. She had wanted to create a place to inspire people to fill their homes with beauty, and perhaps she had achieved a tiny portion of that goal, although a grand opening and one day did not prove anything, really. The review would bring people in. The reviewer had said that the customers were *appreciative*, so that was good. And it was no small achievement to have introduced Natalie's art to this part of the world. It helped Bella believe that she had a good eye for art as well as for furniture.

Aaron hadn't yet taken the San Francisco job. If he did take it, he wouldn't start until September. She had a few more weeks to see how her shop went, to test her creative judgment, before she made a decision about staying or moving. Her talent in life was beginning to come clear to her, like a ship arriving through the parting mist. She loved Aaron. She was infatuated with Slade.

But most of all, she cherished the spark of possibility burning inside her at the thought of what she, Bella, could do with her life.

24

.....

Morgan was a time bomb waiting to explode.

After she sweetly, sanely, tucked Petey in bed, she stormed around the house beating pillows back into plumpness, folding laundry, doing anything she could to use up some of the manic anger whirling inside her like a tornado building up from a small funnel into a roaring twister.

Josh had told Natalie he was writing a novel. *What else had Josh shared with Natalie?*

At ten o'clock, she heard Josh come in. She waited for him to climb the steps and peek in at Petey as he usually did. Then he walked into their bedroom.

Morgan was in a nightgown, pretending to read.

"Hey," Josh said.

She intended to be cool about it all, but the sight of him broke her open.

"Oh, Josh."

"What?" Puzzled but wary, Josh perched on the end of the bed.

"Natalie told me."

Josh drew back just slightly, as if she'd punched him. "She told you I'm writing a novel."

Morgan crossed her arms over her chest, partly to calm her shaking. "How could you?"

Josh nodded. "I knew you'd be angry about this. You think I already spend too much time away from home—"

"Wait. You think I'm upset because you're writing a novel?"

Josh almost smiled. "Well, look at you. I'd say you're upset."

"Of course I am—because you didn't tell me, you told *Natalie*!" Morgan couldn't tolerate one more second of his typically male incomprehension. "What kind of husband are you, to share such an intimate, *enormous* secret with another woman? Are you sleeping with Natalie?"

Exasperated, Josh groaned, "Oh, for God's sake, Morgan. Of course I'm not sleeping with Natalie. Don't be fantastical."

"Oh, okay. I won't 'be fantastical.' " The full blackness of wrath settled on her. "So you're not sleeping with Natalie, but you're sharing with her the secret you would share with your wife, if you were truly married."

"What?" Josh ran his hands through his hair. "Now you're just getting overwrought. What does that even mean, 'truly married'?"

Morgan said through clenched teeth, "It means faithful. It means choosing each other over everyone else. It means being *true* to each other in every way."

"Oh, babe." Josh tried to put his arms around her. "Morgan. Come on. I *am* true to you in every way."

She wrenched herself away from his attempted embrace. "You told *Natalie* you're writing a novel, and you didn't tell *me*!"

He hung his head. "Okay. I get it. Look, I'm sorry. I apologize, all right? But, listen, it just happened. It just came out. It was when Natalie was babysitting Petey after the painting party you guys had—"

"The one you didn't come to."

"Okay, *fine*. Guilty as charged." Her words had snapped something in Josh. He walked away from the bed and stared up at the ceiling. "Don't you see, Morgan? I can't do anything right by you anymore. You're always pissed off because I'm always working. I knew you'd go *ballistic* when you found out I'm also trying to write a novel in my spare time—spare time, hell, as if I have any."

"Oh, I see!" Morgan stood up, too, facing her husband. "So it's *my* fault you conspired with Natalie."

"Oh man, give me a break, I didn't *conspire*—don't be so dramatic."

"Dramatic!" Morgan could hear how shrill her voice was. She paced around the room, trying to cool herself down, trying to get to the heart of the matter. "Josh," she said, quiet now, as if she were calm, "why didn't you tell me you're writing a novel?"

"Because of *this*!" His voice broke. The firestorm of her anger had crossed over to ignite his own anger, injury, and fear. "Because I knew you would give me holy hell about it. Damn it, Morgan, I work eighteen hours a day. I suck up to Ronald Ruoff every day, *every day*, 'yes, sir; of course, sir; you're right, sir; I'm sorry, sir; I'll get right on that, sir.' I take wealthy prospective investors out to lunch and pretend I'm something I'm not, and if you don't think that makes me feel like a nasty little lizard, think again."

"I thought you believed in Bio-Green," Morgan said.

"I do. Of course I do. I wouldn't work for them if I didn't, I'm not that much of a tool. I do believe in Bio-Green and their goals, but that doesn't mean it helps me believe in *me*. I'm thirty-five. I don't want to do this for the rest of my life. But I also love you and Petey. I'm trying my damnedest to provide for both of you, to be sure Petey and any other children we have get a good college education. I try to spend some time with Petey, I try to be here part of the weekend to take him out on the lake. Jesus, Morgan, I break my neck getting back here. But it's not good enough for you."

"Josh—" How had the argument turned? How had she become the bad one?

"I want to see if I can write novels well enough to make money, and I think I can. But it takes *cojones* to try to write. It's . . . private, and embarrassing. I could tell Natalie I'm writing a novel because I don't care what Natalie thinks about me. But it makes all the difference in the world what *you* think of me."

"Josh—" The adrenaline whirling through Morgan made her almost dizzy, stalling her at the height of her outrage. She felt she was being cheated somehow, that Josh was spinning this argument on its head. She could understand the sense of Josh's words, she could see her husband's weariness, but she was still *right*, she was still owed something. If he loved her, Josh needed to be the one to make the first move toward reconciliation.

But Josh turned away from her, his entire body haggard and desolate. "I don't know how to fix this, Morgan. I just don't." He strode from the room.

Morgan heard the front door slam. The Escalade started up and roared away.

He would come home. Josh would go for a drive to cool off, and he would come home.

Fatigue struck. She was more exhausted than she'd ever been in her life, except after giving birth to Petey. She slid down on the bed and let sleep engulf her.

Josh hadn't returned home by morning.

Morgan dressed and fed Petey absentmindedly, replaying last night's argument, making funny faces at her son, feeling sick in her heart.

The day still wore its hazy veil of early-morning coolness, so Morgan took Petey outside and settled him in his stroller. He enjoyed a ride around the lake road, and Morgan needed to move while she thought about what to do next.

This was a good time of day for a stroll. Few cars were on the road. The neighbors had already gone to work or off shopping. The trees arching over the road were in full flush, providing an abundant green canopy of shade. By now Petey had made friends with a few of the neighborhood dogs, who ambled out to lick Petey's hand and wait hopefully for him to hold out a few of his Cheerios. Morgan and Petey sauntered along, stopping to chat with neighbors working among flowers, before strolling farther, in the direction of Petey's beloved babysitter's house. Often Felicity or her mother would invite them in for iced tea.

But this morning, both Felicity and Grace were standing in the front yard, crying.

Morgan slowed the stroller, wondering whether she should turn around and protect Petey from the sight.

Then she noticed the teenage boy lying at the bottom of the driveway, huddled against the curb of the street. He was crying and clutching his arm, and he was bleeding terribly from his head and arm. Morgan couldn't comprehend why Grace and Felicity, normally caring, kind people, weren't attending to him.

"Petey." Morgan used her most cheerful mommy voice. "Let's see if we can help this boy. I think he has a boo-boo."

She turned the stroller toward the boy so Petey could see what she was doing, grabbed a couple of baby diapers from the back pocket of the stroller, and cautiously approached the boy, who, she recognized, was Drew Keller, Felicity's boyfriend. Drew was fifteen and cute, in a scrawny way.

Bending toward him, she said, "Drew. It looks like you're hurt."

He struggled to sit upright. "I fell out the window." After a moment, he clarified, "The second story. Felicity's room. C-c-caught my arm on a jagged piece of metal from the storm, and the top window came down on me. I'm trying to get back home, but I can't walk very well. I had to rest. I think my arm's broken." He was trying to snuffle back his tears while blood streamed down his face, onto his clothing. "I know Mrs. Horton wants me out of here. Do you think you could call my mom?"

"Oh, honey." Morgan handed him a diaper she had turned soft-side-out. "Press that against your head. It will slow the bleeding. Do you have any sexually transmitted diseases?"

He looked alarmed. "What? We just had sex *once!*" Embarrassed, he looked down. "The first time." His lips were turning blue. His skin was paling out.

Morgan said calmly, "I'm calling an ambulance. Then we'll call your mom." She hit 9-1-1. "This is Morgan O'Keefe. I live on Dragonfly Lake. There's been an accident at"—she stopped to check the number on the mailbox—"67 Lakeside Road. Adolescent male with bleeding head wound, bleeding and possibly broken arm. He's going into shock. Yes. I'll stay here."

Clicking off the phone, she said to the boy, "Can you extend your arm?"

He looked dazed, unsure. Blood was soaking his hairless chest, flooding down his thin body to puddle around him on the street.

She held up the other baby diaper. "I want to wrap this around your arm to stanch the bleeding."

With his good arm, he was holding the first diaper against his head. He tried to stretch his bad arm toward her but winced, crying out in pain.

She moved toward him, taking care not to step in the blood. "It's fine. I can do it from here. Press on your head harder. Can you see that? You've already slowed the flow. Head wounds bleed like Niagara Falls. It's not a sign of anything terrible. It's just the way head wounds are. It's probably not very deep. You'll be just fine. I'll phone your mother as soon as I've got this attached." She spoke in a mild, firm, reassuring voice as she wrapped the diaper around his arm, which was deeply slashed. She fastened it tightly. "Tell me your mother's number, honey."

His teeth were chattering. "Four-one-three . . ."

She punched in the numbers as he said them. When a woman answered the phone, Morgan said, "Hi, this is Morgan O'Keefe. I live on Dragonfly Lake. Your son Drew is here at Felicity's house. You need to come at once. He fell out the window and broke his arm. I've called an ambulance."

His mother was brisk. "I'll be right there."

"Your mother's on her way," Morgan informed Drew. She took out a baby blanket tucked into the back of the stroller, unfolded it, and draped it over Drew's chest and shoulders. It was lightweight, covered with bunnies, and not very large, but it might give Drew some warmth and also a sense of protection. The blood from the head wound had slowed.

"I'm going to talk to Felicity," Morgan told the boy. "Your mother will be here any minute, and the ambulance. It's under control."

"My mom's gonna kill me," Drew said.

Morgan smiled. "Not until after she's sure you're okay," she promised. She added, "I'm going to leave Petey here. Talk to him, would you? Tell him everything's all right. Don't frighten him." She wanted to keep Drew from sinking away into a shock faint, and Petey was wide-eyed and fascinated.

She walked up the lawn to the two weeping females. Felicity was barefoot and naked except for a sheet covered with bluebirds wrapped around her. Grace was dressed in shorts, sandals, and a tee shirt, as if it were any normal day, but her face was red and tear streaked.

"Grace," Morgan said, "what's going on?"

Grace wrenched her face toward Morgan. "That crazy delinquent raped my daughter!"

Felicity was equally intense. "It was *not* rape! I told you! I sneaked him in the house last night! Yes, we had sex, but I'm fifteen now, and I love Drew." Felicity choked back sobs. "It was the first time. It was the only time. We just fell asleep. We didn't mean for you to see us like that."

Her mother gave an insane laugh. "I'm sure you didn't!"

A car shrieked up to the house, slammed to a stop, and a woman leapt out. She ran to Drew and knelt next to him. Sirens sounded and an ambulance streaked toward Felicity's house, parking next to Drew. Two EMTs jumped out. Morgan walked down to stand nearby, watching as they examined the injured boy. Drew's mother babbled at them the entire time. Up on the lawn, both Grace and Felicity were silent as they watched.

Morgan returned to Petey, who was trying to watch everything at once. "Isn't this interesting? Petey, look, a real, live ambulance! And real emergency technicians." She thought the scene might frighten him—so much noise and weeping and strange people in uniforms and the towering ambulance with its light blinking. But Petey was delighted.

The attendants brought out a stretcher. They put a pressure dressing on Drew's head and wrapped it and his arm, then lifted him into the back of the ambulance. His mother stepped up inside. The driver approached Morgan.

"This is your house?"

"No. It's the Hortons'. I'm a neighbor, Morgan O'Keefe. I'm the one who called in. I understand that Drew was in the girl's bedroom and tried to escape when her mother opened the door this morning. He hurt himself in the process."

The driver smiled just slightly. "Won't be the first time we've attended something like this. Give me your phone number in case we need it."

She gave him her number, and he got into the ambulance. Without the drama of a siren this time, the vehicle pulled away.

Morgan pushed her stroller up the driveway.

Felicity was weeping dramatically into her sheet.

Grace glared at Morgan. "He probably gave my daughter an STD."

"I doubt that," Morgan said. "He told me it was the first time he'd had sex."

Felicity wailed. "It's true!"

"Well, we'll be lucky if we all don't get diseases," Grace continued angrily. She gestured toward the driveway, which ran slightly downhill. "Look at all this blood! It's got to be full of germs and HIV and hepatitis B and God knows what else!"

"I doubt that," Morgan told Grace. "Have you touched the blood?"

"Of course not!" Grace flared her nostrils.

"Felicity?"

"No. It all happened so fast. Mom and Dad *knew* the metal was split on the storm window"—she shot an accusing look at her mother—"but Drew just went out the window so fast, and then he screamed because he'd cut his arm on the metal, and then he fell and hit his head on those stupid stone cupids Mom put in her flowers."

"Blood on my cupids," Grace wailed. "Blood everywhere. And who knows what's in it."

Morgan asked calmly, "Do you have any bleach?"

Felicity and Grace stared.

"Bleach works as a disinfectant on blood," Morgan explained.

"You've got a street drain near your driveway. We'll decontaminate the blood with a mixture of bleach and water, then hose it all down into the drain."

"What do you know about this kind of thing?" Grace demanded.

"I'm a biosafety expert," Morgan told her. "This is my field."

Grace looked worried. "But *blood* in the drain . . ."

"It happens every day, in every home," Morgan told her. She leveled her eyes at Grace. "So do you have bleach?"

"I have bleach."

"Go get it. And put on sunglasses, both of you, to prevent any bleach mist from getting in your eyes."

"I'll get dressed," Felicity said in a small voice.

The two Hortons went into the house. Morgan lifted Petey out of the stroller, carried him away from the driveway, and let him roam around the lawn in his stumbling baby gait. He loved all Grace's outdoor statuary, the elves hidden among the rhododendrons, the fairies among the zinnias.

Felicity came out first, dressed now, in shorts and a top and sneakers. She knelt down next to Petey and chatted with him. Grace came out carrying a bottle of bleach.

"We need a bucket and hose," Morgan told her.

Felicity played with Petey while Morgan supervised, showing Grace approximately how much bleach should go into a gallon of water, helping her carry it and splash it over the precious stone cupids, around the side of the house, and into the drying stream of blood speckling the driveway. She poured the largest amount on the puddle where Drew had lain. Grace attached the garden hose to the outdoor faucet and took turns with Morgan flooding the bleached blood down the driveway, around the corner of the curb, and through the metal grid, down the storm drain. In only a matter of minutes, the sun had dried out the water, and everything was just clean and normal as always.

Felicity's mother sighed, exhausted by the morning. "W the bleach kills my flowers?"

"A moderate amount of bleach can actually help flow gan assured her. "Once the bleach is mixed with all tha' remaining chlorine is not really a problem. Besides, it may even help by killing the bacteria in their stems. Possibly, it will fade their colors for a while, probably not. If I were you, I'd rinse them more with water from the hose, really soak the ground around them."

"Right. Thanks." Grace gave Morgan a wry look. "Wait until Petey is a teenager." She rubbed her hands over her face. "Sorry, Morgan. I should thank you for all your assistance. I don't know what I would have done without you." She tried to laugh but couldn't quite get there. "Drew's a nice boy, but I'm not ready for my daughter to be having sex yet. She's only fifteen. Her father will die. His perfect princess."

Morgan moved a few steps away. This was for the Hortons to deal with. "I've got to get Petey back home for lunch."

"Yes, of course you do," Grace replied, her mind on other matters. "Thank you again, Morgan, for your help."

"I'm glad to help."

The truth was, Morgan thought, as she gathered up her son and said good-bye to Felicity and tucked Petey into the stroller, she had been more than just *glad* to help. Something had switched on inside her at the scene—something had gone very calm, determined, and deliberate. Her mind was equipped for just such dramatic moments when normal people freaked out. When *she* knew exactly what to do.

And suddenly, Morgan knew exactly what *she* should do.

Elation burst within her as she pushed the stroller toward her house. She found herself running. Petey waved his hands and squealed. At home, she unbuckled him, swept him up into her arms, ᵃnd raced inside. She grabbed up a banana and a Tupperware bowl ᵗ Loops, a rare and special treat. She headed for the car.

ᵈrove toward Bio-Green, Morgan played Queen's "We ᵑs," singing along at the top of her voice. By the ᵗ husband's facility, she was zinging with in the lot, unbuckled her son from his her hip, and hurried toward the main lobby, greeted the attendant at the front ᵉ elevators, and punched the button for the

Imogene was at her desk, typing. She looked up in surprise when Morgan crashed into the office in her shorts and tee shirt.

"Hi, Imogene." Morgan gave the girl her best official smile. "I need to see Josh a minute. Play with Petey for me a bit, will you?" Before the secretary could protest, she thrust her son onto Imogene's lap.

Imogene looked scandalized and uncertain. Morgan didn't stay to watch, but as she opened Josh's door, she heard her son say, "Pretty." No doubt he was pointing toward Imogene's sparkly jewelry.

"Why, thank you," Imogene replied, formally. "Would you like to see pictures on my computer?"

Morgan shut the door behind her. Josh looked up from his desk, startled. His hair was rumpled, he wore yesterday's clothing, and he had dark circles under his eyes. He must have slept on the sofa in his office.

Josh stood up. "Morgan. Is everything all right?"

"More than all right. Everything is wonderful. Well, it's going to be." She picked up the office chair in front of his desk and carried it around to the side, so she was within touching distance of her husband. "Josh. I have a plan."

Josh looked worried.

"I'm going back to work. I'm going to take the job they're offering at U. Mass. in biosafety. *You* are going to stay home with Petey and write your novel." She grinned triumphantly.

Josh stared at her. "That's your plan."

"It is."

Josh nodded. "Okay, I can see how you think this will work. I can see the sense of it. But, Morgan, first, you don't have the job. Second, you don't know what it pays. Third, whatever it pays, it won't be as much as I make here at Bio-Green."

"So we sell the house."

"Sell the house?"

"Josh, we don't have to live on the lake. There are lakes all over this area. We can drive to a lake when we want to. We don't have to have a posh house. We don't have to have our huge automobiles."

"Morgan, that's too optimistic. I'm pretty sure an agent will take my book, and he's pretty sure it will find a publisher, but no one has a clue how much money I'll make, if any."

"But that doesn't mean you shouldn't give it a try. Josh, it's important to you. Maybe even *crucial*."

Her husband looked at her with his clear green eyes. His shoulders relaxed. He leaned back in his chair. He stared at Morgan, and he understood. "As crucial as your work is to you."

"I'm not saying I don't love taking care of Petey—"

"I know. I know that." He ran his hands through his hair as he always did when he was thinking, and gazed around his office.

"Do you love it here?" she asked.

"It's a really cool office." After a moment, he continued, "But if you're asking would I give it up in order to write, the answer is yes." Pushing back his desk chair, Josh stalked around the room. "This is pretty drastic. Remember, Morgan, how miserable we were in Boston, living in a dump, struggling financially."

Morgan nodded. "I remember."

"It's not going to be easy," Josh continued, thinking aloud.

"No," Morgan agreed. "Not easy."

"Complicated details." Josh began to name them. "Selling the house. Finding a new house. Dealing with realtors. Packing stuff. Helping Petey cope with another move."

Morgan held her breath.

Josh warned her: "You're talking about radical changes."

"I am."

"Let's break it down." A spark burned in his eyes, that fire of challenge and boldness she'd always loved in Josh, which made him so charismatic. "Why don't you apply for the job? If you get it—"

Morgan was almost shivering with hope. "*When* I get it—"

"—we'll move on to phase two. I'll talk to Ronald about my position here. Maybe I can downsize it. Maybe not, but it's worth asking about."

"Oh, Josh!" Morgan threw herself at her husband, kissing him passionately on the mouth.

Josh laughed through the kiss and gently pushed Morgan away.

"You'd better stop that or I'll take advantage of you all over my desk."

"Well, there's an idea!" For a moment, Morgan desired sex with her husband more than anything she'd ever wanted in her life.

They looked at each other, turned on, elated, mischievous—*connected*.

"Go over and talk to them," Josh said. "You know that's what you really want to do."

"You're right." Morgan laughed. "That's certainly one of the things I want to do," she said, locking eyes with him before she flew across his office and out the door. She grabbed Petey from Imogene and raced through the building, out to her car.

25

·····

The July morning was dense with humidity, the air so thick and moist it was spongy. Natalie woke with a glaze of sweat on her skin. The heat pressed down on her eyelids, as if forcing her back into her swamp of sleep. She struggled to comprehend why she was so hot; the air-conditioning at Aunt Eleanor's worked efficiently. . . .

She wasn't at Aunt Eleanor's.

She was in Ben's bed.

Her eyes flew open. All her senses flipped awake like flowers eager for rain. Next to her, Ben lay on his side, one arm over Natalie's waist, as if to keep her from leaving, although he should know after last night she had no intention of leaving. The warm gust of air ruffling the top of her head was Ben's breath. She glanced down at his strong, tanned arm, each individual hair golden in the morning light. Perspiration glistened along his arm. His room was not air-conditioned. Why bother buying a window air conditioner? He was hardly ever here, he told her last night.

Her eyes wandered the room, noticing what last night she'd been too occupied to see. Ben's room was in an ordinary condo-minium—four square rooms, white walls, venetian blinds over the windows, an oatmeal-colored wall-to-wall carpet, commonplace moldings, hollow-core doors, basic. His bedroom held a double bed taken from his grandparents' house, covered simply with one white bottom sheet; why, he'd asked sensibly, would he need a top sheet in such heat? Natalie had replied—this conversation had taken place late at night, when they were sated from lovemaking—that she couldn't sleep without something over her to make her feel safe. "I'll be your safety," Ben had promised, spooning next to her and wrapping his arm around her.

His arm was still there.

A battered wooden chest stood against one wall, one of the drawers open, a cotton rugby shirt spilling out. In the corner was a wicker chair, its strands unweaving from around its arms and legs and sticking out like antennae covered with discarded clothing. Through the open closet door, she saw proof that he could be organized: All his pants hung together, his shirts together, his jackets together. Around the room, towers of books, journals, and monographs rose, teetering dangerously the higher they grew. Six fat tomes rose on his bedside table. How he managed to turn on the light or shut off the alarm clock without knocking the books on the floor, Natalie could only wonder.

The clock. It was after nine! They'd slept late. Well, they'd been awake half the night. At certain moments, they'd spoken words of love, although occasionally Natalie had coached Ben. "Now," she said, "is when you tell me I'm beautiful." That was during the second time they made love, or maybe the third, and she held herself a certain way, teasing him. He had groaned, "You know you're beautiful." And she'd moved just exactly the right way, to reward him.

He had told her he loved her. Without prompting, Ben told Natalie he loved her. She loved him, too, she'd replied, over and over. She'd never been more nakedly honest with any person. No words had ever meant more. She smiled, remembering.

"Are you awake?" Ben's voice was a whisper stirring her hair.

"Mmm," she answered, wriggling tighter against him.

"Hungry?" he asked.

"Starving."

He released her and rolled on his back. "I've crushed all feeling from this arm," he confessed, rubbing the arm he'd been lying on in order to put his other arm over her.

Natalie flipped over to face him. "Poor baby. Want me to kiss it?"

"If you kiss anything of mine, we'll never get out of bed, and we have things to do today," Ben told her.

"Oh, really?" She nudged him with her pelvis.

"Stop. I'm serious." He sat up, tossed his legs over the side of the bed, and rose. "I've got to take a shower. I smell like a sty."

"I have to take a shower, too. Shall I take one with you?" Natalie offered.

"Natalie, behave yourself." Ben's expression was serious, but his eyes were full of light. "You know what would happen if we tried to shower together. If you want to take one first, go ahead. I'll make coffee." He strode, naked, from the room.

The shower felt wonderful, cleansing and refreshing. She soaped her hair with his shampoo, scrubbed her body, and stood for long minutes rinsing beneath the flood of water. His towels were old but clean, no doubt borrowed from the Barnabys' house. Her hair, almost chin-length now, lay in cooling spikes against her face and head.

She saw her face in the mirror. She looked good. Happy. *Glowing*.

What possible plans could Ben have for today that would propel him from bed so quickly? What "things" did they have to do? Her heart jumped like a startled doe. She forced herself to calm down. She had gotten so bossy in her life on her own, she hardly knew how to act around a man, let alone one as reserved as Ben.

She dressed in the clothing she'd worn the evening before, just shorts and sandals and a pretty, sleeveless cotton top. They were wrinkled, but fresh enough, and anyway, everything got wrinkled in this damp heat.

She followed her nose toward the aroma of coffee coming from the galley kitchen.

"The coffee's ready. Help yourself to juice and cereal," Ben told her, and went to take his own shower.

He'd set out a box of granola for her, and a bowl, and a spoon. She found the milk and juice in the refrigerator and, on the spur of the moment, opened the cupboard door. On the shelf were cans of baked beans and corned beef, and a box of Apple Jacks. For some reason, she loved it that he had Apple Jacks. It helped her spy the boy in this serious man.

She ate her breakfast. Ben came out of the bedroom, dressed in khakis and a polo shirt in a turquoise that made his eyes silvery blue.

"Ready?" he asked.

"Just let me wash the bowls," she told him.

He nodded. "You're right. In this heat, they'd start smelling sour quickly. I'll dry."

She treasured standing next to him, not talking, performing such a humble, ordinary task.

"Now," he said, grabbing his keys up from the counter. "Off we go."

"Okay." She hesitated. "Ben, I don't know where we're going. I'm only wearing shorts. Am I dressed appropriately?"

"Sure," he assured her. "I'm taking you to see my office and lab."

If he'd said he was taking her on a rocket to the moon, she couldn't have been more surprised.

"Oh!" she said, and smiled. "Well!"

"Come on." He took her arm and ushered her out of his condo, down the stairs, and into his car.

His condo was on the outskirts of the small town of Amherst. As he drove along the shaded streets, past grand old Victorian houses and into the maze of the university, he informed her like a tour guide, "This is my regular route. I bike to my office whenever I can."

The university was enormous, sprawling over more than fourteen hundred acres of land, its buildings a mixture of modern and historic, the campus so extensive the streets required traffic lights, metered parking spots, and a university bus system.

Ben parked in a lot in the middle of the campus.

"I'm totally lost," Natalie told him. "I'd wander around here forever and never get home."

"I'll take care of you." Ben took her arm.

His manner had changed; his words were not flirtatious but sounded practical, and Natalie realized that before her eyes he was morphing into Science Man.

"This is Draper Hall." He opened the door into a stately Victorian building. "My office is this way."

She went quietly alongside him as they walked down a shadowy corridor. He unlocked his door and they stepped into his office.

It was a small room with a window looking out on a well-groomed lawn crisscrossed by sidewalks. Along three walls were bookcases reaching to the ceiling. A beaten-up wooden desk, obviously university-issue, sat in front of the window. Behind it was Ben's ergonomic chair, and in front of it was a plain, uncushioned wooden office one. Ben's computer took up a great part of the desk surface, and all around it piles of papers of various sizes and thicknesses sprawled like several giant decks of cards. Yet Natalie could see some order to it all. One pile of manila envelopes. One pile with ring binders, probably student essays. One pile of pads of graph paper with penciled equations slanting upward on the page.

Ben held out his hand. "Sit down." He indicated his desk chair.

"That's your chair."

"Yes, and it's comfortable. I'll sit here."

Natalie hid her delighted smile at this unexpected gallantry. She went around his desk and lowered herself into his chair.

"Now," Ben said. He sat forward, his elbows on his knees, hands on his elbows. "You know we've got an oil crisis."

Natalie said, "Duh."

"Right. What I'm trying to do is to find a way to convert woodmass into biofuel."

Natalie nodded encouragingly. "Okay."

"Woodmass contains a large amount of oxygen and water. We are using pyrolysis—the thermochemical decomposition of organic material—"

"Of course." Natalie tried not to roll her eyes.

"I need you to hear this," Ben told her.

She straightened in the chair. "I'm listening."

"We're attempting flash pyrolysis in an ablative process. We're moving biomass particles at high speed against a large metal mass." A change came over him as he spoke. His words were deliberate, clipped, clearly enunciated, evenly paced, as if he was trying not to rush himself in his attempt to articulate his complicated subject. He folded his arms on his desk, leaning toward her, eyes steady, posture upright—and yet clearly his excitement for his experiment pushed him to an emotional high she'd never seen before, not even when they had made love. He transformed into a flame, burning for this subject, yet held firmly in check by sheer force of will. He would not rush. He would not reduce or diminish. He would do it fully and right.

She nodded, her eyes fixed on his as he continued to explain mechanical reliability, carrier gases, reaction volumes, and commercial applications. She couldn't begin to comprehend what in the world he was talking about, but she struggled as she hadn't since high school to memorize some of the terms, because she *got* it, what Ben was doing.

He was talking to her. He was telling her what mattered to him, what he did daily, what he was thinking about constantly, what made him absentminded and moody and noncommunicative. Just as she found herself in the midst of a group with her thoughts wandering away toward the penumbra on the bottom left side of her current portrait, so did Ben's mind return like a homing pigeon to this biomass stuff.

"I have five graduate students working under me," he said. "I supervise their work. I write detailed applications to various companies, mostly energy corporations, for grants to continue my work. During the fall and spring semesters, I teach three classes and have papers to grade, theses to oversee, and faculty meetings to attend. I'm required to do volunteer work with the students three hours a week; I oversee the chemical engineers club. I attend every conference the university will send me to. I work on papers about our project, which I submit to the most prestigious journals in our field in hopes of getting published, and that's daunting work. I love my work and I'm obsessed with it."

"It's important work you're doing," Natalie said slowly.

She had said the right thing. Ben sat back in his chair, his hands curled into loose fists on his thighs. "I think it is."

"I can't pretend to understand it, you know."

"Probably you'll be able to, kind of," Ben told her, and he was being honest. "You're an artist. You know about charcoal and the chemistry of color."

"Yes, that's true," Natalie agreed.

"Probably you could teach me a few things about chemistry and pigments," Ben told her. "You could never teach me to do what you do—I use real materials and processes, but you seem to pull inspiration out of the air." He paused, searching for words. "The thing is, Natalie—the thing is, I'm boring. At least to most people I am. I can't change that."

Soberly, she told him, "You're not in the least boring to me."

Ben shifted uncomfortably on his chair. "I wish I could explain this. . . . Natalie, I've always dated scientists before. So that we could speak each other's language. And I don't understand why, but no matter how nice they were or how brilliant, or even if they were chemical engineers like me, I always found *them* boring. But you—I never find *you* boring."

"Ah." Natalie sighed. She felt as if she were blossoming like a rose in front of him, the feeling caused by the inexplicable chemistry between them. Probably Ben knew the formula for it.

They talked some more, but he had work to do and so did she. They agreed she'd take his car, drive to her house, and paint. Around five, she'd pick him up to drive to her house for dinner.

In Aunt Eleanor's house, the air-conditioning hummed softly, keeping the air cool and dry, which was just what Natalie needed for her paintings. She drifted into her studio and studied her work—the charcoal of Ben swimming. Yet some unusual atmosphere surrounded her as completely as the conditioned air. It was as if an incense were pumping through the coils of the machine into the air she breathed, wafting her into a sense of bliss, as if she were on some invisible drug.

She realized she *was* on an invisible drug, and it was love.

. . .

"Mom?"

"Natalie. Are you okay?" Marlene's voice went up an octave.

For an instant, Natalie was breathless, stabbed with guilt. It had been over a year since she'd seen her mother, and weeks since she'd phoned her.

"I'm fine, Mom, just fine. In fact, great. How are you?"

"How's Slade?"

"He's fine, too. And, Mom, I've sold some paintings! I got a great review in the *Hartford Courant*."

"Oh." Marlene hesitated. "That's wonderful, Natalie. You really are becoming a success."

"I want you to come see them. I want you to meet my new friends. Especially, I want you to meet a man."

"You do?" Marlene's voice lifted in surprise.

"Of course I do. You know there's plenty of room in Aunt Eleanor's house—"

"I think I'd like that."

Natalie babbled on, "Mom, I like it so much here. I might stay here. Not in Aunt Eleanor's house, but in this area. The people next door have become such good friends. Bella is about my age, and her brother Ben is the man I want you to meet. Her parents, the Barnabys, own the house next door. . . . What? What did you say?"

"I said I'd like that." Marlene sounded shy. "I'd like to come visit. I'd like to meet your friends."

Shocked, Natalie said, "Well, good, Mom. How soon can you come?"

"I'll have to find someone to deal with the dogs. But I'd like to come as soon as possible, if that's all right with you."

"Yes, please do that," Natalie agreed.

"I'll call you right back," Marlene promised, her voice stronger now.

Natalie didn't return the phone to its cradle but sat holding it in her hands, as if the instrument still retained her mother's words— and more than that, her mother's tone of voice, which had been rich with affection. Was it possible that Marlene had changed? It would be strange, Natalie supposed, if her mother *hadn't* changed over all these years. When Natalie was a young girl, her mother's voice had been warm, enticing, adoring. During Natalie's teenage years, Marlene's voice had been strained and curt. Of course, Marlene's life had been difficult then, and it was a pretty safe bet that teenage Slade and Natalie had not filled Marlene's life with joy.

So Marlene had changed—but, Natalie realized, she had changed, too. Watching Morgan with her small son made Natalie understand how a woman can love a child with all her heart at the same time she's being driven mad by that same child. Morgan had to stretch emotionally, from sweet to strict, from practical to consoling, from counselor to cuddler, in the space of minutes. Natalie didn't know if she could ever do that. And now she understood, a bit, all that her mother had done for her and Slade. Not perfectly—and who could do it perfectly?—but well enough.

For the first time since she'd left home, Natalie was eager to see her mother.

26

· · · · ·

Bella had set her laptop computer on the display counter so she could be available in case a customer walked in. She sat on a high stool, a sheaf of notes in a pile beside her, and she had several windows open on her screen.

Her mother had not used a computer to run Barnaby's Barn, but Louise had been organized. She kept a ledger and several accordion files marked with the names of the artisans, each of their works, their asking prices, the dates the pieces were set out for exhibit, the dates they sold, the prices that were paid, the commissions Louise took, the amount and number of the checks sent to the artisans. She also kept, for tax purposes, a record of every paid utility bill—electric, water, heat. Snowplowing in the winter for the parking lot. Lawn mowing in the summer.

Basically, Bella was realizing, her mother's shop had been an endeavor of love. Louise had always made enough money to clear expenses—as long as she didn't pay herself a salary.

That was the past. The question was, could Bella's support itself and Bella's own real life? Her fingers flew from the columns on the screen to the Dashboard calculator. She chewed her lip as she worked.

"Hey."

She looked up to see Slade standing in the doorway.

For once, he wasn't in all black. He wore blue jeans and a snow-white tee shirt that made his black hair shine like ebony. He lounged against the door, cocky, relaxed, slightly amused by what-ever private joke was running through his head.

"Hey, yourself," Bella answered. "What are you doing here?"

"I'm in the area. Scouting for Ralston's."

"Ah. Finding anything?"

"Could be." Slade's eyes were hooded as he stared at Bella, trans-fixing her.

She dragged her gaze away, back to the computer screen. Sliding off the stool, she minimized the page she was on. She stretched. "I'm trying to make a business plan."

"A business plan," Slade echoed.

"Yes, you know. Outgo. Versus income. How much I should spend on advertising, how much of that should be in local papers, how much on Internet sites. I've already listed on Facebook and LinkedIn."

"How'd you do yesterday?"

"Not good. I sold two pieces of Penny's jewelry. A couple came in to look at Natalie's work, but they didn't buy anything."

"You know, in a business like this, you survive from large sale to large sale. You can't expect to sell something every day."

"I do know that." Bella leaned on the counter, picked up a pen, and doodled on one of her notebooks, thinking. "Still. To be pain-fully honest, Slade, I'm just not sure I can make a go of it." Talking to herself more than Slade, she murmured, "I don't know why I didn't take a good, hard look at the money side before. I think I got carried away by the excitement and romance—"

"What if you had a partner?" Slade asked.

She wasn't really listening. "Hmm?"

Slade ambled across the room and leaned on the counter facing her. He crossed his arms. His hands were almost, but not quite, touching hers.

"What if you had a partner?" he asked again, his voice low, al-most a growl.

Bella looked up at Slade. His dark blue eyes were nearly black. His mouth was quirked slightly in that seductive way he had, but she felt tension steaming off his body. His muscles were taut, his hands clenched on the counter, the knuckles almost white.

"You?"

"Why not?"

Bella cleared her throat. "Surely the real question is *why*," she said quietly.

"We'd make a good combination, don't you think?" Slade's voice was warm and tempting.

All she had to do was touch his hand.

She pulled back. She moved away. She came out from behind the counter and walked to the door, stepping just outside to stand blinking in the full blast of the summer heat. She stared out, unseeing, at the parking lot. The towering oak at the side threw a circle of shade over the grass and the bench.

She'd learned so much this summer, and why she hadn't learned it all before now, she had no idea. For one thing, she now knew that she, Bella Barnaby, good, sweet, petite Bella, could want to jump a man's bones simply because he made her weak with lust. But that was not love. That was not even liking. If she *loved* Slade, she could overlook the Morgan incident, which hadn't really amounted to much. But the bittersweet truth was, she didn't love Slade.

For better or worse, she loved Aaron. That meant that one way or the other, she was in for heartbreak, because she couldn't have Aaron and this particular shop on rural 202. But she shouldn't hook up with Slade because she couldn't have Aaron. *Keep it simple*, she told herself, for she'd seen that advice mentioned many times on Internet business plans.

She sensed Slade coming up behind her, and then she felt his hands on her shoulders.

His mouth was at her ear. "Bella. Imagine the possibilities."

It was easier to do it this way, without facing him. "It wouldn't work, Slade. Not you and me. Not in business, not in any other way either. I don't know, I'm not sure of much right now. I've got to check out apartments in Amherst, I've got to check out retail location rents in the town—"

"Why so depressed? Your parents own this building. You don't have to pay rent." His hands tightened on her shoulders.

"I think I do. If I want to grow up."

He tried to turn her around. "I'll help you grow up."

She felt his heat, the force of his sexuality. His physical pull was like a planet on its moons as she turned around in his arms.

She put both hands on his chest and shoved him away more brusquely than she'd intended. "Slade, no. I'm saying *no*."

His eyes narrowed. "Morgan said something."

"Yes, but that doesn't mat—"

"Damn it, Bella, Morgan means nothing to me! *That* was just—silliness."

"I also know that, Slade." Now she put her hands on his shoulders, gently. "It was silliness with Morgan, and it is silliness with me."

It was as if a sheen of ice rose out of his skin, coating his body, veiling his eyes. He had been soft, open. Now he was hard, closed. His mouth became a dark line, bitter, almost frightening. But the worst thing was the glint of pain at the back of his eyes.

She would not say she never meant to hurt him. That would only hurt him more. It would hurt his pride.

He stepped back, out of her reach. He was fully inside her shop and she was outside. Strange. She expected him to push past her now, to stride away, head high, jaw taut, superior and exasperated, to jump on his motorcycle and peel away, scattering the pebbles, tires shrieking.

Instead, he smiled. "You know, Bella, with you it was never silliness. With you, it was never a lie."

Her heart stopped. "Slade—"

His smile deepened. "Don't worry, babe. I'll survive." Reaching out, he touched his fingers to her chin.

He stepped past her with the gallantry of a highwayman, graceful, contained, already thinking of the future, and mounted his motorcycle. He kicked it into life and wheeled onto the main road without disarranging a stone.

. . .

"Well," Bella said, after Slade was out of sight and sound. "Well." She discovered she needed to cry, and no one was pulling into the parking lot, so she reentered the coolness of the building, went to the back of the shop, sat down on a chair, and bent over, holding her hands to her face and letting the sobs shake her. She wasn't even sure why she was crying: pity for Slade? regret for lost possibilities with such an enticing, confusing man? terror for herself? For with a partner, she could probably make a go of the shop, but without one, she was afraid she was doomed.

Or maybe not.

She dried her eyes and returned to the showroom.

Slade had taught her some things, that was certain. But she had taught herself—*realized* it herself—that she had "an eye" for unique pieces of furniture, jewelry, and art. Perhaps the location of the shop was wrong, but Bella's dream of a store filled with exquisite items for people's homes was right. Perhaps some people knew what they wanted to do from the moment they could walk and talk, but others didn't figure it out until later, or when they stumbled across it by accident. Did that make it less real? This felt very real to her.

She had created Bella's. If she was serious about running a business, she had a lot to learn. She needed to take classes, surf the Internet, and, doing things the old-fashioned way, take books out of the library. The thought excited her.

A man entered the shop, so quietly he took Bella by surprise. She was deep in her thoughts and had to straighten her shoulders and clear her throat before saying, "Hello."

Her customer wore a stodgy blue gingham checked suit and a polka-dot bow tie. Perhaps in his forties, he was dignified in an academic way, with a short beard and a slow, deliberate way of moving.

"I have moved here from Santa Fe," he informed Bella in a high, cultivated voice. "As you know, the houses and furniture designs are quite different there. I've bought a nice old historic colonial in Amherst, and I'd appreciate some assistance in furnishing it. I read in the paper that you carry some authentic antiques."

"We do," Bella agreed, stepping out from behind the counter. "Let me show you what we have."

Ben was lying on his stomach on a long table covered with cushions and a soft blue sheet. Natalie was squinting her eyes at him, charcoal in her hand, as she worked on the line and shadow of his back. She had his face mostly done, partially submerged in surging water, his eyes open, his arm straining forward past his head as he appeared to swim.

"Can I take a break?" he mumbled, his mouth obstructed by the blue sheet.

"Sure." He was a good model, capable of holding a pose without twitching, and this pose required concentration and physical effort. Natalie stretched her own arms. "Want some coffee?"

"I need to pee." He jumped off the table and strode, naked, from the room.

Natalie enjoyed the view of his backside.

When he returned, she enjoyed the view of his front side, but as he walked into the room, he was carrying on a conversation, as if she'd been following him around.

". . . so I thought, since Mom and Dad want to travel, but they don't have the money for it without dipping into their retirement accounts, I'd buy their house. I make a pretty good salary, I've got tenure, I've stashed away some savings. You and I could live there—you like the lake, I know, and don't you have to be out of your aunt's house by next spring? We could get married whenever you want. I know women like to fuss over that sort of thing. Summer would be best for me, because I don't have as many classes to teach, or, come to think of it, January would be ideal because that's winter session." He went to the table where Natalie had placed a pitcher of ice water and glasses, poured himself a drink, and took a long swallow. "Dad will want to finish out his teaching contract this coming year, so they could start traveling about the time you move from your aunt's. And Brady will be through high school then, but he'll want to live at home until he starts college, at least through the summer, and probably come home for holidays. With the money I pay for Mom and Dad's house, they'll be able to buy a small cottage, not on the lake but in the area. What do you think?"

Torn between disbelief and joy, Natalie almost collapsed onto the floor. Hands on hips, she asked, "Was there a marriage proposal in there somewhere?"

Ben leaned against the modeling table, crossed his arms over his chest, and groaned. "Do you want me to get down on my knee?"

Natalie laughed out loud. "Actually, it would make for a pretty memorable pose, since you're naked." Sobering, she said, "Ben, we've known each other about three months."

"Okay, how much time do you think is appropriate before deciding to marry?"

Oh no, Natalie thought, *he's going to get out his computer and start searching for statistics*. "I suppose it's different for each individual couple, Ben."

"I agree." He thought for a moment, then said, "Look, let's get engaged, and then you'll have until next spring to change your mind."

"Or you to change yours," Natalie shot back.

"I won't change mine."

"Ben . . ." She walked to the window. "First, would you put on some clothes? I don't think we can talk about this with you naked. At least I can't."

"Okay," he answered good-naturedly, and pulled on his bathing trunks. "Better?"

She shook her head helplessly. "You could put on a bear costume and still look sexy."

Ben walked over and stood close to her, not quite touching. "It's more than sex between us, Natalie."

"I know." Had she ever been more frightened in her life? Had she ever been happier? "It's just so . . ." She studied his face, taking in the clear, healthy blue of his eyes, the familiar lines of his jaw and cheekbones, his expression of honesty. How did anyone *know*? How did anyone *trust*? "Ben, why do you want to marry me?"

"What?" He leaned back, staring at her as if she wasn't making sense.

"I mean, do you think it's *time you got married*? So you can buy your parents' house and start your own family?"

"Well, yeah, I suppose I do. But that's not why I want to marry you."

She waited in silence, her own heart racing, her pulse fluttering in her neck, wanting him to say the perfect words and at the same time having no idea what those words would be.

Ben frowned. "I don't know what to say. I mean, I've never proposed to anyone before." Reaching out, he took her hands in his. "I love you. I'm in awe of what you do. I don't mean just your art, although that knocks me off my feet. What you've seen in my mother, what you've shown in your drawing of her, well, it's amazing. I want to be with you for the rest of my life. It's like you wake up something inside me. I'm more alive when I'm with you. I would never leave you because I couldn't bear to be without you."

Something inside Natalie broke open, flooding her with joy. Tears streamed down her face.

Ben looked worried. "Did I say something wrong?"

Natalie put her fingertips on his lips to hush him. "Ben. You said the perfect thing. I'll marry you. Of course I'll marry you."

Ben pulled her to him. "Thank God."

Natalie lifted her face up to his for a kiss, but he was talking again. "You don't mind living in my parents' house, do you? It's just that I love the lake, and I think our kids would like it, too. It's big for us, but you could have one of the bedrooms for your studio, and we'll need bedrooms for our children, and a guest room, too, for when Slade or your mother comes to visit." He stopped talking, his eyes widening.

"Is something wrong?" Natalie asked.

Uncomfortably, Ben confessed, "I just realized it's almost August. School starts at the end of next month. I'll be a crazy man."

Natalie tilted her head, watching him fondly. "So this is something you need to get done," she prompted. "This plan to get married."

"Exactly." He stopped. "Is that wrong? Does it upset you?"

"No. I'm just learning how you think. I've always been around artistic types, Ben. They're more—*romantic*." She gestured at her clothing, and his. She was barefoot, in stained cargo pants and a black tank top. She'd brushed her teeth this morning, but she wore no lipstick and the only mascara on her lashes was left over from last night. Ben was standing there in his bathing trunks. The morning sun streamed in the window.

"I see," Ben murmured. "You want romance." He grabbed her wrist. "I have an idea."

He led her down the stairs and into the kitchen. He snatched her floppy straw sun hat from the hook and plopped it on her head. He grabbed up the bottle of sunblock she kept by the back door and led her outside.

They went down the steps, across the lawn, and over to the canoe left upside down next to the water. As soon as she saw it, Natalie guessed where he was taking her.

Natalie helped Ben swing it over and shove it into the water. They both stepped inside. They both took a paddle. Ben sat in the bow to steer. Natalie was glad to sit in the stern, to watch his back as he took the lead.

The day was hot, the bright sun painting the water with a silver sheen. Their paddles made a kind of music as they stroked along. Ben had taken the day off from his lab in order to model for Natalie; it was a weekday, most other adults were at work or busy with chores. Summer ferns and foliage fell down the banks like a green filigree, and trees swayed in a playful breeze. They glided along the lake, enjoying the serenity of the late morning.

They arrived at the arch of willow branches reaching from one bank to the other.

"Duck," Ben called.

She bent down as they slid beneath the tickling strands of leaves, and then they were there, inside the small, private cove. Light streamed through the trees, painting the water pale green. From the bank, a frog jumped into the water, affronted at their arrival. The canoe knocked gently against the bank. Ben shipped his paddle and turned around to face Natalie.

He was smiling. "Is this romantic?"

Natalie touched his cheek lightly. "Very."

She expected him to kiss her. Instead, he reached into his trunks' pocket and brought out a small black velvet box.

Inside was an antique engagement ring, one whopping large round faceted diamond surrounded by smaller diamonds, set in platinum.

"Ben!" She was breathless.

"It was my grandmother's. My grandmother Barnaby. She passed it along to me for when I got engaged." Awkwardly, Ben knelt in the bottom of the canoe, which was almost an impossibility with his long legs, and looked uncomfortable. He took Natalie's hand in his. "Natalie, will you marry me?"

Tears glittered in her eyes, making rainbows fly up from the ring. Her heart was racing with joy. "Of course I will, Ben. I'd throw my arms around you and kiss you, too, but I'm afraid I'll tip the boat and we'll both fall out and the ring will get lost in the lake."

"Then I'd better put it on you." He slipped the ring from its velvet slot and slid it onto Natalie's finger.

"Ben, did you have the ring in your trunks all morning?"

"Yup."

"Didn't you worry about being out on the lake with it in your pocket? What if we'd had an accident? What if the ring had fallen into the deep part of the lake?"

Ben's gaze was steady, the expression of a man she could trust. "Sometimes, I think, it's worth taking a risk."

28

Bella hadn't had the best of days.

First, an elderly couple came in, sour-faced and suspicious. The man walked with a cane. He and his wife made a slow tour of Bella's, eyeing the furniture skeptically. The man would then extend an arm and whack the dry sink or table leg with his cane, several times, as if expecting to prove the wood was really pressboard. Bella politely asked him not to hit the furniture because it might leave marks. The man humphed, told her everything in her shop was too expensive, and the couple left.

The hours passed slowly until her next arrival, who turned out to be a very pregnant woman simply needing to use a bathroom. Afterward, she thanked Bella and rushed away.

The third person to enter was a man in his fifties, so dapper and decorous Bella suspected he was a professor at one of the universities. Enchanted by a desk, he examined it inch by inch, squinting, squatting, peering, even sniffing. He asked Bella if she could come down on the price, and she sweetly said perhaps a few hundred. Then he began to grill Bella: What were her qualifications to sell antiques? Did she belong to the Antiques Dealers' Association of America? Did she subscribe to any journals such as *Art and Antiques*? Did she have an associate, perhaps someone older and more *experienced*, he could talk with? Bella struggled to remain polite, and after he left—without buying the desk—she counseled herself that the interaction had not been worthless. She knew she needed to find out about various organizations and antiques magazines. Perhaps she could even start taking some courses.

Another dark cloud on her horizon was the mess she, Natalie, and Morgan had gotten themselves into. Their last get-together had ended so badly, with Morgan storming away, and understandably so. Josh shouldn't have told Natalie about his novel before telling Morgan. As for Morgan and Slade—Bella was glad that Morgan had told her about Slade's pass. It hurt Bella's pride, but deep down, she wasn't really surprised. Most important, it had helped her sort out her feelings about Slade and Aaron. Slade had been such fun, bringing such a sense of *romance*. Slade was a summer breeze, enticing, playful, inconstant. Aaron was the earth beneath her feet, and the sun and moon as well.

She was flicking off the lights, preparing to close the shop, when the phone rang.

"Bella?" Morgan's voice was surprisingly cheerful. "Could you come over for a drink right now?"

Surprised, for a moment Bella didn't speak.

"I've asked Natalie. She's coming, too. I want to apologize to her, and to you—"

"No apologies necessary—" Bella began.

Morgan cut her off. "Fine, but come anyway. As soon as possible, okay?"

Something good had happened, Bella could tell. Her spirits lifted. "I'll be right there."

Aaron had gone down to the Cape to sail with his brother. Bella drove home, showered, slipped into a clean pair of shorts and a tee shirt, and headed next door to Morgan's.

Morgan was on the deck, setting out a board of cheese and crackers. Her long brown hair was loose, falling around her shoulders, transforming her from athlete into model. She wore khaki shorts and a casual blue linen shirt.

"Hey, Bella!" Morgan kissed Bella on the cheek as she came up onto the deck.

"You seem happy," Bella remarked warily.

"Oh, I am!" Morgan did a little spin. "I'll tell you about it when Nat gets here."

"I'm coming!" Natalie called, running across the lawn in a blue sundress.

Bella gawked. Natalie in blue instead of black? Wow.

Natalie skipped up the steps. She hugged Morgan. "I'm so glad you phoned. I've been miserable since—"

"I know. I have, too," Morgan said. "I don't want the three of us ever to split up, even if we argue. Did you ever hear that the Chinese character for disaster is the same as the one for opportunity?"

"Morgan," Bella said, "you're not quite making sense."

Morgan laughed. "What I'm trying to say is that what you told me, Natalie, about Josh's novel— Well, wait!" She dashed into her house and quickly returned carrying a tray with champagne flutes and a bottle of Perrier-Jouët.

"What are we celebrating?" Natalie asked.

"Everything! Wait till you hear!" Morgan poured the frothy liquid into the glasses and handed them around. "All right, ladies, here we go. (A) Josh spontaneously, without coaxing, decided to have a boys' night out with Petey. That's a *first*. He's taking him to see Daddy's office, to Fresh Side for dinner, and to the library."

"Ergo, our girls' night out," Bella said.

"Oh, it's more than that. (B) He's getting ready to become Stay-at-Home Dad!" Morgan lifted her glass high. "Here's to me! The new assistant director of hazardous waste management at the University of Massachusetts!"

"Get *out*!" Natalie shouted. "When did this happen?"

"Yesterday!" Morgan waved her hands. "Sit down, sit down, I'll tell you all about it."

"I didn't even know you were planning to take a job," Bella said.

"I've been keeping my eye on the U. Mass. site all along," Morgan confessed. "Then, when there was the blood spill at Felicity's—"

Natalie demanded, "The *what*?"

"The blood spill." Morgan's tone was matter-of-fact. "Felicity's boyfriend injured himself climbing out of Felicity's window—"

Bella sipped her champagne as she listened to Morgan recount the events of the adolescent drama at the Hortons and the satisfaction Morgan felt that spurred her to initiate the interview at U. Mass. She heard the authority in Morgan's voice, her knowledge and experience clear in every word.

"I discovered the director of the Environmental Health and Safety Office knows my old boss at Weathersfield. I've got the perfect qualifications, plus I'm *here*. Perhaps they were desperate, but they called today to offer me a full-time position. Josh is going to talk with Ronald Ruoff to tell him he has to resign because we can't both work full-time. Josh will take care of Petey and work on his novel. He's got an agent who's very optimistic about selling it." Morgan paused to sip her champagne, then continued. "Even better than all that, it's as if Josh and I are falling in love again. We talk and talk and make love like we used to. It's heaven. It means, of course, we're going to have to put this place on the market."

"Oh no!" Bella cried.

"I know. We love it here. I'll be making a decent salary at the university, but nothing like what Josh makes at Bio-Green."

"Maybe he'll make a killing with his book," Natalie suggested.

"Maybe, but we can't count on that. We're going to sell this place and buy something smaller, not on the lake. But near here, of course, so we can come visit as often as you'll let us."

"Well," Natalie said slowly, "I won't be *here* after next spring. Aunt Eleanor's returning then." She met Morgan's eyes, and then Bella's. "Oh hell," she said. "I can't wait. Morgan, I don't want to spoil your big announcement, but I have a couple of my own."

Morgan perched on the side of a chair impatiently. "Tell."

"A New York gallery has contacted me. They read the reviews and they want to carry me. I'm going down to New York to meet with them."

"Oh, Natalie, what fantastic news!" Bella cried. She hugged her friend, carefully, so she wouldn't spill their champagne.

"It's all because of you, Bella," Natalie said. "I owe it all to you for hanging my work in your gallery. I owe it to *both* of you, for believing in me when I hardly believed in myself." She raised her glass in a toast. "Here's to you, Bella, for discovering me."

Bella's eyes teared up. She was happy for Natalie—and she was thrilled for herself. She had helped a friend, and she had proved to herself that, truly, her judgment was worthy.

The three women toasted.

Morgan said, "You said you have two announcements."

Natalie's grin was like a flash of sunshine. "Ben asked me to marry him. I said yes."

"You're going to marry Ben?" Morgan and Bella exploded from their chairs. They grabbed Natalie and all three hugged and jumped up and down like teenagers at a rock concert.

Morgan poured them more champagne. "Natalie," Bella said, "you're going to be my sister-in-law."

"How cool is that?" Natalie's laugh was contagious.

"Where are you going to live?" Morgan asked.

"Next door," Natalie told them. "Ben has already talked to Louise and Dennis. He wants to buy their house. We expect to get married in January. Ben says that's a quiet month at the university, so we can have a honeymoon. We plan to move into the house sometime in May."

Bella's jaw dropped. Ben had talked to *his* parents? Ben and Natalie were going to live in the *Barnaby* house? Where was Bella supposed to live?

"Bella," Morgan asked. "What are you thinking?"

Bella forced a smile. "So much change . . ."

Natalie nodded, her face somber now, too. "I know. More changes to come, too, enormous changes."

"But we won't let anything change our friendship," Morgan declared. "Listen, I've never had such close friends as you two. This has been an amazing summer, and something quite unusual has happened here, on Dragonfly Lake. I mean the three of us meeting and influencing one another's lives. Even if I leave this lake, I still need the two of you to be my best friends. I want to be your best friend, too. Okay?"

Natalie reached out and touched Morgan's arm. Very seriously,

she said, "I've always wanted to be the best friend of an assistant
director of hazardous waste management."

They all laughed.

Morgan aimed a look at Bella. "Are you with us, Bella?"

Bella smiled. "Always."

The three women sat on the deck while the sun sank lower, bur-
nishing the gray clouds with a dull silver gleam. Around them the
birds were settling in for the night, calling out and answering. Even
the trees seemed to be settling their leaves for sleep. As darkness
fell, a slight breeze stirred the air, drifting across the lake, lightly
brushing against their skin, teasing their hair, cooling the backs of
their necks. Lights came on in houses all around the lake, flicking
into brilliance like fireflies, here and here and here. So many families, Bella thought, so many people with their own dreams and
struggles.

At last the women rose. Natalie and Bella helped carry the
empty bottles and glasses and plates into Morgan's house, then went
away, calling out, "Good night."

At home, Bella peeked into the living room. Both her parents
were reading.

"Hi, guys." She perched on a chair. "I've been talking to Natalie
and Morgan. Natalie's engaged to Ben."

Louise beamed. "We know. Isn't it grand?"

Dennis cocked his head thoughtfully. "Ben wants to buy the
house."

"I know. I'm glad for them, and for both of you." She paused, her
eyes full of melancholy. "I guess I'm kind of sad for myself. I love this
house so much."

Louise reached over to pat Bella's hand. "You'll have your own
place soon enough. Oh, that reminds me. Aaron phoned. He's back
in Amherst. He'd like you to call."

Aaron. His name was like a fresh breeze in a stuffy room.
"Great, thanks." She hurried up to the privacy of her room and
called Aaron.

"I thought you were staying at your parents' tonight," she told him.

"I missed you," Aaron said. "Any chance you could spend the night? I could come get you."

"I'd love it," she said. "I've got a lot to tell you."

As she had many times before, Bella packed a duffel bag with toiletries and a change of clothes. She ran out as soon as Aaron's car turned into the drive.

"Hey," he said, his voice warm with affection. Beneath the overhead light, his nose glowed with sunburn and his cheeks were rosy. He smelled fresh from a shower and shaving cream.

"Hey." Leaning over, she kissed him. "I'm glad to see you. Good day sailing?"

He laughed. "Oh yeah. The wind was perfect."

"Nice and even?" she asked.

"Not at all. It was gusting from the southeast, a real challenge. We got up some speed, too, and almost capsized." He slapped the steering wheel. "Damn, it was fun."

She'd never been much of a sailor, and Dragonfly Lake had its moods, but nothing ever *challenging*.

While he drove back to his apartment in Amherst, Aaron raved on about the sail. Bella studied his profile in the flickering light from the street lamps. He looked like a Roman emperor. A centurion. Although what was a centurion? She'd forgotten. She meant that he looked classical, wise, and strong.

Aaron parked on the street, hefted her duffel bag on his arm, beeped his car locked, and taking Bella's arm in his, walked with her up the sidewalk and into the apartment building. It was just after ten o'clock. The building was silent; people were settling down for the night.

In his living room, he turned on the lights. "Want a drink?"

Bella shuddered. "I think I'll get myself a nice, cool glass of water. I've been drinking champagne all evening with Morgan and Natalie, and I've had quite enough alcohol for a while."

"Want to go to bed instead?" Aaron asked.

She grinned at him. "I always want to go to bed with you. But tonight, I'd like to talk awhile."

"Okay." Aaron got himself a cold beer and flopped down on the sofa. "About anything special?"

She kicked off her sandals and sat at the opposite end of the sofa, bringing her bare feet up and stretching out her legs so she could put her feet on his lap. "Lots of special things," she told him, looking up through her lashes.

He ran his hand over her ankle and up to her knee. "Shoot."

"Well, Morgan got a job at U. Mass. in the biosafety department, or something like that, involving waste management, and if you can imagine, she's absolutely over the moon about it. And Josh is going to quit Bio-Green and they're going to sell their house and buy something more modest so they can live on Morgan's salary while Josh writes his novel."

"Wow. I had no idea Josh was writing a novel. What's it about?"

"It's sci-fi, that's all I know. And, Aaron, Ben and Natalie are going to get married! They're going to buy Dad and Mom's house and live there, and my parents will buy a more manageable house and do some traveling."

"I can't say I'm surprised," Aaron said. "I mean about Ben and Natalie."

"I'm so happy for them. For all four of them. Especially for Ben, because Natalie's wonderful, and he deserves someone who loves him and can deal with him. But that's not all." She set her glass on the coffee table, drew her legs up beneath her, and took a deep breath. "I'm going to give up Bella's and go to San Francisco with you."

Aaron stared at her, speechless.

"Oh, Aaron, I love you so much." Bella leaned toward him. "I want to make a life with you. I want to make you happy. I want to watch you work and create your buildings and become famous."

"Wait." Aaron frowned. "You're going to give up Bella's? Why this sudden change of mind?" He didn't sound happy.

Bella drew back, surprised at Aaron's reaction. "I thought you'd be thrilled."

"Well, I'm not. Not unless you can tell me why you've decided to give up Bella's."

Bella struggled for a moment, wondering how to answer. "The romantic reply would be that I love you so much I want you to be happy and I want to be with you. And that *is* true. Perhaps it's the first reason. But it's not the only reason. I've had a lot of time to think. What if I *do* have an eye for antiques and art? Shouldn't I train it? Shouldn't I educate myself? If I did, I'd certainly be able to do a better job of talking to my customers. I want to take some courses in art history and antiques. . . ."

Aaron sat quietly for a moment. "Wait a minute. Listen to me. What if I turned down the San Francisco job? There will be other jobs. I could find something west of Boston. Then you could take some time to give Bella's a chance—"

"No," Bella insisted. "You want that job. I need more education. In a way, Aaron, you and I are doing similar things, supplying human beings with beauty in their life. Only, you've had your education. I need mine. I need to learn more."

"You have a natural gift, Bella," Aaron assured her. "Look what you did with Natalie's paintings. You haven't studied art retail, but somehow you knew she was good, and you hung her paintings and they sold. You did the same with Penny's jewelry."

"I didn't know about furniture," Bella reminded him quietly.

"You're wrong. I think you do know a lot about furniture. Why do you think Slade Reynolds spent all that time going antiquing with you? Because he was trying to get into your pants?"

"Aaron!" Bella flushed.

"You think I didn't notice? I'm not blind. But in a weird way I respect Slade. I don't think he spent *all* that time helping you just to get you into bed. He could tell you're a natural. He admired your judgment."

"I'm stunned," Bella said. She put her hands on her cheeks, giving herself a moment to think everything through. Lifting her head, she looked at the man she loved. "Aaron, I can't believe you would give up San Francisco for me."

"I'd give up anything for you," Aaron told her. "It just took me a while to realize that."

Bella smiled from ear to ear. "Me, too," she said. "I mean, I'd give up anything for you. I finally got it that going to San Francisco wouldn't mean giving up anything. I want to go. I've already checked online. They've got first-class schools there."

"But what about Dragonfly Lake?" Aaron asked. "I thought you didn't want to leave it."

"It will be here," Bella told him. "We can come back. I want to move on. Most of all, I want to be with you."

Aaron took her in his arms and held her close. Bella snuggled against him, loving his strong embrace, his warm male aroma, his muscular chest supporting her giving softness. She had never felt more at home.

29

When she first saw her mother getting out of her truck, Natalie almost didn't recognize her.

Her mother had been transformed. Marlene's hair, once a long, stringy gray, was now a multihued caramel color, shaped to fall in flattering layers around her face, bringing out the blue of her eyes, which Natalie was surprised to see was the same dark blue of her own eyes. She'd always thought she'd gotten that blue from her father.

"Mom! You look amazing!" Natalie raced out to hug her mother.

Marlene accepted the embrace, saying almost shyly, "You look pretty wonderful yourself, darling."

Natalie grabbed up her mother's suitcase and led her into the house. "Have you ever stayed at Aunt Eleanor's? It's fabulous."

"I stayed a couple of nights a long time ago. My little sister does have style. I'd get awfully lonely out here, though."

"But there are people all around."

"Eleanor doesn't own a dog," Marlene pointed out. "Although," she continued with a twinkle in her eye, "people can be nice, too."

"Mother." Natalie almost dropped the suitcase on her foot. "Don't tell me you have a boyfriend."

Marlene looked coy. "Hardly a *boy*."

"Well, Mother." Natalie was astonished. This was an entirely new Marlene. "Come to the kitchen. I have lunch waiting. Tell me everything."

Natalie had placed a posy of dahlias in a small white pitcher at the center of the table. That was her only "fancy" touch. She hadn't seen her mother for over a year, and the Marlene Natalie had known would have scorned "fancy." "I made ham and cheese sandwiches. What would you like to drink? I have fresh iced tea."

Marlene was turned toward the large glass door and the lake. "That all sounds perfect. Have you enjoyed yourself here?"

"You have no idea. I have a lot to tell you." She set the plates on the table. "We'll eat outside this evening when the sun isn't so direct. It's hot out there."

Marlene settled in a chair, took a sip of iced tea, planted her elbows on the table, and scrutinized Natalie. "You're happy."

In the face of her mother's warm attention, Natalie let it all spill out. "Oh, Mom, I'm in love with the most wonderful man. His name is Ben. You'll meet him tonight. He's a good man, Mom. We're going to get married." She held out her hand to show off her engagement ring.

"My," Marlene said, holding her daughter's hand, turning it this way and that. "That's a whopper."

"I know. It was his grandmother's."

"What does he do?"

"He's a scientist at U. Mass. A chemical engineer. I'm not sure what that means, but I'm learning."

"Attractive?"

"*Dreamy.*"

"Does he treat you well?" The question had years of weight behind it. The question had the ache of the husband and father who had been there, then left and never returned.

Natalie kept hold of her mother's hand. "Yes. Very much so. I can trust him, Mom."

"That's good." Marlene patted Natalie's hand, an unusually affectionate touch. Marlene had usually been more physically comfortable with bulldogs.

Natalie cocked her head. "You look happy, too. You look—different. What's up?"

"We're talking about you." Marlene blushed and took a dainty bite from her sandwich. "Mmm. Delicious. Honey mustard."

"Don't try and change the subject. Tell me about this—'hardly a boy' friend."

Marlene's cheeks grew rosy. She looked down at her lap, playing with her napkin, folding it into careful little squares. "His name is Joe. He's retired from a hardware store. Widowed. Not bad looking, although he's thin as a beanpole."

Natalie had never seen her mother so girlish, so coy. "Does he live near you?"

"Across the street, down the road a bit. That's how we met. He raises the best sweet corn in all Maine. I told him I'd trade some of my pickled beets. He guesses that I use something more than dill and onions in my beets, but I won't tell him my secret." After a moment, Marlene looked smug. "Yet."

"Does he have a dog?"

"He raises long-haired dachshunds."

"Get out!" Natalie burst out laughing. Her mother had always scorned any of the smaller breeds of dogs, considering them puny, yappy, and fussy.

Marlene laughed, too, shaking her head at her own opinions. "Well, they were his wife's dogs. They're getting old. He's learning about my bullies." Her head raised, her back straightened, her chin lifted in pride. "It might please you to know that I've been accredited by the American Kennel Club. I've been showing two of my bullies at the New England Dog Shows. I'm pretty sure I'm going to be able to enter Westminster next year."

Another surprise. Another tilt of the world, toward the sun. "I didn't realize you were interested in showing."

"I wasn't, at first. I wanted a protective animal who would be gentle with my children, and bulldogs are great for that. They look more frightening than they are. Once I had Winston and Jennie, I fell in love with the breed."

"I remember," Natalie said softly.

"You were so jealous of those dogs." Marlene laughed and lay back in her chair, remembering. "But I was concerned about Slade—you, too, of course. I was afraid he'd stay at home, feeling obligated to take care of me, be the man around the house, that sort of thing, and he's as stubborn as you. I needed to show him, and you, too, I could be fine on my own, so you could both have your own lives."

Natalie's mouth dropped. "You kept getting more dogs just so we could leave?"

"Not *just* so you could leave. No. I loved those dogs. I love the ones I have now. I love breeding them. I finally saved enough money to build the kind of kennel I want for them, with a special whelping room. Lots of bulldogs have trouble whelping."

Natalie remembered the dogs running all over the house, jumping up on the sofa, drooling on the rugs.

Marlene rose from the table. "I want to get my purse. I have some pictures to show you."

As Marlene went into the hall, Natalie settled her chin in her hand and allowed herself a moment of silent awe and gratitude that felt almost like a prayer. Her mother looked so different. She was *happy*. She wasn't weary, ragged, round shouldered with exhaustion as she had been when Natalie and Slade were children. But wasn't that part of it—the children had grown up and Marlene now had the time and money to care for herself?

Marlene came back into the room with a photo album in her hand. "Here's my new sweetie pie."

She passed the album to Natalie, who expected to see a photo of Joe, Marlene's beau. Instead, a bulldog stood there, posing for the camera.

"Cara Mia," Marlene said. "She's my brood bitch. Two years old and in fine health."

Natalie only half listened as Marlene extolled the virtues and characteristics of her prize animal. What fascinated her was Marlene's enthusiasm, her dedication, in spite of the various difficulties and challenges. Marlene had raised bulldogs for twenty years, and it still lit her up inside as she talked about them. What had Louise said when Natalie was drawing her? *How clever of your mother to turn a passion into a way of making a living.* Something like that. Watching her, Natalie understood for the first time that she might have gotten some of her good looks from her father, but she'd received her love for her work straight from her mother's genes. Slade had, too; his love for antique furniture was an obsession. Perhaps there was a gene for professional intensity; perhaps someday scientists would discover it. Bella's languorous sister, Beatrice, didn't have it; Ben did, a deep vein running straight through him, like Natalie's love of painting.

"Don't you have any photos of Joe?" she asked her mother.

Marlene laughed. "You know, I don't. Which is a shame, because he is a fine-looking man. He's bald, but his head is a lovely shape."

A *lovely* shape? Natalie's heart lifted. For so many years, her mother had been entrenched in a deep, dismal rut of loneliness and sorrow because her husband had left her. Was it possible this Joe might become permanent in Marlene's life? Was it possible her mother might have pleasure, and trust, and companionship? The thought pierced Natalie with a hopefulness that was almost painful.

After lunch, Marlene went upstairs to take a nap. Natalie began preparing for the evening. She'd invited the O'Keefes, the Barnabys, and Aaron to dinner. Ben had agreed to grill salmon on the deck for her. She marinated it in soy sauce, brown sugar, lemon, and garlic and put it in the refrigerator. She'd made a cold rice salad that morning while waiting for her mother to arrive. She stirred up biscuits for a berry shortcake and stuck them in the oven. She prepared the spring leaf lettuces in a bowl, ready for dressing at the table. She wouldn't paint today. Later, though, she would show her mother her work.

At five-thirty, she woke her mother. They both took showers and dressed. Natalie wore her blue sundress and sandals; she'd told her guests the dinner was casual. She hoped it would be cool enough to eat on the deck.

Marlene wore a loose lavender sundress and long, dangling silver earrings. Earrings! When had her mother ever worn jewelry?

"Mother," Natalie said. "You look fabulous."

"Joe gave me these earrings," Marlene confessed. She tipped her head forward so Natalie could inspect them. They were long, slender twists. "I just phoned him. He's taking care of the dogs. They're doing just fine without me. That's the nice thing about bulldogs. They can be a very quiet, contented animal, and, of course, they adore Joe. I have them in the house now because it's air-conditioned. They're in the kitchen. Joe will probably let them in the living room this evening when he watches the Red Sox."

"Ben's parents have a yellow Lab," she told her mother.

"Good dogs."

"And a cat named Bossy."

"*Cats.*" Marlene sniffed dismissively.

The doorbell rang and everyone arrived: Bella and Aaron, Morgan and Josh, Louise and Dennis, and best of all, Ben. They settled on the deck, where Natalie had set up two tables with plates and utensils. Conversation flowed naturally. People leaned against the railing, chatting, complaining about the heat, waving at boaters who sailed past on the lake.

Eleanor's tables were round, impossible to push together. Natalie had actually considered putting out place cards at the tables because she wanted her mother to sit near one of the Barnabys, so she could get to know the family. But place cards would just be weird, she decided. When the salmon was ready and people drifted naturally into chairs, she was relieved to see that Ben sat on one side of Marlene, Louise on the other, and Dennis across from Marlene. Natalie sat at a table with Bella, Aaron, Morgan, and Josh.

At first the conversation centered on the Red Sox, who were doing well this year. Natalie had tried for a while to work up the interest to support the Yankees in their feud against the Red Sox, if only for the sake of a good-natured argument, but in fact she didn't really care about baseball, and as usual, she found herself talking with Bella about which of the new players had the best body. Of course, no one, new or old, could replace Jacoby Ellsbury for sheer gorgeousness and charisma.

From time to time, Natalie leaned back in her chair to listen to the other table. How was her mother doing?

"... bulldogs are always described as 'walking muscle,'" Marlene was saying.

"Mother," Natalie called over. "How long have you been talking about your dogs?"

The rest of the table shushed Natalie.

"I'm fascinated," Dennis assured her.

"Especially since our dog is waddling blubber," Louise added, laughing.

So it was good, Natalie thought. They were all getting along. *The in-laws*.

Later in the evening, as Natalie went in to prepare the desserts, the others got up and moved around, some bringing in dishes, her mother leaning on the railing, talking with Ben and Morgan.

Bella and Aaron helped Natalie carry out the shortcakes. Everyone exclaimed in delight except for Morgan and Marlene, who were too engrossed in conversation to notice. They sat together at a table, leaning toward each other as Morgan described, in much the same tones Marlene used to talk about her dogs, an autoclave.

"Autoclaves are steam sterilizers used for high-level disinfection," Morgan was saying.

"Like a pressure cooker?" Marlene asked. "My mother had one of those for canning."

"Exactly. We can use them to sterilize lab equipment for reuse and waste materials, anything infectious or with blood—"

Natalie plunked Morgan's plate down in front her, saying with sweet sarcasm, "I've always thought a dinner party on the lake was the perfect time to discuss lab equipment for waste materials."

"Well, darling," Marlene told her daughter, "I need to learn about autoclaves. I'd love to be able to afford one big enough to do the dogs' bedding."

Natalie laughed. "Well, then, ladies, enjoy your conversation."

In spite of Natalie's citronella candles, by the time they finished dessert, the bugs were beginning to appear, so the group carried plates into the kitchen and settled in the living room for coffee. This time, Ben sat on the sofa, and after Natalie had finished setting out the sugar bowl and milk pitcher on the coffee table, he patted the spot next to him. She snuggled up to him happily.

Bella was on the opposite sofa, snuggled up to Aaron. She looked older somehow. Perhaps it was the new hairdo, pulled back in a knot.

"While we're all here," Bella said, "we've got an announcement to make." She paused for effect, then, with a smug look, turned to Aaron. "I'm moving to San Francisco with Aaron. I'm going to en-roll in art and furniture history courses this fall."

"Bella!" Morgan looked stricken. "You're moving away? I thought you loved it here."

"I do. We'll come back often to see everyone. Besides, Morgan, you told us you and Josh have to sell your house and get something smaller, not on the lake."

"True," Josh said. He and Morgan had settled on cushions on the floor, leaning against the wall. "Besides, Morgan will be working all the time."

"And so will you." Morgan nudged her husband playfully.

A noise sounded in the driveway. A vehicle arriving. Not a mo-torcycle, but perhaps a van. A moment later, a knock sounded on the door, and before Natalie could rise, Slade walked in.

He wore khakis and a white button-down shirt, and he was not alone. A woman was with him, a rather stern-looking young woman wearing a business suit.

"Slade!" Marlene cried.

"Hey, Mom." Sauntering over, he leaned down to kiss his mother and give her a quick hug. Straightening, he looked around the room. "Hey, everyone." He returned to the woman and put his arm around her shoulder. "I'd like you to meet Dina Hannoush."

Dina nodded politely. She could be pretty if she didn't look quite so judgmental. Glasses hid her green eyes.

"Dina's father sells Turkish rugs," Slade informed them. "That's how I got to know her. We recently connected and decided to start our own shop together." His smile at Dina indicated something more than professional interest.

Slade went around the room, introducing everyone, keeping a possessive hand on her arm.

Natalie said, "Slade, Dina, would you like some coffee? Or anything to eat?"

"Coffee would be lovely," Dina said. When she spoke, she became softer. Her voice was deep and melodious, hinting at a gentler self within her severe shell. "Can I help you?"

Natalie rose from the sofa. "No, it will just take me a moment." She went into the kitchen.

Slade said, "I'll grab a couple of chairs from the dining room."

Natalie found two more cups and saucers, poured the coffee, and carried them back toward the living room. Slade had a dining room chair in his hand and waited for her to go first. As Natalie passed her brother, she arched an eyebrow. Slade answered her with a nod that, surprisingly, held no mischief. Why, Slade looked *happy*.

Slade set the chairs in the group, and Dina sat down. Slade sat next to her. Natalie handed them each a cup of coffee.

"Nat told me Mom was coming for a visit, so I thought I'd better get out here and see her," Slade told them. "And I wanted you all to meet Dina."

"Slade," Marlene said, "I'm so glad you came. I can't tell you how wonderful it is to see both my children in the same room again."

Natalie looked at her mother while she was answering a question of Slade's about, of course, her bulldogs. Marlene glowed as she talked, and Natalie realized with a leap of her heart that the next charcoal she would draw would be of her mother.

. . . . .

Summer Breeze

A NOVEL

Nancy Thayer

A Reader's Guide

Nancy Thayer on The Perfect Man

In Nathaniel Hawthorne's short story "The Birthmark," a flaw is removed from a woman's face and she dies, because a perfect person can't live.

But modern-day women still cherish the dream of the perfect man. In some novels, they ride horses, own castles, give diamonds. In real life, we hope they're employed, have all their teeth, and behave with kindness to dogs, cats, and offspring.

I write about contemporary lives and people like the ones I know, with problems, flaws, hopes and dreams common to us all. I could invent a perfect man—but first, I'd have to figure out what the heck that means.

In *Summer Breeze*, I had the pleasure of writing about four *good* men. Even though he is a bad boy, I include Slade in that category. Can I tell you how many of my readers *love* Slade? My sister called me to protest because Bella chose Aaron when she could have had sexy Slade. But seriously, would you want to *marry* Slade? Would you really want to get pregnant, blow up like a turnip, give birth and not have sex for a few weeks, all the while worrying that Slade was flirting, or worse, with the delivery room nurse? (Not that I'm picking on nurses for flirting. My sister is a nurse. I worship nurses.)

No, I think we must rule out Slade as a candidate for the perfect man. But wait, maybe not! Maybe the question is: The perfect man for what?

Naturally—and I mean that in a few ways—we want our perfect man to be sexy. We fall in love with men in real life and in fiction because they've got serious sensual power that draws us to them. Of course not every woman feels that for every long-lashed man with bedroom eyes, which is, after all, a good thing.

Slade is sexy, but he's also a player, a charmer, and a bit of a wheeler-dealer. He's not completely trustworthy. He makes choices we might not approve of. He's the man our mothers warned us about, which is no doubt part of his appeal.

There's something inherently delicious, something inherently *alive*, something basically good in wanting to be bad, just for a moment, a moment out of time. Perhaps there are times when imperfection seems like just what the doctor ordered. We want to leave behind our routine lives with grumpy husbands, unpaid bills, whining children, critical mothers-in-law, dust balls under the sofa. Isn't that why we read?

But if in real life we want a man for more than a toe-curling fling, we want someone reliable, generous, capable, and well, *good*. True, we want that *zing* when we fall in love with a man. Each time we look at him, we want our hormones to light up like fireworks on the Fourth of July. But eventually, we'd really need a man who would lovingly give our kids a bath and put them to bed when we have to work late. *And* hang up the wet towels. Am I asking too much? Well, a girl can dream . . . or write fiction.

Summer Breeze characters Aaron, Ben, and Josh are sexy, too. They're also smart, kind, and dependable. But are they perfect?

Josh kept an important secret from his wife, Morgan. He told Natalie the secret—was he a bad husband? Or was Morgan a less than perfect wife?

Ben's a scientist obsessed with his work, which makes him seem distant and, as he puts it, "mentally underground." He does his best to express himself with Natalie. But will that be good enough for a long-term relationship like marriage? Will he talk to his children?

In my humble opinion, Aaron is the best of the lot. Not only is he intelligent, handsome, and patient, but he truly wants Bella to find the work that will make her heart sing, and that was the starting point for this book, as it is the foundation of my life. I want the work I love and a good man. I want my women characters to have all that, too.

Perhaps I treasure the work I love and my good man because I once, long ago, knew a Slade and can still pick up a book or pop in a DVD and see a Slade.

My own daughter—my intelligent, feminist daughter, married to a wonderful and handsome man, with three children—surprised me when she told me she would choose Slade over Aaron. Perhaps it had something to do with the passage where Bella and Slade are looking at Mr. Wheeler's furniture:

"Bella wanted to kiss Slade . . . Among all this antique furniture, she felt caught in a dream: She was the maid, he was the master; she was the peasant selling flowers, he was the soldier. He was the pirate. She was his plunder."

Does this antiquated image thrive in all our feminine dreams?

Let me ask you: if you were Bella, who would you choose: Aaron or Slade? Or how would you describe your perfect man? Email me at nancy@nancythayer.com to let me know, and I'll post the results on my website.

Questions and Topics for Discussion

1. Bella is so attached to her home that she considers breaking up with Aaron so she can stay at Dragonfly Lake. Why do you think she feels this way?

2. Do you identify with Bella's fear of change? Why does she finally decide to move to San Francisco? Would you have made the same decision?

3. While Bella finds comfort and nostalgia in the gargoyle cabinet and family antiques, Morgan feels trapped and isolated by the design of her luxurious new house. How can the appearance of a house affect the mood and family relationships within it? What is the difference between a house and a home, and does it have anything to do with furniture?

4. On the day that Natalie and Ben decide to stop talking about science and art, Natalie comments that their work is "the most interesting part of us, or the *defining* part of us." Do you agree? What would you identify as the *defining* part of yourself: the roles you play, your interests, your personality traits, or something else entirely?

5. Why does Natalie and Ben's relationship work despite their different interests?

6. Slade, the bad-boy, wheeler-dealer antiques aficionado, tells Bella that he would give up his playboy lifestyle to be with her. Why do you think he makes that declaration? Do you believe him?

7. How does Slade's decision to bring Dina Hannoush to the dinner party at the end of the summer reflect on his character?

8. Although we often don't see it, Josh struggles with pursuing his dream, supporting his family, and spending enough time with his wife and son. How well does he manage the balancing act?

9. Is Josh right to conceal his novel from Morgan? How would you have handled the situation?

10. While Natalie's exterior is that of a sleek and sophisticated New Yorker, she often believes that her thoughts and feelings are those of a child. Does the summer represent a growing-up process for Natalie? How do her attitudes towards Marlene, her mother, reflect her maturity?

11. Which of the characters do you identify the most with? Why?

12. The lakeside community seems like such a wonderful place to live. What is your ideal community?

Read on for an excerpt from

ISLAND GIRLS

A NOVEL

by Nancy Thayer

Published by Ballantine Books

Arden's half-hour television show for Channel Six, a local Boston station, was called *Simplify This,* which Arden privately knew was a ridiculous title because, really, nothing in life was simple.

She couldn't remember when she'd last had a vacation, and even when she had a weekend off, she'd worked, tapping away at her laptop or considering DVDs prospective entrants had sent her, or reviewing call sheets or expenses. Even watching television was work because she recorded and savagely studied competing shows, comparing theirs to hers, searching for what she was missing, what she could improve. Reading books and magazines: same thing. Even exercise was work for Arden because she had to keep her thirty-four-year-old body in shape for the merciless cameras that made everyone's butt look ten inches wider and ten pounds heavier. Same with having her nails and her hair done. She was fairly certain she worked when she slept.

Simplify This expressed her hard-won life's motto: to simplify your life, to stuff useless old family heirlooms like grandmothers' tea sets and framed photos of relatives so distant you couldn't remember their names into neat cardboard boxes, tidily labeled and piled in the attic or basement, or given away to the second-hand shops so you could claim a tax deduction. As you did it, you vanquished the ghosts of the past, the should-haves and could-haves, the expectations of parents, the dreams of childhood. Then your present life was clear and spacious, facing forward, not back.

Arden had spent her adult years simplifying. She had created a television show and her own life's battle cry out of the desire to simplify her odd, complicated family (if you could even call it that), which was like a jigsaw puzzle with the pieces scattered by the winds.

Today she parked her posh little Saab convertible in her reserved spot in the station's lot, whipped through the glass doors, nodded to the security guard, and strode down the corridor to her private lair. She unlocked it, stepped inside, leaned against the door, and kicked off her high heels.

It was a hot day for early May. Arden stripped off her suit jacket and unzipped her tight skirt. She collapsed in the wonderfully padded chair behind her desk, put her feet up, and stabbed the message button on her answering machine.

Messages: The dry cleaner said the stain wouldn't come out of the lavender silk dress. The masseuse reminded her she'd changed the time of her appointment. Marion Cleveland understood that all entries to Arden's *wonderful* show should be sent by mail with a DVD, but Marion was a *close personal friend* of Ernest Hilton, the program director of Channel Six, and so Marion thought Arden wouldn't mind Marion phoning directly because Marion's house would be *perfect* for *Simplify This*.

Four forceful thuds sounded at her door, and before she could speak, Ernest Hilton barged in, followed by a tiny wide-eyed brunette.

"Ernest." Arden swung her legs off her desk and straightened in her chair, yanking her shirt down over the undone zipper of her skirt.

"Arden." Ernest hauled a chair from the corner of the room, moved the stack of folders off it onto the only empty space on Arden's desk, and set it next to the visitor's chair facing Arden. He gestured to the size zero to sit.

I'm not going to like this, Arden thought. She knew Ernest well enough after six years of working with him. He was fifty, jovial, and fat, and he never appeared in front of a camera.

"I'd like you to meet Zoey Anderson."

Arden smiled. "Hi, Zoey." The young woman was dazzling, with long dark hair clipped loosely to the back of her head and enormous dark eyes. Her dress was a simple sleeveless sheath of linen, at least two sizes smaller than what Arden wore, and Arden was slim.

"So here's the deal," Ernest continued, after Zoey gave a brief smile. "Channel Six has been bought out. New management. Now new show." He held up his hands and spread them in a banner. "*Simplify This from A to Z*. Get it? From Arden to Zoey."

Arden's heart turned to ice.

"What the numbers are telling us, see, Arden, is that we're not getting any of the younger demographic. You've captured the marrieds, the empty nesters, the first new homes in the suburbs, but no one under thirty watches *ST*."

"I wouldn't say *no one*," Arden objected.

"Time to move on, any old hoo." Ernest slapped his hands on his mammoth thighs. "Things get old fast. Gotta change."

"*ST* has excellent ratings," Arden reminded him. "The ratings show—"

"Of course, of course," Ernest interrupted. "But they could be even better, and they will be once we've got Zoey on board. She can work with the under thirties. Who needs help simplifying more than they do? They live in lofts, share apartments, don't know how to do their taxes or keep records, trip over all the wires for adapters for their thousands of devices. . . ."

Zoey spoke up for the first time. Her voice was high pitched and girly girl. "One week I'll do the youngies, and the next week you can do the oldies." Arden was surprised Zoey didn't put her finger in her dimpled chin.

The youngies, Arden thought, inwardly moaning. *The oldies*.

Another tap at the door. Once again it opened before Arden could speak. Sandra, her secretary stuck her head in.

"Sorry, Arden, but you've got an emergency phone call."

Arden stared. She had no husband, no children. She didn't even own a pet. "Thanks, Sandra." She nodded toward Ernest. "Excuse me. I'd better take this."

Her mother spoke. "Arden? Honey?" Her voice sounded different. It didn't crack with its usual take-charge, *You know I've found the perfect house for you*, Boston real estate agent's pizzazz.

"Mom? Are you okay?"

"I'm fine, darling. But, Arden, . . . your father died."

"My father died." Arden repeated in robot tones, trying to make the words compute.

"Oh, that's so sad." Across from her, Zoey's enormous eyes filled with real tears.

"He died on the island," Nora continued. "I've spoken with Cyndi and Justine. The funeral will be on Monday."

"Mom, can I call you back?" Arden asked. "I've got people in the office. I need just a minute. . . ."

Her mother clicked off.

"I have to go to Nantucket," Arden reported in a stunned monotone. "My father died. The funeral is Monday."

Ernest nodded lugubriously and got to his feet. "Terrible thing, terrible thing," he intoned, although for all he knew, Arden's father could have been an ax murderer. "Take all the time you want, Arden. In fact, you've got a lot of vacation due you. Why not take a month. Or two. Or three? I'm sure Zoey can handle it. The timing is just right; she can start her part of the series, and then in the fall we can segue you back in."

Arden sat dumbfounded, staring at her boss and his new, *young*, discovery. She knew how Ernest worked. With some degree of accuracy, she could interpret his every mouth crimp or eyebrow lift. Terror struck: was she losing control of her own show?

That would be a horrible thing, a betrayal of her and the years she'd put into *Simplify This*, and into this station, but as Arden sat quietly smoldering, there stood little Zoey with her eyes full of tears.

Lucky little Zoey, who wept when someone's father died. Obviously, Zoey's father had never abandoned her and her mother.

Arden could imagine Zoey's life clearly: parents who adored each other and never divorced, brothers and sisters who were *real* siblings, a father who was a strong disciplinarian but fair, a mother who attended the school plays where Zoey had the leading role.

Nothing like Arden's mess of a life. Or like Arden's oh-so-charming disaster of a father.

She had always assumed she would somehow get more of him later. My God, Rory Randall was only sixty and in good health. He golfed, he played tennis, he swam! How could he be dead? Arden still had so much to say to him, so many difficulties needed to be discussed and settled—*he* had so much to say to her, she knew he did, she knew! She was his *first* daughter, his first child. Because of that, she was special! Her mother had made a mistake, someone had gotten their information tangled; Rory Randall might be ill, perhaps in the hospital with a minor heart attack, but not dead.

Emotions shifted within her like fractures in the earth, warning of a tidal wave surging her way. Arden reminded herself she was a pro. Some people in the station considered her practically a goddess; she was gorgeous, clever, energetic, invincible. If she allowed herself to display anything except expertise bordering on disdain, everyone in the station from the janitor to the CEO would think she'd broken down because of Zoey's arrival. It wouldn't matter that Arden's father had died. Everyone knew Arden's only love was her work.

She would not humiliate herself.

"I'll pencil in another meeting for next Wednesday," Arden said decisively. "I've got to leave now."

"Of course." Ernest and Zoey went out, closing the door respectfully behind them.

Arden zipped up her skirt, then grabbed her purse and jacket. She slipped her feet back into her murderous high heels and trotted out of her office to her secretary's desk.

"Sandra, I've got to go to Nantucket for a week. My father died. You can reach me by cell."

"Oh," Sandra began, "I'm so sorry—"

But Arden didn't trust Sandra. She knew the moment she was out of the building, Sandra would be gossiping about her with the other employees and interns. Really, there was no one you could trust.

Atop those impossible heels, she stalked, head high, out of the station. She got in her car, fastened her seat belt, and drove away. She didn't allow herself to cry.

Meg Randall sat in her ancient Volvo tapping her fingers impatiently on the steering wheel as she waited for the car ferry to bump into its place in the pier so the vehicles could be unloaded. She considered herself one of the most moderate, gentle, easygoing women she knew, but at this moment she felt as impatient as Secretariat stalled behind the starting gate.

The steamship *Eagle* rumbled, shuddered, and groaned into its berth. Chains clanked as the dockworkers raised the ramp into place, jumped aboard, and waved the cars off. With a flash of triumph, Meg drove onto Nantucket.

She was here before Arden!

It had been years since she'd been on the island. She'd never been old enough to drive here before, but her car carried her with perfect assurance down Steamboat Wharf, through the cobblestone grid of town, and along the winding narrow lane of Lily Street, into the driveway of her father's house.

She stepped out into the sunshine and looked around. The street, with its houses clustered closely together, its narrow brick sidewalk, and tidy trimmed privet hedges, lay in timeless peace beneath the morning sun. It was very quiet.

Meg stretched. She had actually arrived before Arden, and she passionately wanted to have first choice of bedroom. That was why she'd hardly slept last night, and had left Boston before six a.m. to make the nine thirty ferry from Hyannis. Meg was going to claim the back bedroom overlooking the yards, lawns, and rooftops of the other houses in the village.

She beeped her station wagon locked, reached in her pocket, and took out the small key to the front door. It lay in her hand like an icon, like a treasure. It *was* a treasure. She had never had a key to this house before. Even though she had lived here, she had never belonged.

White clapboard, three stories high, with a blue front door sporting a bronze mermaid door knocker, the house was similar to the others

in the neighborhood. The driveway next to the house was short, ending at a privet hedge centered by a rose-covered arbor. Already some
of the pale roses were blooming. On either side of the front door, blue
hydrangeas blossomed, and pink impatiens spilled from the white window boxes.

A storybook house. A house with many stories.

Meg went up the eight steps to the small porch, took a deep breath,
and opened the door.

Cleaners had been in; she smelled lemon polish and soap. Ignor-
ing the first floor, she took the stairs to the second floor two at a time.
Like all old Nantucket houses, this one rambled oddly around rooms
with fireplaces or closets built in at odd angles. But the path to the bedroom, *her* bedroom, was embroidered into her memory like silk thread
on muslin.

Here it was, at the back, with the morning glory wallpaper and
two walls of windows gleaming with light. An old-fashioned three-
quarter mattress lay on a spool bed, covered with soft old cotton sheets
and a patchwork quilt in shades of rose, lemon, and azure, echoing the
colors in the hand-hooked rug covering most of the satiny old pine
floor. An enormous pine dresser stood against one wall, still adorned
with the posy-dotted dresser scarf that had been there when Meg was
a child. This room had no closets, only hooks for clothes, but that had
never mattered to Meg. She had cherished the room because of the
slightly warped, ink-stained wooden desk and creaking cane-bottom
chair placed against the back window, where she could sit and write or
contemplate the starry sky and dream.

When she was a girl, for a year this had been her bedroom. Then
Arden got into one of her jealous snits, claiming that since she was
the oldest, she got first dibs. Meg had to take the side bedroom, which
should have delighted her. It was twice as large as the odd back bedroom, and actually decorated. The theme was mermaids, and Meg's
mother, Cyndi, who at the time had been the current Mrs. Randall,
had gone a bit wild, draping the windows with mermaid curtains, covering the twin beds with mermaid sheets and comforters, softening the
floor with a thick Claire Murray mermaid rug. Even the bedside lamps
were held up by mermaids. It should have been a young girl's paradise.

It just made Meg cranky. She wouldn't give her older, snotty half sister Arden the satisfaction of showing she preferred the back room, and she *really* wouldn't beseech Arden to exchange rooms with her. She just accepted it. She was used to acceptance as a way of life.

Then their father married Justine and adopted Jenny, and Meg got to spend one blissful summer there. The next summer was when what Arden and Meg called "The Exile" began. After Justine took over, Meg and Arden didn't get invited to spend any time at all at their father's house, not one summer month, not one summer day.

But that was then, and this was now, a new stage in life, a new day. Years had passed.

Meg would pretend to be selfless, thoughtful, taking the small back bedroom, allowing Arden one of the big front rooms. Jenny had the other front bedroom, years ago done up in pinks and greens.

She needed to unpack quickly, before anyone else got here. She needed to spread her belongings out all over the room, claiming her territory.

She clattered down the stairs and out the front door to the car. She regarded the number of cardboard boxes filling the open hatch, took a deep breath, reached in, and hefted the first heavy box.

Most of what she'd brought to the island was either books or notes or steno pads filled with research. In spite of the terrifying fact that she'd have to spend three months living with the two women who disliked her most in the world, Meg was thrilled to be here, because at last she'd be able to focus completely and solely on writing her book.

Because it was the last day of May, the humid heat of island summers had not yet arrived. Still, after Meg made a few trips up and down the steps carrying the boxes, her clothes were damp with sweat. She sank down on the top step of the stoop to catch her breath and gather her long, wild strawberry-blonde curls into a clump high on her head. The cool air on her neck felt sensational.

A soft breeze drifted over her skin, tickling her slightly, making her senses stir in the most pleasurable way. Leaning back on her elbows, she sighed deeply, closed her eyes, and breathed in the salty island air.

And allowed herself to think of Liam.

PHOTO: ©JESSICA HILLS

NANCY THAYER is the *New York Times* bestselling author of *Heat Wave, Beachcombers, Summer House, Moon Shell Beach, The Hot Flash Club, The Hot Flash Club Strikes Again, Hot Flash Holidays,* and *The Hot Flash Club Chills Out.* She lives in Nantucket.